'I don't know really where to start with this one! It was so strange & weird, yet I totally mean that in the good way!'

— ANNE BONNY BOOK REVIEWS

'For a thought provoking, original serial killer thriller, you could do no better than *Hellbound*, which due to its social commentary reads more like literary thriller than a bog standard serial killer read.'

— AJOOBACATS - VINE VOICE

'I thoroughly enjoyed this story and can honestly say that I've read nothing comparable to it.'

— BENJAMIN E. SAWYER - AUTHOR OF THE FAMILIAR

'Would I recommend this book? A million times over I would, with bells on! Twisted, irresistible, powerfully addictive this is a must read for those of you who are drawn to the dark side!'

— CRIMEBOOKJUNKIE.CO.UK

'Prepare to be shocked, both emotionally and politically as McCaffrey's novel comes to its unexpected conclusion. This is a book which you must read.'

'This is a remarkable novel, I don't say that lightly... If you're a fan of thought-provoking, psychologically thrilling stories, read this. I highly recommend it.'

'The ending is pure gold. I'd read it again tomorrow just for THAT!'

'Obadiah Stark is an exceptionally brilliant, unforgettable evil and horrible character... I loved him!'

'This is one extraordinary book.'

'A brilliant book.'

'Very imaginative and there's a hint of Stephen King in there.'

'Hellbound' is on my top ten list of books I would read over and over again… the writing is outstanding.'

'I rarely give 5* and this one deserves them for being so very different.'

'Brilliant is a word that doesn't do this book justice.'

'Well written, compelling to read and has its moments of real tension.'

THE TALLY MAN

BOOK ONE IN THE HELLBOUND ANTHOLOGY

DAVID MCCAFFREY

First published in 2014* by:
Britain's Next Bestseller
An imprint of Live It Ventures LTD
27 Old Gloucester Road
London.
WC1N 3AX
www.bnbsbooks.co.uk

@BNBSbooks
www.davidmccaffrey.net
ISBN 978-1-910565-86-5
Cover designed by Miacello Designs ©

The Tally Man was originally release under the title **Hellbound,** though is otherwise
unchanged

For my Piglet, Gruffalo and Baby Moo Man

FOREWORD

As an author, I've been asked to write forewords on occasion and have usually passed, simply because writing takes up so much of my days that to stop everything and read another author's work becomes a burden. Yet, when David McCaffrey asked me to write the foreword to his updated version of Hellbound (now titled The Tally Man), I was delighted.

First, because David was my writing coach student years ago when he began this amazing novel; and second because he is a good guy and the world needs more like him.

As to The Tally Man, the story's central character is not a nice guy, in fact he makes Hannibal Lecter seem somewhat pleasant.

How do you punish pure evil? How does one condemn a soulless being who has no capacity for caring?

Read The Tally Man... you'll enjoy the trip.

Steve Alten, NY Times & International best-selling author of MEG.

The whole course of human history may depend on a change of heart in one solitary and even humble individual – for it is in the solitary mind and soul of the individual that the battle between good and evil is waged and ultimately won or lost.

M. Scott Peck

PROLOGUE

SEPTEMBER 7TH

18:38

Inishtooskert (*Inis Tuaisceart*), The Blasket Islands (*Na Blascaodaí*)
    County Kerry, Ireland

OTHER THAN EXTENSIVE RUINS OF ANCIENT STONE BUILDINGS AND the prison, the only thing of any particular note on the island was the colony of European Storm-petrels that resided there.

Inishtooskert was inhabited until 1953 by a completely Irish-speaking population and was famous for the literary and linguistic heritage of its former inhabitants. These islanders were the subject of many anthropological and linguistic studies towards the end of the 19th century, so much so that many books were written to record much of the inhabitants' traditions and ways of life. The archipelago was named the Blasket Islands, Blascaodaí in Gaelic.

It is strongly believed that the word had linguistically

travelled down the ages from the Norse word '*brasker*', which meant 'dangerous place'.

The archipelago consisted of six principle islands; the Great Blasket Island, Beginish, Inishnabro, Inishvivkillane, Inishtooskert and Tearaght Island. All of the six islands inhabitants were evacuated to the Irish mainland on 17th November 1953 under mysterious circumstances. Some believed that they were abandoned due to the serve weather which beat the islands on an almost daily basis, ensuring that the population would consistently be in danger of being washed out into the raging sea, still in their houses, still in their beds.

Others, who had embraced the mythology of their Gaelic upbringing, believed that they were spirited away by the Slaugh, a band of the unsanctified dead who fly above the earth, stealing mortal souls. Unable to enter into the light of the sun, they can only come above ground at night when there is little to no moon. During those times, they would often hunt the hapless and unlucky, claiming many a victim. Most who encounter a member of the Slaugh were never heard of again. Those who were strong enough or lucky enough to survive were believed to never be the same.

Others simply believed that the inhabitants had relocated to Springfield, Massachusetts, where their descendants now lived.

Other than the bird population, however, it seemed that the vibe which emanated from ADX Absolom, by virtue of its occupants, was enough to convince all species of insect and mammal to find habitation elsewhere, either on the other islands or on the mainland.

If man had such attuned intuition, then it would be very likely that, other than the employees of the prison service, no one would ever visit the island at all.

This appreciation only added to the reputation of ADX

Absolom, unofficially referred to as the Alcatraz of the Blasket Islands.

The maximum-security prison was situated on the Dingle Peninsular, an archipelago at the most westerly point of Ireland. Known to the Irish as '*An Fear Marbh*', the land mass resembled a sleeping giant.

To the guards who worked behind its stone walls, it was simply called '*The Dead Man.*'

The prison covered thirty-seven acres and contained four hundred and ninety cells, each one reserved for men convicted of the most violent crimes in need of the tightest control. Each inmate would spend their life sentence in their cell – essentially a concrete box with a four-inch wide sliver of window.

Furnishings were limited to a concrete bench built into one of the walls, a toilet that stopped working if blocked, a shower that ran on a timer to prevent flooding and a sink missing its plug to prevent it being fashioned into a weapon. In return for good behaviour, the prisoners had the opportunity to have a polished steel mirror bolted to the wall. A radio and television – all controlled remotely, so the inmate did not actually come into contact with them – were additional rewards to be earned.

Only recreational, educational and religious programming was permitted.

———

RICHARD SABITCH, THE WARDEN OF ABSOLOM, ENTERED THE Death House, a €300,000 lethal injection facility located in a nondescript building outside the main compound.

Looking around, he verified that everything was prepared.

This afternoon's execution was a big one, and the last thing Sabitch needed was a subpar performance in front of the media.

Lined with green tiles, the Death House had the sterile appearance of a hospital bay, bare of equipment except for a stainless steel sink in one corner and a white folding screen. Soon it would contain a large gurney equipped with five Velcro restraints designed to pinion the prisoner, along with four guards. The curtain remained closed across the windows of its three viewing rooms. Intravenous tubes passed through a small opening in the wall, which led into the executioner's chamber. A camera recorded everything, ensuring that the prisoner would not purposely be subjected to any pain during the procedure.

The two men who would perform the execution flanked the warden.

"Sir, We've just got the call. We have a go."

The warden took a deep breath. A direct line with the Department of Justice was always maintained during executions. The Prime Minister retained sole authority to grant a last-minute stay of execution.

In the case of the death chamber's impending prisoner, the warden knew none would come.

The man he was waiting for was being prepared in a room adjacent to the Death House. He had been transferred from Sector 17 – a group of cells designed to hold the most dangerous of Absolom's prisoners.

It currently holds two prisoners.

After this day was over, there would only be one.

————

OBADIAH STARK IS STRAPPED TO A GURNEY SHAPED LIKE A crucifix, his bare arms secured onto boards projecting from its sides.

The blue, prison-issue trousers and top stencilled with his identification number contain a clean-shaven forty-four-year-old with emerald eyes.

A doctor and nurse prepare both his arms with a 2% Chlorhexidine solution, ironically intended to reduce the risk of infection. Two fourteen-gauge cannulae are inserted into the prepared brachial areas and covered with transparent, adhesive dressings to hold them in place. Flushed with a heparin/saline solution, the nurse hangs a 1,000-millilitre bag of normal saline from a stand, connecting it to the cannula in his left arm and hurries away.

Throughout all of this, Obadiah's eyes never lose their silent annoyance at these intrusions into his personal space. As the Irish Medical Organisation forbids medical staff from participating in executions, the doctor and nurse will stand behind the white folding screen and monitor Obadiah's heart rate via the ECG electrodes attached to his chest.

Three of the guards exit the room, leaving one at the head of the gurney.

Obadiah strains to look at the doctor's handiwork. Nodding his haughty approval, he turns his attention to the other man in his presence.

Father Michael Hicks has been delivering Holy Communion to death row inmates for more than 20 years. He has been in the worst of them: Tadmor Military Prison, ADX Colorado, Bang Kwang, al-Ha'ir, Katingal. Throughout all his years in service, he has often been in the presence of evil, but today is the first time he has ever felt it.

Casting a glance over to the warden, who nods approval, Father Hicks steps up to Obadiah and begins the Apostolic Pardon and Viaticum.

"The Lord is my shepherd, I shall not want. He maketh me to lie down in green pastures and leadeth me beside the still waters."

The doctor attempts to administer Ativan and Paxil, sedatives intended to ensure that Obadiah remains relaxed.

"No," Obadiah states, shaking his head.

"It's protocol, Mr Stark. It will make the process more comfortable."

"I said no," Obadiah repeats.

The doctor looks over at Sabitch to seek instruction.

"It's his choice," the warden advises.

Acquiescing, the doctor moves back behind the folding screen.

Father Hicks continues. "He restoreth my soul; he leadeth me in the paths of righteousness for his name's sake. Yea, though I walk through the valley of the shadow of death, I will fear no evil; for thou art with me, thy rod and thy staff comfort me."

Under the intensity of Obadiah's stare, the priest's confident tone begins to falter. He feels like an insect under scrutiny in a jar. "Thou preparest a table before me in the presence of mine enemies; thou anointest my head with oil, my cup runneth over."

"Hey Padre," Obadiah interrupts calmly. "Let me take this one. 'Surely goodness and mercy shall follow me all the days of my life, and I will dwell in the house of the Lord forever.' "

Father Hicks tries to hide his disquiet at the sarcastic recital of the 23rd Psalm, silently calling on his faith to strengthen his resolve.

The strap-down guard shifts uncomfortably at Obadiah's indifference towards his impending execution. By this time, death row prisoners are usually pissing in their prison-issue pants.

"May I ask who you ticked off to get stuck in this hell-hole?" Obadiah enquires.

"Faith brought me here," the priest replies assuredly.

"Well, can I be so bold as to offer you some advice? Consider it a parting gift. Think of this place not as a prison, but a leviathan. Your faith alone won't cut it. The beast himself will come along and rip it from your soul. You have to fight to keep it in here."

Unsure how to respond, the priest simply smiles and nods his head. Silently indicated to do so by the warden, the guard approaches the gurney from behind and pushes Obadiah's head down roughly against its surface, placing the final Velcro strap into place and testing its security with a gentle tug. The prisoner gives no indication that the restraint bothers him.

"Are you afraid, Father?"

"Only for your soul, my son."

"My soul?" Obadiah's quizzical tone is genuine, despite its cold, emotionless delivery. "You believe my soul is tainted with evil?"

"I do." The priest moves closer to Obadiah, trying to prove his absence of fear. He does it more for himself. "But through no fault of your own. There are people in this world who simply respond with hatred in the presence of goodness. They do so, not with blind malevolence, but simply because they lack awareness of their own evil and wish to avoid understanding it."

"You believe I'm this way because I made a choice to extinguish the light in people's lives? Because it revealed my darkness, therefore my pain of self-awareness? Au contraire, Padre. Think of me as an inevitable stage in human evolution. My pure entropy simply conflicts with your naïve vision of goodness. Extremes such as you and I have to be locked in combat. It is as natural for evil to hate good as it is for good to hate evil. Wouldn't you agree?"

Father Hicks counters with what he feels is a convincing argument to Obadiah's rhetoric. "That may be so. But for every soul you destroyed, you offered yourself as an instrument of salvation in another. Your evil deeds therefore only served as a beacon, warning others away from its shores."

The three guards re-enter the room, ready to shuffle the gurney into the death chamber.

Obadiah smiles, his face taking on a youthful, disarming appearance. The condemned man's voice is laced with dark promise as he continues. "Remember Father, evil is simply 'live' spelt backwards. It's a presence more ubiquitous in the world than you realise. Do not the international relations of realpolitik advise politicians to disavow absolute moral and ethical considerations in politics in favour of a focus on self-interest, political survival, and power?

"We live in a world where world leaders justify their perspectives by laying claim to a 'higher moral duty', under which the greatest evil is seen to be the failure of the state to protect itself and its citizens. Even Machiavelli believed that it is safer to be feared than loved. He knew there are traits considered good that, if followed, will lead to ruin, while others considered vices, achieve security and well-being."

The priest retaliates. "But refusing to acknowledge the weakness in your own personality made it easy for evil to take hold."

"Possibly, but acceptance of that ignorance would have to be meant because my soul would never go lightly otherwise. Is that not true, Padre?"

"So, what of guilt? Remorse?"

"Guilt? What is guilt, other than a sack of bricks to be set down when you deem it necessary. To acknowledge my guilt when that curtain opens would be to admit I regret the things I've done. I don't. If God was so concerned about it, he wouldn't have given man free will, allowing him a 'get out of jail free card' to commit the most atrocious acts, sometimes in his name and then provide him with the opportunity to repent. The man's obviously a sadist. I merely took my free will, laid down my sack of bricks and freed those individuals from a pointless existence."

"And on whose authority was it pointless? Yours?"

Obadiah considers the curt reaction an achievement. "Well, seeing as this moment is all about me, no one else's authority matters, does it? You know as well as I do, that if God is responsible for everything, then he is ultimately responsible for evil. That's not my burden to bear, nor is it yours. But bear it you will, as it's your vocation to do so. To compensate, your primitively feeble, religious mind will attempt to explain away the unknown. You'll try to convince yourself that they do not exist, these people you mention, who respond with hatred in the presence of goodness. By the same measure, you'll never accept there are some who exist to destroy light, simply because it's in their power to do so.

"Smug offerings of redemption hold no meaning for me, Father. Take a good look in the mirror when you get home. I'm the antithesis of you, and you of me. Wrap that thought around you tightly when you're alone in the dark. Close your eyes, and you'll see me there."

Unable to find an appropriate retort to the compelling argument, Father Hicks stares at Obadiah with a sorrowful look. He wonders where his impressions of such a malevolent world came from, surprised if his sentiments were not directly related to his experience of family. If that was the case, then Father Michael Hicks wept for Obadiah Stark as a child.

"Do you wish to stay, Father?" Sabitch asks from the doorway as Obadiah is wheeled past him towards the death chamber. "I can have one of the guards escort you to the witness room."

The priest shakes his head. "No, thank you, Warden. If the man has a redemptive path, it lies elsewhere. His soul now rests with the Almighty. May he have mercy on it."

Making his way to the exit, Father Michael Hicks never looks back.

———

OBADIAH'S APPEARANCE IS ONE OF SOMEONE RELAXING IN THE sun as his gurney is secured into place.

The guards give the prisoner one final check before taking their place outside the door.

The witness room is full of representatives from CBS, 60 Minutes, Sky News, BBC, France24, CBC, Al Jazeera, Telesur and other news outlets from around the world. The execution of a man considered a superstar in the netherworld of crime is something that commands a great deal of airtime.

Also present are relatives of Obadiah's victims. They take up the front four rows of chairs, wishing to see his death up close. They are bound by the hope that his death will be a painful one. They know, however, it will be merciful compared to the suffering he inflicted upon their loved ones.

Sabitch checks his watch and nods, indicating his desire to begin. At that moment, Obadiah's eyes spring open, his smile gone. His green eyes reflect the light from the death chamber, giving him the impression of a possessed soul.

The curtain opens, presenting the execution room to the witnesses. Some women begin to pray, others cry, their husbands and partners pulling them close to provide comfort.

The warden instructs the technician to raise the gurney on its hydraulic rams until it's positioned almost vertically, allowing Obadiah to view his audience.

The execution begins.

"Obadiah Stark, you have been found guilty on multiple counts of murder and have been sentenced to death by lethal injection. Have you anything to say?"

Sabitch waits patiently for a response.

Staring through the viewing window to the faces beyond, Obadiah's expression is steady as if carved from stone.

"I provided a blessing to those people," he replies, his voice tinged with a cold, metallic quality. "A blessing from the pointlessness of existence. You should be thanking me."

Through the speaker in the death chamber, Obadiah

smiles upon hearing the weeping caused by his comments. He sees a few men rise to escort their wives from the witness room, expelling expletives and desires for him to suffer in his direction.

"Would you gag the prisoner, please?" Sabitch orders. The guard complies, placing a wide leather strap over Obadiah's mouth.

He doesn't resist.

The two executioners behind the one-way glass simultaneously press a button each, beginning the manual injection of three chemicals.

Sodium thiopental, a short-acting barbiturate, used widely as an anaesthetic, causes unconsciousness very quickly when injected into a vein. Pancuronium, also known as Pavulon, is a muscle relaxant, paralysing the diaphragm and arresting breathing while the Potassium chloride finishes the job by inducing cardiac arrest.

The men performing the execution are from the Correctional Department and have literally been trained to just push a button. Only one of the two buttons pressed is operational. A computer within the equipment scrambles the circuits randomly, so neither one knows which of the buttons did the job.

Once pressed, the machine activates six syringes - three of which hold the lethal medication; the other three contain a harmless saline solution.

Currently, the sodium thiopental does not seem to be doing its anaesthetic job.

The tension is palpable as the room's occupants wait for the infusion devices to complete their cycle.

Obadiah expels a low, serpentine hiss, audible through the gag, the final, precious breaths of air slowly being released from his lungs. The witnesses stare in apprehension as his eyes begin to slowly shut, the thief of their sons and daughters falling into an eternal sleep.

Sabitch nods towards the doctor, the execution apparently having reached its grim, theatrical conclusion.

Obadiah's eyes are closed, his expression one of peace.

The monitor sounds the asystole alarm, signifying no cardiac electrical activity. The doctor places his hand over Obadiah's right wrist, feeling for a radial pulse.

As he palpates the area, Obadiah's eyes snap open. In the witness room, some of the people in the front row cry out in shock at the unexpected revival.

The doctor takes a breath and moves back once Obadiah's eyes have closed for the second time, holding his wrist again. He waits for thirty seconds to ensure he can feel no further radial beats, looks over to the nurse for acknowledgement that the ECG is not picking up a rhythm and then nods to the warden.

Obadiah Stark is dead.

As the curtain closes across the viewing window, the warden instructs the medical staff to begin the final preparations of the body for transfer to the pathologist for the autopsy. It is standard procedure following an execution.

In the viewing area, reporters and cameramen pack up their equipment and begin filing out of the room. Some try to catch a few of the departing relatives for their thoughts on the execution. Most are met with silence or waved away with a "no comment."

A few stop and expel their vitriolic feelings of anger, condemning the authorities and the justice system for taking so long to apprehend him.

Joe O'Connell, an investigative reporter for The Daily Éire, has been amongst the throng of media in the witness room.

At six foot two, his height and athletic frame ensure he stands above most of the news-hounds he arrived with.

O'Connell has followed Obadiah's murderous career from the moment he committed his first killing in Ireland. The reporter has two reasons for being there; one, to get details on the execution for his column tomorrow; and two, to gather as much information as possible for the book he plans to write on the disease that was Obadiah Stark.

Running his hands through his brown, grey-flecked hair, Joe turns to see who's left in the room, his blue eyes noting a guard by the door and an elderly couple sitting directly behind him.

He scribbles a few notes on his pad, places it in his pocket and stands to leave. He considers approaching the couple to see if he can obtain any quotes to use tomorrow, but as if sensing his intent, the woman raises her head, displaying tear-streaked cheeks. Realising he is unlikely to get anything printable from her, or her male companion, he decides against it.

Moving towards the exit, Joe shivers once. The sensation makes him stop and look around the room, but he sees nothing unusual and continues on.

It reminded him of his childhood when his mother used to say that someone must have stepped on his grave.

There has to be evil so that good can prove its purity above it.
Buddha

1

SEPTEMBER 15TH

18:54

Fenit (*An Fhianait*)
County Kerry, Ireland

IF INISHTOOSKERT WAS ONE OF THE MOST DESOLATE PLACES IN Ireland, Fenit was, by contrast, one of the most tranquil.

Meaning 'The Wild Place', it was anything but. With a population of just four hundred and thirty, the small village on the north side of Tralee Bay and just south of the Shannon Estuary was enclosed from the Atlantic by the and extended northwards from the Dingle Peninsula. As well as being home to a lighthouse, a castle, a golf club, an angling club and a football team, Churchill, the harbour, had a contentious claim to fame.

Saint Brendan, born on Fenit Island and one of the early monastic saints and a navigator, was believed to have discovered America before Christopher Columbus. It was alleged that Columbus used Saint Brendan's manuscript from his earlier travels, 'Navigatio Sancti Brendani Abbatis', to locate what became the United States.

Many of Fenit's occupants simply believed it was a religious analogy.

———

Joe O'Connell tossed his keys on the table and threw himself into the leather chair with a weary sigh.

The drive home from work had been a bitch, doing little for his mood. Because of an accident closing the R551, traffic had been diverted to the R558. With every single car in the country apparently deciding to be on the road at the same time, his usual ten-minute drive had taken an hour and a half. He'd promised himself he would check the news later, making a personal bet it had probably been some tosser on a mobile phone who'd caused it.

The panorama of Tralee Bay spread out before him, the wispy lights of the last few fishing boats making their way back into the marina still visible.

The tide, on its way in, gently rocked the boats already berthed. They rose and fell in a gentle, rhythmic fashion. Announcing the imminent arrival of night, the smudged sky polarised the window, allowing Joe to see his reflection.

In his thirties and with boyish good looks, he was beginning to get crow's feet that framed his blue eyes; eyes that missed nothing. Wearing his usual work clothes of a shirt, tie, dark blue jeans and wearing glasses, he had the look of an accountant rather than a reporter.

It had been just over a week since the execution of Obadiah Stark, and he still found it occupying his every thought.

Though his job demanded he report on the detritus of society, the image of someone being put to death was difficult for him to let go of.

He'd never seen anyone die before.

Using his sullen thoughts as an excuse, he snatched a

bottle of Jack Daniels from the counter while walking through to the kitchen. Pouring himself a straight shot, he flexed his neck from side to side as the malty warmth of the bourbon slipped down his throat. Already he could feel it warm his stomach and relax his mood. Rotating his shoulders in circular motions to work out the cramps, he poured another drink and moved back to the window.

Now shrouded in twilight, he found himself wondering how many of the harbour's inhabitants would still be discussing the events at Absolom. His column in The Daily Éire had gained him a press ticket to the execution which locally had been the equivalent of receiving front row tickets for The Pogues. Joe had found it disappointing that, instead of being interested in the more intelligent capital punishment debate that had raged ever since ADX Absolom's conception, they were only concerned about whether Stark had begged for forgiveness?

How many of the families present had left due to the stress of being in the presence of their loved ones' killer?

Had he soiled himself during his final moments?

Were his final words vitriolic?

Joe conceded that bound to the tedious routine of living in a fishing district, they had little else to entertain themselves with other than gossip and rumour-mongering. But now it was over, he wasn't sure how he felt about capital punishment.

Growing up with staunch Catholic parents, the adage of 'an eye for an eye' had been instilled in him from an early age. Graduating from university with a degree in Criminology, Joe had gained the perspective that such an axiom meant everyone would end up sightless.

'Then again,' he thought to himself, 'an eye for an eye in the kingdom of the blind meant a one-eyed man would be king.'

Add to the equation his job in investigative journalism,

and he had enough insight to metaphorically straddle the fence of the capital punishment argument.

The obvious benefit was that the criminal would no longer offend. With money not an inexhaustible commodity in the current economic climate, it could be better spent on alternative resources such as health care and employment.

It didn't seem to work as a deterrent, so that left only retribution as a justification for it – punishment in proportion to the offence.

On the other hand, you could tease out a cogent argument concerning the potential for a miscarriage of justice.

And then there was the ethical acceptability of the death penalty. Whatever the position, Joe knew that there had been no anti-death penalty activists present outside Absolom when Obadiah Stark had died. There had been no question of the man's guilt or whether he'd deserved his fate.

For Joe, that silently spoke volumes.

'Still,' he thought. 'Thinking someone deserves to die and watching them die, are two completely different things.'

The lighter cast the study in a flickering glow as he lit a cigarette. Stopping at the desk, he randomly flipped open the file lying there.

He looked at it whenever he had found himself doubting whether putting Obadiah Stark to death had been the right thing to do.

The file put it into perspective for him.

Through a bluish haze of expelled smoke, the face of an attractive young woman, late twenties and brunette with large brown eyes, peered back at him.

Ann Marie Sutcliffe.

Obadiah's fourteenth victim.

Over his years with the paper, he knew he'd developed an uncompromising vision of society. It had been out of necessity, to remain unbiased for his reporting. Therefore, during his career, he had lied, flirted, blackmailed, terrorised and stolen to get information. He had collected details, documents and quotes from every, solitary person he had ever interviewed and kept them all in files in his study.

So far, he had never referred to them again.

The biggest of those files was the one in front of him.

Mostly illegal but detailed and well organised, an anonymous contact in the Gardaí had regularly fed Joe information and details on Obadiah Stark's victims. Their deal had been such that, if Joe promised not to sensationalise events, his contact would give him as much as possible.

And Joe had been true to his word, always reporting the facts, not the conjecture. And yet despite his unusually guarded professionalism in this one instance, he sometimes wished he'd done what a paper had done a few years before in the United States when they'd managed to get access to what were thought to be sealed police files.

Using the details within it, they had come up with the perfect nom-de-plume for Obadiah Stark. One that would sell papers and allow the killer to be perfectly burnt into the public's consciousness - The Tally Man.

It was believed that Stark had begun his murderous career in America around 1988, committing eighteen murders in six years. The crimes appeared motiveless; his victims seemingly without a 'victim trait' - police talk for arbitrary killing.

Each killing had increased in unnecessary violence, the level disproportionate to the last. Throughout it all, Obadiah eluded capture; the police had been left no evidence to pursue until twenty-four-year-old Sara Morgan.

Surviving her attack after being left for dead and suffering horrific facial injuries, Sara's detailed statement ultimately led to the serial killer's media-friendly nickname.

One more murder occurred in the United States after Sara's escape, followed by nothing for six months until a body was found in an alleyway in Slane, Ireland.

Being a small town situated on the north bank of the

Boyne, they were not accustomed to dealing with serious crimes. The Gardaí enlisted assistance with the investigation from their neighbouring constabulary twenty-eight miles away in Dublin. When another victim was discovered in a cave outside of Ardfert, a decaying city near Tralee, they knew they had a problem.

With the modus operandi matching descriptions they'd received from the Federal Bureau of Investigation and Interpol, it was clear that The Tally Man had arrived on Irish shores.

Joe subsequently discovered that Stark's choice of country wasn't arbitrary.

Obadiah had been born here.

He flicked through the file, stopping at the photographs that had corroborated the escaped girl's description. Taken the night of his arrest, they showed Obadiah, naked from the waist up, his arms behind his head. His sun-kissed back bore the large outline of a tattoo in the shape of a tombstone. The detail on the stone was exquisite, emphasising every slant and curve of its surround and pedimental sculpture. The intricate use of shadow helped to accentuate the depth of the work, causing the stele to look almost three-dimensional.

The rationale for the Gardaí taking a photograph was not to admire its design, but more to catalogue the details contained within it.

As accurately described by Sara, where the epitaph would typically be were twenty-seven, small, tattooed score marks. They were laid out in groups of five; four vertical lines and one diagonally through the middle of them all.

This design was duplicated five times within the tattoo, with two scorings set apart from the others.

Twenty-seven tallies signifying twenty-seven dead souls.

Three more JD shots and many cigarettes later, Joe's mood had taken a turn towards the melancholic. He wondered why he did it to himself, poring over the murder details repeatedly?

Wandering over to the stereo and flicking it on, he clumsily browsed through his CDs until he came across Beggars Banquet by The Rolling Stones. With Mick Jagger's gravelly tones blasting the opening lines of 'Sympathy for the Devil' through the speakers, Joe sat down and closed his eyes.

The song's lyrics, married up to a samba-like beat, took him back to Obadiah's chilling pastiche moments before his death.

He saw Obadiah Stark, the scar on the national psyche, smiling from his gurney, defiant in the face of death.

Obadiah had represented a perfect conduit for everyone's irrational fears about evil. His existence had been comparable to someone turning off the night-light and leaving their children in the dark, listening to creaking on the stairs.

Joe knew that people like Obadiah Stark rarely happened. Yet through all his time writing about the man, he knew he had come no closer to understanding what had made him tick.

Maybe the pathologist performing the autopsy had seen the answer when he'd cut him open.

Joe imagined it surreally visible after they'd removed his skull, a message stamped across his meninges – The reason for me killing all those people was because…

Men like Obadiah Stark didn't spring out of nowhere, he mused. Nor were they sent by the devil. They were merely a childhood disaster waiting to happen - one that had approached for years and no one had done anything about. And the families, punished through their losses, naïvely took comfort in the naive belief that his execution would ensure that no one repeated such incomprehensible crimes again.

Joe's train of thought forced him to consider his book. If it were ever going to be taken seriously, he would need a specialist. Someone who, as Jagger was querying in the background, knew the nature of Stark's game.

He would have to look into that at work tomorrow.

Finishing his drink in one mouthful, Joe switched off the stereo and climbed onto his bed, fully clothed.

He found himself revisiting his final piece on The Tally Man, as he fell quickly into a drink-assisted sleep.

'Was Obadiah Stark so neglected as a child, that he became incapable of any emotional empathy?

Individuals such as these are unable to judge something to be cruel if cruelty is all they have known.

Current research by the NSPCC suggests up to one million children are trapped by neglect and deprivation. With parenting proven to be the most critical element in a child's life, is it fair to blame the now-deceased parents of Obadiah Stark for their son's crimes?

The haunting sight of watching a man killed, albeit legally and with the full support of the justice system, has challenged my logic between locking someone up and throwing away the key or metering out what could be classed as poetic justice.

I find myself convinced that the death of Obadiah Stark was the right thing to happen, that such a man could never have been rehabilitated or offered a chance at redemption.

But I find myself wondering if we have the right to make such a decision and whether his execution represents a much larger problem we continue to refuse to face – that of deciding what defines justice.'

'We must develop and maintain the capacity to forgive. He who is devoid of the power to forgive is devoid of the power to love. There is some good in the worst of us and some evil in the best of us. When we discover this, we are less prone to hate our enemies.'
Martin Luther King, Jr.

2

08:26

The goal of theodicy is to show how God could have created the world despite all its evil.

Whether a religious individual or not, most would agree that evil doesn't exist in Heaven and that Heaven is better than the present world.

Whatever the definition, evil would not exist there in any form. Any damned souls would go to Hell, suffering never-ending torment for all eternity.

But no one in their right mind would choose eternal punishment over Heaven, only to repent the moment they arrived in Hell. That would leave God with a problem: if he let the repentant leave, Hell would be empty. If he didn't, he would be unjust for continuing to punish them.

However, repentance is more than stating you'll do whatever is necessary to get out of Hell. It involves acknowledging guilt, a desire to change behaviour and, ultimately, showing remorse. The Bible defines it as accepting Christ's sacrifice as substitutionary punishment for your own wrongs and agreeing to love God.

To quote Shakespeare, 'Ah, there's the rub.'

In reality, people in Hell would never repent, having had

their entire lives on Earth to do so. It is inconceivable that any punishment for those souls in Hell would ever change their minds. But a Hell comprised of those who would never repent poses a hypothetical notion.

Would not a person repentant in Hell have taken the opportunity to do so on Earth before they died? And would a man unable to feel remorse, labelled by the Diagnostic and Statistical Manual of Mental Disorders (DSM) as a sociopath, even be allowed entry into Heaven?

If he was, would his sins be forgiven?

———

THE SMELL OF OZONE PERMEATED THE AIR, SLOWLY TEASING Obadiah from his reverie.

Nearby wind chimes, announcing a breeze, gently played their lonely sound. He sat and glanced around, blinking as he took in the unfamiliar environment.

The room was large - white walls and beige carpets. A mahogany bureau stood against the far wall, joined by a set of wardrobes. Photographs were visible beside the bed on which Obadiah lay. One was of an attractive, brown-haired woman, another of a young girl, possibly aged three or four.

The one that caught his attention was the one with three people in it - the woman, the girl and a man. He reached over and snatched the frame from the bedside cabinet.

In its background was a bright, cerulean expanse of ocean. Boats were visible on the horizon, children and adults present in the milieu.

The three people in the photograph's foreground were smiling genuine smiles. It depicted an obviously happy period, the man draping his arm around the dark-haired woman's shoulder, the young girl, with her long, red hair flowing to her shoulders, squinting as if the sun were in her eyes. The man appeared relaxed with their company, his eyes betraying the love he felt for them.

The photograph told a lie. Obadiah couldn't remember the last time he'd felt love for anything or anyone. But given that it appeared to be him in the photograph, he realised that was a problem.

He didn't know the woman, the child or the location. Nor did he recognise where he currently was.

Though panic wasn't an emotion Obadiah was familiar with, he knew anxiety, despite having conditioned himself to avoid such distracting, human frailty.

Climbing out of bed, he walked to the window to better orientate himself. Drawing back the curtains presented him with a vista of greenery and blue skies. The horizon implied an ocean was nearby, the sounds of seagulls searching the shoreline audible through the open window. The sun was filtering through the leaves of the trees directly outside the window, creating dappled sunshine on the ground below and jumpstarted a memory of a childhood home similar to this one.

But this couldn't be home.

Obadiah searched his mind, trying to ground the creeping disquiet he felt rising. He remembered his final moments, strapped to the gurney as lethal chemicals were infused into his bloodstream. He could still recall their pinprick-like sensation as they'd coursed round his cardiovascular system, making the entire journey in approximately twelve seconds.

The sight of the people in the witness room, crying, angry, satisfied, was burned into his mind's eye. Acerbic emotions had come off them in waves, as he had slowly drifted off into the darkness.

They remained almost tangible in the air. It was as if only moments ago Obadiah had been there, in Absolom, waiting his turn to die.

And he had died.

The quintillion of synapses in his brain had simply ceased to spark off each other.

But what of his soul? Father Hicks had tried to convince him that his soul, however dark, would be redeemed after his death and live on beyond his mortal body.

Is that why he felt alive now?

Perhaps when his body had died, his soul had been released and become independent. Though once residing in his body, developing, it had needed death to be free.

Not being a religious man, Obadiah had not believed Father Hicks' last-minute attempts to convince him that beyond the veil of life there existed a better place. He'd simply thought there'd be darkness, silence and the end of consciousness. Yet here he was, able to sense, touch, feel and hear.

Obadiah had never really considered what Heaven and Hell would be like. He'd had no doubt that if such places did exist, he would never have been spending the rest of eternity in Heaven, but in an especially reserved section of Hell. Whether his expectation had been the lowest circle of Dante's Inferno or Milton's Tartarus, Obadiah Stark hadn't expected Hell to be like this.

So, if I'm not in Hell, he considered, then where am I?

The distant sound of laughter broke his musing. Looking down, he saw he was dressed in only blue pyjama bottoms. Grabbing the shirt on the back of the chair by the bureau, he moved towards the door, passing a mirror as he went.

What Obadiah Stark saw in the reflection was not only beyond his brain's ability to process, it was impossible.

The image beckoned him to move closer as if taunting him to check its genuineness. He ran fingers over his back.

His skin was smooth, unblemished. There was no sign of the scars you would receive following removal by dermal enhancement; a process he knew was similar to being splattered with hot fat.

It had been there when he'd died, the image such an integral part of him that being without it was something Obadiah had never considered. It had been as much a part of him as his skin.

And now, his record of achievement, his tally, was gone.

It was as if the tattoo had never existed.

––––––––

THE SMOKY SMELL OF BACON WAFTED THE AIR AS AOIFE STARK cracked open two eggs, recoiling as hot oil from the frying pan splashed onto her arm.

A little girl stood on a chair by her side.

"Be careful not to get too close, Ellie," she warned.

The little girl nodded. "Okay, Mummy. You be careful too."

"I will, chicken. We don't want Daddy to have to take us to the hospital 'cause we burnt ourselves, do we?"

"No. His breakfast would get cold."

Aoife smiled at her daughter's astute observation. She was always amazed at how realistic her view of the world was. Not concerned with actually injuring herself, she was more worried about her father's breakfast going uneaten.

At four and a half years-old, Eleanor Stark was the mirror image of her mother in every way other than her long, strawberry red hair. Her green eyes, full of life, were wide with concentration as she clumsily mixed the contents of the bowl in front of her. The smears of flour on her button nose and across her cheeks gave the impression of someone wearing tribal war paint. Her mission, to ensure that the eggs and flour in the bowl before her were beaten into submission, was of the utmost importance.

Lumps would not be tolerated, the marks on her black t-shirt and blue jeans a testament that she meant business.

By contrast, her mother, red pyjamas and a black dressing

gown disguising her curvy figure, was less battle-damaged; brown hair, tied up in a ponytail, hung just over her right shoulder. Known as Eva to her friends, her thirty-eight-year-old face, while not hitting the exclamation button for beauty, came awfully close to it.

She looked at the clock on the wall.

Nine-fourteen.

It was unlike him to sleep so late. Usually, he was up before the sun and his daughter.

Scraping the bacon and two eggs on a plate, she tussled Eleanor's hair.

"Go and check on your Daddy, sweetie. Tell him his breakfast is ready."

" Please leave my pancake mix. I haven't got all the lumps out yet."

"Don't worry. I won't touch it."

Ellie climbed down from the chair, wiping her hands on her jeans. "Oops," she remarked, not having realised how dirty they were.

She looked up at her mother with wary eyes.

"Come here, you," Eva said playfully, wiping her daughter's hands with a damp cloth before gently hitting her on the bottom. "Go and cover your Dad in flour."

The little girl skipped towards the stairs, humming a tune Aoife didn't recognise as she went. She stopped when she was on the third step.

"Daddy's already up. Quick, hide!"

Ellie liked to hide whenever she hadn't seen either of them for a while, either when they came back from work or stumbled downstairs on a morning. Eva had always thought it was adorable. And she had got better at hiding too, having always hidden in plain sight when she was younger, not realising that she could be seen through the gaps in the clothes horse or when underneath the table.

As she raced off to conceal herself in the cupboard, Eva

cleaned her hands and put some cutlery by the plate of food. Walking around the breakfast bar that housed the cooker and hob, she stood to welcome her husband as he came round the corner of the stairs that led from the kitchen to the first floor.

Obadiah recognised her as the woman from the photographs, noting the look on her face - one of interest and familiarity, not fear or panic. Not the look of someone with a stranger in their home.

"Morning, Obi. You're just in time for breakfast."

Eva moved towards him and leaned in to kiss him on the cheek. He instinctively pulled away at the alien gesture, noting her surprised expression as he did so.

"What's the matter? Are you okay?" The hurt in her voice at his reaction was apparent.

"Who are you?" Obadiah demanded. "Where am I?"

Eva took a few steps back, startled by his sudden behaviour. "What do you mean?"

"Where am I?" he repeated sternly.

"Obi, you're scaring me."

Obadiah marched forward and grabbed Eva's arm, betraying his usual sense of logic and introspection. "I want to know where the fuck I am."

"Let go of me, Obi," Eva insisted. "You're hurting me."

He released her, surprising himself at the acquiescence. He'd never thought that a woman giving him an order would garner anything other than an unfavourable response. Yet, something in her voice made him relax his grip.

Obadiah rubbed his temple to massage away the pressure he was feeling there.

"Obi, you need to go and lie down. Have you taken your tablets this morning?"

He stared at Eva, his expression one of blank acknowledgement. "What day is it? What date?"

Eva's voice took on a gentle, concerned tone. "It's Saturday. Saturday the eighteenth of March."

She moved back towards him, gently touching his forearm. "I think I should call the doctor. He said if you ever complained of feeling unwell in any way, we had to let him know."

Obadiah sat down on a step. Eva knelt on the floor in front of him maintaining her contact with his arm.

"No, no doctors. March eighteenth? That means it's been seven months. It seems like only a few minutes ago. I must be... the priest must have been right."

His random comments confusing her, Eva leaned closer. "Obadiah, what are you talking about? Who was right? What priest? I'm calling the doctor."

She rose and hurried towards the bench where the phone sat. Halfway through dialling the number, Eva felt his hand firmly on hers.

"I said no," Obadiah insisted. Looking in her eyes, Obadiah saw fear. But it wasn't the fear he was used to seeing. Not the fear he had savoured so often in the past, as he had moved within kissing distance of his victims, allowing them to burn the image of their destroyer into their minds. This fear was different.

It was fear for his wellbeing.

He still possessed the black void where his soul belonged – utterly free of internal restraints, with no pangs of conscience. People always assume that conscience is universal among human beings. This made Obadiah's hiding the fact that he was conscience-free, effortless. Though he could recall his crimes, he felt neither guilt nor shame. Without such emotions, most people would feel deaf and blind.

To him, they had been the bastion of his dark heart.

Obadiah began backing away, moving towards the archway which led to what he guessed must be a front door. He had to get out of the house. The thoughts coursing through his mind were almost overwhelming. Every murder he had ever committed - brutal and violent; were available to him in graphic detail.

But the images and memories didn't concern him. It was the lack of emotion his presence was causing which had him bewildered.

She should have been frantic about him being there, screaming hysterically or quietly praying not to be hurt. Instead, she was showing concern for his wellbeing.

To Obadiah, the whole situation was surreal in the extreme.

During his life, he had learnt to whip up other people's reactions to hatred and depredation. They'd been amongst his most revered talents, enabling him to kill a large number of unsuspecting people before his capture and execution. He'd prided himself on his lack of conscience, its absence allowing him to take lives and then sit back safely and watch in satisfaction as the whole country jumped. That had been true power.

Yet the woman before him was offering aspects of interaction that Obadiah had never experienced – love, concern, empathy. Emotions he'd avoided growing up to condition himself for survival, were now confronting him unconditionally and unbidden.

He had always been the one with the control in a situation, every variable accounted for.

In this situation, he was the unknown quantity.

As he opened the door leading outside, Eva ran towards him. "Obadiah, where are you going? You're not even dressed."

He glanced at her momentarily, before slamming the door and racing down the path.

As he jumped the fence, Eleanor opened the door to the cupboard where she'd been hiding, seeing her cheeks stained with dried tears.

"Mummy, where's Daddy gone? He sounded angry. He's poorly again, isn't he?"

Putting her arm around her daughter, she pulled her close and whispered softly. "I don't know, baby. Don't worry, he'll be back."

Dr. John Franklin, BS.c. (HONS, PH.D. M.A., M.CLIN, PSYCH. A.F.Ps.S.I.

Subject: Stark, Obadiah James (a.k.a. The Tally Man)
Classification: Serial Killer

Intro: Between the years 1988 and 2003, the subject murdered no less than twenty-seven people (U.K. and U.S.) as verified by the Gardaí and the Federal Bureau of Investigation (FBI). Subject was captured in May of 2003 at Dublin airport attempting to flee back to the United States. He was remanded in custody until his trial with all extradition requests by the U.S.A refused by the Irish Government. He was subsequently tried and sentenced to death at ADX Absolom.

Purpose of Study: To identify social, physiological, and psychological factors that could lead to better profiling of serial killers.

Methodology: Forensic evidence, crime-scene reports, interviews with FBI and Gardaí investigators over a three-year period (2007-2010) as well as a direct subject interview. Additional biographical information was gathered from schoolteachers, judges, solicitors, psychologists and correctional staff currently employed at ADX Absolom. Credit is to be given to Warden Richard Sabitch, who was instrumental in arranging the private session with the subject.

Subject classification: During the mid-1970s, the FBI agent Robert K. Ressler coined the phrase 'serial killer' after serial movies [1]. Supporting this, Akira Lippit argued that, 'Like each episode of a serial movie, the completion of each serial murder lays the foundation for the next act which in turn precipitates future acts, leaving the serial subject always wanting more, always hungry, addicted [2].

Investigators describe three types of killer who commit multiple murders; the mass murderer who kills several people at one time, spree killers who go on a rampage with knives or guns, killing one person after another; and the serial killer, who dispatches victims one at a time, sometimes with a gap of several years between murders. Serial killers pose a special problem for criminal investigators because their motives are often far less obvious than those of someone who commits a single murder.

Obadiah Stark fits firmly into the serial killer category. His crimes took place over a period of sixteen years, taking the lives of twenty-seven people known to the authorities (this figure is based upon Obadiah's 'tally', located on his back in the form of a tattoo. It is suspected his number of victims is greater than twenty seven, but this will be touched upon later in the report).

Psychopathology: Prior to the commissioning of this report, a request was made by this author to perform an electroencephalogram on Obadiah to assess possible enhanced brain activity. The intent was to evaluate the possibility of whether patterns that define serial killer behaviour are linked to the mind.

The request was refused by both Warden Richard Sabitch and Obadiah himself.

A medical examination of Obadiah after his arrest revealed a biochemical imbalance present in his blood and urine tests, identifying a condition called pyroluria. Though widely contested in the medical profession, pyroluria is believed to be an inborn genetic abnormality in the haemoglobin causing the production of the protein kryptopyrrole 3. The condition is also thought to be responsible for a wide range of behavioural conditions such as schizophrenia, depression, paranoia and certain types of violent behaviour, though this remains mostly theoretical.Present in up to 70% of diagnosed schizophrenic and depressive patients, it has also been found in the blood of alcoholics, children with learning disabilities and in approximately 10% of the non-psychiatric stressed population. It is also common in most cases of lung cancer. Certain ethnic groups such as the Irish show an increased percentage of pyrolurics 4. This is interesting given Obadiah's family background

Subject history: Obadiah James Stark was born 21st November 1966 in Kerry, Ireland. He was raised in a working class Catholic household by his biological parents. Subject's father, Eli Stark, worked at an iron works in Kerry. Subject's mother, Aideen Stark *née* Reed, worked as a cleaner at a local school. Anecdotal reports from neighbours indicated that Subject's father was prone to beating Obadiah and his mother. Police records for Eli Stark indicate numerous arrests for drunken behaviour.

One report highlighted an incident where Obadiah had to be admitted to hospital having been knocked unconscious following Eli shunting him into a wall.

Discussion with neighbours and former schoolteachers describe a child who would spend a great deal of his time alone. Records attained from the local church confirm Subject served as an altar boy between the ages of seven and ten. Neighbours confirm subject had established a friendship with Thomas Jacques, a fellow churchgoer whom he was often seen with after service.

Excerpt taken from interview with Thomas Jacques (altar boy at the same time as Obadiah):

"He was a bit of a loner. He never really talked about what went on at home, but I had an idea. I just felt bad for him, so one day I invited him fishing. We spent an hour together by the lake. He was very fidgety. We started messing around, skimming rocks. He managed to hit a duck near the shore. Next thing I know, he's in the water, had grabbed it by the neck, beat it to death against a tree trunk, then tore off its head. I remember laughing, but really I was scared. He seemed unfazed by the whole thing, almost calm. I avoided him after that. Thankfully he moved to the States."

Additional information: Eli Stark's acceptance of a job for Gerdau SA at its Atlas Steel unit meant that Obadiah moved with his parents to New Orleans in 1979. There he attended St Anthony's School in the Jefferson Parish, one of many in the Roman Catholic Archdiocese of New Orleans.

Despite the opportunities such a change of location may have presented, police and medical records indicate that Eli's pattern of alcohol-fuelled violent behaviour increased during this time.

They had been there less than a year when Aideen Stark died after apparently drowning whilst in the bathtub. Evidence pointed to her having fallen asleep after drinking heavily. The police, suspecting foul play, questioned Eli following the incident and his history of violent behaviour towards his wife.

No charges were brought against him.

One week later Obadiah's father was found dead inside his car. According to the police report, Eli Stark had been the victim of a botched robbery attempt, though there was no evidence that anything had been stolen. His throat had been slashed, his stomach gouged and his spine snapped. The police reported that the attack seemed particularly frenzied for a robbery, with the injuries suggesting a personal attack. Obadiah was questioned in relation to Eli Stark's death, and subsequently released.

He was thirteen years of age.

Following this period Obadiah became a ward of the state, spending time in various care homes. Social workers at the time highlighted that he displayed unpredictable behaviour, often reacting to situations with sudden, violent outbursts. One report recounted a situation where he beat a boy bullying him almost to death with a metal clothes prop following a disparaging remark made against him. Carers at the various establishments Obadiah spent time living in noted that, despite his developing violent, disposition, he also became noted for his ability to manipulate other residents.

Such coercion was noted as involving the promotion of gambling amongst other residents and the encouragement of others to commit theft.

Entries in his social records indicated numerous warnings regarding the aforementioned, as well as cautions concerning violent behaviour. Such behaviour accounted for Obadiah's transfer to different facilities over the course of eight years until he turned twenty-one and thereby no longer the responsibility of the state.

Though such events and actions can perhaps be considered commonplace in an environment where children from broken homes congregate, it may also be suggested that in such places, Obadiah began to understand how his intellect and understanding of human behaviour could be used to satisfy his own needs. In this case, basic power and control over others and a developing narcissistic belief that he was above the law.

It is the author's opinion that all of the aforementioned, his abuse as a child and its subsequent introverting effects on his personality, may well have led to the development of his sociopathic tendencies. However, it is important to note that I also believe these characteristics were already present in Obadiah's personal makeup and simply suppressed, only coming to light when he underwent an emotional trauma.

It is a sad truth that many children suffer physical, sexual or psychological abuse, but a great many do not grow up to be malcontents, murderers, rapists or paedophiles. As discussed under the heading psychopathology, genetic factors may be contributory to a person's development, both morally and emotionally.

Obadiah's relocation to a foreign land and the reaching of his threshold of endurance for suffering at the hands of his parents may have only compounded his feelings of alienation.

In Obadiah's case, this alienation then channelled him towards a destructive path consisting of murder.

References

1 Ressler, Robert, K and Tom Schachtman (1992) *Whoever Fights Monsters*, St. Martin's, New York.

2 Lippit, Akira Mizuta (1996). *The infinite series: fathers, cannibals, chemists...* Criticism: 1-18.

3 Kraus, R.T. (1995) *An enigmatic personality: case report of a serial killer.* Journal of Orthomolecular Medicine 10, 11-24.

4 Hoffer, A (1995). *The discovery of Kryptopyrrole and its importance in diagnosis of biochemical imbalances in Schizophrenia and in criminal behaviour.* Journal of Orthomolecular Medicine, 10 (1):3.

'The death penalty is certainly pro-life to those would-be victims if a convicted killer is released. And in this day of ultra-liberal courts, anything is possible. The death penalty is appropriate punishment for capital crimes, and is also the ultimate form of deterrence: people who are executed can never murder again.'

Bob Meyer

3

SEPTEMBER 16TH

07:15

Denny Street, Tralee (*Trá Lí*)
County Kerry, Ireland

FIRST PUBLISHED IN 1904, THE DAILY ÉIRE WAS NOW IRELAND'S
biggest-selling regional newspaper.

Save for a brief interruption when the Black and Tans
destroyed the paper's presses during the War of
Independence in 1919, The Daily Éire had always prided itself
as being on hand to break the news and report the most
important events from not only Ireland but the rest of the
world. Such prestige had made it not only a bastion in the
publishing industry of Ireland, but a working environment
considered one of the best by most of its employees.

―――

JOE WASN'T SURE IF IT WAS THE HANGOVER THAT HE WAS NURSING
or his book proposal diverting his focus, but the office hadn't
looked an encouraging sight to him from the moment he'd
arrived.

On his way into work, and despite the fact he knew he shouldn't even be behind the wheel of a car after drinking last night, he'd made a quick stop at McDonald's to try and shake himself out of his alcohol-induced reverie.

Three cups of coffee later, he was still feeling the caffeine's arrhythmic effects as he put his bag down beside his chair and perused the surroundings.

A labyrinth of brown desks around him were already filling up with the early risers, their black computer monitors blinking to life as they began performing their daily wind-up routines of hectic communication and frenzied motion, all in pursuit of that looming deadline.

Joe had tried never to feel the pressure of deadlines. His view of them was that they were something to aspire to, not be dictated by.

Surrounded by various papers, photographs and reports haphazardly decorating the surface of his desk as well as an in-tray stacked high with jobs to do, he sat down and flicked on his computer. Given that his workspace was pretty much the same all year round, he couldn't use his book as an excuse for not tidying it. Besides, he liked to think of his desk as user-friendly; if you stepped back and looked at it from a distance, it all made perfect sense.

Tapping in his username and password, Joe winced as the message notification flashed up on the screen, informing him of 57 e-mails in his inbox. His hangover recovery not yet in full swing, he tilted back in the chair and began massaging his temples.

His piece on Obadiah's execution had brought with it all the ethical baggage he had expected with a state execution. The whole situation had ignited a capital punishment debate in the country, with even staunch Roman Catholic Bertie Ahern throwing his opinion into the arena.

Joe had caught him on Sky News that morning, arguing that criminals were real people who had lives and a capacity to feel pain and fear. He had smiled, hearing the former Taoiseach insist that 'what is being overlooked is the mental suffering that the criminal suffers in the time leading up to the execution.' The faux drama of him asking a reporter how he would feel knowing he was going to die tomorrow morning at 08:00, was forced to the point of being comical.

Joe had to agree there was no such thing as a humane method of putting a person to death. Having seen the horrific process firsthand, he conceded that, regardless of the crime, every form of execution was a terrifying and gruesome ordeal to witness. It would be hard for anyone to believe that the relatives of Obadiah's victims had enjoyed watching him die.

There was no doubt that such an act had a brutalising effect on society as a whole, numbing them to the inhumanity occurring in the world. Yet while he didn't believe they'd enjoyed Obadiah's execution, they'd certainly taken comfort from that fact that the death penalty, being the bluntest of blunt instruments, had removed any last vestiges of the man's humanity and any possibility of rehabilitation which may have existed.

Just one more act resulting in cultural anathema, Joe thought.

Though the country currently had a mutual understanding unimaginable since the 1960's, Obadiah's actions had reminded people of the atrocities committed by various loyalist gangs at the height of The Troubles. Paramilitary activities of abduction, torture and murder on random Catholic civilians had been common occurrences, with some crimes arguably as brutal as Obadiah's murders. It could at least be argued that during The Troubles, people were killing for something they believed in.

Obadiah Stark had killed merely because he was a monster and one of the most dangerous human predators on the planet.

The thrum of the office brought him back to his environ,

and he began deleting emails without opening them. Reading the first few lines of them in the viewing pane provided him with enough information to know whether or not they were going to be relevant.

An envelope slapping onto Joe's desk caused him to jump. Alison Climi was walking away by the time he registered who had dropped it there.

Alison, long mahogany hair, a slight but curvy figure and a thirty-six-year-old face that was gentle yet attractive, flicked a gaze back at Joe as she moved back towards her corner of the office. Her column, the 'tits and arse' section as Joe called it, was all showbiz and celebrity gossip. Yet despite the potential shallowness of her clientele, Alison always seemed to make her pieces project more depth than they probably deserved.

Joe knew she was married, but that didn't stop him continuously flirting with her whenever the opportunity arose.

She had never said she was happily married.

In fact, he often thought she deliberately encouraged him to come onto her just to appease her ego. She certainly always dressed the part; low, v-necked sweaters and short skirts that had encouraged many of the men in the office to start a pool on the colour of her knickers. Though she had yet to perform her interpretation of Sharon Stone, so he didn't know for sure, Joe had ten euros on them always being black.

Seeing her caused him to momentarily forget his hangover. Grabbing his fourth cup of coffee of the morning, he walked over to her at her desk and sat in the chair opposite her.

"Mornin'," Joe chirped.

"Hey," Alison said back at him, not looking up.

Idly flicking through the piles of papers in front of him, he quickly scanned some of the information.

"I thought Jennifer Aniston was seeing Gerry Butler?" Joe asked casually.

"She was," came the playful reply, as Alison slammed her hand down on top of the pile. "About five years ago. And, just like all the rest, you'll just have to wait until tomorrow's edition to read all about it, no pun intended."

"Oh, I can hardly wait," he said sarcastically.

"Don't you have something to do?" Alison enquired with as much implication as she could manage.

Joe seemed oblivious to the hint. "Of course, but nothing that can't wait until you call a time-out and let me know I'm getting on your nerves."

"Okay, you're getting on my nerves," she said laughing. "I have work I need to get on with. The world won't wait forever to find out about Jen and her beau you know. Besides, don't you want to know what is in the envelope I gave you? The postmark said London, I think."

"London? My reputation must be preceding me," he replied, striding across the floor to his desk.

He noticed the package had been posted from Mayfair as he tore it open and removed the contents. A note and a business card were paper-clipped to a booklet advertising a criminal profiling service, run out of London. The company, Behavioral Relativity Service (BRS), offered a service which reflected the field of criminal anthropology's 'multidisciplinary composition and theoretical plurality, presenting an authoritative focus on the theoretical concerns surrounding the causes of crime, their interrelationships and the criminal process to the addressing of the actual crime and its perpetrator.'

The note was signed by Victoria Carter, head anthropologist of the BRS.

Writing to offer her assistance to Joe, she'd been following his pieces on Obadiah Stark during his murders, arrest and execution and had heard he was intent on writing a book on Obadiah's life and crimes.

Placing the note and booklet on his desk, he pinched the bridge of his nose and slumped into his chair. He knew he should feel flattered that someone with such experience would want to meet and possibly work with him.

Joe knew his book would need someone like her to lend it credibility. He was determined not to fall into the trap of stereotyping Obadiah as the nice, quiet boy next door who, by the light of the full moon had mutilated his victim's naked bodies because they reminded him of his father whom he hated with a passion.

Though without a doubt a sociopath, in Obadiah's case, the word was more a description than an aetiology.

The man had certainly projected callousness and been able to manipulate other human beings without guilt, displaying the kind of narcissism that isolates someone from basic feelings and emotions. But to really understand how his level of dysfunction had alienated him from his fellow human beings, Joe knew he needed a specialist in the area of the 'cause and effect' processes precipitated by such narcissistic disorders.

He was still flicking the business card between his fingers when he heard his name shouted across the floor.

"O'Connell. You got a minute?"

Putting the card in his pocket, he walked into the office at a measured pace, closing the door behind him.

Lit with plain, hazy fluorescent illumination, the blinds drawn across the windows filtered subdued incandescence in slats across the room.

Joe sighed blissfully at the numbing effect the subdued lighting had on his head, sitting down in the seat opposite his editor.

Ciaran Walsh was in his late forties, slightly overweight but possessing the broad shoulders of someone who had once been lean and fit. His brown eyes peered through his steel-rimmed, black glasses. As well as being known as a nice guy, he was softly spoken and casual, dressed in a blue shirt; no tie, no jacket and black trousers completed with meticulously polished shoes.

Ciaran had a reputation in the office for being a man of stringent self-control and punctuality. Many of the staff saw him as the eye of the hurricane; calm in the face of the chaos that was a press room. Always coming across as if he had any situation under his complete control, Ciaran Walsh was someone who was not only a good editor but a decent human being. Joe knew he often played upon those most principled characteristics to get what he wanted and sometimes he felt guilty about it. He liked his boss but had never been one to fall into line easily, often trying to find holes in other people's logic as to why he should do something a particular way.

Joe knew he often came across as belligerent and that the only reason he still had a job was that he was damn good at it. His editor knew it too. Joe was one of the most proficient journalists Ciaran had working for him.

During his eight years with the paper, his crime reporting had gone from commenting on local delinquencies to being one of the country's leading sources of information on not only local criminals and their activities, but on international crimes and their after-effects, both politically and emotionally. Ciaran always expected good work from Joe, but even he was still surprised by his ability to gather information from witnesses, victims, and most intriguingly, the criminals themselves in some cases. Not only did Joe seem to understand the bureaucratic ways of things, but he could get under the skin of the people he was investigating, often coming back and producing a piece of journalism that was not only factually accurate but imaginative and powerful.

Though Ciaran didn't want to know how Joe gained most of his information, he did know that not once in eight years had Joe O'Connell produced a mediocre piece of work for The Daily Éire. It was that reason and Joe's knowledge of the crimes which had convinced Ciaran to offer him the prestigious job of reporting on the execution of Obadiah Stark.

As he spoke in his melodic Gaelic tone, he looked serious but thoughtful. "So, how are you? I know we haven't really spoken since the prison."

Joe shrugged his shoulders, not used to answering questions from his editor that required emotional honesty. "Okay. You know, just getting on with things."

"There's no shame in admitting that watching someone die, regardless of what they've done, is a pretty big deal. I don't know how I would feel about it."

Joe could feel his boss's sincerity as he spoke, his voice soft and empathetic. "Well, he didn't writhe around in agony. He just looked like he'd fallen asleep, albeit suffering what appeared to be a myoclonic jerk halfway through."

Ciaran looked at Joe quizzically. "What's a myoclonic jerk?"

"You know when you're just falling asleep, and you're dreaming you're riding a bike, and you fall off? You wake yourself up by jumping in your sleep as you bang your head in your dream. That's a myoclonic jerk. Obadiah had what looked like one, just before he actually died. It was creepy, actually."

Joe stared at the floor for a moment, playing back the moment in his mind when Obadiah had looked at everyone in the viewing chamber. It had almost been as if something had momentarily interrupted the execution process.

"Interesting," Ciaran replied, moving his empty coffee cup absentmindedly across the desktop.

Looking back up, Joe smiled halfheartedly. The whole conversation had him uncomfortable. Sensing his unease, Ciaran quickly moved onto his reason for asking to see him.

"Anyway, I received a phone call from Margaret Keld this morning."

Joe quickly straightened up in the chair, his interest piqued and his discomfort forgotten.

"Really? And…?"

"… and, she's agreed to your request for an interview and is willing to meet. She laid down a few stipulations, but nothing that will pose a problem, I don't think."

Ciaran sounded almost triumphant as he delivered the news.

Joe looked surprised. "To be honest, I never thought she'd agree to talk to me. I mean, she's turned down every interview request ever made since her daughter died."

Ciaran took the opportunity to remind Joe of his responsibility. "Well, it's good news for you that, for whatever reason, she's changed her mind. But remember Joe, I had to pull a lot of strings, considering it has nothing to do with anything that will benefit this paper. One of her provisos was that the interview is not exploitative, purely factual. She doesn't want her daughter's name being used as a promotional tool."

Joe knew Ciaran was referring to his book, an independent piece of work, neither sanctioned nor opposed by the paper and one that required Joe to use many of The Daily Éire's resources to make it feasible.

Margaret Keld's agreeing to an interview was the first step.

Victoria Carter would be the second, but he was going to keep her to himself for the time being. Ciaran and the paper had no monetary gain from the book deal, and if working on it infringed on his actual reporting duties, his editor could intervene and stop him pursuing it. So far, it hadn't come to that, and his editor had gone out of his way to be helpful.

Therefore, Joe knew he had to show his appreciation.

"Thanks, Ciaran. It means a lot. I won't let it get in the way of my job."

Joe meant what he said, but knew that it would require a lot of work in his own time.

Still, fortune and glory are never supposed to come easily.

The ringing phone on Ciaran's desk broke the moment. Joe thumbed back towards the door, indicating his intent to leave. Picking up the phone, Ciaran nodded and greeted the caller with his surname.

As Joe left, he heard his editor sigh before the door closed behind him.

The office was now in full flow, every desk and cubicle diligent with ambitious individuals, eager to be the next candidate for Sky News or the BBC.

Many of the people he worked with had made no secret of the fact they were using the paper as a proverbial stepping stone to something better, at least in their eyes.

He looked around at the various outcroppings of monitors, noting the numerous pairs of eyes and flurries of hair which were all that remained above the many terminals.

Alison looked busy scrolling showbiz copy in her corner, the financial team of Wilson Graves and Mike O'Hare could be heard talking about the most recent Bank of England interest rate cut, their voices just audible above the low murmur of the television above them.

All around, the snicker of keyboards filled the air, suddenly sounding to Joe like the loneliest sound in the world; the sound of monotony.

Placing his hands in his pockets, he casually weaved his way between desks until he arrived at his own. He fished the card out of his pocket and began to dial Victoria Carter's number. The call connected on the fourth ring, putting Joe through to a messaging service.

The brief message, detailing that Victoria was currently away on business and would be back on the 18th September, provided Joe with a melodic tone and perfect diction; quintessentially English.

He waited for the telltale beep for speaking.

"Hi. My name is Joe O'Connell. I work for The Daily Éire. I received your parcel this morning, offering your services regarding my book. I'd like to take you up on your offer, so please ring me back when you get this message. Cheers."

Hanging up, he found himself imagining the face that went with the voice. She sounded like she would be a slight, fragile specimen, but he knew well enough that perception of someone rarely matched the actuality of their appearance.

Still, that English voice of hers had sounded damn sexy.

Checking the time, he decided to prepare his notes for a meeting with Margaret Keld. Her cooperation was necessary, not only for his actual narrative but also for ensuring the collaboration of other relatives. Joe knew he had to treat any interaction with them sensitively.

Even though Margaret Keld's daughter, Obadiah's second victim in Ireland, had been murdered over seven years ago, he knew that feelings, both personal and political, still ran strongly regarding the Gardaí's lengthy investigation into the killings. Though eager to pursue an alternative career and hopefully secure a financial deal, it was important to Joe that the book be taken seriously by his peers as a point of reference for the Obadiah Starks of the world.

His time covering the murders had given him an insight afforded to few others. And though it had taken him to dark places and left him with images he would rather be without, they had also provided him with a dichotomous understanding that had allowed him to see human monsters like Obadiah for what they were: social chameleons. Able to use the facets of peoples' leftover emotions to fashion something appealing to them which they would then use to bait the hook that would eventually snare them.

Settling into his chair, Joe scribbled down a few ideas he

had for the interview. How this one went would dictate the responses of the other relatives to his request for their thoughts.

He found himself wondering if such a tragedy could convince someone that there comes a time when there's no longer a point searching for an understanding as to why some things happen.

Would Margaret Keld really be interested in a book attempting to unravel the complex nature of her daughter's killer?

After all, Joe thought, he was dead. What would insight into his mind offer them now?

'Death - A punishment to some, to some a gift, and to many a favour.'
Seneca

4

08:49

From the moment he'd woken up, the hairs on Obadiah's neck and arms had been prickling as if subject to static.

Something was out of place.

During his viaticum, Father Hicks had hinted that Obadiah's only salvation would be to accept God's forgiveness or suffer for all eternity.

He had made no such admonishment.

For this refusal, Obadiah had expected to find himself in a dark, inhospitable place, distant from God and in extremis as he was tortured in ways his blackest nightmares could never imagine - a punishment reflective of his soul.

He currently saw none of those things.

His path leading from the house was tapering into a tree-lined grove. The low morning sun flashed through the branches, striping the path and casting long shadows ahead of him, as though indicating his destination. Sessile oaks either side were a blanket of autumnal golden fire, their colours rustic and faded. The leaves seemed to possess an inner light of pure yellow, burning brighter than the sun. Interspersed with the Sessile's were small filmy ferns, their previously dull, green leaves now a brilliant crimson.

For a moment, he wondered if he was still dying and the two minutes it took for the injections to manifest their effects were translating into abstract time.

Closing his eyes, he recalled the sensation of Velcro straps, the tilting of the execution table and the pin-prick caress of needles being inserted into his veins. Moments later, he'd been somewhere which reminded him of his childhood home. But if death was a dream-like state such as this, death wasn't something he would be worried about.

As if to reinforce the reality of his surroundings, Obadiah touched the trees and tarmac. His every breath drew in the fusty odour of mouldy leaves and damp earth, evoking the smells of sage and pine. Underneath, their aroma was subtly being overridden by the fragrance of decay, as countless organisms actively broke down spent vegetation and returned it to the soil.

All these sensations, supported by the bracing air tightening his face, collectively told him he wasn't dreaming.

As the avenue became more urbanised, Obadiah approached what appeared to be a town. He stopped and leaned against the corner of a wall, his face dropping as a look of puzzlement skittered across it.

Clusters of brick buildings faded into the distance, surrounded by folded hills of vibrant green. Streets ahead of him dazzled in their array of painted washes, picturesque shops and bar signs. He saw lovers walking hand in hand, the woman laughing at something the man had whispered in her ear. Another couple sat on a bench, murmuring. A man walked slowly down the street, hands in his pockets, his attention focused on a distant point ahead. A woman pushing a pram across the street waved her thanks to the driver for stopping.

Everywhere he looked, people were going about their mundane, human lives.

The sights before him fuelled his confusion. He tried to

take in every detail of the environment, studying each scent and ambivalent action.

A lion studying cattle on the prairie lands.

He began travelling slowly towards the throng of activity, moving past the shopfront displays. Catching sight of a figure mirroring his steps, he leaned into the plate glass. Obadiah saw the white shirt and blue pyjama trousers, hair cut close to his scalp and a face clean-shaven. His eyes reflected the light from behind him, appearing colourless in the sheen of the glass.

Purveyors of the soul that told everything about a man.

In this case, they spoke of a man very much alive.

Turning away from the window, Obadiah gathered his thoughts as he moved on past cafés and sandwich bars. The smell of coffee and croissants assaulted his senses to the point of being overwhelming. He heard a train in the distance, rattling across tracks and ahead of him spotted a marketplace where people milled about in front of bookstalls and fruit and vegetable stands. Near the horizon, a church spire pointed heavenward.

Making his way to the centre of the town, Obadiah positioned himself on a bench while continuing to gaze at the golden glint of streets and shops in the morning sun. All around him life buzzed and shone with promise. It was the opposite of his habitat in Absolom for almost a decade and a complete contrast to all he'd ever known.

Yet he was still trying to shake the sensation that this location was familiar.

The house. The town.

It was almost as if someone had taken a description from his memory and interpreted it as best they could, but in the process had lost something. For all intents and purposes, it looked remarkably similar to Killarney in Kerry where he'd grown up.

Somewhere he'd tried very hard to forget.

But if that was the case, how did he get here?

Okay. What the fuck is going on?

An attractive, red-haired woman passed by, distracting him from his thoughts. Her slim, toned legs and shapely hips were accentuated by the tight fit Levis she wore. He found himself aroused at the sight of her, despite his current predicament. Then again, he hadn't seen a woman in years, so maybe it wasn't that strange.

But despite her physical appearance, all he saw was meat.

Someone plainly waiting to be a victim.

She glanced at him, embarrassed by the attention he was giving her. Reactions such as those and the growing whispers and stares he was accumulating, forced Obadiah to realise he was unsettling the populous.

In pyjama trousers, a shirt and no shoes, he looked every inch the unfortunate. If he were to go any further, he would need some clothes.

As he sat contemplating how to obtain some, he heard someone call his name.

Looking around, he noticed a man approaching, tall and thin with an unusually chubby face and a confused expression. His hands were gesticulating wildly at the surrounding environment as though he couldn't believe Obadiah was sitting there.

"Obadiah? Jesus, man. What's the craic? Why are you sat in your fuckin' PJ's?"

He sounded genuinely concerned, his manner free as though addressing a close friend.

Obadiah stared at the man with a dark expression, his right hand blocking out the now high sun's glare. He didn't like his casual tone. Nor did he look remotely familiar. His accent however established that Obadiah was indeed in Ireland.

He studied the man as people continued to walk past, muttering under their breath and adhering to the sociological theory of defusing responsibility.

"Do you think he's sick…"

"… poor man. He must be homeless…"

"… if his family know? I know his wife… go over? No way. What happens if he's drunk?"

The stranger moved around to face Obadiah.

"You must be freezing? Does Eva know you're here?"

He moved to sit beside Obadiah before noticing the look in his eyes. Suddenly feeling uncomfortable, he decided to remain standing, shifting awkwardly from foot to foot. Despite this, his tone remained laced with worry.

"You feelin' okay, mate?"

"You know me?" Obadiah's voice was soft, yet subtly accusatory. He didn't like what the stranger represented - an unknown quantity.

The man's eyebrows wrinkled in confusion. "What do you mean? Jesus, have you been drinking or something?"

Obadiah's eyes held their obsidian darkness. He was in no mood for civilities. However, the encounter had now provided him with an opportunity - both for attire and possible answers.

Realising this, Obadiah softened his tone slightly. "I don't suppose you could see to it to loan me some clothes?" he asked, faking his friendliest smile.

The man returned the gesture and placed a hand on Obadiah's shoulder, cheerfully jostling him as he spoke.

"Of course I can. Christ, my car's over there. You can tell me what happened to you on the way."

He pointed southwards towards a series of side streets. "Wait here. I'll pull up over there."

As the stranger jogged away, Obadiah returned his attention to the town, now bustling with people.

The sun was at enough of an apex that it appeared to be setting the buildings alight, as though the town was determined to present itself to the world.

A horn sounded just ahead of him. The man had returned and was idling by the kerb, his face full of eagerness for Obadiah to climb into the vehicle so he could assist him with his misfortune.

At that moment, a piece of the puzzle fell into place.

He has no idea who I really am.

———

THE JOURNEY TO THE STRANGER'S HOUSE WAS BRIEF.

Obadiah said little, preferring to project the impression of someone vulnerable and confused.

Confused he was.

Pulling up at a small cottage, the man invited Obadiah in as though they were friends and journeyed upstairs to find some clothes. As he waited, Obadiah softly padded around the living room, reconnoitring his environment.

For the second time today, he noticed a photograph that piqued his curiosity.

Apparently taken on a night out, it showed a group of people, men and women, jeering towards the camera with their arms around each other, drinks held high in the air. A woman, second to the left, Obadiah recognised as the woman he had encountered this morning. Beside her, he saw himself, smiling as he mouthed something to the cameraman.

Interesting.

Aware of his host returning, Obadiah turned towards the living room door, having taken hold of the picture frame. He ran his tongue over his teeth, gently biting the front of it.

The man was explaining that he was sorry if the clothes weren't very stylish, but they were all he could find.

Obadiah positioned himself in front of the doorway, holding the picture frame by his side. His breathing was slow and even, his demeanour relaxed to the point where his heart rate was bradycardic.

As the man turned into the living room, Obadiah grabbed him by the throat and propelled him against the wall. The clothes dropped to the floor, the man trying to grab at his attacker's hands, but finding a grip like steel.

"Jesus Christ, what the fuck…?" His voice was tremulous with shock.

Obadiah leaned in close. "Shhhhh. I simply want your attention. I'll release my grip and allow you to take some deep breaths and calm yourself. If you try to run, you'll be telling God in heaven that you never saw evil so personified as you did in my eyes. Do you understand?"

The man nodded frantically, the colour draining from his face with the understanding that the person he thought he knew, was also very dangerous.

Obadiah relaxed his hand and took a small step back. "Who are you?" Obadiah's tone remained quiet, yet laced with insistence for an answer.

The man swallowed audibly as he rubbed his neck. "What? Mark. Mark Thorne. For fuck's sake, Obadiah. What's got into you? You must be ill, mate. Let me call Eva, and she can come and get you."

Obadiah ignored him and continued. "How do you know me?"

"I'm a friend of your wife's. We went to school together. I introduced you both."

Mark's hands were shaking violently as adrenaline flooded his brain and body's stimulus centres.

"I'm not married," Obadiah replied matter of factly. He held up the photograph. "When was this taken?"

Mark paused as he tried to recall the time period. "Erm…

two years ago. We all went to Portugal. Don't you remember?"

"Two years ago, I was in Absolom, in a cell with a three inch by three foot long slit for sunlight." He moved closer to Mark, his eyes never blinking.

"Absolom? What're you talking about? You're sick, man. Let me help you. We can call Eva and deal with it together."

His tone failed to hide its pathetic, pleading quality.

"And where are we?"

"Killarney. We're in Killarney."

Obadiah barely reacted to the confirmation that he was in the place of his childhood, his only movement the release of the picture frame which shattered on the floor.

He couldn't explain why Killarney looked so different from how he remembered but then again, he hadn't been here for over thirty years.

"Please let me go, Obadiah. What's with all the questions? I don't understand why you're doing this."

"Ah, the eternal refrain of humanity. Pleading ignorance and begging for help."

Obadiah moved so quickly, Mark didn't have time to react. The vice-like grip was back around his throat once more, causing him to become frantic and aggressive.

"For god's sake, man. Let me fucking go, I mean it." Trying to sound intimidating, he simply sounded like a wilting flower.

Obadiah tightened his grip, pulling Mark close. "Do I look like someone who cares what God thinks?"

Grabbing his head with both hands, Obadiah snapped it around, the accompanying sound like a tree limb breaking.

Mark's body seemingly hung in mid-air for a moment, before sliding down the wall and crumpled in a rag doll heap at Obadiah's feet.

The house became silent once more. The ticking of a clock

in the passageway and the insectile hum of distant traffic outside the only sounds accompanying the moment.

Obadiah sniffed belligerently before picking up the clothes and holding them up one at a time - dark blue Diesel jeans and a white T-shirt.

Obadiah nodded at Mark's good taste in legwear before stripping off the shirt and pyjama trousers and changing into them. He caught sight of his back in the mirror behind him as he pulled on the T-shirt. The absence of his tally still confused and frustrated him in equal measure.

Not only had his chance at death been stolen from him, but his shrine had also been taken.

Dressed, Obadiah stepped over to Mark's body and removed his trainers. Checking the size, he sat on the floor to put them on before rising and picking up the house keys from the table by the door.

Venturing outside, the street remained quiet, the occasional passing car the only sign of activity. He locked the door and posted the keys through the letterbox, taking in a deep taste of the clean, morning air before setting off back in the direction of town.

He considered taking Mark's car but quickly dismissed it. Having spent so long behind concrete walls, he was enjoying the opportunity to walk freely.

Approaching the town again, he noticed it was busier than when he'd left. People wore casual clothing, making the most of the unbroken sky and the uncharacteristically warm autumn weather. Aside from Dublin, Killarney had always been the most popular of tourist attractions in Ireland. Its historical exposure had begun when Queen Victoria had visited in 1861 and had continued ever since. Indeed, the place had spawned Hugh Kelly and Brendan Moloney. Obadiah smiled wryly that its most famous son was currently walking amongst them and they had no idea.

He knew they had tried hard to forget that one of the

world's most infamous serial killers had grown up in the same town as Michael Fassbender.

With the streets becoming crowded and hot, Obadiah returned to the bench he'd initially sat on and once again studied the passers-by.

Their movements and actions reminded him of flies, trapped behind a window, struggling to find a way out of their prison of glass. Their behaviours were random and manic, as they haphazardly flitted from one window to the next, never appearing to stop long enough to take in any information.

Within this chaos, Obadiah noticed the red-haired woman again.

Carrying bags of shopping, she was more focused than the others, seemingly set on a particular destination. Obadiah stood and proceeded to copy her route, weaving between parked cars in the lot like a Great White honing in on its prey. She fished a set of keys from her bag as she approached a shop, currently empty and cloaked in darkness.

He realised she was either opening up or she owned it - most likely the latter.

His footsteps light as though cushioned, Obadiah steadily made his way towards her, using her blind side to avoid acknowledgement of his presence.

His mind was focused, the initial caprice of his arrival here now tempered by the opportunity presented to him.

Who was he to deny his true nature? In the absence of the reason for his being here, why not test its boundaries?

She saw Obadiah's approach reflected in the window and turned to face him, her expression one of curiosity as to the approach of a handsome stranger.

Using the opportunity to get close, Obadiah smiled, flicking his tongue across the front of his teeth before bringing his elbow round and catching her directly on the jaw.

He grabbed her as she slipped to the floor, gently guiding

her down. He glanced around, ensuring no one had witnessed him, before plucking the keys still clenched in her left hand and locating the one that opened the door.

He dragged her body into the cool, darkened shop and positioned her against a wall, closing and locking the door behind him.

He scanned outside a second time before carrying Red towards the rear of the shop, propping her in a chair in such a way that she couldn't fall off in her unconscious state.

Obadiah grabbed another chair and sat opposite, studying her face.

Her complexion was like porcelain, almost alabaster, in contrast to her fiery hair. The V shape of her lilac sweater trailed a path to a suprasternal notch delving deeply into the border of her sternum, her breasts below rising and falling gently in her cataleptic state.

He could have watched her all day and night, the perfection of her face a direct contrast to the sights he'd seen for so long at Absolom.

But he had a job to do.

If the answers he required didn't come freely to him, he would use his new environment to entertain him instead.

Obadiah gently slapped Red's cheeks to bring her round. She murmured slightly as reality slowly returned, her body tensing with the veracity of her situation and how she'd arrived here, flooding over her in waves.

She worked her aching jaw from side to side, suddenly noticing the throbbing in her head. As she spoke, she tried to hide her fear, but the slight tremble in her voice seeped through.

"Please, you can take the money. Just don't hurt me. You don't have to do this."

"I don't have to, no." Obadiah smiled a baboon's smile that stretched from ear to ear. "Forgive my manners. I didn't ask you your name."

Red's eyes began to moisten, but her voice became steadier. "Susan. Susan Sheridan. Please, let me go. I haven't seen you. I won't say anything to anyone. This isn't necessary."

Obadiah's green eyes flashed with intent as he stood and wandered over to the counter, randomly opening drawers and cupboards.

Red glanced feverishly toward Obadiah and then the door, trying to calculate if she could make the distance.

Obadiah sensed her intentions."I didn't tie you down. Therefore, I would strongly advise you not to try to make a run for it. Stabbing someone in the back is so... uncivilised." His voice was playful yet menacing as he continued scanning the area.

Opening the drawer behind him, he smiled before grabbing a knife and closing it again.

Obadiah returned to his seat, not at all surprised to see her still sitting there. She could possibly have made it if she'd seized the moment.

Coulda, woulda, shoulda, he thought, playfully pricking the ends of his fingers with the knife. He had to admit that the smell of her fear was exhilarating. He hadn't experienced it in so long - not in such a raw, unbridled fashion.

Tears silently streaked her face.

"No crying, please. It's a waste of suffering."

Susan repeatedly sniffed before finding her voice. "You're going to kill me, aren't you?"

Obadiah's eyes appearing to glint, despite the absence of any direct light. His expression caused Susan's breathing to become more rapid, as though suddenly deprived of oxygen. The realisation of what was about to occur was the most surreal sensation she had ever experienced.

"Please... I'll give you anything you..."

Already bored, Obadiah's hand snapped out like a coiled snake.

The knife swung in an upward arch, effortlessly slicing through the soft of her neck. Susan gasped quietly before the blood flowed freely from the now gaping wound. Her eyes developed a peaceful, distant gaze as her head slumped down to rest on her chest.

Obadiah wiped the blood which had splashed his face with the back of his hand. The coppery smell of Susan's blood slowly filled the air.

Whatever the reasons for his emancipation from Absolom, why had he been returned here - to the place where his torture had begun?

The country, never mind the town, was a constant reminder of who he could have been if his childhood circumstances had been different. Had he been destined to become this way, or did his father take a child and manufacture a monster?

He was saddened that the two souls he'd liberated so far could not be part of his now-absent tally.

Obadiah found himself wondering what Dr Franklin would have to say concerning this disappointment. At the time, he'd found it amusing, though interesting, that someone would want to devote so much time and effort trying to understand what made him tick.

Franklin had believed Obadiah was a loner, suffering from a narcissistic personality disorder with the potential for explosive violence that could be linked all the way back to his childhood.

Obadiah didn't doubt any of that. But as far as he knew, Franklin had missed the one fundamental understanding making his crimes unique.

Obadiah Stark had killed for no reason more complicated than he chose to.

His liberation from Absolom hadn't changed that aesthetic.

He looked at Susan's motionless body for a few moments, wondering how long it would take for someone to find her before moving to the door and stepping outside, knife in hand.

The sun was maintaining its persistent campaign of attempting to inject warmth into the cold chill. The wind had risen slightly, stirring the leaves on the trees, the current ignorance of Obadiah's campaign of horror ensuring the morning remained as motionless as a painting.

Here, Obadiah was apparently an unknown quantity, his history unrealised by the people living in the place where he'd been born.

That, compounded with his lack of understanding about everything, did not sit well with him.

He had been ready for death, had prepared himself, and someone had stolen it from him. Therefore, by his reckoning, he didn't really have anything to lose.

He hadn't wanted a second chance. After all, you only felt guilty if you thought you'd done something wrong.

His mind focused, he decided that if he couldn't understand this place, he was going to make damn sure it understood him.

Denying him his death had been a grave mistake and one that many would now suffer for.

He randomly approached a lady trying to get into a car, grabbing her by the hair. Swinging her around by her ponytail, Obadiah slammed her into the nearby vehicle.

Ignoring her cries as she slipped to the floor, Obadiah leaned over and sliced the knife across her face, neatly popping her right eyeball and severing her nose in half. She squealed and grabbed for her face as he cut across her neck, her body going limp almost instantly.

A couple ahead had already started their car, having witnessed Obadiah's actions and were accelerating away. He picked up the woman's body as though it was weightless and threw it into the car's oncoming path. The driver of the vehicle swerved to avoid it, acting on instinct despite knowing that she was already dead.

The front of the car crumpled as it ploughed into a parked Mercedes, the red automobile sliding sideways before striking the vehicle next to it. In his dazed state, the driver didn't notice Obadiah coming up beside his window, his hand holding a stone that was subsequently launched through it, striking the man in the face.

Obadiah reached in and roughly pulled him through the shattered glass, its serration slicing a wound in the top of his head. The female passenger was slumped forwards, her head bleeding from the impact to the dashboard. Obadiah knew she was already dead.

The knife in hand, he brought it up towards the man's hands pitifully trying to protect his face, slicing fingers off neatly below the knuckle. Its journey continued on and came across his cheek, widening his mouth into a clown's grin. Obadiah quickly stabbed it into the other side of his face, the muscles making a soft sighing sound as they met resistance with the knife. His mouth severed wide, the man shuddered as he passed a final fluid-filled breath.

Obadiah paused, considering his next move while surveying the ensuing panic. Coupled with the buildings around him, cathedrals of shimmering glass and brick and shining with life in the bright sun, the whole situation was almost heavenly.

He saw people pathetically attempting to barricade themselves inside shops and cars. Many souls were hurriedly leaving the location on foot, not looking back in case they caught his attention.

Tightening his grip on the knife, he ran towards the nearest pedestrian, gathering speed as the woman with the pram tried to flee Obadiah's charge. He wasn't interested in finesse or meticulous detail. He just wanted them to die. Their only crime: being in his presence.

The woman with the pram didn't get very far as Obadiah bounded up with dancer-like precision, grabbing her from behind by the throat. Kicking the pram out of the way and ignoring the cries from within, he brought the knife down in an overhead motion. It entered the woman's stomach just below her sternum.

Sliding to the floor, she tried futilely to hold in her stomach and protect her head at the same time, thereby failing to intercept the foot travelling to her face. Obadiah's kick to her head shattered her skull.

She called out for someone to protect her baby from between the disjointed fragments that had once been her jaw. Obadiah's final kick broke through her fragile latticework of ribs, puncturing her lungs and forcing blood to explode from the wound in her abdomen.

The pram remained stationary on the path. The newly orphaned baby continued crying, sensing the fractured emotion in the air.

A man altruistically charged Obadiah from his left side. Gesturing towards the pram with a bow, as though encouraging him to pursue it, Obadiah kicked it again, this time into the road. The baby screamed in conjunction with the sudden violence of movement.

Twisting to the side as the man shoulder-barged him, Obadiah grabbed him by his hair and began stabbing him in a brutal frenzy. The knife repeatedly penetrated his lower abdomen and groin area, some of the incisions so deep that his ileum poked out through various apertures.

The man cried out, more from shock than pain, before falling silent. His eyes slowly collected a glazed expression of bewilderment and peace in equal measure, before stilling themselves and staring towards the sky.

Obadiah's heart was racing with the exertion of his

actions, but he quickly managed to slow it to its normal rhythm. Looking around, he realised that little more was necessary for what he wanted to accomplish.

Keeping hold of the knife and ignoring the receding sounds of terror, he scanned the now emptying streets for somewhere he could wait for the authorities.

Somewhere less fussy.

Spotting a pub just a short distance ahead he began a leisurely walk towards it, wiping his hands lazily on his jeans. The few people who remained on the street ahead parted with his coming, as though he were Moses waving his staff. He knew they were wondering if they were next to die, but Obadiah was past his desire for inflicting suffering. Now, he simply wanted closure.

Ahead on Main Street, he noticed The Laurels. A traditional Irish pub, Obadiah remembered it from his childhood. The red signage emblazoned with yellow lettering was enticing to Obadiah.

Though he'd never had a drink in there, having left Ireland before he was old enough to legally partake, the memories it sparked were so powerful he felt almost obliged to have a tipple there.

As he made his way through the doors into the virtually-deserted pub, the tiled floors and beamed ceilings spoke of rustic Irish heritage, an obvious nod to the old ways. Approaching the bar, he noticed the numerous alcoves and dimly lit corners, their offers of seductive seclusion inviting to the new customer.

But not Obadiah. He wanted to be in plain sight for when they arrived to take him.

The red-faced proprietor approached the bar, the smile on his face beginning to fade and replaced by one of fear as his eyes registered the blood on Obadiah's T-shirt and the knife he had placed casually on the bar.

"Barkeep, a pint of Guinness, please."

The man continued staring at Obadiah, uncertain of how to respond to his polite request.

His reply was preceded by a long pause. "... certainly."

As his Guinness was being pulled, Obadiah glanced around the saloon. The few customers it had contained were hurriedly leaving, the muted televisions on the walls now the only signs that the place was open for business.

They needn't have left on his account. His moment had passed, and now he merely wanted to wait for the Gardaí in peace and have a quiet drink while he did so.

As the pint appeared in front of him, Obadiah admired the shamrock shaped into its head. He had always been intrigued as to how bar staff learnt to do them. Did they go to a class, or was it something they just picked up?

His first mouthful was like honey gliding down his throat, warm and soothing. He drank almost half a pint in one go before placing it back on the bar and closing his eyes, as if to savour the moment he knew would be fleeting.

He heard the sirens in the distance and knew the building would soon be surrounded by armed and unarmed Gardaí officers, trying to make contact with him and to discuss his surrender peacefully.

He felt no fear. He had faced horrors in Absolom that no one in this place could ever comprehend or even understand, on an emotional level or any other.

Though considered rebarbative himself, Obadiah positioned paedophiles and child murderers as the lowest form of detritus on an evolutionary scale. So strong were his feelings on such revolting examples of humanity, that while being briefly held on Ellis Unit in Texas, before his incarceration in Absolom, he had made contact with one Santiago Margarito Rangel Varelas after learning he was also a guest there.

Obadiah discovered from a guard that Leanna Williams, his two-year-old stepdaughter, had died from multiple brain haemorrhages following kicks to the head. She also had numerous broken ribs and had been sodomised - all injuries inflicted by Varelas, who had informed the police she had fallen at home.

Two weeks later, Varelas had been found dead in his cell, having been beaten and choked to death with his own penis. No one knew how access had been gained to his cell, nor was Obadiah ever implicated in the incident.

Personally, Obadiah had thought he should have had his mouth stitched to the arse of a fat, truck driver, but the phallic suffocation had sufficed.

Through that, his life and incarceration, throughout everything, he had mentally prepared himself for the day when his suffering would all be over, and he could finally rest.

He'd made his peace with the world and had accepted his afterlife would either be blackness or suffering.

Either of which he had been fine with.

Yet, he had ended up here, his childhood home and the site of his own personal nightmare. It held no fear for him now. But once it had and all been because of what it stood for: his torment at the hands of his father.

This had been his Hell.

And someone had seen fit to return him to it. Either for a sick joke whose punchline he wasn't privy to or because someone had broken him out of Absolom and thought he'd want to hide out here in this pathetic excuse for a reality check.

Whatever the reason, Obadiah had just proven he would never accept it. Someone had wasted his or her time.

The Tally Man was no one's puppet. The only rules he played by were his and his alone.

Outside, he heard Gardaí cars pulling up, the drivers

shouting instructions and information to their colleagues. Obadiah knew there would be at least half a dozen officers armed with both Glock .22's chambered for a .40 S&W cartridge with a standard magazine capacity of fifteen rounds and Remington 870 P shotguns with standard four round tube magazines under the barrel.

He noticed the proprietor on the phone, probably talking to one of the Gardaí outside, describing Obadiah's appearance and position within the pub. He knew they would be fortifying their places around the perimeter to ensure he didn't escape.

He had no intention of trying.

Finishing his Guinness, Obadiah stood and smoothed out imaginary creases in his t-shirt. Picking up the knife from the bar, he stared at the proprietor and winked before walking over to the window. He knew they wouldn't have had a chance to set up snipers yet, so felt safe enough. He saw the armed Gardaí where they crouched, weapons pointed downward in a safety position. They had the visors down on their helmets, their Kevlar vests black and bulky.

The street was deserted but for the Gardaí, their cordon visible a few hundred yards in both directions. Obadiah's mind remained unfettered, the scenario playing out before him inconsequential.

The proprietor coughed, radios on the Gardaí vests broadcast muffled voices laced with urgency, the electrical buzz of the televisions in the background, it all echoed around him as though eager to see the outcome of this inevitable showdown.

Obadiah appreciated the symmetry. The circumstance had been much the same when he'd been apprehended the first time around. Then, one man had put the pieces together regarding Obadiah's actions and had managed to outsmart him, something Obadiah had been impressed by.

Not many had ever risen to the task of challenging his

intellect, no one except Kevin O'Hagan. Obadiah had ensured that good ol' Kev had been left with a parting gift before being overwhelmed by officers, subsequently ending up in the high-security prison where he had expected to die.

Today would be less dramatic. He had no intention of resisting apprehension. Even if he'd wanted to be here and had been happy at his good fortune, he could never tow the line, even if he tried.

Being a killer was in his blood. It was all he knew.

Normality was an alien concept to him.

As the Gardaí shifted stances outside, Obadiah decided that now was the time to make his final bow. Whatever his reason for having been brought here, they would just have to manage without him.

Moving to the door, he heard a voice call outside for him to stand down and come out with his hands held high. Opening the door, Obadiah was greeted with bright sunlight reflecting off parked Gardaí vehicles and the stifling smell of petrol fumes. Guns rose almost immediately as he stepped over the threshold of the pub, his hands by his side, the knife still brandished in his left.

"Down on the ground! Get down on the ground, now!"

Obadiah stepped forwards slightly, his expression relaxed. "Officers, please. If you knew who I was, you'd have already fired."

One of the Gardaí moved towards Obadiah, his posture casual to imply trust. His arms extended, he held his hands out in front of him. "Sir, come on. There's no need for any trouble. We can talk about this."

Obadiah smiled at the officer and repositioned his grip, lunging forwards, the knife now above his head.

A gunshot rang out, slamming into him like a concrete fist and driving him back towards the open pub doorway. Voices rang out to hold fire as Obadiah slumped down the door and onto the ground, his body twitching from a chest wound as he bled out.

And so the day fades away, and I begin to wake...

As the light began to dim, he saw shadows, approaching him with waving arms and timbre-like voices. He felt a great weight upon his body but felt no pain. He heard the rushing sound of the ocean as though a seashell was being held to his ear.

As everything began to fade into incandescence, he smelt ozone and heard the sounds of seagulls, calling out for food overhead.

The dark shapes before him morphed into angelic figures, fluttering in a breeze that had suddenly risen. Wind chimes sounded their lonely collisions as he felt the ground soften and plume around him, moulding to his body as though he were sinking into a cushioned hole.

Succumbing to the gentle reverie, Obadiah Stark closed his eyes and settled into his never-ending sleep.

———

HE STIRRED SLIGHTLY AS A BREEZE GENTLY CARESSED HIS FACE, encouraging him to rise from his slumber.

When he opened his eyes, Obadiah saw a white expanse above him, finished with a light fitting in its centre.

He bolted up in bed, feverishly glancing around him. The beige walls and fluttering curtains projected a mocking familiarity. The smell of cooking food tickled his nostrils as he dived out of bed, grabbing the picture frame on the bedside cabinet.

His breathing was rapid, his mind frantic as he tried to understand what had just occurred.

A female voice from somewhere beneath him distracted his concentration.

Obadiah covered the ground to the door in two broad

steps, flinging it open as he hurtled towards the stairway that he had only walked down yesterday.

Reaching the bottom, he saw a small girl covered in flour and a raven-haired woman in a black dressing gown.

His breath caught in his throat.

"Morning, Obi. Ellie was just coming to get you."

Dr. John Franklin, BS.c. (HONS), PH.D. M.A., M.CLIN, PSYCH. A.F.Ps.S.I.

Subject: Stark, Obadiah James (a.k.a. The Tally Man) cont.

Theme classification: Just as the serial killer can be categorised under three particular types, so can these types be further broken down into distinct themes in order to better search for patterns of behaviour. According to Holmes and Holmes $_5$ (1998), four themes (one divided into two clear-cut groups) exist which classify a serial killer as one of the following:

1. **Visionary**: Suffering from a break with reality, the visionary serial killer murders because he has seen visions or heard voices from demons, angels, the devil or God telling him to kill a particular individual or particular types of people.
2. **Mission:** The mission killer is focused on the act of murder itself. He is compelled to murder in order to rid the world of a group of people he has judged to be unworthy or undesirable.
3. **Hedonistic:** This type of sexual killer is subdivided into the following two groups:
4. **Lust:** The lust killer kills for sexual gratification; sex is the focal point of the murder, even after he has killed the victim.
5. **Thrill:** The thrill killer murders for the pleasure and excitement of killing. Once the victim is dead, this murderer loses interest.
6. **Power/Control:** This type of killer derives pleasure

and gratification from being able to exercise control over the victim, and consider themselves a 'master' at what they do.

During my time with Obadiah Stark, this author came to the conclusion that he fits firmly into the power/control classification of serial killer; killing for the derivation of pleasure and control.

Obadiah displays neither incoherent nor delusionary behaviour, instead coming across as an articulate and highly intelligent individual with a typically sociopathic personality, lacking internal control, guilt or conscience, but with a need to control and dominate others.

The subject knew the difference between right and wrong, but elected to ignore the distinctions.

Theme selection criteria: Obadiah Stark's motives centre on his need for dominance and control over his victim. A majority of post-mortem reports performed on his victims indicated injuries consistent with torture. Tease cuts, contusions and ablations were also present on many of the victims' bodies. There were also signs of gagging and restraints, demonstrative of the need for Obadiah to exert power and control. No signs of sexual assault, or evidence that body parts were taken away, were noted. Furthermore, with no link established between any of his victims, it appears that their selection was purely arbitrary.

Classification subtext:

Twenty-seven deaths are attributed to Obadiah Stark - eighteen of which were committed whilst in the United States over a period of six years. Evidence indicates that the subject ceased killing for a period of six months during 1993 for reasons no one has been able to ascertain. During this time period, it is believed the subject left the United States and relocated to his home country of Ireland where he recommenced his murders, committing a further nine over ten years and making him the most prolific serial killer in Ireland's history and indeed the world.

Interestingly, Obadiah Stark was not labelled 'The Tally Man' until 1993, when Sara Morgan, a twenty-four year old woman who survived her attack, described the tattoo on his back. The media subsequently acquired the description and thus the tabloids had their selling point.

Excerpt taken from interview with Obadiah Stark (dated 17th April 2010):

"You call me a sociopath. That's simply a word for someone who evinces certain personality traits. But given that one in every twenty-five people are sociopaths, perhaps "sociopathy" is a normal personality variant which serves mankind well in your struggle to survive and procreate across the countless millennia.

"Make no mistake about it. You need the sociopath. We are useful and the world knows it. For example, in a combat unit, who would be the sniper? Who could sit in a tree waiting all day to kill a perfect stranger in cold blood? The sociopath, of course. What about James Bond? Literature loves him, but is he not a sociopath with his licence to kill? What about the surgeon who can cut into human flesh without feeling anything—no hesitation, nerves, or fear?

"Sharks, lions, tigers, alligators... all have senses designed to locate the weakest prey and seek them out, removing the wheat from the chaff if you will.

"Severe weather patterns kill thousands with water or wind... the earth's way of keeping the human population down to a manageable level. When that happens, God works in mysterious ways. Wars rage in Afghanistan, men kill countless hundreds of other men and who weeps for the

collateral damage? You love the man who kills complete strangers because he gets paid to do it, but you hate the man who does it for free. Like a shark, I'm just thinning the herd, you pack of fucking hypocrites!"

Offender profile: Obadiah Stark is cognitively intact, possessing an above average intelligence (IQ estimated at 120-130). His vocabulary, sentence complexity, capacity for conditional thinking, memory, perceptual complexity and capacity to view matters from multiple perspectives all support this assessment.

The aforementioned qualities contribute to the aspects of his character that supply him with his sociopathic behaviour. Coupled with his propensity for impulse control and good organisational and planning skills, such attributes make him more dangerous than the average sociopath.

A review of Obadiah's previous crimes indicated that his primary source of pleasure and personal security come from his desire for the power and control torture and murder bring with them. Using the DSM – IV (Diagnostic and Statistical Manual of Mental Disorders, Fourth edition) [6] and Hare Psychopathy checklist [7] (a psycho-diagnostic tool incorporating a clinical rating scale to assess factors of an individual's personality such as superficial charm, grandiosity, need for stimulation, pathological lying, manipulating, lack of remorse, callousness, poor behavioural controls, impulsivity, irresponsibility and failure to accept responsibility for one's own actions), this author attempted to understand how the autistic spectrum can be applied to the psychopathology of Obadiah Stark.

Paradoxically, though the subject meets some of the criteria for autism (namely impaired social interaction skills and a repetitive and stereotyped pattern of behaviour), he doesn't score highly enough on the Hare PCL to be clinically labelled a sociopath.

This is atypical of the subject. Despite Obadiah's narcissistic lifestyle and attitudes, he is culturally sophisticated. This dichotomy makes him more sinister, dangerous and less subject to his immediate environment and hence less predictable. A loner with an ever-present potential for explosive violence, Obadiah Stark will readily impose his will onto others, with violence his primary problem-solving device (see additional information in Section One).

My sessions with the subject identified someone extremely defensive in his manner of thought and quick to take offence, whilst at the same time careful and calculating with his responses. Such traits signify that the subject is too rigid and controlling to have socially pleasurable interests and activities, preferring to use his crimes as the pleasurable activities that additionally meet his need for power and control. Fundamentally, Obadiah Stark is a mass of contradictory behavioural structures and emotional responses. Taken alongside the previous section's discussion on Obadiah's psychopathology, this information supports the illustration of an individual with extreme egocentricity and a ruthless disregard for the rights and feelings of other human beings.

References

5 Holmes, R.M. & Holmes, S.T. (1998) *Serial Murder (second edition)*. Thousand Oaks, California: Sage

6 American Psychiatric Association (2000) *Diagnostic and Statistical Manual of Mental Disorders (fourth edition)*. Washington D.C. American Psychiatric Association

7 Hare, R.D (1991) *The Hare Psychopathy Checklist*. Multi-Health Systems, Niagara Falls Blvd, North Tonawanda, New York

'The man's fuckin' Satan. When he was dead, they should have shoved a stake through his heart, buried him, and then dug him up a week later to stab him again, just to be sure.'
Richard Keld, father of Obadiah Stark's second victim in Ireland.

5

SEPTEMBER 16TH

11:56

Blennerville (*Cathair Uí Mhóráin*)
Tralee, County Kerry

A SMALL VILLAGE AND SUBURB OF TRALEE, BLENNERVILLE HAD
formerly acted as Tralee's port due to its connection to the
town centre by a ship canal.

It was also the main exit point of emigrants during the
Great Famine (1845 – 1852) and home port of the famous
emigrant barque, 'Jeanie Johnston'.

Approximately one million people died while a million
more had left Ireland during this period. The cause of the
famine, a potato disease known as potato blight, ravaged a
third of the population, all of whom were entirely
dependent on the crop for food. The situation, already
volatile, was further exacerbated by political, social and
economic factors that remain the subject of historical debate
to this day.

A watershed in Irish history, its effects permanently
altered the island's demographic, politically and culturally,
for both native Irish and the resulting diaspora, establishing

the famine into folk memory and creating a dividing line in the Irish historical narrative.

———

JOE HAD HAD MANY OPPORTUNITIES OVER HIS YEARS AS A journalist to feel guilt and self-loathing for what he did.

His no-holds-barred approach to obtaining information often left him with a hollow feeling inside, so much so that he sometimes wondered if he'd traded his soul for a scoop and hadn't realised.

He justified his actions by telling himself it was important the public were given all the necessary information to understand what had led up to the crime, irrespective of who got hurt in the process. Further solace was taken in knowing that those he was reporting on should have felt guilty in spades, more than enough to balance the scales.

Today, he didn't feel quite so single-minded.

He had suffered from guilt, but whether it was because of the byline identifying a victim's relative or a broken promise not to use a quote, he couldn't work out. But it had never been the guilt which ate away at your insides. It had been more like how you felt after overindulging in too much chocolate - easily corrected with an apology or a re-evaluation the next day.

Yet somehow he felt that if he didn't treat this interview correctly, he would feel guilt that wouldn't be so easily remedied.

Checking his watch, he placed his shoulder bag on the floor and leant back into the sofa. The creaking, full grain leather was accompanied by a mild release of an earthy smell reminding Joe of getting into a brand new car for the first time.

As he waited for Margaret Keld to return, he became aware of his hangover receding, causing his body to crave food as a counterbalance to his plummeting blood sugar. He was feeling a little sluggish and silently hoped he could start the interview as soon as possible.

Before leaving the office, Joe had been on the receiving end of a friendly reminder from Ciaran to tread carefully during his interview. Joe knew his editor didn't want anything negative ricocheting back on to the paper from any of the relatives he was hoping to speak to. Given the fact that so little time had passed since the execution, the people of Ireland needed space to move past Obadiah's crimes and his association with their country.

They needed the time to dream of better days ahead.

In spite of the reasons for his visit, Joe's welcome into the house had been more cordial than he'd expected, though he could tell from the moment Margaret answered the door that she didn't like him or what he stood for. He accepted the only reason he had access at all was not his celebrity as a journalist, but because Ciaran had given his own personal assurance that her daughter's name would not be sullied or her character besmirched in Joe's book.

The living room he had been ushered into was swathed in shadows. The blinds were closed, giving it the unnatural feeling the slated sunlight provided with its contrast of dark and bright. Photographs adorned the walls of Margaret and two people who, upon closer inspection, Joe recognised as her husband and late daughter captured in happier times - before The Tally Man.

A flat-screen television hung on the chimney breast above a faux log fire which was currently unlit. Weaved anaglypta wallpaper gave the room a timeless appearance, the shadows from the blinds adding larger patterns to its embossed weave. A smell of melted molasses drifted into the living room from the open kitchen door. A spider's web hanging in the corner wafted lazily in the breeze as Margaret moved in carefully, carrying a tray containing tea and a plate of biscuits.

"You can be my guinea pig. I haven't baked in a long time, so I'm not quite sure what they'll be like."

She set the tray down on the table in front of Joe.

"Do you take sugar, Mr O'Connell?" Her tone was polite but curt.

Joe leaned forwards. "No, thank you. And it's Joe. May I?" He gestured towards the biscuits.

"Please, help yourself," Margaret insisted as she poured tea into two small, plain china cups. Placing a cup in front of him, she sat down opposite in a matching leather chair.

Her greying hair was tied neatly back into a ponytail, exposing a round, heavily lined face. Brown eyes stared down at the cup of tea she was holding in her hands, as though she were waiting for it to reveal the answer to an unspoken question.

Dressed in a pale blue shirt and long, pleated black skirt, Joe thought Margaret looked as though she'd forgone any interest in displaying vibrancy in life and had instead chosen to utilise colours reflecting her heart – empty and alone.

He rubbed his hands together vigorously to remove any crumbs before reaching into his shoulder bag beside him and removed his dictaphone. He shook it gently from side to side to indicate its significance.

"Do you mind if we record this?" he asked, swallowing the last of his biscuit.

"No, that's fine," Margaret replied quietly.

Joe pressed the record button and set it down on the table in front of them. He rested his notepad on his knees and scribbled a heading on the page – M.Keld interview. 16th September 2011.

Lacing his fingers, he took a deep breath before speaking. "Mrs Keld, I appreciate you taking the time to talk to me. I know you've spoken to my editor, but just for the record, the whole purpose of this interview is to get an idea of your feelings concerning your daughter's murder and the subsequent linking of it to Obadiah Stark. I assure you that my book will not glorify his crimes. Is that okay?"

"You can call me Margaret and yes it's okay." Her voice was now strong, as though she'd mentally prepared herself for his questions, a direct contrast to her appearance and demeanour.

Joe took another sip of tea before leaning back into the sofa, trying to take on a relaxed posture to make his subject feel at ease. Though he already had abstract information concerning his initial questions, he knew it was essential to follow a logical chain to lead Margaret into answering his more difficult questions later on.

"So, the night when your daughter went missing, when did you realise something was wrong?"

Margaret paused for a moment. "Kizzie always rang me when she was on her way home from work, without fail. She was good like that. If her mobile battery went flat, she would ring me from a phone box. So, that night when I didn't hear from her, I just knew something had happened."

Joe smiled sadly. "Kizzie? Was that your nickname for Katherine?"

Margaret's face seemed to glow slightly as she recalled the origins of her daughter's name abbreviation. "Yes. It was her father who actually started calling her that when she was a little girl. I was never quite sure where it came from, but it always sounded cute, so it sort of stuck."

"And after what happened to Katherine, how did you feel?" Joe knew it was an abstract question, but he had to give the book contrast against the details of Obadiah's crimes; he had to offer some human emotion.

Margaret hesitated as if searching for the correct words. "I felt crushed. I am not sure if you have children, Mr O'Connell, but when you lose a child, your heart cracks open a chasm so deep, you know it'll never heal. To know you'll never hold them again, hear them laugh again, never see them dance again. The grief is relentless."

Her eyes took on a distant expression before continuing. "When I got to the hospital to identify the body, she was just lying there in a gown as though she'd fallen asleep. Of course, the nurses had done their best to smarten her up. I asked them to let some sunlight into the room. I didn't want to be holding her for the last time in darkness.

"As the nurse opened the blinds, a sun-catcher in the shape of a rainbow on the window caught the sunlight. And you know, the room was filled with brilliant flashes of colour. The walls, the floor, the ceiling, the sheets covering her. And that was my final memory of my daughter. Not the fact that someone had tortured and stabbed her to death. My final, lasting memory was of her bathed in a rainbow."

Joe wasn't sure how to proceed after Margaret's recollection. He noticed she had refused to call him Joe – keeping it formal. Needing to know more on her thoughts of her daughter's killer, he tried to phrase his next question delicately, but couldn't think of a way to soften its intention.

"When were you made aware that your daughter was the latest victim in a string of murders?"

She thought for a moment before replying. "It was a few days after Kizzie's death. The Gardaí came to see me and informed me that a suspect in many crimes in America was also a suspect in my daughter's and another girl's murder."

"They didn't tell you anything about the man they were referring to?"

"Not at that time, no. It was a few weeks later, when another girl had been found, that his name was released, linking him to Kizzie and all the others."

Joe could tell Margaret was being careful to not mention Obadiah's name, as though speaking it out loud would summon his presence.

"And how did you feel once he was caught?"

"At the same time, relieved and appalled. Relieved that no other family would have to suffer the loss that we had."

"And appalled, because...?"

"… because it had taken so long to catch him. The man had been murdering people on both sides of the world for nearly twenty years, and no one had ever come close to stopping him. He'd made a joke of the world's law enforcement. If they'd done their jobs right in the States the first time around, my daughter wouldn't have died. Then again, I could say the same for the Gardaí. They were just as incompetent."

Joe held Margaret's gaze. He had to admit, he agreed with her.

Obadiah had made the police forces look like the Keystone Cops. But her opinion was jaded by ignorance and a refusal to accept that the man they'd been up against was a knowledgeable and proficient individual. Obadiah had felt no empathy for any of his victims and Joe suspected, for no other human being. His lifetime spent scrutinising people's emotional reactions combined with his intellect, had endowed him with the extraordinary ability to lie and manipulate people. With his handsome, everyday appearance, he had been able to blend in and be innocuous. Even on death row, he had shown no sorrow or regret. The only emotion he'd ever seemed to express was one of frustration at being caught.

To him, it had meant he'd been outsmarted.

"I understand you, and your husband separated not long after Katherine's death. He certainly spoke some powerful words after Stark was executed."

Joe again felt compelled to push her on about Obadiah. He knew she was being evasive in addressing it.

Margaret glared at him, as though offended by the question's personal nature, but almost as quickly appeared to compose herself before responding.

"Richard struggled after Kizzie's death. We both did. But he found it much harder. She had been his little girl. They were so close. He became so full of hatred and bitterness that his whole personality appeared to change overnight. He slept less and drank more. He started not turning in for work, and when he did, he wouldn't be sober. He would fall asleep in her bedroom, holding her picture. Don't get me wrong, Mr O'Connell, I felt like I was dying every day. But Richard, he just couldn't accept she was gone. We began arguing all the time, about the police, about his drinking, about redecorating her room. Everything just became a fight. So we split up, and he moved back to Belfast where he'd grown up. We spoke on the phone, but the first time I saw him again was the day of the execution."

Joe nodded slowly, taking in Margaret's expression. He felt a slight twinge of what he could only describe as self-loathing at his line of questioning. He could see that she was struggling with her recollection of her daughter.

Scribbling a few notes on his pad, he decided to focus on the day Obadiah died.

"The execution? You were there?" Joe knew she had been, but wanted to hear what she would say.

Margaret's emotional leakage was noticeable, even for someone not looking for it. It was apparent that recalling the event filled her with repulsion.

"Yes, I was there. Richard accompanied me, though we were separated at that time. I'd never even been to a prison before, so that was stressful enough. But seeing him up close for the first time... it was horrifying. I hadn't attended his trial, so this was the first time I'd seen him in person.

"He looked so... normal. Like someone, you could walk by every day in the street. I found it hard to believe that he could have taken my Kizzie's life and so many others. But when he spoke... that was when I knew he was a monster. His voice held no remorse. He wasn't sorry for what he did.

He was just... apathetic about the whole thing. He deserves to suffer. I hope they really make him suffer."

Joe frowned at Margaret's present tense terminology.

"Make him suffer? How do you mean?"

Her eyes widened for a microsecond with a flash of fear, before she composed herself and spoke after a short pause.

"Those in charge of his soul in Hell. I hope they make him suffer for all eternity for what he did."

Joe stared at Margaret intensely.

For reasons he couldn't explain, he suddenly knew she was hiding something. Whether it had been something virtually imperceptible in her tone, her sentence repetition or an electrical current she'd given off - he didn't know what, and he couldn't explain how he knew.

He just knew.

In that moment's pause, before she had answered him, he had seen her honesty waver like a flame in a draft.

Joe had no doubt that she wasn't trying to deliberately mislead him. She was a truthful person who had merely just provided him with a false answer in an emotive situation as to what she'd meant. He had sensed her realisation at what she'd almost implied by accident and knew she had then made a conscious, considered choice to alter what she had subconsciously wanted to say.

He was no Paul Ekman, but even Joe could sense her leakage of emotion she was trying hard to conceal.

He jotted on his pad the words 'Hiding something?' and heavily underlined it.

Joe raised his eyes to see Margaret brushing crumbs from her lap. Her momentary loss of composure had now been replaced by his original impression of her as strong and focused.

Joe swallowed hard. Was he misreading her statement? Or did she know something? If she did, he had no idea what it could be. The man was dead.

"How did you feel, knowing that your daughter's killer had finally been brought to justice?"

Margaret's face took on a hard expression, her voice full of venom."Justice? His execution wasn't justice, it was mercy.

Did he suffer in pain and anguish like my little girl had? Did he cry from the pain that I'm sure his other victims had suffered? I know you were there, Mr O'Connell. Do you think his death was inhumane, or practically relaxed?"

Joe considered his answer carefully. "I think that there's no humane way in putting a person to death and that, as a society, we have a voyeuristic urge to observe such acts. I don't know if I believe in the adage of *lex talens*, but I do know that his suffering will have been brief compared to that of your daughter and that there's no real way to ever compensate or balance the loss of a child at the hands of another."

Margaret nodded her satisfaction at Joe's answer. "Evasive, Mr O'Connell, but I understand your wish not to upset me, and I appreciate it. Ultimately, no punishment would have ever been enough for that man. His torment was brief. Mine is never-ending."

Her eyes began to moisten slightly as she fought back the emotions bubbling beneath her composed façade.

Excusing herself, Margaret left the living room and went upstairs, obviously struggling with the discussion concerning her daughter's killer.

The guilt Joe had been fighting to avoid slowly crept up on him like a moorland mist, embracing him at the ankles and then crawling up his legs and across his stomach, provoking a feeling of nausea.

He stood and tried to shake it away, telling himself that his questions were necessary to provide a balanced argument for his book. He needed the human emotion to counteract the veracity and repellent detail that Obadiah's story entailed.

He clicked off the dictaphone and returned to look at the

photographs adorning the walls, taking note of Margaret's face. He hadn't particularly paid attention to it on his arrival, but thinking back to his place sitting opposite her, he could now see that where she had once been youthful-looking given her late forty-something age, her face had now lost its innocence.

Her small, animated features had developed lines and creases from the anguish she'd endured, her cheekbones pulling her face down into an almost permanent expression of sadness. Realising the physical toll her daughter's death had had on her, the psychological stress notwithstanding, ushered Joe towards the realisation that he hadn't understood anything about Obadiah Stark in the sense that his legacy hadn't died with him, but was everlasting.

And yet Joe couldn't avoid the recurring sense that Margaret was hiding something. On the one hand, he could accept that her sentence structure when she'd been discussing Obadiah's suffering was a by-product of her ongoing pain at her daughter's loss.

But the nosy, journalistic side of him couldn't shake the feeling that her face had given away a lot more than her speech pattern ever could have.

He turned as Margaret re-entered the room, smiling at her as he moved back towards the sofa. She made no attempt to sit back down. Her eyes were red and swollen.

"I'm sorry, Mr O'Connell, but I can't continue our interview. I thought I'd be okay after so long, talking about Kizzie and… him. But it's still too raw. I do appreciate what Ciaran told me you're trying to do. But I don't think I can talk about it anymore, certainly not at the moment anyway."

Joe nodded his understanding. Though he was slightly annoyed that she'd decided to cut the interview short, he understood her reasons. Besides, he had enough to get started and was eager to get back to the office to see if he'd had a response from Victoria Carter.

He projected his most sympathetic voice. "I understand, Mrs Keld. I appreciate your time today and honesty in what must be a difficult subject for you."

Margaret smiled her appreciation at his acknowledgement.

"I'll let myself out," Joe stated, dropping his notepad and dictaphone in the bag and collecting it from the floor. Smiling his thanks, he moved towards the front door and stepped outside.

The nearby birds in the trees welcomed his entrance back into the bright sunshine. Joe was about to walk through the gate when he felt compelled to turn around.

He found Margaret Keld staring at him, her face full of what he could only describe as anguish. He got the distinct impression she wanted to say something, but the thought was quickly intercepted by her shutting the door.

As he climbed into his car and drove away from her house, Joe slumped back and let out a sigh.

The house and those around it faded away in the rear-view mirror as he recognised the exhaustion he felt from his poor night's sleep and lack of substantial food – all alcohol induced.

His body sagging in the car seat, Joe wound down the window, embracing the blast of fresh air that engulfed his face. He stared through the windscreen, his mind trying to distinguish between his own interpretation of Margaret Keld's comments and what, if anything, lay behind them.

"... a monster... no remorse... no sorrow or regret... I hope they really make him suffer."

'To appreciate heaven well, it is good for a man to have some fifteen minutes of hell.'
Will Carleton

6

08:56

Had Obadiah awoken with his head sewn to the floor, he wouldn't have been more surprised than he was right now.

As déja-vu went, this was the most absolute definition imaginable.

Déja-dead.

Trying to process what was in front of him forced Obadiah to wonder if he was experiencing a vivid dream. The woman from the photograph, the smell of breakfast, the filtered sunlight through the window and the time on the clock.

All were a perfect representation of what had gone before.

Subconsciously massaging the wound-free areas on his body where the Gardaí had shot him, he slowly advanced down the stairs and moved towards the breakfast bar.

His eyes never flinched from the woman before him, but she merely returned his stare with a warm expression, pushing a strand of black hair back behind her ear.

"You're just in time for breakfast."

Eva's confirmation was met by silence.

"Obi?" she questioned gently. "Are you okay?"

Obadiah held her gaze. His respiratory functions seemed to have slowed imperceptibly, his breath caught in his chest.

"Is this a joke," he managed to gasp, his tone dark and laced with menace as he gestured around the kitchen.

"Is what a joke?" Eva asked in amusement.

"This," he emphasised, repeating his sweep around the room.

"Obadiah, what's the matter with you?"

Concerned, she moved closer to him and took his hand which he quickly snatched away. Running them both through his hair and clasping them behind his neck, he blinked rapidly as though trying to clear his vision.

Obadiah was quickly becoming less confused and slowly approaching bewilderment.

The little girl on the bench looked at him with a curious expression. "Daddy, why are you sad?"

She continued to stir her bowl of mixture as she spoke.

Obadiah was wordless. He couldn't believe any of this. Was he going mad? Had the drugs used to execute him damaged his mind before death?

"This has got to be a fucking joke!" His outburst promoted a shocked look from both females.

"Obadiah! That's enough." Eva quickly moved closer to her surprised daughter and held her by the shoulders. The little girl had stopped mixing whatever was in her bowl and was staring at Obadiah with widened eyes.

"What's with you?" Eva persisted. "If you're sick again, you need to tell me, not behave like this."

"What the fuck are you talking about?"

"Go sit in the room, Ellie. Now, please."

The little girl stepped down from her stool at the sound of her mother's firm but gentle interjection. Slowly, she walked past Obadiah into the room to his left, confusion concerning the sudden outbursts of emotion apparent in her eyes.

Eva followed in her daughter's footsteps, stopping in front of Obadiah. "Obi, what is going on with you? You've been up five minutes, and already you're acting like a monster, scaring your daughter and scaring me. Tell me, what's the matter?"

He found himself backing away from her, simultaneously wiping the beads of sweat accumulating on his forehead.

He needed space to process what was happening.

Eva moved closer, her tone softening as she sensed his discomfort and confusion at something she wasn't privy to. "Obi, what is it?"

Obadiah ignored her implied concern. "You know," he responded, placing his palm on her chest and forcefully pushing her back. "Now I think about it, I'm not feeling too good. But you or someone else is obviously messing with me, and it's a big, fuckin' mistake."

A burning need to understand rose in his gut, intent on consuming him. Wearing just the pyjama trousers he'd awoken in, he stormed through the house, out the gate and onto the road, ignoring Eva's calls of concern from the door.

He increased his speed and headed in the direction he'd followed yesterday, needing to see the consequences of his actions.

He knew their inertia, or a lack of it, would reinforce his wavering certainty of whether the promnesia he was experiencing was coincidental or something more insidious.

As he headed down the avenue, the smell of the autumnal trees and the breeze on his skin teased him with an elemental joke he was not yet privy to. And for the first time since his childhood, Obadiah Stark was feeling something he had long ago determined he would never experience again.

Fear.

His pace never slowing, he followed the dips and curves of the avenue until he saw the town ahead of him. Obadiah stopped and scanned the surroundings, the cold air biting at his half-naked torso. His shoeless feet were numb, but he didn't care. He wanted to see the effects of the carnage he'd wrought when last here.

He was immediately disappointed.

People were going about their daily routines, as they had done yesterday. And they were going about them with the distinct lack of a Gardaí presence.

The buildings, shaded in hues of turquoise, yellow and orange, should have been cordoned off following his actions. The town should have been under surveillance, with law enforcement a very tangible presence. Yet, they were conspicuous by their absence.

Taking in the details of every person who walked by him, Obadiah scanned their faces for signs of anxiety or apprehension at his presence. He had expected his profile to be plastered all over the news. But other than a passing interest at his semi-clad appearance, no one seemed to care he was there.

Seeing a newsagent, Obadiah strode over and snatched one of the tabloids from the rack outside. The front page headline protested about the number of soldiers killed in Iraq to date and the Government's lack of progress in their withdrawal from the country. Conceding that his performance yesterday may not have superseded such political fare, he thumbed to the next pages. A Page 3 girl and an article on an approaching decade of doom for the UK under Conservative rule greeted him, but still, he saw no mention of his name or events.

His reverie was abruptly broken by the sound of someone calling his name. Turning he saw a man jogging towards him, his right hand raised in acknowledgement. For what felt like interminable minutes, everything around Obadiah seemed to freeze, with sounds becoming muted and slowing to an imperceptible hum.

Then like a recoiling spring, it all became unstuck and returned to a normal rhythm.

"What the hell...?"

The man before him should have had his head facing one

hundred and eighty degrees in the opposite direction. That was where Obadiah had left it. Yet his rounded face and lean frame were not contorted in any way.

"Obadiah? I thought it was you. What's the craic? Why are you half naked, man?"

His heart thudding loudly in his chest, Obadiah glanced around, curious to see if he was involved in a set-up to identify him before a team of officers could move in. But all he saw were the human cattle, running ignorantly about their urbanised pasture.

Letting the newspaper fall to the ground, Obadiah began backing away, his eyes fixated on the man before him. Unable to establish a rational explanation, he began to find it difficult to breathe again, as though a great weight were suddenly pressing down upon his chest.

He realised he was caught in a circumstance he couldn't control, an experience alien to him. As incredulous as it seemed, he appeared to be experiencing the exact same day that he had yesterday.

Everything happening around him had happened before.

Mark looked at Obadiah, his eyebrows furrowed in puzzlement. "You okay? You look all fucked up."

Obadiah felt anger rising from the pit of his stomach. The man standing before him meant that everything he'd accomplished yesterday had been erased and reset, the obdurate universe conspiring to rob him of everything and define it merely as prologue.

In this reality, where Obadiah Stark was once again standing in his hometown of Killarney, The Tally Man had never existed.

The increasing bustle of people flitting about him began to feel like insects stinging at his brain. Ignoring the man before him, Obadiah turned around and broke into a sprint, eager to get back to the house which was now the only place he now believed he could feel at ease.

Shouts for his attention from the man who should have been dead, faded into the background as he pushed himself faster, welcoming the accompanying shortness of breath.

———

OBADIAH COULDN'T REALLY REMEMBER THE JOURNEY BACK TO the house.

His feet had begun to bleed from his lack of shoes, every step he took now a biting ache. The day slowly brought with it shadows and the cold, his anxiety replaced with a need to feel warm again.

Staring up at the house, he regained his breath, imagining what might be waiting for him inside. The woman and child who seemed to know him were the biggest conundra of all. Being back in his childhood home was unbelievable enough, but that two people appeared to know him but have no awareness of his history was mystifying.

Fuck, this is all wrong.

When he'd been strapped to the gurney in Absolom, he'd believed that that was the end - his end.

But it had been denied him.

Yesterday hadn't been the opportunity he'd initially thought, but a trick leaving him now with an insoluble problem.

Obadiah left the front door ajar as he strode through the hallway and back into the kitchen. He saw Eva standing with her back to him, the telephone conversation sounding heated and desperate. As if sensing his presence, her face displayed momentary shock as she noticed him before she slammed the phone down on its receiver and raced over to embrace him.

Moving away, Eva held him at arm's length. "Where the hell have you been? I've been worried sick. I nearly called the Gardaí, thinking you'd had an accident. What's going on,

Obi? Why did you leave like that? And Jesus, you're freezing cold!"

She hurried upstairs and returned with a blanket which she put around his shoulders. Obadiah held it by the corners but remained fixed to the spot. He didn't have the slightest idea what to say.

"What's your name?" His voice was firm, its insistence for an answer explicit.

"Eva," she replied sadly. "It's Eva, Obi." She moved forward to hold him again, but Obadiah stepped back.

The hurt broke over her face like ripples on a lake.

"I don't know you. I don't know the child. I grew up in this wretched house, but I don't know who you people are."

Eva's eyes welled with tears at his matter-of-fact statement.

He paused before continuing.

"My name is Obadiah Stark. The media call me The Tally Man. I murdered twenty-seven people over sixteen years and was executed in ADX Absolom on September 7th 2011. I expected to be burning in Hell, but instead found myself here, with my tattoo signifying my life's work gone. I don't know who put me here and I don't understand why. I don't know if God or the devil is playing a game with me. But here I am.

"Yesterday, I walked into town, murdered five people and was shot by the Gardaí for my troubles, which was fine. I hadn't wanted the second chance. I only wanted out of this shithole called life. But then this morning, I wake up, and I'm here again, with no bullet wounds, and everything exactly the same as it was yesterday. A man whose neck I snapped yesterday, just waved at me for fuck's sake.

"I do not care for another soul on this planet. I have never loved anyone and have only ever been interested in one thing – increasing my tally of victims. But you don't understand any of this, because as far as you're concerned, the man I have just described isn't the man you know, is it?"

Eva didn't reply. As though frozen to the spot, her face had developed a profound sadness that Obadiah was unable to quantify. It was as though her world had just begun to crumble before her and all she could do was watch, unable to influence the outcome.

"Obadiah, you're sick. You're really sick, and you need to let me help you... let us help you - as a family. The hospital told us that if it progressed further, you might begin to have delusions or hallucinations. Why didn't you tell me sooner? We can't wait with this thing, you know that!"

Her voice had begun to crack, the emotion becoming too much for her to contain.

Obadiah closed the distance between them, feeling oddly calm in what was a potentially provocative situation. But killing was the furthest thing from his mind.

"I'm not ill," he stated with a chuckle. "I'm a predator who preys on the human stain. I am a beast. When I left this house earlier, I found myself considering the age-old philosophy of what death actually is and what the consequences of our action s in life may hold. Is Hell a manifestation of the suffering we have caused others? Is Heaven somewhere where a person's souls can nurture the smallest desire to change? Then I realised I didn't really care, other than this doesn't feel like Hell to me. I don't know what the fuck this is. Father Hicks believed that the saddest example of humanity could become the greatest. I am going to prove, right now, that he was full of shit. I control my own destiny, no one else."

Obadiah had turned his back to Gill as he spoke, knowing she would be too afraid to move. At this moment, he felt as comfortable as he ever had. In control, with someone hanging on his every word, whether they wanted to or not.

Eva moved to stand in front of him, tears flowing freely down her face. She reached out to take his hand, but he rebuffed the offer and stepped back slightly.

"Obi, you've never hurt a soul. You're surrounded by people who care about you and who just want to help. Please, let me help you."

A smile broke over Obadiah's face as he found himself fascinated by her persistence to help him. Though she obviously didn't know him as The Tally Man, she appeared to know him as Obadiah Stark, sick with what he could only guess was some sort of brain tumour.

For a second, he considered whether this could be true. Could his entire existence as a sociopath have been merely a carcinoma-induced delusion?

No. The sensation of taking the lives of the people he'd killed had been too visceral, the feeling of incarceration in Absolom too tactile an experience to be anything other than real.

"I know you think you know me, but be thankful you don't."

Without the slightest hint of emotion, Obadiah turned from Eva and letting the blanket fall from his shoulders, walked back to the front door, out of the house and towards the cliffside that he'd observed that first day from the bedroom window.

Reaching its precipice, he felt the primal force of the sea as it crashed upon the shore, its momentum carrying fret and spray towards his forty-foot apex.

In his mind's eye he could see the faces of all his victims beckoning him to join them, their appreciation at what he had given them in death, etched onto their faces.

The sound of Eva calling out his name as she approached grated on his nerves, the child's voice more serene in its pleas for his attention. He faced them and saw her and the little girl she'd called Ellie clutching at each other, their faces contorted in importunate desperation.

Turning away, he closed his eyes and stepped out into the enticing nothingness, its embrace cool and weightless.

As he fell, his body was suddenly racked with pain. Mere seconds stretched into what seemed like minutes as Obadiah spasmed from the white-hot needles burrowing their way into his upper back with movement akin to insects beneath his skin. He tried desperately to reach the area being affected but was unable to bring his flailing arms around far enough to make contact, stifling a cry of anguish as his body suddenly thrashed about as though he were a marionette whose strings had been cut.

He focused his mind on dying, but the pain was unrelenting, refusing to allow him a moment's respite.

And then just as abruptly, he felt himself slipping away into stygian blackness while his world burned dazzlingly bright in contrast, light and dark having the battle to see who was superior.

Obadiah Stark felt as though he would have nothing more to think about as the darkness enveloped him.

Then he thought he began to feel a slight breeze on his face and heard what sounded like seagulls.

He heard the sound of a child calling his name, smells tickling his senses.

And it all began anew.

Dr. John Franklin, BS.c. (HONS), PH.D. M.A., M.CLIN, PSYCH. A.F.Ps.S.I.

Subject: Stark, Obadiah James (a.k.a. The Tally Man) cont.

Victim history:

Obadiah's first murder is believed to have been committed in 1988 at the age of twenty-two, eighteen months after being released from state custody. Although no forensic evidence was found at the crime scene linking Obadiah to the murder, nor were there any witnesses' forthcoming, during one of my interviews with the subject he alluded to one of his tally marks being specific to the victim but refused to elaborate.

The victim, Lauren Tolson, was found on 10th October 1988, just off Highway 90 in Louisiana. This highway connects the West Bank to the East Bank on the north (via the Huey Long Bridge) and to St. Charles Parish on the west. Her throat had been slashed, the cut going so deep as to almost sever her spinal column. There were no signs of sexual assault. She had been rolled inside an old carpet and left at the bottom of an embankment, approximately five hundred yards from the highway. When discovered, Lauren's body was in the later stages of decomposition, with forensics estimating she had died three weeks earlier on 19th September 1988.

If this author is to assert Lauren being Obadiah's first victim, then the crime showed an already brutal and uncompromising approach towards killing. Lacking the finesse he would later develop and hone, it is clear from the severity of the knife wounds that the subject felt neither remorse nor hesitation at taking a life, ensuring that death was quick and disposal of the body equally as capricious.

Though speculation remains concerning Lauren Tolson as Obadiah's first victim, there is no doubt that the subject's next victim was Angelina Tegan, a 27 year-old housewife from Monticello, Baton Rouge. Married, with two children, her body was discovered on the 24th of November 1988 in a brownfield site just outside Monticello, her body half-submerged in a pool of water with hands and legs still bound together. Her body was partially clothed, though once again no signs of sexual assault were present. Her throat had been cut almost through to the vertebrae and she had multiple stab wounds to her abdomen. This increase in ferocity indicates that the subject had still not developed the patience he would eventually demonstrate, instead inflicting the mortal wounds in a frenzied manner that implied anger or frustration.

When questioned by this author, Obadiah freely admitted murdering her, stating that though he'd found the location distasteful, he knew that the environment's industrial nature would help mask or destroy any signs of physical evidence.

Monticello, an area of Louisiana not comprised of an overly affluent population, is home to many people in the East Baton Rouge parish who earn an average $49,000 a year. To Obadiah, such a working class family environment presented the perfect opportunity for him to 'take from his own' as he put it during our conversations concerning Angelina's murder. She represented someone that he could value as an opportunity, but devalue as a reminder of where he'd come from.

With feelings of emptiness by this time probably more chronic than acute and despite being only his second murder, Obadiah may already have been attempting to fill such emotional voids with the pain of others. It is of interest to note that, at this time, he was already honing his ability to compartmentalise his own socially dissociative symptoms, characteristics which would act as a barrier to him interacting with his potential victims in a friendly manner. This learned partitioning of his sociopathic side would later develop into an ability to hide his murderous pastime within a façade of charisma.

Both murders highlight Obadiah Stark's highest value and singular desire already in its infancy - control. Though he would later develop this to feed his need for order and perfectionism, at this point in his career he was already projecting himself as the sole source of his internal strength. On a basic level, Obadiah's actions represent a perfect example of man's need, from a biological standpoint, to achieve power and control. With society and the media reinforcing such a belief by providing rewards for dominance and promoting an ideal that power can often be gained through violence, Obadiah Stark chose to demonstrate such an evolutionary process. He understood that the effective use of violence could provide him dominance and gain him a measure of control.

Put simply, taking responsibility for defining his own destiny under his own terms, he had already chosen to use the pain of others to guide his way. And he was doing it with no more regret than if swatting a fly.

Excerpt taken from interview with Obadiah Stark (dated 17th April 2010):

"Once I had chosen them, there was no escape. They were dead as soon as I laid eyes on them. And yes, I used them to satisfy my every desire, enjoying the fact that I held their lives completely and utterly in the palm of my hand. That's a power you can't buy. You have to take it. Did I feel bad about the first one? It was certainly the most challenging, but then

the first of something always is. Did it plague my consciousness? No. After all, you only feel guilt if you've done something wrong."

'We lie only when we are attempting to cover up something we know to be illicit… There is no need to hide unless we first feel that something needs to be hidden. We come now to a sort of paradox. Evil people feel themselves to be perfect. At the same time, however, they have an unacknowledged sense of their own evil nature. Indeed, it is this very sense from which they are frantically trying to flee.'
M. Scott Peck

7

SEPTEMBER 27TH

23:18

Denny Street, Tralee (*Trá Lí*)
County Kerry, Ireland

CRIMINAL ANTHROPOLOGY IS BETTER KNOWN AS OFFENDER
profiling, the method by which links can be made between
the criminal and the crime - characteristics and physical
appearance amongst other traits.

Though its birth is often debated, it is thought Johann
Kasper Lavater was amongst the first to proffer a link
between the criminal and their facial structure. Widely
derided in the in the late 19th century, other professionals
such as Cesare Lombroso and Raffaele Garofalo believed that
criminals were born with detectable physiological differences.
Add some misconceived social Darwinism to the mix that
considered certain species possess a moral superiority over
others, and you had a heady misrepresentation of what
constituted a criminal.

More modern adaptations of the theory of criminal
anthropology and its relation to the study of physiognomy
have allowed it to find its place in modern-day profiling,

discovering actual links between illegal activities, galvanic skin responses and chromosomal abnormalities.

————

SLEEP JUST WASN'T COMING.

Thoughts gently ricocheted off the wall of Joe's mind, creating a circumfused hum inside his head that prompted him to massage his eyes with the knuckles of his forefingers. The low, background buzz of the television he'd left on in the living room drew his attention, seducing him further away from the embrace of sleep. His head ached from staring at the computer monitor for virtually three straight days.

Since his interview with Margaret Keld, he'd managed to gain face time with the relatives of Wendy Dutton and Niamh Kelly – Obadiah's third and fifth victims on Irish shores. Securing the family's participation in his book hadn't been easy. Mark and Susan Dutton had flatly refused an interview until Ciaran had once again intervened and reiterated what it was that Joe was trying to do with his book. Despite his burgeoning inferiority complex towards the necessity for Ciaran's interference, he was grateful for the assistance.

Once the Duttons had agreed to an interview, Mary and Robert Kelly had followed suit. Because of this, he'd ended up working flat out, editing his column during the day while writing until the early hours of the morning on his book. Getting back from work earlier today, Joe had decided to take a break, permitting himself an early meal and shower before climbing into bed. But despite it now being past eleven, he couldn't shut his mind off. He particularly kept going over and over his meeting with Mark and Susan Dutton.

He'd expected it to be difficult, especially given that their animosity towards the 'sloth-like' intervention of the Gardaí during their daughter's murder investigation paralleled that of Margaret Keld's. Because of this, he had taken a slightly different approach with his questions, realising that to acquire their honest opinions on Obadiah's execution, whether they considered it just punishment for his crimes or their feelings on law enforcement inadequacy, he would have to be slightly more aggressive in his approach. And though eventually forthcoming, just like Margaret Keld, Joe felt that something was 'off' about their acerbic focus on the inadequacy of Obadiah's punishment in the eyes of the law.

The Duttons had been almost excitable when the interview had turned towards their feelings on Obadiah's execution. They'd begun by explaining that they'd always felt strongly that the ends did not justify the means, regardless of what the Bible said about an 'eye for an eye.' When the interview drifted towards how their daughter, Wendy, had suffered, they'd begun to contradictorily preach that the justice system was broken and that current application of the death penalty was insufficient to ensure a just punishment for the crimes it was applied to.

Echoing Bertie Ahern weeks earlier, Joe had put forward the juxtaposition that Obadiah would have been able to feel emotions the rest of us are capable of feeling and that there was no such thing as a humane method of killing someone, therefore wasn't the suffering equal for both the victim and the perpetrator? Following a heated discussion and accusations of Joe being a heartless bastard, he had been politely thrown out of the house.

Letting out a huge sigh, he told himself to relax and tried to clear his mind, but no matter how many times he turned over in his bed, he couldn't get comfortable.

The interview with the Kellys had gone slightly better. With the family offering him a little more substance other than disbelief in the justice system, he'd found himself interested in their belief that Obadiah Stark's reckoning was out of their hands and in the hands of a higher power. Though Joe had thought they'd come across as too comfortable with Obadiah's punishment, he couldn't deny that the religious slant the interview had taken had provided him with an interesting springboard upon which to place his analysis of Obadiah's behaviour and driving forces. Still, despite his Catholic upbringing, the Kellys telling him that the soul of their daughter's killer was getting what he deserved left him a little ill at ease.

"For crying out loud."

Sitting up in bed, Joe flung the duvet off his legs and mussed his hair. If he weren't asleep by now, he wouldn't be for hours so he may as well get some work done.

Slipping on a t-shirt and jeans, he left the bedroom and sat down at his desk. Flicking on his laptop and the desk lamp, he glanced back at the television and saw Michael Landon walking down a dusty road as credits rolled across the screen. An angel with a perm, he thought. So very eighties. Redirecting his attention to the computer monitor, he skimmed over his work from earlier, finding himself quietly pleased with the results:

Serial killers are often seared into societal consciousness by the constant pontification of the media and public hysteria. With every aspect of the killers' and victims' lives documented and pored over exhaustively, it is no wonder that frequent discussions take place on the whys and wherefores of how they became killers and whether the punishment they ultimately received is punishment enough.

Conversely, it isn't often public or personal outrage which engages tabloid readers or stimulates debate, nor is it the ongoing debates around how they could do what they did to those poor, unfortunate souls. The one question that rules above all else in the quest for understanding merely is why? Why did that person grow up to become a monster?

We need to know their motives, the lead up to their violent act. We need to understand what pushed them into taking those first, dark steps down the road of cruelty and hatred towards life. There must be a reason, however nebulous, which caused them to feel that what they were doing was right and just. Were they hugged too much or not enough? Was it for money, power or sex? Whatever the elusive answer, it could never be the answer. That one reason, above all else that singularly focuses on the many individual emotions, beliefs, desires and ideals driving them to do what they did. And if it was ultimately ever proffered, would we even understand it?

Making a few minor edits and deciding that maybe it would be his preface, he clicked on the save button and rose from the desk.

The kitchen floor was cold as he grabbed himself a glass of water. He considered taking something to help him sleep, but decided against it. He had never been a big pill fan, instead preferring to let nature run its course.

Cradling the glass in his hands as he walked back into the living room and placing it on the table, he dropped into the sofa, putting his head back and closing his eyes. If this was an example of things to come, Joe wasn't sure if he'd be able to keep up a high standard for both jobs. One of them would inevitably end up showing a lack of productivity, but he couldn't allow it to be his job at the newspaper.

The book was a luxury he'd been afforded the opportunity to develop. And as helpful as Ciaran was being, his understanding would only go so far if the column began to suffer.

Maybe he shouldn't have started the book in the first place. Being around crime and criminals was bad enough, never mind having eaten, slept and breathed Obadiah Stark for more than two years. To have decided to spend more time in the killer's psychological company and write a book on what made him tick was, in hindsight, not his best decision. But as with most things, it had seemed a good idea at the time.

Reflecting on the interviews so far, he wondered if he was merely reading too much into them. Maybe they weren't hiding anything, that it was just a mechanism for venting such profound grief that they would never find closure for. Perhaps he was being too much of a reporter and looking for things which weren't there.

He couldn't blame them for wishing further suffering on Obadiah's soul. They and so many others had lost that which was most precious to them, and now they faced only ongoing pain. At least, he conceded, Obadiah's plight had been brief.

Joe finished his water and turned off the television mid-news bulletin. He decided he would try his bed again. If he lay there long enough, he knew he would eventually fall asleep from boredom if nothing else.

To help him on his way, he poured himself a generous short of Jack and drank it in one mouthful. Tablets he didn't care for, but Jack would never let him down.

Its warmth filtered into his stomach as he climbed into bed. He rubbed his eyes hard, causing phosphenes to dance across the blackness behind them. As he saw his own blood cells move through the capillaries of his retina, they momentarily merged with images of Obadiah's victims before moving out of his visual axis, leaving him with a twisted montage of innocent bodies lying brutalised on the floor.

Their physical corruption lulled him into a fevered sleep.

———

THERE WAS A LOW BUZZ IN THE NEWSROOM.

Reporters bustled around Joe as he wove between them with the precision of an ice skater. It could be a hazardous place for those not accustomed to its frenetic activity, especially as the days crept closer to a deadline. Joe had often found inspiration from the electricity that such an environment produced, channelling its energy into his work.

He had woken at six thirty, feeling refreshed after eventually falling to sleep.

Good old Jack, he mused. That guy had known his shit.

After showering and dressing, he'd grabbed his laptop and had headed up the R551, arriving at his desk in good time.

Quiet when he had gotten there, it now it looked like an eruption of human beings had taken place.

"O'Connell!"

The shout across the room was barely audible above the activity around him. "Someone's in the conference room for you."

He quickly topped up his coffee and made his way to the opaque, glass covered wall at the far end of the newsroom. Walking in, he was pleasantly surprised with the sight that greeted him.

The long, slender legs, accentuated by the tight-fitting skirt she had on which stopped just above her knees, were only slightly less distracting than her generous breasts which added shape to her button-down, white shirt. Her blonde hair was tied back in a ponytail, complementing the oval shape of her face. She had a fine nose, slightly sun-kissed skin and large, almost cat-like eyes, coloured the deepest shade of blue. Her lips were full and the colour of faded coral.

"Hi," he said, flashing his most appealing smile.

Legs stood and moved towards him, extending her hand. "Mr O'Connell? I'm Victoria Carter."

Joe's smile grew wider, so much so that he thought he was probably starting to look a little foolish. "I wasn't expecting you. After I left a message, I guessed you got tied up with work, and I didn't want to pester you with phone calls."

As he took her hand, he caught the slightest hint of perfume, subtle yet stimulating. Her hand was warm and gripped his firmly.

"Well, I was travelling to Ireland anyway with work, and I

have family here, so I figured it would be an ideal opportunity to meet you."

Her clipped, English accent gave her the sound of an old-fashioned headmistress. He found it an added pleasantry to an already appealing presentation.

"Lucky me, then," he replied. "I have to say, I appreciate your offer of assistance. I mean, I've followed Obadiah Stark for years, but know I've only scratched the surface as to what made him who he was. Any guidance or input you could give me would be great."

Victoria sat back down and indicated for Joe to join her. "Well, it would be my pleasure. It'll be nice to be involved in someone else's book for a change rather than writing it myself."

Joe knew she'd had a few books published, some of which were often referenced as amongst the best examples of dissecting what criminal profiling actually was. He actually felt a little awed sitting in her presence, with her offering to help him. In his line of work, he'd often had brief contact with celebrities and academics, but Victoria Carter was quite an opportunity.

Hot and smart.

"So, how long do you think you'll be here for?"

"I'm not sure yet. It depends how involved we get in your work and how long my other responsibilities take… maybe a few weeks. In all honesty, I'm looking forward to working with you. Though my work has brought me into contact with some of the most dangerous and most evil people on the planet, Obadiah Stark is particularly fascinating. He was a walking contradiction of social acuity and psychopathic tendencies. I saw this as an occasion to work with someone who was driven enough to attempt an understanding of his desire to kill. I must confess, I have a certain affinity for Obadiah Stark."

Joe resisted the adolescent urge to punch the air, instead opting for a more dignified "Well, that's great."

Reluctant to leave her, he checked his watch. "Listen, I have to get back to work, but if you're free later, we could grab a beer and discuss what you need from me and what I should be looking for. What do you think?"

Victoria stood and smiled. "That would be nice. I'll go and get myself freshened up and meet you back here at five thirty?"

"Five thirty sounds grand, Victoria." He offered his hand again, feeling that it was far too formal, but there was little else he could offer seeing as they'd just met.

"Okay then," she said taking his hand. "And it's Vicky."

"Vicky," Joe repeated before nodding and turning to move through the door back into the newsroom. He held it open for her as she brushed past him, leaving behind a slight wake of perfume that teased his nostrils. She smiled at the courtesy before heading towards the lift wheeling her black suitcase.

"Jesus, who was that?" David Cadman grabbed Joe by the shoulder. "She's hot, man."

Joe shrugged his colleague's hands away. "She is going to be my assistant for the next few weeks. And while you're invading my personal space, did you find out what's happening tonight?"

"Yeah, we're all going to meet at The Greyhound and head on from there. Why don't you ask the MILF you've just slobbered over to come?"

"One, you don't know whether she has kids. Two, I did very little slobbering and three, I'm not sure if her first night out in Tralee wants to be with a whipdick such as yourself."

"Please, she'll love me. How could she resist?" David stated with a grin.

"How could she resist a delusional financial columnist? Give me a minute with that one..." Joe replied, smiling as he headed towards his desk, ignoring the retort behind him.

His meeting with Victoria had stimulated his curiosity about her work. He'd Googled her name when he'd first received her message. Retyping it into the search engine, he saw hits totalling 1,790,000. To save time, he clicked on her Wikipedia page.

Born February 15th 1975, she'd grown up in Surrey, England and was considered one of the most eminent criminal profilers of the 21st century. Following an education at Oxford, she'd moved to the USA, becoming an undergraduate at the University of Chicago and leaving with an advanced degree in behavioural science, psychology and research methodology. She'd worked for the Pat Brown Criminal Profiling Agency in Washington for six years before leaving and becoming one of the few individuals to be employed by the National Centre for the Analysis of Violent Crime (NCAVC) in Quantico as a research specialist without a background in the FBI. She'd left two years later to start her own company in London, the Behavioural Relativity Service.

Not bad for a thirty-six-year-old, Joe thought.

He clicked on a few other websites, including the BRS's own, but found mostly the same information. One thing that struck him as unusual was that there was little to no mention of her family, other than where she was born. Then again, he considered that, given her high-profile position amongst the criminal world, she would probably not want to advertise details relating to her family for reasons of protection. Besides, he could find all that out and hopefully more when he met her for a drink after work.

May fortune favour the brave.

The phone ringing on his desk prompted Joe to close down the Internet. He picked it up on its second ring.

"O'Connell."

Hearing the voice on the other end immediately gave him goosebumps, such was the resonance of discomfort in it. The man calling him obviously had something to be concerned about.

"Mr O'Connell? Joe O'Connell, who covered the execution of Obadiah Stark?"

The voice was laced with a sense of urgency.

"That's correct."

"I need to see you as soon as possible. I have something I need to tell you. You need to know so others can know about…"

The voice became distant to the point that Joe thought they'd been cut off."Hello? You still there?"

"I'm here."

"Can you give me an idea as to what it is?" He knew what the reply would be, but it was in his nature to ask questions he already knew the answer to.

"Not over the phone. We have to speak in person tonight."

Joe winced. Bollocks. Of all the nights for a potential scoop to fall into his lap.

"Tonight… isn't fantastic for me. Can it be tomorrow morning?"

The explosion of emotion caught him a little off-guard. "No, it fuckin' can't be tomorrow morning. I'm risking my job just talking to you now…"

"Okay, please relax," Joe soothed, realising that his biological desires towards Victoria had temporally dulled his senses. "Who do you work for?"

"That's not important at the minute. Tonight. Nine thirty. O'Dywers on Ashe Street. Booth at the back. Don't be late."

The voice had become more insistent, unspoken secrets leeching from his every word.

"O'Dwyers got it," Joe acknowledged, scribbling the address on a Post-it. "I'll be there. We can talk completely off the record unless you say so. Okay?"

The line had already gone dead.

Placing the receiver in its cradle, Joe leaned back in his

chair. He'd had many contacts, informants and grasses over the years, all providing small details to his investigations for the paper that added just that little bit of reliability, which was quite a contradiction in terms given the fact they were mostly criminals.

But this call had been different, almost melodramatic. That said, despite his occasional wavering morality when it came to a story, he would never consider not following up on it just in case it turned out to have been true. Even someone as selfish as Joe couldn't cope with someone's death on his conscience.

Noting the time as a quarter to three, he decided to do the research now on his current story concerning money laundering amongst Government officials before meeting his mysterious caller.

He grabbed his coat from the back of his chair and shouted over to Cadman as he swung his arms into the sleeves. "David, I won't be making it tonight. Something's come up?"

"What, your dick? It's about time." He laughed as though his retort made him the next Peter Kay.

"Póg mo Thóin," Joe snapped back, Irish for 'Kiss my arse', shutting down his computer and grabbing the Post-it from his desk.

He would ring Victoria from the car and apologise. Hopefully, she would say she was actually tired from her trip and that she didn't mind at all if they rescheduled.

Of all the times... fuckin' Obadiah Stark. Even dead, the guy just couldn't help ruining people's lives.

'Are they real or is it Memorex?'
Gillian Macbeth-Louthan

8

08:34

Waking up for the second time when you thought you'd died really put things in perspective.

The discomfort on his back prompted Obadiah to jump out of bed and stand sideways in front of the mirror.

Designed by himself, the intricacies of the tattoo were as familiar to him as his own skin. The elegant representation of a tombstone rippled as he arched his back in various directions, trying to establish a clearer look.

Within it, memento mori were once again visible - four inch long lines with a diagonal score across them and one standing alone. Obadiah wasn't sure which was stranger – the fact that the tattoo hadn't been there when he'd first woken up here, or the fact it had just reappeared without its original twenty-seven tallies.

He guessed the six tallies must represent the six people he'd murdered when first arriving here; the pain when he jumped, the markings being re-branded into his skin.

So the only anomaly remaining was the purpose behind its reappearance with its less than original quota.

Obadiah lightly caressed the pigmented areas, noticing the dermal tenderness despite the absence of an inflammatory response to the surrounding cutis. The ablations felt fresh, the occurrence a subtle change to the supernal recall he was experiencing, enforcing his suspicion there was more to his being here than he yet understood. If everything else in the world around him was to be exactly the same, as he suspected it would be, the only challenge now was how to motivate himself in such a repetitive setting.

Experience so far showed his actions had no effect on the ultimate outcome. It was now more than simple déjà vu. His sense of recollection was too strong. It was the when and the how which eluded him, obfuscating an endgame he was not yet party to.

Perhaps to begin understanding why he was here, he needed to embrace it as another stage in his evolution. The stimulus would be refreshing if nothing else.

No more fucking about…

Glancing one final time at his back, he slid the mirror aside to reveal a wardrobe. Pulling on some underwear, a black t-shirt and dark blue jeans, Obadiah moved towards the stairs, his emerald eyes sparkling with new-found expectation.

———

ONCE DOWNSTAIRS, HE HAD APPLIED HIS MOST CHARMING SMILE and told them they were all to go out together – as a family.

Eva had been slightly resistant, but eventually succumbed and had gotten dressed in a baggy jumper, long, tanned skirt and brown knee-high boots.

Cleaning the flour from Ellie and putting on her dark blue winter coat, gloves and wellingtons, they had left the house together and walked to the town.

Obadiah's desire to see the repetitive behaviours and incidences he knew would occur was less than compelling. More overwhelming was his curiosity to experience them with Eva and Ellie, to see how their addition to the equation would alter the dynamic. He wanted to see what this existence, for want of a better word, was offering him. He imagined emotions he had rarely given credence to would be available to him.

Obadiah wanted to feel them, court them and toy with them. Maybe even learn from them. He had never claimed to be omniscient.

The sky was cerulean as they made their way down the tree-lined avenue. The autumnal edge in the air that Obadiah recognised well prompted Eva to clutch the jacket to her throat. Linking her arm through his, she sidled up against him for warmth, her closeness offset only by Obadiah's stillness. He wondered what kinds of noises she would make if he ripped out her throat. The curiosity crawled beneath his skin like a parasite.

Ellie kicked through piles of crimson leaves on the pavement as Eva spoke.

"What's on your mind, Obi? You seem a little... distant today."

He kept his response short. "Do I? Nothing of consequence."

Eva gave him a wry smile. "Okayyyy, Mr Loquacious."

They walked in silence the remainder of the way to town, making their way down College Street, Eva occasionally calling out for Ellie to be careful.

They stopped outside Miss Courtney's Tea Room, the café Obadiah recognised as Susan Sheridan's establishment. Wondering if their arrival there was serendipitous, Obadiah looked through the window, observing his former victim moving about the few tables already occupied.

"Come on. Treat me to a coffee and a doughnut. I feel a cheat day coming on."

Eva pushed Obadiah playfully by the shoulder. "It was your idea to come out..."

Intrigued by the thought of being in Susan's presence again, knowing she would have no recollection of her death at his hands, Obadiah opened the door and gestured for Eva and Ellie to move ahead of him.

"Why thank you, sir," Eva emphasised with a smile and a cheeky wiggle of her hips as she motioned Ellie towards the table by the window.

Eva removed Ellie's coat before doing the same herself and sitting down.

Standing by the window, he took in the view. His outline appeared black in the glare of the sun, as though his very soul were momentarily visible. As expected, everyone in the café remained blissfully unaware they were in the presence of death.

The tables were dressed with linen tablecloths, the tea and coffee served in china. Obadiah noticed that the pieces were all different, augmenting the air of eccentricity and charm to the café that subtly distanced it from the more sharp-edged modernism of other establishments.

Obadiah actually felt a sense of relief at being in an environment which could allow him to preserve his self-image of perfection. He had spent his entire life conditioning himself to be acutely sensitive to societal norms, always finding it fairly easy to outwardly live a life which appeared above reproach. His murderous proclivities aside, Obadiah had always enjoyed the pretence of being normal. He slowly realised it might be a pleasant diversion to embrace this role he'd been assigned.

His expression remaining thoughtful, Obadiah sat down and studied Eva.

She had a handsome, sun-kissed face, defined by good bone structure. Framed by her coffee-coloured hair and slightly freckled across her cheeks, the light cascading through the window gave her an ethereal shimmer. Eva's brown eyes locked with his as he stared, her smile forcing him to subconsciously respond in kind. Smiling wasn't something that had often had a place in Obadiah's life.

Ellie was sorting packets of sugar in the bowl as Susan Sheridan approached and stood beside the table. "Morning, folks. What can I get you?"

Eva skimmed across the menu. "Hi, can I have a tall Latté and a glass of blackcurrant for the munchkin and… Obi, what would you like?"

Obadiah, intrigued by the scenario's normality and Susan's lack of recognition, paused briefly before asking for a black coffee. Eva gave him a quizzical look as she spoke. "Oh, and a jam doughnut please."

She smiled knowingly at Obadiah.

"Ellie, would you like anything else?"

The little girl, now stacking the sugar packets, replied with a decisive, "No, thank you, Mummy."

Susan smiled as she moved towards the kitchen, leaving Obadiah with Eva's curious expression.

"Since when do you drink black coffee? You always said it made you twitchy."

"I fancied a change," he replied with a shrug.

"Well, that's refreshing to hear, given everything that's happened recently. Isn't that right, Ells?"

The little girl spoke without looking up. "Yes, you've been grumpy recently, Daddy."

Obadiah felt a spark of curiosity. Her innocence was refreshing.

"How would you prefer me to be?" The lack of emotion in Obadiah's tone went unnoticed by the little girl.

"Happy, like you used to be before you were sick. Today, you seem sad."

Her pile of stacked sugar packets collapsed, eliciting an exaggerated sigh. Then she was lost again in her reorganisation.

Children had always been intriguing to him, if only

because they taunted him with realisations of what his childhood could have been.

Eva thanked Susan as she returned to place their drinks on the table before turning her attention to Obadiah. "So, what brought on this sudden desire for impulsive behaviour? I might get to like it if it extends beyond this tea room."

Her enticing smile and pout were lost on him."Let's just say recent events have given me pause to consider my behaviour."

"Obi, you're very strange today." She picked up one of her daughter's sugar packets and poured it into her cup, stirring it methodically. "But that's one of the reasons I fell in love with you."

She leaned over and kissed him on the cheek before turning towards Ellie and playfully mussing her hair.

Obadiah prickled with electricity at the contact. It had seemed so long ago that he'd almost forgotten what being in the presence of unbridled, fearless emotion was like. His sudden feelings made him uneasy. He began to perspire and tried to initiate a conversation to divert his discomfort.

"I want to see a doctor today."

Eva's focus immediately shifted back to Obadiah. "Why, do you feel sick?"

"No, I just want to chat with someone about what's going on up here." He tapped on his forehead as he spoke, suspecting that part of understanding who he was supposed to be here may involve understanding what was supposed to be wrong with him. He'd guessed he had a tumour of some description but needed to know more. How big, where it was, the symptoms it could cause.

Eva reached for his hand. Obadiah allowed her to grasp it. "Obi, you'd tell me if something was wrong, right?"

"Of course." His answer was clipped. He found the realisation that he had no idea what he was supposed to do in this type of situation disconcerting and enticing in equal measure. He accepted that evolution of any kind was a penetrative, violent act, metaphorically speaking.

"Do you want us to come with you?" Eva's grip tightened on Obadiah's hand.

"No, I'd prefer to go alone."

His emotionless, matter of fact response caused Eva's brow to crease with mild disappointment, but she knew better than to push him for a rationalisation. A saddened "Okay" was her only response as she relaxed her grip.

Obadiah sensed her upset and tried to ignore it. However, realising the identity and location of the doctor were not known to him, he quickly proffered a response. "I just want to talk to someone alone."

Though his tone had softened, Obadiah offered no physical contact to complement his words.

"No, it's okay. I understand." Eva brushed muffin crumbs from her sweater.

"Exactly," Obadiah responded with a lifeless tone. "However I would appreciate the company on the way."

Eva smiled appreciatively as she turned and gave Ellie a kiss on the forehead. "We'll walk with Daddy to the doctor's won't we, Ells?"

"Yup," came the reply between swallows of juice.

Obadiah nodded, suddenly eager to get moving. Not having considered looking for a wallet at the house, he pretended to check his pockets before raising his eyebrows at Eva in insincere apology.

"What a shocker, Obadiah Stark. You think you're royalty, carrying no money around on you," Eva said as she rose from the table to pay the bill.

Obadiah found himself left staring at Ellie.

She was gazing absentmindedly out the window, playfully twirling her straw around the rim of the glass. He could see she resembled her mother in many ways, her bone structure, her slender neck and small nose. And yet, he was amazed to notice that he could see himself in her eyes; emerald green. The sheer incredulity of her being his daughter, even if only in this afterlife existence, had Obadiah imagining a million different scenarios simultaneously.

Would she hold his hand if he offered it? Would she allow him to pick her up? Would she ask him to read her stories at bedtime, take her to school, go to the cinema?

All the things he had desired so desperately himself as a child, things never offered. He'd sought to replace those desires with more inventive pastimes but had never forgotten what it had felt like to want his father to offer a hand to him with an intent behind it other than chastisement.

"Are you scared?" Obadiah leaned forward slightly as he spoke.

Ellie looked at him over the rim of her glass. "Scared of what, Daddy?"

"Scared of me."

"You're silly," came her reply with a giggle.

His thoughts on the charade of giving him a child and the purpose it could serve were broken by Eva's return to the table.

"Okay, we ready?" she said, placing her purse back in her bag and pulling out Ellie's chair.

"I'm ready," Ellie proclaimed as she jumped up from the table, knocking over the glass in the process.

The accident prompted the café's occupants to stop their conversations and for a moment, focus all their attention on Obadiah and his companions.

Eva had already bent down to begin collecting the shattered pieces, Ellie crouching by her side, offering apologies. Obadiah made no move to assist them, preferring to stare back at the inquisitive people who had deemed his area of the café their focus of attention.

He took a few steps forward towards the nearest table, his physique seemingly growing with each movement.

"Is there something I can help you with?"

Though a question, its meaning was apparent, despite the softness of his tone. Accompanied with mumbles and nervous twitters, the café's patrons slowly turned their interest away from Obadiah and began subdued conversations.

Susan had arrived with a dustpan and was sweeping the remaining fragments from the floor as Eva stepped up to Obadiah and gently touched his elbow.

"Come on, you. Let's go before you upset the natives."

Eva ushered Ellie out the door and into the biting air. Obadiah sensed all eyes of the café on him as they moved past the window and onto College Street.

The businesses around him hummed with activity, reminding him of ants in a bivouac. The people hurried in and around the pavements and shopfronts, never seeming to spend any significant amount of time digesting what they saw, always being driven to move on to the next spectacle without any understanding as to why.

He found it tedious, as though they were all moving in slow-motion and he was moving in real time.

Obadiah walked slightly apart from Eva, her attention more focused on Ellie's safety than his proximity. As they ambled past McSorley's and onto Plunkett Street, he found his memories prickling at some of the sights around him.

He hadn't paid much attention since his arrival here, his focus having been directed towards understanding the why, not the how.

But now, in a more relaxed state, he realised that many of the sights around him were acting as stimuli for childhood memories.

The Killarney Art Gallery, the Grand Hotel and St. Mary's Church on Main Street: they all began to pull at his subconscious like a magician pulling handkerchiefs from a hat. He tried to piece the elicited memories together like a jigsaw. It was so long ago since he'd last been here that Obadiah knew he wouldn't be able to form a complete picture. Oddly, the memories which were the most powerful were the ones of least significance; the smell of damp pavements, the haze of lights in shop windows, the cold sensation of a breeze on his face.

And yet, despite their emotive pull at his mind, it all felt different, and not merely because he had returned here in the strangest of circumstances.

It was different because he was sharing it all with someone else. Eva was his first, voluntary companion he'd had since his friendship with Tom Jacques.

And he found himself wanting to share himself with her in a way that wouldn't result in her death.

As they turned onto Cahernane Meadows, off Muckcross Road, Obadiah noticing the doctor's surgery just up ahead. Nothing looked familiar, but then again he'd never really been allowed to visit a doctor's as a child in case they asked him awkward questions concerning bruises on his body.

"Drs Fiona O'Brien and John Gantly," he read out loud from the sign.

"Obi, are you okay?" Eva questioned.

He began to walk towards the entrance, dismissing her with a curt, "I'm fine."

Eva loosened Ellie's coat before taking her hand.

"Is Daddy okay?"

The concern in her daughter's tone pulled at Eva's heart.

"Daddy's fine, sweetie. He's just anxious is all."

Their presence triggered the surgery's automatic doors, and they moved through to stand beside Obadiah at the reception.

———

OBADIAH HAD LET EVA DO THE TALKING, GIVEN THAT SHE'D appeared to know the girl behind the desk personally.

He had stood impassively while she inquired about any spaces in Dr O'Brien's schedule. After a brief phone call, they were told she would see Obadiah briefly in the next ten minutes and would they kindly take a seat in the waiting room.

Eva and Ellie had decided to do some shopping while he waited.

Sitting down, Obadiah had amused himself by imagining the reactions of the people around him were they to know who he was and what he did. The desire to show them was still there, pulsating beneath his skull, but he remained controlled. He was much more interested in what the doctor had to say about his physical condition here. Obadiah was beginning to think it strange that he had no actual symptoms when his name had been called from the reception desk, advising him the doctor would see him now.

Fiona O'Brien's office was relatively large, housing the usual medical equipment one would expect; a long, black examination couch, a shelf stacked with medical journals and textbooks, a hand-wash basin in the corner, a device for measuring height and a desk with a computer and the obligatory sphygmomanometer where the doctor sat.

The only thing incongruous in the room was him.

Dr O'Brien was a slight, well dressed, middle-aged lady, with greying hair and a pleasant expression. She had welcomed Obadiah into the room as though they were old friends and motioned towards the chair by her desk while she washed her hands.

"So, what can we do for you today, Obadiah?" Her Irish lilt and warm delivery were oddly relaxing.

"I want you to tell me what's wrong with me?"

Though taken aback by Obadiah's direct manner, she

moved her chair a little closer to him. "Has something happened?"

Obadiah couldn't help but smile. "You have no idea, Doc. I just want it explained to me again, so I have it clear in my mind."

Fiona settled back into her chair and clasped her hands together. "Look, I know it can be a great deal of information to process. What specifically would you like me to go over?"

Obadiah leaned forward. "Tell me everything."

His emotionless tone surprised her, but she accepted that people deal with things in different ways and that perhaps, this was Obadiah Stark's way of coping – compartmentalising his condition.

With a sigh, she began. "Okay. You were diagnosed with a Glioblastoma multiforme – the most common and aggressive type of brain tumour in humans. Nine months ago, you underwent multimodality treatment consisting of an open craniotomy with surgical resection of as much of the tumour as possible, followed by a course of chemo-radiotherapy, anti-angiogenic therapy with bevacizumab, gamma knife radiosurgery. Your symptomatic care is with the corticosteroids. By the way, I see you have kept your hair short since the operation. It suits you.

"Usual symptoms include nausea, vomiting, headaches and possible hemiparesis. The main symptom, however, is progressive memory loss, with personality and neurological deficits due to the tumour's temporal and frontal lobe involvement. The symptoms, of course, depend greatly on the location of the tumour, which in your case is in the frontal lobe. This can affect your ability to recognise future consequences resulting from current actions, to choose between good and bad actions... previous research has identified that some patients find it difficult to suppress unacceptable social responses... all higher mental function involvement. As your frontal lobes also play an important part in retaining longer-term memories, memories associated with emotions, symptoms can include finding it difficult to modify emotions that fit socially acceptable norms.

"Two months ago, scans showed your tumour had returned. Other than further chemotherapy, which you refused, our options are limited. Forgive my bluntness, Obadiah, but the fact we're having this conversation again is a little worrying. Is everything okay?"

Obadiah, ignoring her questions, crossed his arms as he processed what she'd said. He wasn't sure if what he'd just learnt helped him understand what had happened to him. If anything he was slightly more confused.

Difficulty recognising consequences, inability to choose between good and bad actions, unacceptable social responses... all aspects of his personality as defined by every psychologist who'd ever attempted to get inside his mind. Yet, in life, he'd had no tumour.

Or had he?

No, all the tests carried out on him at Absolom would have picked something up. He had suffered headaches, but didn't everyone? Nausea and vomiting... generally, he had a strong constitution. He'd felt nauseated recently, but figured it was related to the process of actually dying. Hemiparesis... never that he could recall, but yesterday when he'd jumped from the cliff, he'd experienced pain and numbness down one side. He had attributed that to his tattoo supernaturally reappearing.

In the words of Lewis Carroll, curiouser and curiouser cried Alice.

Taking several breaths and pressing his head back against the chair, Obadiah waited a moment before speaking. "Prognosis?"

Fiona O'Brien smiled apologetically. "Three to six months."

Obadiah clenched his jaw. "And this surgery was nine

months ago?"

"Yes." She waited for a beat before speaking again. "Is there anything I can do?"

Silence permeated the room, accentuating the ticking of the clock on the desk. Obadiah stood up while this latest piece of the puzzle bounced around his mind, trying to find its logical place. If all he'd just been told was true, he could be facing a slow, painful death from a growth, potentially the size of a grapefruit, in his head. That was if he could even die here. For reasons still beyond his comprehension, he appeared to have jumped from the proverbial frying pan.

Maybe this was his actual punishment. Had he been spared death by lethal injection only to face a possible death considered more appropriate to his crimes?

Was his mind being rotted away so delicately, that he couldn't tell what was real or not anymore?

Maybe he'd always been here, and life before had only been a dream.

Returning to Fiona's question, Obadiah bent forward and placed his hands on either side of the doctor's chair. His inappropriate closeness forced Fiona to lean back, her expression one of increasing concern for her wellbeing.

"Obadiah, please sit back." She failed to hide her anxiety.

"You medical people are all the same. I had to listen to a pious, sanctimonious arsehole only a few days ago. He was telling me all about death as well. That didn't turn out exactly as I imagined, so I can't see how this could be any different. Why would I be spared death, only to be placed in an afterlife where I'm dying anyway, albeit slower? You ask if there anything you can do? Can you turn back time and allow me to die the first time around?"

Her eyes projected blankness.

Obadiah leaned in closer and grabbed her by the chin with his right hand. "I didn't fucking think so."

He mused as to whether she'd still hold her dumb-arse

expression if he crossed the ends of the stethoscope around her neck and pulled them taut. He could just place his knee on her chair to give him leverage and really put all his force behind it. Maybe he could even cut through her neck. Decapitate this stupid bitch who thought she knew everything.

His heart pounded in his chest as his face hovered over hers. The doctor's eyes glanced furtively at the door behind him, wondering if someone would hear her if she shouted. Once upon a time, she would have already been dead. Now, with everything else going on, he just couldn't be bothered. The mystery unfolding before him seemed intent on consuming all that he was and had been.

Fiona O'Brien swallowed audibly, her anxiety rapidly becoming unbridled fear as she saw in Obadiah's eyes darkness that seemed barely contained. He slid his nose along the side of her neck, taking in her scent as though a tiger confirming a kill.

Fiona, her eyes shut tight, worked her head frantically from side to side, trying to evade the dehumanisation of her person. Tears rolled freely as she tried to comprehend how a straightforward appointment, with one her fondest clients, could have so quickly turned in to the most fearful experience of her life.

"I am going to tell you something important," he said tonelessly, still holding her face. "On a scale of one to ten, it's a ten. It's 'I just worked out how the fucking universe works' important. And after I've told you, I want you to explain it to me, like I'm a two-year-old. Do you understand?"

Fiona nodded quickly.

Obadiah leaned forward again and whispered in her ear. "I murdered the owner of Miss Courtney's Tea Room two days ago. Slit her throat from ear to ear. It was beautiful."

The doctor was pale, her eyes wide with fear and shock.

She was afraid to call out, even if she'd been able to. Obadiah let go of her face and paced around the room.

"She wasn't the only one, of course. I murdered quite a few people that day. And then, the strangest thing happened. I woke up the next day, and everything was the same. No one was dead. They were all going about their business as though nothing had happened. So I killed myself. And guess what… I woke up and found that everything was still exactly the same. This is now the third day I've experienced, where everything is the same as it was the day before and the day before that. I can't seem to die or change anything for twenty-four hours. But that isn't the best part. Four days ago, I was executed by lethal injection in ADX Absolom – my reward for being one of the world's most notorious serial killers. And then I found myself here - Heaven, Hell, who the fuck knows. I have a wife, a child. I live in my old childhood home in the town where I grew up and have just learnt that I have an inoperable brain tumour.

"By the way, doc, the tumour? Would you, in your medical opinion, consider it evil? I'm guessing you would, seeing as you probably define any defect in the structure of the human body that prevents us from fulfilling our potential as human beings as evil. Of course, if evil is an illness, it's not only a disease; it is the ultimate disease. Maybe that's my punishment. The ultimate disease afflicted with the ultimate disease. Poetic, don't you think? So anyway, doc, you tell me, which part of what I've just told you do you want to explain first?"

Fiona shook her head, an indication that she could neither comprehend what she had just heard nor knew the answer. Obadiah snorted his disdain at her pathetic response.

"That's the thing about this place. No one has a fucking clue what I'm talking about."

He stopped his pacing and paused in front of the doctor, her body almost curled into a foetal position in the chair.

"Close your eyes."

She didn't hesitate, despite the waves of terror crashing over her. Seconds seemed to stretch into minutes, as she considered what she'd just heard; as she waited for some violent act to take place against her. And then, there was nothing.

No sound, no presence, no movement.

She slowly opened her eyes, expecting to see Obadiah's face hovering over her. But she saw no one.

The door to her room was open, the muffled sounds from the corridor and distant reception assuring her that life was still continuing. There were no screams or cries for help.

She tentatively rose from her chair and moved slowly towards the open door, wiping snot and tears from her face. A practice nurse walked past, paying no attention to Fiona as she moved down the corridor and into the reception area.

The waiting area was beginning to fill up now, the majority of the people waiting to be seen elderly, though a few children were present with their parents.

She couldn't see him anywhere.

Attempting to compose herself by straightening her skirt, Fiona approached the receptionist behind the glass panel who was just completing a phone call. She smiled at Fiona but received nothing in return other than a look of distress.

"Obadiah Stark. Did he just come through here?"

"Yes, Doctor. About two minutes ago. Is everything okay? You look dreadful."

Fiona tried to smile a reassuring smile. "I'm fine. Was anyone else with him?"

"No, not that I could see. Are you sure you're okay?"

"Yes, thank you, Kay. I'm just tired. Give me a few minutes before sending in the next patient if you don't mind?"

Fiona O'Brien slowly walked back to her office and shut the door, trying to process what had just happened.

———

As he walked up the road to meet his 'family', Obadiah knew he should despise what was happening to him.

But he didn't.

He had approached his being here all wrong. His anger at being cheated death had clouded his ability to see the opportunity before him. Whatever had occurred at the moment of his execution, the fact remained he was somewhere he could go unnoticed without a pretence.

If he desired to kill, so be it.

It would all reset the following day, with no consequences.

If he chose not to, he would be able to experience life in a way he'd never thought possible. Free from recognition and implication.

He was actually proud of the self-control he'd shown with the doctor. And this tumour he was supposedly dying from… if each day began anew, what was the worst that could happen?

Yes, here he could be who he'd always conditioned himself to be.

No-one.

'The darkness drops again but now I know that twenty centuries of stony sleep were vexed to nightmare by a rocking cradle. And what rough beast, its hour come round at last, slouches towards Bethlehem to be born.'
William Butler Yeats

9

SEPTEMBER 28TH

20:06

O'Dywers, Ashe Street, Tralee (*Trá Lí*)
County Kerry, Ireland

EVIL CAN BE SUBTLE, INSIDIOUS, CAPABLE OF INFILTRATING THE most secure of philosophies and ideologies, planting its 'vicious mole of nature' in even the most righteous of minds.

Oligarchies and organisations can be founded with the noblest of aspirations in mind and yet find themselves becoming the most capricious of despots, with their power resting amongst a small segment of society - the wealthy, royalty, military and corporate.

But what constitutes an evil act? To answer that, it must first be defined what evil actually is.

Is slapping one's child considered evil? Were the acts committed at Auschwitz during wartime evil? The rape and murder of children?

Is it the act which is evil, or the person who commits it?

DAYLIGHT WAS A DISTANT MEMORY BY THE TIME JOE ARRIVED AT O'Dywer's.

Despite the time of year, the air was warm as he finished the last of his cigarette outside the entrance to the pub. Anyone who smoked in Ireland nowadays was pretty much made to feel like a leper, the social ostracising akin to being an endangered species. Joe was immune to the attention it now brought. He had only ever been a social smoker anyway and given he was about to have a pint, it was his excuse for having one now.

The open fire to his right was burning as Joe stepped through the doorway, the crackling of embers and coal adding to the relaxed atmosphere the pub always held. He made his way down the narrow walkway adjacent to the bar, stopping long enough to order a pint of Guinness before removing his coat and taking a seat on the brown, velvet banquette in the empty booth at the bottom as instructed by his mysterious caller. He had deliberately arrived there early in the hope he could control the situation when, or if, his furtive guest arrived.

The Guinness was refreshingly cold as Joe took a long drink, emptying half the glass. He realised he hadn't been here in a while. He'd always preferred O'Dwyer's around this time, its early evening occupants mostly consisting of regulars ruminating over the newspaper or talking about their day at work. The sounds of the hushed conversation and the smell of brewed hops and whiskey were comforting.

Joe leaned back, letting out a huge sigh of frustration at his being here instead of a booth somewhere with Victoria Carter. He began to irritate himself further with the thought that this meeting might be a complete wind-up. It wouldn't be the first time.

Feeling his eyes becoming heavy, he closed them and let the gentle murmur of social interaction wash over him. Then, what felt like almost immediately, a presence made itself known by sliding onto the bench opposite. Glancing at his watch, Joe realised he must have dozed off.

The man before him was stocky and built like a rugby player. Middle-aged with auburn hair thinning on top, he had the intense stare of someone who took life exceptionally seriously. His black coat with its wide collars buttoned almost right to the top, made him look like a spy from an old 1930's movie.

Joe rubbed his eyes and quickly centred himself, shuffling forwards on the bench slightly.

"Hello," he said firmly. "Can I get you anything to drink?" His journalistic instincts kicked in, knowing he could get more from someone if they felt at ease.

The stranger glanced from side to side, quickly checking behind him and towards the bar before speaking. "No, I'm fine."

His Belfast-accented voice was strong, the voice of someone used to have people do as he told them.

"So, mate. Can I ask who you are?"

He paused before speaking. "Peter Stamford." His hands were clasped in front of him, the thumbs thoughtfully working around each other.

Joe took another mouthful of Guinness as he assessed his company. So far, he wasn't giving much away.

"So, Mr Stamford. Why am I here? Just so you know, I turned down a date with an attractive woman, so I hope you're going to blow my mind."

The man didn't react to Joe's flippancy. "I work at Absolom, Mr O'Connell. I was one of Obadiah Stark's strap-down guards."

Joe shifted in his seat. "Okay, you have my attention."

Stamford leaned towards Joe, his breath smelling like he'd already frequented a pub before arriving here.

"You were there, when he died, at the back of the room. What did you see?"

Joe smiled at the direct nature of the question. "Straight to the point. Okay, what did I see? Well, I saw one of history's most infamous serial killers strapped to a table, receiving a cocktail of non-recreational medications, while most of the world's media and a dozen or so people who wished him dead looked on. Am I missing anything?"

Stamford smiled a knowing smile. "You're missing everything."

"Oh, really? Okay, let's assume for the sake of argument that you're not jerking my chain. What did I miss?" Joe did little to hide the intrigue in his tone.

"What do you really know about Absolom, Mr O'Connell? Did you know that we pretty much provide an environment where the inmates eat, sleep and defecate in their cells and only leave them for one hour a day? With the full support of the Government, we have ensured that the prisoners can never allow themselves the audacity of hope that they will ever see the light of day as free men."

"That's quite a profound statement," Joe said quietly.

Stamford ignored him and continued. "We perfected the tradition of behaviour modification. Strip searches, metal detectors and constant video surveillance are standard practice at the prison. Yeah, they're deemed excessive and humiliating by the Irish Human Rights campaigners, but really, they only serve as intimidation techniques. Because of a previous incident some years ago and picketing by those pain in the arse bleeding hearts, Sabitch had to abandon the strip searches that were a daily part of the program. Then, the same Government which had supported many of his methods suddenly baulked at such extremes, probably due to media pressure, forcing him to agree to acknowledge the prisoner's human rights. Their human rights! I mean, seriously!

"Joe Fort imprisoned on drug trafficking charges; the only Irishman ever convicted of terrorism for hire. Santiago Margarito Rangel Varelas murdered his two-year-old stepdaughter with kicks to the head. Upon investigation she also had numerous broken ribs and had been sodomised, all injuries Varelas told the police she'd sustained having fallen at home. Stuart Swango, physician and serial killer. David York, serving 135 years for child molestation. Mohammed Rassim, one of the four former al-Qaeda members sentenced to life imprisonment in 2007 for their parts in the London July 7th bombings. The list goes on. I can't think of one inmate there who deserves the slightest modicum of leniency or compassion. And then you had Obadiah Stark." Stamford hesitated for a moment as though thinking. "He never showed signs that any of those measures had a deterrent effect on him. He was simply an empty, black hole of a human being. I hesitate to even call him a man, as he seemed to lack the most basic of human emotions. There was no empathy, no remorse, not even hatred. Varelas demonstrated anger at his incarceration, denying he'd committed a crime. Stark didn't emote at all. You simply couldn't gauge the man for a baseline. He never caused any trouble, but you could see it in his eyes. It was more than darkness. It was simply... emptiness, as though he had no soul."

Stamford's voice slowed as though recalling Obadiah had forced him to experience a profound disquiet. "Stark was kept in Sector 17; call it an 'ultramax' within the supermax. A group of cells where there's virtually no human contact whatsoever, not even with the guards. Almost the entirety of Stark's incarceration at Absolom was spent in Sector 17."

Joe's expression remained impassive as he finished his pint and wiped his top lip. "Okay, I can count at least four violations of civil liberties going on at Absolom, but assuming I actually give a crap that they're happening to criminals, why should any of this interest me?"

"It should interest you, Joe, because you're not reading between the lines. What I've just told you illustrate what a well-oiled a machine Absolom is. There are no mistakes or oversights. It has a perfect record for a reason. Which is why what I'm going to tell you is all the more disturbing."

"Go on," Joe instructed, quietly becoming more excited at Stamford's building exposition.

"I told you I was one of the strap-down guards at Absolom. Well, after an execution, there's all the procedural stuff. Determination of death of the inmate, reading of a statement by the warden notifying the witnesses the execution is complete, contacting the media regarding the carrying out of the sentence, etcetera, etcetera. Then, after all the witnesses have been escorted from the death house, the intravenous lines are supposed to be crimped closed and disconnected, but not removed. This is to allow a review by the county coroner if necessary. First red flag – all the lines were removed from Stark the minute the room was sealed. I know this because I was assigned to the room for security. Then, after the body has been tagged and placed in a body bag for removal to the mortuary, all the unused chemicals are documented on a CDCR form as to why they weren't used and then transferred to a locked fridge to await disposal. Red flag number two – I spoke to the Intravenous Sub-team a few days after the execution. They'd completed an inventory of all the supplies and drugs used. I asked them for their records regarding the amounts used during Stark's execution. None of the medications used for an execution - Sodium thiopental, Pavulon and Potassium chloride had been released from the pharmacy on the day of the execution. When I questioned them, they said it must have been a clerical error, and they would look into it. Drugs used for lethal injection do not suffer from clerical errors, Mr O'Connell.

"Red flag number three – the Record Keeping Sub-team is supposed to meet with the team leader to check all the documentation, which is then given to the warden for inclusion in the Master Execution File. Seventy-two hours after this, the warden writes an after-action critique of the execution - what went well, compliance with regulations – and then a death certificate is issued along with a warrant of death. None of the documentation concerning Obadiah Stark's execution is in the Master Execution File. Not a single document."

Joe felt confused. "But Obadiah has a death certificate. I know, because I checked as a matter of course for the article I wrote after his death."

"But he shouldn't have," Stamford interjected. "Not if his warrant of death hadn't been released."

Joe suddenly needed another drink.

"So, Mr Investigative Journalist," the strap-down guard said, leaning back on the bench. "Riddle me this - how does someone who's been executed by the state have a death certificate issued, despite there being no legal documents concerning his actual execution and why does he have all evidence of the drugs used in his execution, lines and all, removed from his body and omitted from the inventory?"

"Okay, so we have a few examples of clerical oversights. At the end of the day, Stark is still dead. Dead is dead."

Stamford slammed his palm against the table, causing Joe's empty glass to jump. "You're not getting it, mate. They're hiding something. Shite, I'm risking my livelihood just being here with you. Be a journalist, do yer job. If something illicit is going on at Absolom, someone needs to find out."

Joe raised his hands in a submissive manner. "Easy, friend. Do you have any proof? Something that will stand up to scrutiny?"

"Other than what I've told you, no. Officially, Obadiah Stark was executed on September 7th, 2011. Unofficially… well, that's where you come in. If I were you, my first port of call would be the warden at Absolom."

The pub door opened, a cold gust of wind accompanying the man and woman who'd just entered. Peter Stamford shot an anxious look in the door's direction before he shuffled from the booth. "I have to go."

Joe stood to try and slow his departure. "Wait, I need more." He went to grab for his sleeve, but Stamford had already moved beyond his grasp and was fast approaching the door.

"Dammit."

Joe grabbed his coat and moved to intercept him on the street. He thought he knew every facet of Obadiah Stark's life and death, but his understanding had just been turned on its head by a stranger.

Joe burst out the pub entrance, scanning the pavement on either side of him, but he saw no sign of the guard. Standing in the night air, a chill of paranoia washed over him. First, he had relatives acting strangely when he'd interviewed them, now he had a prison guard suggesting that they may be more to Obadiah's execution than he could have ever realised. Intuitively, he knew that somehow the two were connected, but he had no idea how. He had lived and breathed Obadiah Stark for two years and yet even in death, his ability for misdirection and obfuscation were still in play.

The rules of the game had just been changed – a game Joe hadn't realised that, until this very moment, he was playing.

Dr. John Franklin, BS.c. (HONS), PH.D. M.A., M.CLIN, PSYCH. A.F.Ps.S.I.

Subject: Stark, Obadiah James (a.k.a. The Tally Man) cont.

Victim history continued:

During 1989, Obadiah was in Louisiana, living in a flat located in St. Helena's Parish, Baton Rouge.

A fairly small parish, Obadiah committed four more murders between the months of March and December 1989. Julie Robinson, Hazel DeMarco, Tammy Porto and Claire Jackson all lived within a ten-mile radius of Obadiah's place of residence.

At the time, Obadiah had gained part-time employment for a local real estate agency where he organised portfolios for the proprietor. He also obtained a job working behind a local bar, the latter job providing a perfect location to observe and meet women. Now offered a large playground to prowl and pretend to live a normal life within and having been freed from not only his parents' influence but also the authority of the state, Obadiah could now do whatever he wished and go wherever he liked, without danger of reprisal.

During this period, all evidence points towards Obadiah projecting the image of a quiet and hard-working employee. He had a number of girlfriends during this period, many of whom are reported as having described Obadiah as an almost introverted character until you established a rapport with him when he seemed to come out of 'his shell' and exhibit a personality that was both charming and self-effacing.

This is supported by a small number of people who socialised with Obadiah, saying that he seemingly thrived on the opportunity to share the common interests he had, namely reading and sports. Conversely, some of his fellow employees recall that Obadiah was seen to be a loner and often arrogant at times.

A perfect example of Obadiah's social skills and interpersonal manner presenting themselves in order to purely serve his desires and need for manipulation, it also illustrates the paradoxical nature of the sociopath; the more sophisticated they are in regards to their behavioural control and ability to project a normal life, the more dangerous they are. Indeed, Obadiah's relationships with women supported his deceitful pursuit of a relatively normal existence.

It was 17th March 1989 when the body of Julie Robinson, a 25 year-old student from Louisiana State University, was found in a secluded part of the campus. She had been stabbed eighteen times and left in an overgrown section of the grounds. The subject admitted to her murder during our session together, marking it as the first time he had confirmed his long-suspected involvement. Later that year, on the morning of 2nd July 1989, Obadiah stalked and murdered 28 year-old supermarket worker, Hazel DeMarco. Her body was found four days later in a field just outside St. Helena's Parish. One particularly disturbing aspect of her murder was that, during her autopsy, the coroner determined that she had not died from the multiple stab wounds to her body, but from strangulation. This meant that she had been alive when Obadiah had decided to make her death more intimate by physically using his own strength to take her life.

During the interview, Obadiah admitted he had expected her to die from the stab wounds, but that when she hadn't, he decided to finish her "the old fashioned way. Up close and personal."

Asked by this author if he could recall anything specific about Hazel, such as clothing or her physical appearance, Obadiah stated he couldn't remember any details and responded by saying "she was just another peasant. What the fuck do you want me to say?... one less burden on the societal system if you ask me."

The increased police presence in St. Helena's Parish did little to deter Obadiah's thirst for killing, nor his continued façade of a reliable and trustworthy employee, his calculating nature providing a further layer to his virtual anonymity - anonymity that led to another murder only months later.

The last time anyone saw Tammy Porto alive was on the evening of Thursday 28th September 1989. She was reportedly seen driving home after leaving her friends at a local bar. A man seen in her car was later identified as her boyfriend and subsequently ruled out as a suspect when it was established that he had been dropped off by Tammy earlier in the journey, for which he had an alibi.

Her remains were discovered on Monday 6th November by some ramblers in a field four miles from where she lived and less than three from Obadiah's house. Markings found on some of Tammy's ribs and sternum indicated immense pressure had been applied to the murder weapon in order to cause such trauma to the skeleton.

During all of this, Obadiah's routine of normality continued unabated, with the now increased media focus on the spate of local murders neither affecting his progress at work nor murderous proclivities. He continued to socialise and date girls, ignorant of the fact that these aspects of establishing and maintaining interpersonal relationships, social awareness and communication skills, were also dichotomous, at once sensitising and desensitising Obadiah's ability to relate to other people.

Regardless of his criminal conduct or social situation, Obadiah was learning to cognitively isolate himself in relation to the murders. His increasingly idiosyncratic thoughts, behaviour and deliberate indifference, all contributed to his colleagues at his place of employment noting that Obadiah was becoming more aloof and arrogant, supporting the theory that at this stage in his 'becoming', he had already begun to compartmentalise what he considered his normal life and his murderous one.

By now, the police knew they had a serial killer on their hands, but because of the distance and time between the murders of Lauren Tolson and Angelina Tegan and the most recent three victims, the police couldn't be certain that they were linked. Obadiah was routinely interviewed by the police in connection with the murders, but his charm and ability for emotive disarmament meant that he was never considered a suspect.

Excerpt taken from interview with Elizabeth Barlow (fellow employee at real estate agency):

"He always seemed kinda shy... almost humble. He never looked you in the eyes when talking to you... really intellectual. You could never have believed he could do the things the press reported him as having done. I mean, he was a regular 'boy-next-door' type, ya know? If I'd ever been walking down a dark alley at night and turned round to find Obadiah Stark behind me, I would have been relieved. He was that normal... good looking too."

It was around this time that Obadiah chose to have applied the now infamous tattoo that would be the primary factor in the choosing of his media nickname. Obadiah told me that he'd decided to get the tattoo in order to "see, every day, the fruits of my labour. This way, their lives would forever be remembered and recorded throughout history. I gave them immortality. They would never be forgotten."

He ended his year with another 'tally' added to his tattoo; the murder of Claire Jackson, an 18 year-old student from Southern University. Her body was found on 22nd December

1989, washed ashore off the Amite River, a tributary of Lake Maurepas.

Partially decomposed, Claire was discovered with the knife used to murder her still embedded in her sternum up to its hilt. No forensic evidence was found due to her body's time spent in the water, though they were able to establish a probable two day window as to her time of death.

Excerpt taken from interview with Obadiah Stark (dated 17th April 2010):

"Many people would find it difficult to comprehend hurting someone and then feeling nothing... no regret, remorse or guilt. I'd found my niche... you have no idea how it feels to have control over the lives of others. I'm not sadistic. Yeah, I enjoyed the power I had over others, but I didn't take pleasure in their humiliation or hurting them. My pleasure came from slipping through the cracks, in being invisible, in killing without getting caught, in manipulating others into serving my own ends.

"When you're a skilled manipulator of people, you know that most humans fool themselves constantly—that's partly why they're so easily fooled by me."

'I think one's feelings waste themselves in words; they ought all to be distilled into actions which bring results.'
Florence Nightingale

10

14:56

The sky was a mixture of light blue hues and cumulus clouds which the sun was fighting to burn away as Eva and Ellie led Obadiah back towards the centre of town, having just left Killarney National Park.

The park, one of Ireland's remaining few which had been continuously covered in woodland since the end of the glacial period, had the accolade of being home to the country's only remaining wild herd of native Red Deer. They had managed to spot one, much to Ellie's squealing delight, while walking across one of the surfaced paths to Muckross Island.

Obadiah had always appreciated nature's innate ferocity to survive. Such an environment appealed to the feral aspect of his personality, reinforcing to him that even the most innocuous and inconspicuous forms of life could take hold and threaten to alter the world around them forever.

The park itself held a perfect illustration of this. It almost seemed illogical that something as simple as animal grazing could present perhaps the greatest threat to its ecology.

Grazing had caused damage to the terrestrial habitats and with the extinction of the park's natural predators such as the wolf and Golden Eagle, had caused the spread of rhododendron, a fairly common plant. Spread easily by seed dispersal, the plant shades the ground flora and prevents regeneration of native woodland species. As light cannot penetrate the dense thickets, few plants can survive beneath it, and therefore the park's oak woods couldn't regenerate. That such an inoffensive plant could hold sway over the life and death of an ecosystem amused Obadiah.

A naturally-occurring phenomenon following its natural evolutionary course and therefore destroying life.

He could relate.

Eva's voice broke his introspection. "So, what do you fancy doing tonight? I thought we could pop over and see Mark. He's rung a few times and invited us over for a few drinks, and Ellie's going over to my mother's, so when we get back the house would be empty..." She left her insinuation hanging in the air.

"Mark? Thorne?" Obadiah, ignoring Eva's suggestive tone, recalled the man's death at his hands his first day here. He had momentarily forgotten that everything had reset since then.

Shit. I've already killed him once.

"I think I'll decline."

Eva ushered Ellie towards her and stopped to button her coat collar. "Has something happened between you two?" she asked Obadiah. "I thought you got on well."

"There's nothing he could say to me that would be remotely interesting."

Eva stopped, a look of disappointment falling across her face as she took note of Obadiah's contemptuous smile. "Since when did you become such an arrogant arse? He's been nothing but kind to us since you fell ill."

Irritated at her tone, Obadiah stepped towards Eva, his large frame seemingly reducing hers by a size or two and forcing her to lean back on her heels before he began walking again. She sighed with frustration before quickening her pace to catch him up, pulling Ellie hurriedly beside her.

"Don't walk away from me, Obadiah. What's got into you? Ever since you left the doctors, you've been quiet. What is it? What did she say?"

He smiled. "Nothing interesting. Doctors... they always think they're the smartest person in the room. In this case, she was wrong. It was me." he replied.

"So," Eva pushed, ignoring Obadiah's reply. "What is it then? We know the situation, the prognosis. We agreed we were going to try and carry on as normal as possible."

Obadiah remained silent as he stopped for a second time and turned to face her. He noticed her expression change suddenly, as though she had momentarily seen into the darkness through an open door to his soul. Deciding not to enter, she drew herself backs and gripped Ellie's hand tighter.

"Obi, you're scaring me. Don't spoil our day together, please?"

Obadiah pursed his lips in frustration. When he'd begun his journey of becoming a master of his craft, the first lesson had been to swallow your pride. After all, how could you hope to be the best at what you do if you weren't willing to learn from those who'd gone before? Therefore, he could be patient and wear another mask if necessary, even if it meant tolerating Eva's inanities. He already had so many faces, thus maintaining one of a loving father and husband shouldn't pose too much of a problem.

"I'm... sorry." The words almost caused him physical pain, but he forced a broad smile to sell them, indicating acquiescence to Eva's request. Cautiously put at ease by his demeanour, Eva returned a small grin and sidled up to Obadiah, laying her hand on his arm. He made no response.

"Look, we don't have to go to Mark's if you don't want to. After I drop Ells off, we can just get a bottle of wine and stick on a DVD."

His irritation rapidly becoming boredom, Obadiah was surprised to find Eva's suggestion appealing. He remembered the last film he'd seen was The Towering Inferno in 1974 when he'd been seven years old. He'd bunked out of school with Tom Jacques to visit the cinema on East Avenue and had found himself lost in a burning building with Newman and McQueen. It was one of the few times that Obadiah could remember actually being a child.

"That sounds good, actually," he responded genuinely.

The wind had begun to pick up as they walked through the centre of town and towards the avenue leading home.

Home.

It was fascinating that Obadiah was already using that word to describe the house he'd woken up in over the past three occasions. Despite having grown up there, he'd never considered it home. Home was a word which held connotations well beyond bricks and mortar. It implied a place of security and warmth, something never guaranteed when he was young.

Yet now, perhaps he could instead describe it as the place where something was waiting to be discovered. Where, in fact, he was finding a hidden part of himself.

Ellie had run ahead of them both, ignoring Eva's chasing pleas to be careful, as Obadiah once again took in the surrounding panorama.

As a child, he'd given little thought to the world around him, his efforts often taken up with merely avoiding a beating from his father. It had been at a relatively young age when he'd realised he was different, that the rules of society need not necessarily apply to him. But now, back here, he understood that he had perhaps been unkind to his childhood memories. Beginning to wonder if taking the time to appreciate the beauty around him could have lessened the pain he'd suffered on an almost daily basis, he considered whether it could have changed who he'd become.

Perhaps finding something pleasurable in his childhood could have tempered his apathy towards all that became his formative years - the ultimate tipping point for his rebirth as The Tally Man.

Almost at once, Obadiah felt it brushing across every pore of his skin, the change in the flow of air around them.

Something was about to occur.

The world seemed to slow to a third of its average speed, the movement of life becoming an out of body vision that he could not interact with.

The red Audi was accelerating up the avenue, its driver on his mobile phone. Ellie was heading out to the middle of the road, trying to grab hold of some branches that she had the intention of sweeping leaves with. Herself unaware of the approaching car, she'd bent down, smiling with victory at the collection of her prize.

Eva's face had slowly contorted into horror with the fear of what she could see about to happen. She was looking towards Obadiah, screaming, but he heard no sound, only a dull thrum of virtual silence burrowing its way into his brain.

Eva was moving towards her daughter, and at that moment, he experienced something profound - as though his very soul had suddenly become a battleground for something more significant.

Moving with the speed of an athlete and the precision of a dancer, Obadiah scooped Ellie up and bounded onto the other side of the road, the car missing his legs by inches as it careened onto the pavement.

Eva had begun to scream, her cries for knowledge her daughter was safe piercing Obadiah's ears. Ellie held him tightly, chilled tears falling against his neck, warm, fast breaths causing goosebumps across his body. Her tiny body was shaking with the adrenaline coursing through it.

Obadiah's expression leaked nothing of the satisfaction he felt at Ellie not having died. He was still trying to comprehend it as Eva approached, virtually snatching Ellie from around his neck and gripping her in a vice-like bear hold.

"Oh my god, Jesus, Ellie. Baby, are you okay? It's okay, sweetie, it's okay..."

Her voice was frantic as she held her daughter's face in her hands and looked into her eyes.

"Oh baby, we thought we were going to lose you. You know never, ever to go into the road. What were you thinking?"

Eva's voice was not angry, simply direct.

Ellie didn't speak, her voice restricted by the enormous sobs that were escaping from her in between gulps of air. She was holding tightly onto Eva's neck, as though afraid her mother would disappear.

Obadiah stood motionless by the side of the road, his gaze having fallen on the car mounted on the pavement, its driver shaking as he tried to open the car door.

Though impassioned, he could feel his frustration at having been inconvenienced by such a random act of unpredictability. Usually, such careless, human behaviour stimulated feelings no more intense than mild amusement.

Today was different.

Today, he'd been part of a new experience, teaching him a new facet of his personality. Yet this creature before him had seen fit to interrupt Obadiah's education by just not looking where he was going.

It would be a pleasure to kill him slowly.

As the driver approached with his arms outstretched in a conciliatory gesture, Obadiah intercepted him in two strides, grabbing him by the neck and throwing him to the ground as he gasped an apology.

"I'm sorry, I'm so very sorry. I didn't see her? Is she okay?..."

Obadiah ignored the tremor of fear in the man's voice.

"You have no idea what you've just done, you pathetic worm," Obadiah spat as he tightened his grip on the man's neck and leaned in closer. "I am not a man with whom to fuck."

The driver tried to pull himself free of Obadiah's grip, but it tightened like a vice. He leaned down and stared into the man's eyes, his face serene and at the same time, maintaining a dark expression that was barely comprehensible.

Ellie's voice resonated through Obadiah. Having climbed down from her mother's arms, she was standing behind him, her arms outstretched in a pleading fashion.

"Daddy, don't hurt him. Please, can I have an up? I'm frightened... I need a cuddle."

Still holding the man by the neck, Obadiah stood before Ellie. Her face was red and tear-streaked, her slight body shaking with all the emotion running amok through her. He found himself caught in the shimmering pool of her eyes, captivated by a little girl's purity of thought.

Impassive, he struggled against the sensation fighting to flood his brain.

Why had he saved her? Why had he risked his life for someone who was of no consequence to him? He had no bond with her, only a flimsy excuse for acknowledgement of her presence. Yet, he found himself continuing to wonder why he'd interceded at all. He'd never before considered saving another person's life, believing his power was in taking it, not granting it.

But the power he felt at having granted someone a reprieve from death was almost as intoxicating.

Ellie had slowly moved in front of him, holding onto his leg as she began to cry again. Obadiah looked down at her and then stared at the man he held in the grip of his right hand. He sensed Eva approaching and looked up to see her wiping her face with the heel of her palms. Her eyes were red, face drained of colour and wracked with fatigue due to the emotional toll.

A few cars that had been passing moments following the incident had stopped just ahead, their occupants having left their cars and walking over to offer assistance.

"Obi," she sniffed. "Let him go. Don't make it worse. I just want to go home."

"Make it worse? You honestly want me to let him go, consequence-free?"

He found the concept of not hurting him hard to assimilate.

"What will it solve?" Eva had moved to pick up Ellie in her arms. "Just thank God she's okay."

Obadiah sneered at what he considered weakness. He found himself struggling to even contemplate not hurting the man.

Pulling him up to his feet, Obadiah drew the driver so close, their noses were virtually touching. He smelt the alcohol on his breath.

"You're the luckiest fuck in the world," he stated coldly. "I can smell the drink, you know. So, if you even consider moving from here before you've reported yourself to the Gardaí, I will hunt you down, I will find you, and I will kill you."

He moved the man around so that he could whisper in his ear. "And whatever you imagine it would be like... it'll be much worse."

Obadiah released his grip, letting the man drop. He stepped over the crumpled heap as Ellie reached out from her mother's arms towards him. He hesitated, uncertain how to react, but interested to see how it would make him feel.

He took her from Eva, arms wrapping tightly around his neck as she pulled her face into the space between his neck and shoulder.

Speaking from her position, her voice was muffled.

"I'm sorry, Daddy. I'm sorry I ran into the road. I didn't mean to hurt anyone."

Obadiah initially had no response. Such a sincere apology was alien to him.

Ellie pulled onto him tighter, his arms remaining supportive beneath her small body.

"Sssh… it's okay. Don't worry."

He heard himself say the words but didn't understand why or where they'd come from. He'd always had the ability to say the right thing, using it to lure people into his confidence. But the strange thing in this instance was that he thought he actually meant it.

Obadiah felt his head beginning to throb at the sheer nature of the implications his thoughts suggested. Eva was beside him, trying to gently lead him away from the road and onto the pavement, his arms still supporting Ellie as she clung to his neck.

Obadiah remained focused on the driver of the car, now sitting on the side of the road, his head in his hands. He looked up just as they passed by him and became transfixed by the look in Obadiah's eyes. As though the stare exerted a physical effect on him, he appeared to shrink back, his face expressing defeat and weakness simultaneously.

Obadiah stopped and held the gaze for a beat before continuing on, ignoring the queries around him from concerned passers-by wishing to render assistance.

He needed to be home. He had to work through the myriad of thoughts that were cascading through his brain.

————

By the time they'd arrived home and settled Ellie down after her bath, it was dark.

Though still upset by the earlier events, she'd been perfectly happy to snuggle down on the sofa and watch

Octonauts with her stuffed Snoopy and a glass of warm milk.

With Eva getting Ellie ready for bed, Obadiah had sat on a chair in the dining room, trying to establish a new baseline for his emotions.

Returning from upstairs, Eva pulled a chair up in front of Obadiah, forcing him to switch his attention. She had a look in her eyes that he momentarily found hard to place. Her hand slowly moved to his leg and journeyed up. Obadiah felt himself immediately stiffening. He hadn't expected this, nor had he accounted for it. The last time he'd been with a woman was before his being caught. He had picked her up in a bar and taken her back to his apartment. The sex hadn't been particularly good, but it had been enough of a distraction to keep him focused on what he'd needed to do at the time, which was avoid getting caught.

He began to find focus difficult as Eva reached out and touched his face, stroking it gently with the back of her hand.

"You saved our daughter. In my book, that deserves at least a little recognition."

Her face was intense, full of desire for what she was instigating. The contact felt electric, his skin painfully developing gooseflesh at Eva's touch.

She leaned forward and kissed his face, moving down to his lips. They were both beginning to breathe hard as she climbed onto his lap, her legs straddling his.

Her kisses became more passionate and powerful. Obadiah found himself unable to resist the raw passion flowing from Eva's body, cupping her breasts roughly then reaching down behind her, pulling her tightly into his crotch.

Her hands began unbuttoning Obadiah's jeans, seeming to move effortlessly across his body. Every intense feeling he'd ever had, murderous or otherwise, wanted to explode from his body.

The anticipatory rush he felt at having contact with a

woman after so long was barely containable. He realised with some measure of disdain that his body was telling him that he'd been missing something he'd never noticed gone – essential human contact.

Captured in the moment, he stood with Eva wrapped around his waist and moved over to the wall, slamming her up against it with a ferocity that made her cry out. He reached up and ripped down her underwear, feeling her warm skin against his bare torso and groin.

In a quick motion they became one person, Eva's surrender to the moment acknowledged by a gasp.

Pulling down on her shoulders, Obadiah continued to want only her flesh, unconcerned about what had passed before. He was interested only in the now.

For the first time for as long as he could remember, he felt alive.

As Eva gyrated against Obadiah's hips, he felt his frenzied desire rising until it was containable no longer. As they both leaned into each other, their panting, heavy breaths filling the air, he sensed their bodies relax simultaneously.

Eva, her body quivering, her legs still locked around Obadiah's waist, remained supported by him as though she were weightless.

His mind relaxing, he began to see a myriad of images flash before his eyes.

All the crimes he had ever committed were there, vividly represented in his recall. And now, following one of the most human and natural of moments that someone could ever experience, Obadiah Stark became cognitive to an expression his narcissism had always defended him against.

He'd only ever felt it once before as a child, conditioning himself from that point onwards to never suffer it again.

But now, shaking from a moment of purity, his grandiose self that had been protected by arrogance and hubris had been broken down, revealing a crack in his internalised being.

He knew he was still a monster, and felt no need to deny the fact.

But for that one moment, Obadiah Stark briefly imagined himself in the eyes of others and the feeling of shame now flooding through him prompted tears to roll down The Tally Man's cheeks as he pulled Eva towards him in a tight embrace.

'Make the lie big, make it simple, keep saying it, and eventually they will believe it"
Adolf Hitler

11

SEPTEMBER 29TH

11:08

Inishtooskert, The Blasket Islands (*Na Blascaodaí*)
County Kerry, Ireland

EVERYBODY LIES.

A lie's sole purpose is to mislead. It can be subtle, carefully weaving its way into the most tempered mind, or it can be massive, instantly destroying all those around with its implications.

Yet, by the same token, lies can also fail. Those who perpetrate the lie may not always be prepared to be challenged on it.

Emotions can also reveal a lie. Though a person may try hard to ensure words that would give away the lie are not used, expressions are more difficult to control.

Lies can be told for the noblest of reasons. And if this is the case, when does the lie become an acceptable one?

Can the deceit of the one ever be for the good of the many?

And if it is, and we accept it as such, are we then complicit in the lie?

———

A SKEIN OF RAIN DANCED ACROSS THE SURFACE OF THE WATER AS the prison launch made its way across the Atlantic Ocean towards Absolom, turning the island grey before blotting it out.

It was almost as though the storm was tethered to the stern of the boat. The landmass itself that was Inishtooskert, ruggedly beautiful, jutted out into the sea.

The Blasket Islands were said to house some of the most varied archaeological monuments in Western Europe, mostly because the peninsula's remote location allowed for remarkable preservation. Alongside the fact that the archipelagos were also famous for accommodating the filming of Ryan's Daughter and Far and Away, one could be forgiven for not believing the original Norse meaning of the word Blasket – 'a dangerous place'.

The prison itself, surrounded by a containment wall forty feet high and patrolled by armed guards twenty-four hours a day, stood on the island like a black spider waiting to ensnare approaching prey within its concrete web. Silhouetted against the darkened and sodden sky, Absolom housed three watchtowers. That was the extent of its perimeter security. Nothing more was required - the vast expanse of water surrounding the island itself did the rest.

Joe had heard an urban legend that there was a blanket of proximity mines just below the surface, but this had never been substantiated.

The rain pounded against him as he bounced in his seat with the rise and fall of every wave, trying not to vomit over the orange lifejacket he wore. After visiting the office early to inform Ciaran where he was going, he had called Victoria and arranged to meet her in the afternoon. He would have liked to tell her about his meeting with Stamford if only to justify why he'd blown her off the other night. He would also have liked her to have accompanied him to Absolom, given her background in criminology and experience at noting deception leakage, but Joe knew that obtaining visiting permission was a colossal pain in the arse unless you were a politician or an insistent reporter. The only reason he'd been granted permission to visit again was that he'd informed Richard Sabitch he was doing a follow up on Obadiah Stark.

His desire to find out if there was any truth to Stamford's suggestion that the warden was possibly complicit in a conspiracy was too great. Though what the nature of such a plot could be, he couldn't begin to guess.

As the launch slowed and broadsided towards the dock, Joe noticed flowers in the earth surrounding the outside of the prison. He then glanced up at the vast concrete construction that was Absolom, coil after coil of flesh-tearing razor wire sitting atop its containment walls.

The contradiction was difficult to process.

Stepping from the boat, he removed his lifejacket and tossed it towards the guard who'd been sitting alongside him for the journey. Aside from a cursory greeting, Joe hadn't engaged him in a conversation for fear of having the guard see him bring up his breakfast. Catching the life preserver, he shot Joe a disdainful stare and silently turned to head back into the cabin.

Securing his coat to counter the bitter wind blowing across the island, he made his way towards the huge iron gates forming the entrance to Absolom. Out the corner of his eye, he saw guards swivel on the containment wall, watching him meticulously. Like crows on a wire. He suddenly felt like an insect being scrutinised in a jar.

The sky had darkened in the time it had taken to reach the gates, as though the heavens were warning him it was a place best left untouched. He felt the desperation, and hopelessness Absolom represented emanating through its walls. He had experienced the feeling before while watching Obadiah being put to death.

It wasn't something he'd been in any hurry to experience again.

Buzzing the intercom, he waited a few seconds before a metallic-tinged voice responded.

"Hello."

"Hi, Joe O'Connell from The Daily Éire. I'm here to see Warden Sabitch. He's expecting me."

The intercom went silent, so he turned and stared into the rain. Working the fatigue out of his eyes with a thumb and forefinger, he noticed the island of Beginish in the distance and observed some of the local storm petrels fluttering in flight and dipping towards the ocean in the hope of scooping plankton from the water's surface.

Local folk stories told that petrels were the harbingers of stormy weather, hence their names. They were more commonly known as 'Mother Carey's Chicken's', Mother Carey being a supernatural figure who personified the cruelty of the sea, while the birds were thought to be the souls of dead sailors.

As clouds continued to gather over the island, it seemed the petrels were living up to their reputation.

The door alarmed behind him and he stepped through into the antechamber between the outer doors and the entrance to the prison courtyard. As it slammed shut, he imagined how it must feel to be a criminal, realising that this was your last stop in life.

The thought made him shiver.

Another buzzer sounded, and the inner door opened.

Richard Sabitch stepped though as it locked behind him and extended his hand towards Joe. In his late fifties, stocky and balding, he had a mahogany sheen to his skin, as though recently on holiday. Eyes that appeared too small for his face seemed to drift across Joe's body, as though taking in every aspect of his person. Joe hadn't considered it at the time of the execution, but seeing him now, he realised he looked like a fat weasel.

He didn't like him.

"Mr O'Connell, good to see you again. I realise we didn't speak during your last visit, but I want you to know I'm a follower of your work."

Joe squeezed Sabitch's's clammy hand tightly for three shakes and then released his grip. "Thank you for agreeing to see me, Warden. I appreciate you're a busy man."

The warden smiled as he ushered Joe through the huge door. "It's my pleasure."

Joe found his forced smile nauseating. As they stopped at a security desk contained behind three inches of bulletproof glass, Sabitch nodded to the man built like a bull behind it. He looked at Joe without acknowledging him and pressed an icon on a touch screen panel which released the electronic lock on the door to their right.

The warden led the way down brightly-lit corridors, reminiscent of a hospital. The harsh lighting exposed the stark blandness of the paintwork. The dark blue and plain white colours, separated by a distinct line which ran the horizontal length of the corridor, suggested to Joe an analogous reference to the differences between the prison inmates and the guards, wardens and visitors; bright white above the line representing the life the population of the prison cells could have had - clear and untouched by darkness; blue below representing the shadier aspects of their lives, alluding to the fact that they'd become tainted by a blacker element which had contaminated their own once bright light.

A place where the endless journey towards death couldn't be escaped.

Joe was ushered through two further sets of secure doors with a guard watching from a security booth. As the final gate slammed shut behind him with a thick, metallic clank, the prison seemed to close in.

He began to feel claustrophobic.

Then, passing through another set of heavy doors, he found himself in a softly lit, carpeted hallway. It seemed an implausible contrast to where they'd just left, almost homely in its presentation. They passed a number of insignificant doors before Sabitch opened one of them and gestured for Joe to enter, steering him towards the chair placed in front of a desk.

Cool, but not cold, the air in the room held a hint of incense. The door shut gently behind them, and Sabitch moved behind his desk and sat down.

He stared at Joe for a few moments before speaking. When he did, his mood was immediately less cordial.

"So, Mr O'Connell, what can we do for you today? I have quite a busy schedule, as I'm sure you can imagine. I understand you wanted to discuss my views on the death penalty for a follow-up article. I'm surprised that you didn't feel they were immediately apparent, given that I'm warden at a facility which has put to death thirteen prisoners over the last fifteen years. It seems to make this interview moot."

Joe didn't fail to notice the exasperation in his tone. "Well, I figured a piece covering the ethics of being on death row, the moral arguments it raises for and against, would be a good way to conclude the articles I'd been doing. As you know, after Stark's execution, there were a lot of protests concerning excessive delays being a violation of a prisoner's human rights. Those kinds of discussions are what the readers want."

He could see Sabitch's irritation at the mention of prisoner's human rights. "Ah, the classic bleeding heart's take on the death penalty," Sabitch said with a smirk. "How quickly they forget what these people have done. I often wonder would they be so concerned if they knew how we torture prisoners and how it's a part of the death row phenomenon if it had been their sons and daughters raped and murdered."

"The death row phenomenon... you're referring to execution following a prolonged delay constituting cruel and inhuman punishment? I've read about that. I gather you don't agree with it."

The warden's answer had no bearing on what Joe had come here to find out, but he was interested nevertheless.

A long pause came before a reply. "Absolom is the place the world sends its prisoners it wishes to punish the most. Think of it as a clean version of Hell, the Harvard of the prison system. There are fewer than five hundred prisoners here, and they are sent here because they're too violent to be anywhere else. That should tell you everything you need to know."

Sabitch gestured towards Joe. "Shouldn't you be writing all this down?"

Caught momentarily off-guard, Joe fumbled into his pocket and pulled out his notepad. "Sorry, I'd been counting on my photographic recall," he responded glibly.

Sabitch swaggered a smile before continuing. "You honestly think that I'm concerned about some naïve, ignorant protestors who only sleep better in their beds at night because of this place? They seem to miss the fact that any delay in a prisoner's execution is ultimately caused by the prisoner themselves. They petition and appeal only to be granted last-minute stays, but it's an attribution argument. If the prisoner's causing the delay, they really have little basis to complain that their human rights are being violated, do they?"

"A valid argument. So, how did you feel about Obadiah Stark?"

"Stark?"

The name hung in the air like a bad omen. "I can't actually think of an appropriate word to describe the man. I'm not sure if you were aware of this, but Stark was kept in Sector 17, the highest level of confinement we have... virtually no human contact, not even with the guards. He was one of only two prisoners kept there, the other being Nader Yousef, the mastermind behind the 7th July bombings in London."

Joe frowned. "Virtually no human contact? Doesn't that illustrate what we just discussed?"

"You ever meet Stark?" the warden asked, reclining back in his chair. He acknowledged Joe's negative response with a nod before continuing. "He had that Charlie Manson look. He just had the eyes. Charismatic certainly and definitely one of the most intelligent people I've ever met. Not just IQ smart, but perceptive smart. Whenever you spoke to him, you could see that it was a powerful person you were looking at, physically and intellectually."

"So, you kept him in a place where he couldn't give any orders?" Joe interjected.

"Precisely. Stark was the real deal. Yes, the chance that he could physically harm someone was non-existent, but his intellect meant he could get inside your head. To me, his mind was his most dangerous weapon."

"You make him sound like Hannibal Lecter," Joe said with a smile.

"Hannibal Lecter is fictional. Obadiah Stark was very real and very dangerous. A sociopath such as him had no desire to be understood or psychologically dissected so that his motivations could be rationalised. He lived to kill, pure and simple. His level of intelligence made him impenetrable to any standard test one would use to perform a psychological autopsy but had no bearing on his actions. You could argue someone with such a high IQ would know that killing is wrong, but that wasn't why he did it. He simply did it because he could."

Joe rolled his tongue around his cheek thoughtfully. "You admired him?"

Sabitch's mouth twitched. "I admired his purity of thought. The man could have been a genius in any field he chose, but he decided to become a killer. It seems a waste of a life to me, but then that's what this place represents. An environment of hopelessness and hindsight."

Joe found Sabitch's responses unsettling. He was a guardian in the justice system and therefore not necessarily cheerful, but Joe had imagined he would be less blasé. He decided to manipulate the conversation towards his intended purpose.

"Stark's execution… did it go as planned?"

"Like clockwork," Sabitch replied assuredly. "There were no incidences before the execution, all the medical and security aspects of the process went smoothly, as did the actual drug administration. It was fairly textbook."

"Textbook…" Joe repeated. "An interesting noun to describe someone's death."

Sabitch sighed theatrically. "I assure you, Mr O'Connell, their deaths are more humane than those visited upon their victims. In my opinion, if anything, they're too lenient."

Ignoring the warden's obvious irritation, he decided to pursue his reason for being here. "May I ask what happens to the prisoners following an execution?"

The warden slowly dropped his head, took a deep breath and spoke. "Lines are removed from the prisoner, the body is moved with care and dignity and placed directly into a post-mortem bag, the facility is cleaned, and a staff debriefing is performed. All standard procedure."

"Is it standard procedure to subject prisoners to strip searches and constant video surveillance? What about sleep deprivation? Would you condone it?"

Sabitch's smile disappeared rapidly. "What is it you're getting at, Mr O'Connell?"

"Nothing. I imagine those rumours are just that… rumours." Having goaded him to try and get a reaction, Joe hesitated before continuing. "What I'd really like is to see a copy of Stark's master execution file."

Sabitch paused. Joe knew the reason why. He'd seen it many times before. People paused before they answered a potentially implicative question because they were trying to process their well-rehearsed lie in their heads before speaking.

"That's confidential. I'm sure you can appreciate the necessity to keep such information from falling into public hands. Especially given the sensitive nature of the death penalty."

Joe nodded. "I do, certainly. In that case, would it be possible to speak with the contract mortuary? Their insight into what happens to the prisoner following the transfer of the body would provide a good sense of closure to the whole subject."

Again, Sabitch hesitated. "Once again, that information is privileged. I must say, I feel that perhaps this was a waste of time for both of us. I thought you wanted to discuss the intricacies of the death penalty, not allude to its moral ambiguities of which we both know there are many. I figured you for a more broadminded reporter. Perhaps I was mistaken."

"No, you're right. I am fairly broadminded. It's just there are some events you find yourself involved in that never seem to sit comfortably. Call it a gut feeling… reporter's instinct. For instance, if I was to say to you, why were all the IV lines removed from Stark's body immediately following his execution, what would you say?"

Joe noticed Sabitch's face flush slightly, as though he was a child caught doing something naughty. He momentarily shrunk back into his chair and then almost as suddenly, regained his composure and stood up with a grand gesture.

"That is not only an absurd accusation but offensive. This facility has a perfect record, Mr O'Connell... for a reason. I run a tight ship. Nothing goes on here that I don't know about. Therefore I would warn you that making slanderous accusations is not in your best interests."

Joe remained seated but leaned forward. "Are you threatening me, Warden?"

Sabitch forced a half-smile. "Threatening, no. Merely advising you that should you decide to pursue this line of questioning outside of this office, you will find yourself facing many... difficulties."

The warden had his hand outstretched, gesturing towards the door. "Now if you please, I'm a busy man."

His tone had regained its affability.

Joe remained seated, ignoring the indication to leave. This was getting interesting. "Warden, who provides a prisoner's death certificate following their death? Is it you personally or a doctor?"

Sabitch appeared to baulk at the question. "It's the doctor who completes the paperwork. I simply oversee the legal aspects of the process."

Joe smiled. "So, when you say legal aspects, you mean to ensure that everything is above board, so to speak?"

"Exactly. What does this have to do with Stark?"

"Nothing. Everything. You write an after-action critique following every execution, is that correct?"

Sabitch breathed an irritated "Yes."

"So, all the details of his execution will be in there?"

"Yes, but it's confidential, I told you. Please, Mr O'Connell, I'm very busy."

"I know, but is there any chance anyone else could get their hands on it? A guard who isn't particularly fond of you perhaps."

"I don't have disgruntled employees," Sabitch replied a little too quickly. "All documentation concerning the prisoners and executions is locked away. Only myself and one other have access to it."

"The other being...?" Joe inquired.

"The other being my senior guard. Now, I think we're done."

Sabitch's tone had an air of finality about it.

Joe remained silent and motionless. "You don't feel it's enough, do you? Execution, I mean. You feel they get off lightly."

Sabitch became piqued. "I do, yes. They're monsters. Some of the crimes they've committed are beyond comprehension, so much so that sometimes you wonder if there's any punishment severe enough. But here I am, custodian of them all. I ensure that they are given the best treatment possible, regardless of their crime. You try to be non-judgmental and sometimes it's hard. Some of their stories are genuinely tragic... parents took children and manufactured monsters. You weep for them as children. But as adults, you believe that the punishment does in no way fit the crime. And Obadiah Stark, he was the worst of them all.

"No, he didn't rape children, molest women, or eat his victims. He simply butchered them, sometimes in the most horrific ways imaginable, but compared to most of the atrocities men are in here for, his were fairly pedestrian. Yet the reason I consider him the most dangerous man we ever had here, is because he never tried to justify his actions. He didn't claim insanity, messages from the Devil or that he'd suffered as a child; I know he did, he just never used it as an excuse. Obadiah Stark was a monster because he felt no remorse or guilt... there was nothing. Every other prisoner here, regardless of what they did, when they get that date, they begin to question their lives and their actions. They may not apologise for or express pity towards their victims, but they consider how different their lives could have been had they taken a different fork in the road. Stark... he accepted death in the same way he murdered those people, with righteous indignation. That made him more than dangerous. It made him believe he was God-like."

Joe held the warden's stare for a few beats before rising and extending his hand. "Well, thank you for your time. It's been most illuminating."

Sabitch paused before shaking his hand curtly. "I hope you got everything you needed."

"Oh, I did." Joe moved to the door without looking back.

Sabitch's hand on his shoulder made him stop and turn to face the warden. "You're a smart man, Joseph. I told you before, I read your work, and I do enjoy it. I hope you're able to continue it. You rarely get your facts wrong, so I can't say I'm too concerned about any of this making the press."

The silence between them lingered in the air. The absence of words didn't hide from Joe that the warden knew what he'd been up to.

You just showed your hand, you dodgy son of a bitch.

He condescendingly slapped Joe on the back, forcing him out of the door. "Have a safe journey back. The waters around Absolom can be treacherous."

Joe smiled as he made his way back down the corridor, hearing the warden's door close behind him.

He had his interviews with the victims' relatives, the conversation with Stamford, and now his meeting with Sabitch. All of it put together told him that something big was being hidden concerning Obadiah Stark's execution. But he needed more; perhaps speak to the coroner, more interviews with relatives.

Someone would give something major away. It was just a matter of time.

Returning to the main door leading out of prison, Joe

found himself wondering what could possibly have been so important about Stark's death. That should have been the end of it all.

It now appeared that The Tally Man's death had been only the beginning.

Dr. John Franklin, BS.c. (HONS), PH.D. M.A., M.CLIN, PSYCH. A.F.Ps.S.I.

Case Number: 01020541/27

Subject: Stark, Obadiah James (a.k.a. The Tally Man) cont.

Victim history continued: During the course of 1990, Obadiah continued his murderous pastime, adding three more tallies to his tattoo; Meredith Clements, Helen Christian and Christina Cole.

Twenty-eight year-old Meredith lived with her husband in Shenandoah, East Baton Rouge, approximately 10 miles from Louisiana State University and worked at Oschner Medical Centre, which was about three miles away from her home. At approximately 20:34 on Monday 12th February 1990, witnesses reported seeing Meredith standing by the driver's side of Obadiah's car before walking away. Her remains were found six months later in woodlands not far from her place of work, the body so decomposed that identification was only possible through dental records and personal belongings.

The body of thirty-six year-old Helen Christian was found off an incline on Interstate 40 by a street cleaner on 23rd May 1990. The coroner stated that Helen had died the previous day. She was killed by a knife wound to the base of her skull which had penetrated her brain and a second wound that had penetrated her lungs and ruptured her heart.

Obadiah's final murder during 1990 was on Thursday 18th October, the last time anyone remembered seeing thirty-two year-old Christina Cole alive.

In his statement, a patrolman recalled having encountered Christina and her husband on Highway 226 after their car had run out of gas. They were arguing and she was insisting on making her own way home. Police reports surmised that at some point during her lone journey home, she encountered Obadiah Stark. Her body was found five days later in Meeman-Shelby State Park, Tennessee. Partially clothed, with no signs of sexual assault, Christina's remains were face down and covered with scrub bushes. The autopsy identified she had been stabbed fourteen times in the neck and sternum and her belly slit open.

Now convinced the murders were linked, the police created a task force. Put together in Louisiana, its main focus was to compile a list of suspects. Using a computer reference system and despite the limited forensic evidence they'd managed to collect thus far, a list was produced with thirty four names on it.

Obadiah Stark was number twenty-eight.

During this time, the subject had left his job at the estate agency and had moved to Jonesboro, Arkansas, where he'd obtained employment as a pharmacy driver at the Surgical Hospital. His credentials forged, Obadiah's credibility was never questioned. Appearing to have secured the job based purely on his charm and ability to manipulate, his employment later proved to be a source of major embarrassment for the hospital during investigations following his arrest.

Appraisal of police reports and evaluations point towards Obadiah becoming less capricious and more structured, his merciless enthusiasm to torture and murder succeeded only by his logical and well organised thought patterns. It must be said that during this author's interview with the subject, his thoughts continued to be well structured.

That his mind remained full of potential for scheming and violence supports the theory of Obadiah Stark's God-like desire for control over others.

Excerpt taken from interview with Obadiah Stark (dated 17th April 2010):

"The street is my world. You all live such sheltered lives, hiding in your warm beds under your twilight skies. I don't expect you to understand what this means... seeing what I've seen – mankind, the beast, the animal. There's no hunting like the hunting of man. Once you've done it for long enough and gotten to like it, you never really care for anything else.

"What I did is was a wakeup call to the world, telling them that terrible things don't only happen in faraway places... they happen right here, on your doorstep. I was born no different from anyone else and that's what makes people afraid. They look down at me and see a fool; they look up at me, and see a God; they look straight at me and see themselves.

"People will read these interviews and say 'it's because he suffered as a child' or 'sins of the father magnified one hundredfold'. But the truth is, they say those things because it makes them feel secure, believing that only exceptional circumstances can create a monster. I simply set out to prove that if one can do what God does enough times, one can become as God is."

Yet this egotistical attitude was tested towards the end of 1990, when Obadiah experienced what can only be described as the only singular moment in his adult life that he'd ever felt anything resembling a human emotion.

Thomas Jacques, his childhood friend and fellow altar boy, was hit and killed by a drunk-driver one evening whilst walking home. The driver, Richard Bullen, married with three children, served eight months for manslaughter and received a $400 fine. Witnesses recalled seeing Obadiah at Thomas's funeral.

In September 1991, Bullen's naked body was found in the woods near his home in Virginia. Forensics later determined that his lower spinal column had been severed with a screwdriver which was found at the scene. Paralysed, Obadiah had stripped him of his clothes and proceeded to remove his genitals with a pair of shears. He had then applied salt to the wound before finally setting him on fire.

No one was ever held accountable for the murder.

With no link known between the subject and Thomas Jacques at the time and no forensic evidence, Obadiah wasn't considered to be a suspect in the killing. My meeting with the subject represented the first time anyone had admitted to Richard Bullen's murder, with details of the murder revealed that only the killer could have known.

Following this author's interview with Obadiah Stark, this case is now classified as solved. Though Obadiah had not seen or spoken to Thomas Jacques since leaving Ireland, it appears his death had a profound effect, something this author witnessed him allude to during our time together.

Excerpt taken from interview with Obadiah Stark (dated 17th April 2010):

"Bullen... that irresponsible prick deserved to die. He should have never been allowed to have a family. If I had the time over, I would have made certain he'd suffered more. I'm still not sure he quite understood why he was dying that day. I mean, I told him it was for Tommy of course, but it didn't seem to sink in... even when I cut off his nuts and replaced them with salt. Mind you, the screaming was awfully distracting.

"Tom Jacques was probably the closest thing to a friend I ever had. I think I creeped him out the day I killed the duck, but I actually enjoyed being around him. He was a genuine, gentle person who just seemed to have a calming effect on

me. How can I put it... he didn't stimulate my primal urges to kill. I think initially, when we moved to the States, I might have actually missed his company. Of course, then life got in the way and I found my true destiny. But back then, everything seemed much simpler when I was with him. I look back now and find it hard to believe that it was me who felt those things. Perhaps I would have killed Tommy myself eventually if he'd still been alive. I don't think I would have wanted someone reminding me of who I was or who I could have been."

'Remorse: beholding Heaven and feeling Hell.'
George Moore

12

08:27

Obadiah woke suddenly, recognising Eva's presence beside him, at once familiar and calming as he took note of her body.

Curvy, skin as smooth as ivory, it glistened slightly with morning perspiration. He allowed his eyes to take in the curve of her breasts, the shape of her leg hanging over the blankets and momentarily felt a sense of peace, unlike anything he'd ever known.

Rolling over, Obadiah placed his head into the pillow, taking a deep breath and smelling his own perspiration. Eva stirred and slid her body out against his, stretching silently as he moved to the edge of the bed.

Obadiah looked down again at her face, her eyes closed, lips slightly parted. He recalled their fevered lovemaking, the musky smell of their bodies together and the release of emotion which had flooded through him.

Emotions that forced him to realise his journey here had taken a very different path.

Slightly disorientated, Obadiah climbed from the bed and stood by the window. As Eva moaned her subconscious disappointment at the removal of his bodily warmth, he tried to ignore the sound of his heart pulsing in his ears, the nagging discomfort he noticed in his shoulder blades.

Everything hadn't reset as it had before. Therefore, what had changed? What was so special that he was now living another day?

A next day.

When he'd initially found himself here against all logical explanation, he had felt only disappointment at realising he was somehow experiencing an example of what could only be described as a perfect, almost Stepford life. He still had no idea why he had been deemed worthy of this accolade. He hadn't wanted it. He didn't want it. But after the incident with Ellie and his subsequent night with Eva, Obadiah found his dissatisfaction being replaced by a feeling he could only equate to fulfilment.

During his time as The Tally Man, the very notion of it would have made him feel physically sick. Now, all he could think was that the previous three days repeating must have served a purpose leading to this.

But to what end?

Obadiah scratched at his shoulder as he moved out of the bedroom and down the stairs to the kitchen. As he looked around, the ticking clock on the wall marking the beats of his memories, he sensed the house was a different beast to the one he'd grown up in as a child. Where it had once been a place eliciting only feelings of desperation, now it seemed to radiate hope. It was almost as though it had deliberately redesigned itself to educe such feelings from him.

His dreams as a child made manifest.

Preternaturally, Obadiah became aware of the oncoming pain before it hit him, causing him to suddenly grab his head, the pulsating, pounding sensation intent on blasting through his skull. He frantically massaged his temples, eventually feeling the discomfort slowly ease.

How can you feel pain if you're dead?

Obadiah found himself wondering this notion as his left arm began to tingle, the sudden pins and needles sensation causing him to tighten and relax his hand as he tried to restore the feeling in his extremities.

Massaging his arm, he thought back to last night. A sentiment he'd never considered open to manipulation had been enticed by his weak desire for flesh in the most carnal of ways.

And boy, had taken pleasure in its release.

Shame had been an emotion Obadiah had considered a violation of his own, self-designed social values. Yet he knew, without question, that it had been shame he'd felt being with Eva and not guilt. There were no internal conflicts about whether or not he'd violated his own values. He had none. Being with Eva was forcing him to wonder whether his own dark, narcissistic nature was his mind's way of defending itself against shame, against everything he'd done.

Had one, pure moment of intimacy forced his arrogant, grandiose self to be broken down by the antithesis of another version of himself – a weak version?

A human version?

And, if so, who had been freed?

An internalised Obadiah Stark who had been hiding in shame ever since his father had first broken down his confidence? Or a man who'd taken manipulation to the next level?

"Morning, Obi." Eva stood behind him, her hands resting on his shoulders. He hadn't even heard her come downstairs.

Sidling around and pulling out the chair next to him, her brow suddenly furrowed with concern as she looked at his face. "Are you okay? You look pale."

His arm still tingling, Obadiah abruptly ceased the massage and folded his arms across his chest, staring at the floor as though not seeing it. His focused stare was like that of a man lost in thought.

"Do you believe that you can do something so terrible it can never be forgiven?" His gaze remained fixed, as though on something in the distance. Or the past.

"Obi, what's the matter? What a bizarre question to ask first thing in the morning. What's with the weirdness? You feeling okay?"

" I feel fine," Obadiah replied tersely, ignoring the pain he still felt in his head and on his back. "But tell me. Do you believe in second chances, regardless of what you might have done?"

Eva placed her hands in her lap. "I don't know really. You know I'm not a religious person. I guess we all have things we wish we'd never done or would do over if we had the chance. Why? What's happened?"

Obadiah's momentary silence promoted Eva to lean closer. He looked at her, his eyes lacking the intensity he'd projected only yesterday."Who do you see when you look at me? Tell me honestly."

Eva laughed until she realised he was serious. "I see the man I fell in love with. Someone in pain. Someone who's supported his family despite his health. Someone who overcame a terrible childhood to become a man who makes me very proud."

Obadiah remained expressionless. "Proud."

He let the word hang in the air for a moment, considering its dichotomous nature given his past.

"You know, some people can look at someone and see whatever they want to see because they see whatever's in them. People are just mirrors."

"What have you been reading? I don't understand what you're trying to say."

"What if I told you I had a dream last night... I dreamt I killed people, lots of people. I did it with a smile. And in my dream, it felt good. It felt... right. What do you think that says about me?"

Eva touched Obadiah's arm gently. "I think it means the tumour is causing you to have vivid nightmares. We were warned it could happen. It's not real. We've had a rough few weeks granted, what with all that's happened. But everything's okay now."

Obadiah could hear the sincerity in her tone and allowed it to momentarily wash over him. He wanted to believe what she was saying. He tried to believe that last night could have actually been real and not some sort of game he was subconsciously playing with Eva.

Obadiah desperately wanted to believe it. He scratched roughly at his shoulder, beginning to feel irritated.

"You don't understand what I'm trying to say."

Standing, Obadiah continued raking at his skin, the discomfort he felt increasing.

"Let me see that," Eva responded, trying to shift the momentum of a conversation that was making her uneasy.

She moved over to Obadiah, lifting his t-shirt and examining his shoulder blade as she gently caressed the area with her fingertips.

"It's red, but I can't see anything."

Obadiah shrugged Eva away and moved to the mirror in the hallway, raising his t-shirt back up as he walked. He turned sideways on, noting the fresh ink present to his surface dermis. Five new tallies, the surrounding tissue inflamed as though just applied, reflected back at Obadiah.

"That's impossible," Obadiah muttered quietly as he turned towards Eva. "You don't see that?"

She stepped closer and examined his shoulder again. "See what? There's nothing there."

Obadiah examined his reflection again, touching the area to assure himself that it was real. "You can't see a tattoo?"

Eva stifled a smile. "Tattoo? Obi, you don't have one, and

you certainly don't have one on your shoulder. Why, have you been keeping secrets from me?" Her tone was playful, but Obadiah's expression remained serious.

"I must be going fucking crazy." Obadiah pulled his t-shirt back down and moved back to the table, placing his hands on its surface and bending over while taking a deep breath.

Eva was beside him, stroking his head. "Oh, Obi. Maybe we should see someone about..."

"I don't want to fucking see anyone," Obadiah interrupted, slapping her hand away. "I don't need catharsis, I need answers."

"Answers for what? Obi, please listen to me. You need help. The last few weeks, you have to admit, you've been feeling a bit low. And what with Ellie nearly being killed a few weeks ago... it's a lot of stress, especially when you're not one hundred per cent."

Obadiah frowned. "What do you mean a few weeks ago? That was yesterday."

Eva shook her head sadly. "No, Obi. It was two weeks ago."

"No, it can't have been. It was yesterday..." His mind struggling to process what he was being told, Obadiah straightened up defiantly.

"No, it wasn't. I think you need help. You're getting worse."

The fear in Eva's voice was evident. Obadiah couldn't believe what he was hearing. How could two weeks have passed and him not know?

What the hell...?

Obadiah quickly began trying to grasp sight of what had been slowly emerging since his execution. With no frame of reference for his death to compare to, he could only assume that this is what it was like.

But the reappearance of his tally... that had significance.

In life, it had been his paradigm, his pathway leading

towards self-actualisation. In death, it must mean something else entirely. He just didn't yet know what it was or the purpose it now served.

Eva looked at him searchingly. "Obi, I don't understand what's going on."

The anger he had momentarily forgotten while with Eva last night suddenly boiled up in him. He bolted up the stairs and quickly changed his clothes, all the time considering whether Eva was the constant that influenced everything which happened to him. She must be important in this whole situation. Therefore, the only way to know for sure was for her to die. If everything started again, he would have his answer. If not, he would be no worse off.

To hell with the afterlife and conforming. If I go to Hell, so be it. Better to reign there than serve whoever's fucking with me here.

As he walked back down to the kitchen, even Obadiah was surprised at the vivid nature of his violent desires. Whereas last night Eva had represented a portent of redemption, something he'd never imagined possible, now she was a focal point for his fury.

He found himself imagining hurling her across the floor and beating her with his bare hands until her face splintered, her flesh burst and blood-spattered from her ruined mouth.

Obadiah could almost hear her cries of anguish, and he couldn't help but smile.

Eva had moved into the living room when Obadiah grabbed her by the hair and threw her behind him, her body skidding across the laminate flooring. She looked up in horror as he reached down and pulled her back up, his large hand wrapped across her chin.

"You know, you almost had me there. For a moment you had me believing I could be someone else... someone better. Fuck, I actually woke up thinking that I'd had an epiphany.

But this whole situation, you're lying to me... it just won't do."

Eva's tears ran over Obadiah's hand as she spoke, her voice trembling. "Obi, I've never lied to you. I love you. Why are you doing this?"

"I'm doing this because it's who I am." As he spoke he seemed to freeze for a moment, his voice momentarily laced with real sadness. "I was a monster who dreamed he was a man and loved it. But now the dream is over, and the monster is awake."

Shaking his head, his face taking on a blank expression, Obadiah shoved Eva around by her shoulder over to the kitchen table, her body smashing into a chair. Stumbling to regain her footing as he marched towards her, she looked at him in shock, unable to process what was happening.

"Obadiah, listen to me. You're not well. This isn't you... please."

Ignoring Eva's pleas, he grabbed her by the arm and picked her up from the floor.

"Obadiah," she begged, despite his hold on her arm and then her neck. "Please, I know this isn't you. You're getting worse. Please, listen to me. I love you... we love you, Ellie and me. You're not yourself..."

His hand gripped her face, covering her mouth as his face darkened. "STOP IT!" he screamed, instantly ashamed at his loss of control.

Never before had he allowed emotion to overtake him in such an aggressive manner. The pain in his head had intensified, as though molten metal was being poured into his skull, oozing across the ménages and reservoirs of his brain.

He wanted to tear off his skin and scratch at his skull.

"This is all a lie, a fuckin' lie. This isn't real, none of it. A wife, a child, a fuckin' happy home life. This isn't me. People like me don't get second chances. I don't know what this is, but I know what it isn't. This isn't redemption. This is punishment. This couldn't be a more perfect vision of Hell if I'd imagined it myself."

Eva, still restrained by Obadiah, gently touched his arm and moved his hand, not frightened by the darkness now present in his eyes. "Obi, we're your family. We want to help you. Please, let us help you."

Obadiah looked intently into Eva's eyes. "Aren't you afraid?"

She replied softly, her hand rising to gently stroke his face. "Only for your soul, Obi."

His face previously etched with rage, softened slightly. His once fiery eyes began to lose their intensity, their arrogance as the words he'd heard moments before he'd died, hit him like a punch to the face. He felt his anger dissipating as though being sucked into a black hole, in its place a growing mortal sense of apathy for all he had done in his life.

Obadiah realised if he were to carry out his intended act of wanton violence, any spark of humanity he had felt last night would retreat into obscurity, taking all hope with it.

The realisation that he could lose the memory of what he had experienced with Eva and Ellie, even if it only constituted a microcosm of human emotion, crashed over him like a tidal wave, crushing all the remaining hatred he was feeling in that moment.

He knew he shouldn't be thinking of Eva. She shouldn't be having this effect on him. Obadiah wasn't sure what he was doing. He felt stunned, unnerved. Surely she could sense his true being, his power?

Yet she hadn't run from him, and neither did she fear him. He realised he was becoming blind to his true feelings. She was masking them, making it so he couldn't set them free. She was threatening to him, but not physically.

An alien, crumpling feeling swept over him, forcing him to fall to his knees. His whole body shook as the intense fear of what was happening to him became a crushing realisation.

He stared up at Eva, his face one of wretched despondency. His eyes no longer seemed filled with hatred, their natural green seemingly searing away the dark. It was almost as though an idealised version of his soul were trying to shine through.

"Help me," Obadiah pleaded. "Please help me."

'Of two equivalent theories or explanations, all other things being equal, the simpler one is to be preferred.'
William of Occam

13

SEPTEMBER 30TH

07:03

Denny Street, Tralee (*Trá Lí*)
County Kerry, Ireland

THE MERE USE OF THE WORD 'CONSPIRACY' CAN SET OFF AN internal alarm bell causing people, educated or otherwise, to shield their minds to avoid the kind of dissonance and unpleasantness such a word generates.

After all, the whole purpose of a conspiracy is to challenge our concepts and beliefs of how the world operates. A conspiracy can alter the very course of history in the most destructive way, or plant doubt in the most incisive and rational of minds.

The driving force behind a conspiracy can be seen as either one individual with power appearing to rival Satan himself, or a private corporation, shrouded in mystery with an almost preternatural ability to manipulate the truth.

Whatever the motivation, the fact of the matter is that the very notion of a conspiracy acts like an event horizon, pulling in everything and everyone around it. Once inside, it will attempt to alter one's very thought processes: only the most ignorant of educated people would dismiss out of hand the evidence a conspiracy presents.

As Sir Arthur Conan Doyle said; Once you have eliminated the impossible, whatever remains, however improbable, must be the truth.

———

JOE THREW HIS BAG ON THE DESK, YAWNED AND DROPPED INTO the chair, flicking the power button on his computer.

His mind was still reeling following yesterday's meeting with Sabitch. The warden couldn't have been more obvious that he was hiding something than if he'd been Rupert Murdoch being questioned about phone-tapping.

That meeting and the one that had occurred a few nights earlier with Peter Stamford had cemented the feeling he'd been trying to shake: the one telling him that something was being covered up about the night Obadiah Stark had died.

Recalling all the conversations he'd had with the relatives of Obadiah's victims and now prison officials, Joe realised they contained too many deflections, too many subtle micro-expressions to be just nerves or apprehension regarding the subject matter.

Lies were being told about Obadiah Stark.

Joe just didn't know why.

Yet.

He had left Absolom last night energised, experiencing the buzz a reporter gets when he knows he's on the cusp of something revelatory and in this case, potentially volatile. When he'd arrived back home, he'd put in a request with one of his former contacts at the port authority for a list of all boats leaving and arriving at the island the night Obadiah had been executed. Joe didn't know what he was expecting to find, but it had felt as though being aware of Obadiah's final journey would provide him with the piece of the puzzle he was missing.

That same buzz had ultimately prompted him to ring Victoria and rearrange their meeting. After a few pleasantries, she'd agreed to meet him at O'Shea's. Joe had figured it was safer to pick someplace catering for both drinkers and those merely desiring a quiet meal.

Tapping in his password, Joe opened up his emails and immediately noticed his request to the port authority had been actioned. He'd received a file from the harbour master at Dunquin (Dún Chaoin), west of Dingle, where all boats departed and arrived when visiting Absolom.

Double clicking on the attachment, Joe read something appearing to be straightforward and unexciting.

Two boats would make the journey to and from the prison on a daily basis, both generally carrying provisions and staff. All the trips tended to take no more than an hour and a half, give or take a few minutes, with an extra, third boat, the Absol, sailing only when it had a prisoner to transport.

Three boats had left for Absolom the day of the execution; the Aperion J29 at 05:02, Absol 17 at 18:06 and Vasel 45876 at 19:03.

The document stated the Aperion and Vasel were the two main boats carrying shift staff to work, with the Aperion retuning back at Dunquin at 06:48 and the Vasel at 20:24.

But it was the time of return for the Absol which piqued Joe's curiosity.

The e-mail stated the Absol had returned to Dunquin at 22:19 - a four hour time difference.

Joe swivelled round in his chair as he contemplated the information. The journeys of both the Aperion and the Vasel had a travel time of around an hour and a half in total. If the Absol was the boat which had sent to transport Obadiah's body back to the mainland, why had it taken over four hours to return?

Joe chewed thoughtfully on his pen, suddenly springing forward and picking up the phone. He flipped open his notepad and found the number for the harbour at Dunquin. It rang twice before he heard a rough brogue.

"Dunquin Harbour."

"Hello. Sorry to bother you. My name's Joe O'Connell. I work for The Daily Éire. I'm doing a follow-up piece on the Stark execution. I need a small section on the Port Authority and yourselves, something emphasising the role you play in the transport of staff to and from the island, movement of prisoners etc., and I was wondering if you had any comments I could use."

There was a slight pause. "Okay. What would ya like to know?"

"Any comments, anecdotes, anything at all about what you do would be excellent. For example, the night of the Stark execution. Big media event, many of the world's media at Absolom. The whole world watching. Did everything go smoothly? Any hiccups, problems, delays of any kind?"

Joe heard papers rustling before the voice returned. "Well, transporting over your lot was a pain in the arse, I can tell ya that. Crammed in like sardines, they were. 'Course, we had all the prison staff travellin' over for their shifts, so ya can imagine it was a little cosy. But, there were no real problems to speak of. Fars I know, everything went like clockwork."

"And after the execution, the transportation of Stark's body. No problems there?"

"No, the Absol left here, picked up his blackhearted soul and brought him back. That's what I was told anyway."

"Told?" Joe quizzed. "You weren't there?"

"Well, I was here for the shift boat leaving, but an hour or so later, I was relieved. So, I picked up my stuff and went home. Nice to have an early night for once." He ended with a chuckle.

Joe lifted his eyebrows. "I gather getting off early isn't a frequent occurrence?"

"No. But I wasn't gonna turn down the offer. You know what they say about that gift horse."

"Yeah," Joe said absentmindedly. "I do. Well, thank you for your time, Mr…?"

"Black. John Black"

"Thank you, Mr Black. Just one more thing. The Absol, carrying Stark's body. What time do you have for it returning to Dunquin?"

"Erm… we have the Absol logged as returning at 22:19."

"22:19," Joe repeated slowly, emphasis the twenty-two.

"That's right," John confirmed cheerfully.

"Do you know why it took the Absol over four hours to make the journey? Were there any reported problems? I mean, isn't it unusual for it to have taken so long?"

"Mr O'Connell, I told ya, I went home. I'm just a minimum-wage harbour master, not a security guard. I keep ma'self to ma'self. Yeah, it took a long time, but the reason for that's none of my business. And to answer ya question…" He paused, and Joe heard more papers rustling. "… nothing's logged in regards to faults, so I don't think so."

"Okay, thank you for your time, Mr Black."

Joe hung up and spun round in his chair again, only more slowly this time, tapping his pen on his chin.

Interesting.

He quickly logged on to Google's weather report to check the weather for the night of 7th September. Though his journey to and from the prison had been in fair conditions, it was prone to sudden changes around The Blaskets. But no; scattered showers, visibility 18.72 km, wind SSW 9.72 km/h.

No chance they'd run afoul of bad weather which would account for the delay.

So, what was it doing for the extra two and a half hours?

Spotting Ciaran in his office, Joe bounced out the chair,

marched through his editor's door without knocking and shut the door behind him.

"Just come in, Joe. Don't let the fact the door was closed bother you in any way."

Remaining standing, Joe suddenly felt like the whole room was watching him through the window.

"So, what is it, ya mannerless fecker?"

"I think I've got a problem."

"I've known that for a long time. What is it? Alcohol-induced liver disease?"

Joe forced a pained smile. "You're funny. But that isn't my problem. Well, not yet anyway." He took a deep breath. "I told you I'd received a phone call the other day from someone who works at Absolom, asking me to meet him. Not unusual, right? I covered Stark's execution; therefore you'd expect someone would want to take a stab at getting their fifteen minutes. But this guy, he alluded to some…discrepancies."

Ciaran's chair moved forward quickly. "Discrepancies?"

"Yeah," Joe confirmed solemnly. "Surrounding the execution."

"Stark's execution?"

Joe nodded.

"Okay, it's not often I'm intrigued nowadays. What did he say?"

Joe leaned against the far wall, as though distancing himself from what he was about to share. "He told me that certain procedural necessities that should have been followed after the execution appeared to have been skipped or omitted."

"Such as?" Ciaran said with genuine interest.

"Well, he told me infusion lines were removed against protocol and that there was an apparent omission in the pharmacy log concerning the drugs used. Assuming he's telling the truth, you have to ask why they would remove the lines? What purpose would it serve unless to maybe hide something? Secondly, omissions in the pharmacy log. Maybe just a clerical error? It's hard to imagine an establishment like Absolom making clerical errors, but there's always a human factor. So were the line removal and the drug omission an error that's not been disclosed due to embarrassment, or something else?"

"Given the media attention surrounding Stark and his death, it would be understandable that if there had been mistakes made and that they would want to keep them in-house. You know this better than anyone. Look at the media shit-storm the guy caused when he was alive..." Ciaran rationalised. "Is this source reliable?"

"He's a senior guard from the prison."

Ciaran pursed his lips in consideration.

"What else have you got?"

"Two things; one, there exists a death certificate for Obadiah Stark." Joe paused for effect.

"And...," Ciaran pressed.

"And, according to my source, no documentation exists in the prison's Master Execution File pertaining to his death. No after-action summary, no warrant of death. Yet he still has a death certificate. So I checked the prison's Post Execution Standard Operation Procedure online, and it states that within seventy-two hours the warden will conduct a critique of the execution, put it in the Master Execution File and then be issued with a warrant of death. Only then is a 'death certificate able to be forwarded to the country from which the inmate was under sentence of death' - in this case, here. So why does he have a death certificate on public record if the procedure wasn't followed?"

Ciaran thought for a moment. "Maybe this 'source' is just out to make some fast euros by pulling your chain. Come on Joe, it wouldn't be the first time."

"I did consider that, but he seemed too genuine. And he

was afraid, as though what he was telling me was bigger than simple administration errors."

"You know," Ciaran said with a sympathetic smile. "Life isn't always as mysterious as it seems, Joe. Sometimes things are just exactly as they are. What actual evidence do you have?"

He considered what he had.

Nothing. No actual evidence at all, other than conversations with relatives that were 'off' somehow, a meeting with a prison guard who was paranoid and a discussion with Sabitch that had wholly consisted of deflection.

He had seen the death certificate but had no way of knowing if there was any paperwork missing from the Execution File at Absolom, other than what he'd been told. That said, why would someone go to the effort of telling him about it unless there was credibility to the story?

"Joe, you'd better not be telling me all you have is a hunch?"

"Not a hunch so much as a strong journalistic instinct that something may be awry with Stark's execution."

"So a hunch then?"

"Pretty much, yeah," he responded submissively. "But if it helps, my hunches always turn out to be right."

Ciaran stared at Joe and sighed with frustration. "You said there were two things."

Joe puffed out his cheeks and exhaled sharply. "After the lines have been crimped and disconnected, but left in-situ, an inmate is supposed to be washed and placed in a post-mortem bag ready for transfer to the contract mortuary."

"Right..."

"Well, I did some checking. A boat left Absolom the night of the execution, the one carrying his body and it took over four hours to reach the mainland."

"So...?"

"So, don't you think it's weird that the boat carrying the dead body of the world's most dangerous serial killer took four hours to make a journey that normally only takes an hour and a half? The harbour master logs have details of every boat that sails to and from the prison; shift details, deliveries, visitors. All journeys take roughly an hour and a half. All except that one. So, where did it go for four hours?"

Ciaran paused before answering quietly. "I don't know. Was there a storm that night... bad weather held it up, or it ran into trouble?"

Joe played with a pencil on the desk. "Nope, I checked. Pretty much clear skies and no record of the boat having encountered trouble."

Ciaran's expression became concerned. "I'm not sure I want to hear any more. The man's dead. Are you implying there's some sort of conspiracy going on at Absolom regarding Obadiah Stark?"

"I never said conspiracy," Joe interrupted. "I maybe implied cover-up."

"Well, whatever you want to call it, I can't think of a fuckin' reason why there'd be either. It's one of the world's most secure facilities with one of the most perfect records. Sabitch has had dinner with the Taoiseach for Christ's sake. But I know you, and you've never been wrong yet, so I'll tell you this, Joe. You damn well better have some fuckin' evidence to back this one up, 'cause if you don't and this blows up in our faces, you'll be all alone, pissing in the wind. I swear to Christ, you won't be able to get a job for the fuckin' Big Issue."

Joe remained quiet, merely nodding his understanding before turning to the door.

"Joe," Ciaran said, causing his employee to stop halfway out the door.

"Boss?"

"Whatever you find or think you've found, be right about this one, for all our sakes."

"I am. Trust me." Joe closed the door slowly behind him.

"I do, son. That's usually the problem," Ciaran said out loud before returning to his computer.

Back at his desk, Joe stared again at the email on his screen, considering his next move.

He had a wealth of evidence, yet no evidence at all. Circumstantial, anecdotal and nothing which amounted to anything considered to be concrete. He needed something to tie it all together. The time lapse was a start, but he needed more.

Revisiting Absolom was out. The warden probably wouldn't see him, and if he did, he wasn't going to admit to a crime. He doubted Stamford would meet him again and the harbour master probably couldn't tell him any more than he already had.

He needed to know where the boat had gone for those missing hours that no one was particularly concerned about. So, he considered, why not go backwards. If the destination of the boat's cargo was the mortuary, why not start there? Reverse engineer his whole, vague suspicion.

Joe rubbed the top of his head vigorously, the potential weight of it all forcing him to consider if he was about to cross his Rubicon.

Wanting to focus, he grabbed a file from the shelf next to him entitled 'Stark – relative's transcriptions'. The folder contained all the interviews conducted with the relatives of Stark's victims, either by himself or other journalists from the media. He flipped it open and began jotting down some aspects of the interviews he'd found unusual at the time. It was time to start gathering what evidence he had, however transparent it may be. Maybe then, he could calm his mind long enough to enjoy his night with Victoria.

There was no way he was going to allow anything to get

in the way of his meeting with her this time. Obadiah Stark had already got in the way of enough of his personal life.

———

JOE WATCHED HER RETURNING FROM THE LONG BAR OPPOSITE them, with a gin and tonic for herself and a Guinness for him – their fourth.

Victoria had the build of a gymnast; slightly broad shoulders, tapering to a narrow waist and great legs. Her face provided further lustre by way of large, encouraging blue eyes. Blonde hair hanging loosely across her shoulders, the slight wave in it suggestive of it having been wet when she'd come to meet him, Joe found himself momentarily imagining her in the shower but quickly pushed the thought away.

He was uncertain whether it was the British accent or her physical appearance which gave her that 'upper-class teacher' sexiness, but there was no denying Victoria Carter was extremely attractive. And though Ciaran didn't have a strict 'no fraternising with colleagues' policy, Joe knew him trying to get her into bed would not be greeted with applause.

Probably not the best idea in the world to be getting shit-faced with her then.

Familiarising himself again with her credentials before leaving the office, he had little doubt that she was one of the foremost experts in her field, having spent most of her adult life trying to get into the minds of the some of the world's most evil individuals. He was still surprised she was so willing to offer her assistance with his book.

Joe had found himself even more impressed to learn that she'd apparently assisted Scotland Yard in drawing up a profile of Jack the Ripper when a local author had offered yet another new theory on his identity. He shivered, momentarily considering how easily Obadiah could have fitted the role of the Ripper had he been alive in 1888.

Sinking into the upholstered chair in front of him, Victoria placed their drinks on the small wooden table. Joe raised his glass in a salutary gesture and took a large mouthful, wiping the froth from his top lip. The remnants of their meal – burger and chunky homemade fries, were being collected by a waiter who thought Joe hadn't noticed him staring down Victoria's top as she'd sat down. Looking up, he realised Joe was watching him and quickly hurried away with an apologetic nod, balancing the stacked plates in his hands.

On his way here, Joe had realised he hadn't spent any real time with a woman since his last relationship had ended eighteen months ago. Since then, he'd practically lived and breathed Obadiah Stark. Back then, Emma had accused him of being obsessed, stating he preferred getting to know a serial killer than spending time with his girlfriend. In hindsight, he realised she'd probably been right, and he still hadn't quite worked out what kind of person that made him.

Maybe the kind of person who would consider that one of the world's most famous prisons had a touch of the Machiavellian about it?

"So," Victoria announced, her cheeks flushing with the sip of her g and t. "You were saying?"

Joe thought for a moment, attempting to redirect his thoughts from Absolom to his book. "Okay, I have the background on Obadiah, the murders, the details, evidence, etcetera. But what I don't have is any context, theories on how the mind of the serial killer works, that kind of thing. I think it might help offset the more unsavoury aspects of his life. I don't mean I want to humanise him and certainly don't want to elicit compassion for him, I just thought any physiological or behavioural aspects could provide some credibility to the narrative. What do you think, Victoria?"

"Vicky," she corrected. "And I think it would provide a good focal point. Studies of serial killers often straddle a fine line between either portraying them as deities or evolutionary misnomers, so it sounds like you're going about it the right way. Have you read the Franklin report on Stark?"

"Yeah, a couple of times actually. His interview provided me with some great insight into his background and the details of the murders... stuff even I didn't know about."

"John's work is an excellent jumping off point," Vicky confirmed. "It would certainly provide your readers with the more rounded picture you're after. What about biological explanations? They might encourage debate amongst the readers."

"What do you mean? I didn't know there were any."

"Well, there's controversial research suggesting a link between human physiology and the brain, that it directly correlates to an individual's levels of aggression and propensity for violence." She paused, noting Joe's slightly bemused expression. "Okay, basically all sensory systems have a thalamic nucleus which receives signals which are then forwarded to the associated cortical area of the brain. Theoretically, if an individual has an impaired thalamus, they may suffer from a lack of empathy, thereby affecting how they process the emotions generated from inflicting pain on others for example."

Joe grinned. "Wow, Miss Carter," he said in an exaggerated fashion. "You've just turned me on with the sexiest justification for someone being a serial killer I've ever heard."

Vicky blushed slightly. "Shut up. It's all highly technical stuff, I assure you."

"Oh, it must be if you're using the word 'stuff' to describe it." He maintained a flirty smile as he raised his glass and took two large mouthfuls.

"Seriously though," Vicky corrected, her smile slowly fading. "Imagine you had no conscience, no feelings of guilt, remorse, concern for friends or family. Shame is an alien concept to you, regardless of the immoral action you've just carried out." She took a sip of her drink and gently placed it back on the Tetley's mat before continuing, her voice so quiet it was barely audible above the background hum of the bar. "Your blood's like ice water flowing through your veins, you have no internal restraints that you even recognise. But you also know that, no matter how intelligent you are, you'll never amount to anything in the upper echelons of society, not unless you become CEO."

Vicky chuckled darkly before continuing. "You know you're different. You're broken. What makes you unfeeling also makes you unable to function in society. And this makes you resentful, envious of those around you. You dream of living life as a human being and instead you simply exist as a monster."

Silence permeated the air, her comments hanging there uncomfortably. Uncertain how to respond, Joe ran a finger around the rim of his glass as he thought. "So, would a sociopath have insight into their own lack of humanity?"

"Well, they know they're different," Vicky replied. "They know they experience emotions in a different way to you and me. Really, all they have in regards to actual emotion is a profound sense of 'one-upmanship'. I guess you'd call it pride. But the characteristics they do possess; deceitfulness, manipulativeness, impulsiveness, disregard for another's safety, these are their actual emotions. Along with the ability to be superficially charming, they end up armed with a paradoxical way to interact with society. Ironically, it also makes them more interesting than most of the people we encounter in everyday life. And because they're more intense, more impulsive, they, therefore, become sexier, more intriguing and, ultimately, more dangerous."

She shook her head as though dispelling dark thoughts and returned to her drink, all the time avoiding eye contact.

Joe leaned his chair on its back legs, recognising her discomfort before tipping it back onto all fours and moving his glass to the side, his elbows resting on the table as he leaned closer to her.

"This can all be applied to Stark?"

"Absolutely. Obadiah Stark is the epitome of everything I've just told you. Despite the unassailability of his character, he represents the pinnacle of what a true sociopath is – free of internal restraints and an unhampered liberty to do whatever they want. Ramirez, Manson, Henry Lee Lucas, they were all in Stark's league, but he definitely takes the prize for being the most successful in regards to his trade. You only have to look at how long he evaded capture to realise that his intellect and cunning far exceeded theirs. And just like them, he's never expressed guilt for his crimes. Then again, Manson and the others were actually insane. Stark's never displayed irrationality... only apathy."

Joe remained quiet, processing Vicky's use of the present tense when discussing Obadiah. He remembered Kizzie's mother doing the same and filed it at the back of his mind. "So, this phallic thing you mentioned…"

"Thalmic," Vicky corrected with a smile.

"Right. Do you believe it?"

"Well, as I said, its only research but not without merit. I mean, if you look at the Franklin report or any of Stark's prison assessments, they all describe someone not only without empathy, but someone who was consciously aware of this vacuum and proud of it, yet displayed no psychotic symptoms, only sociopathic ones. He was completely aware of his actions and actively pursued them. If the suggestion of thalamic impairment is taken as fact, then Stark fits the theory perfectly - the perfect killing machine."

"I imagine he would have made quite the study candidate," Joe asked thoughtfully.

"You have no idea," Vicky agreed.

They both took a drink before lifting their eyes to each other.

"It's all heavy stuff, Vicky. I mean, you sound like you understand him," Joe suggested. "Obadiah, I mean."

She flared briefly at his comment. "Understand him? No. In all the years I've studied serial killers and tried to explain their actions, I've never come close to understanding them. Understanding The Tally Man wouldn't take back the things he did."

Finishing her drink, Vicky looked up at Joe and smiled apologetically, warmth once again returning to her face. "Wow," she said with a heavy shrug. "How did you manage to get me in such a melancholic mood after we were having such a nice time?"

"I'm sorry," Joe responded. "I just find it all fascinating. And it'll all be handy... if I can remember any of it."

"Don't worry. I'll give you the cliff notes tomorrow. I thought they were joking at your office when they said you were obsessed with The Tally Man. I mean, is he all you think about?"

"No," Joe replied hesitantly, considering the irony of Vicky's comment. "I do think about other things."

"Such as?"

"Such as the colour of your underwear."

"Really?" Vicky responded with a coy smile.

He laughed, raising his hands in surrender at the ridiculous nature of his flirting. "Just ignore me. Ol' Man Guinness has apparently settled in for the night. And, on that note…"

He flashed Vicky a wide smile as he moved from the table. "Same again?"

She nodded and shot him a pretend frown, acknowledgement that she knew he was trying to get her drunk.

Joe told the bartender to keep the change as he returned to the table and handed her a drink.

"I'll tell you what," Vicky said with a half-smile. "No more talk about Obadiah Stark or any other serial killer you can think of. Tomorrow, you can ask me as many questions as you like on whatever you like and I'll give you as much as I can for your book, but for the rest of tonight, I want to enjoy your little town. I want to learn more about you, Joseph O'Connell. Think of it as a first date... where would you take me after here?"

"Joe," he corrected. "I even made my parents call me Joe. And we could go to Sean Og's. It's a good craic in there."

"Your place'll have to wait then." Vicky stood up and finished her drink in one before giving him a wink and walking towards the door, her bag slung over her shoulder.

"Shit," Joe said out loud with a laugh, surprised but pleased at her sudden enthusiasm.

Leaving his drink untouched on the table, he followed her out the double doors, eager to forget the sinister theory concerning Obadiah's execution forming in his head.

As he jogged to catch Vicky up, Joe failed to notice the car idling on the other side of the road, its driver taking a rapid series of photographs of him before slowly accelerating up Denny Street.

'All men dream: but not equally. Those who dream by night in the dusty recesses of their minds wake in the day to find that it was vanity: but the dreamers of the day are dangerous men, for they may act their dreams with open eyes, to make it possible'
T.E. Lawrence

14

17:32

He felt empty, an emptiness he'd never before experienced. And it filled him with another feeling he'd never known: dread.

Obadiah had no idea where they were going, only that Eva had said this morning that they needed to get away.

He needed to get away.

She believed wholeheartedly that his flashpoint aggression and descriptions of murder were simply the end result of a man trying to come to terms with a terminal illness. And though Obadiah had allowed her to believe that, he knew his eruption of anger was due to the conflict going on within him, a battle with the prize his very soul.

He glanced over at Eva in the driver's seat before pulling down the sun visor and flipping open the mirror. He saw himself, his emerald eyes seemingly alight with crimson flames as though the battle within him were reflected there. The monster that was Obadiah Stark – or had been Obadiah Stark felt lessened somehow, as though every breath he took expelled one more part of who he had been.

Before he'd found himself here, the shadowy corners of his heart had been sated with desires and projections of strength and power. Now, in a place where he was powerless, with those wants and desires taken from him, he no longer knew how to fill those empty spaces. Even if what he thought he felt for Eva and Ellie was something abstractly related to caring or even love, he had no concept of how to use those emotions for anything other than manipulation and suffering.

"Where do you want to go, Obi?" Eva flicked on the windscreen washer, scraping away the accumulated dead insects on the screen.

"I don't know," he replied distantly. "Where could we go?"

"Well, we could check into a hotel for a few days while we work out what we're going to do," she replied, trying to be cheerful. "Or there's my parents' cottage on Beginish. I mean, there's not much for Ells to do there, but she loves the grey seals and the Arctic Terns, so she'd be okay for a few days. I don't mind sweetie, it's up to you. Whatever you want, we'll do. I just want to understand what's happening."

Obadiah remained expressionless. "You and me both."

Staring out the window, he tried to focus on the images rushing past, all of them blurring into one coalescing backdrop which appeared to almost be painted onto the window. Ellie sang a Disney tune in the back of the car that Obadiah recognised as 'A Whole New World' from Aladdin.

It most certainly is, he thought, turning to look at her.

She stared back at him, beaming a huge smile that threatened to split her face open. Obadiah tried to remain stoic, expressionless. Over the years he'd perfected the art of a crocodile smile, being able to produce a perfect image of kindness and compassion which ultimately served his goal of manipulation. Yet here, in the back of a car in this ethereal no man's land, he found himself unable to stop the genuine response forming on his face. And he felt discomfort at the fact it didn't feel unnatural.

He knew he shouldn't be having these reactions to such

primary stimuli, but Ellie's genuine look of love and adoration was a force more potent than Obadiah had ever experienced. His smile quickly faded as he caught himself unconsciously enjoying a human moment. He promptly turned around and back towards the window.

"Obi, I think maybe we should speak to someone else," Eva announced with a sigh. "The things you said, maybe they mean you're getting worse. It's something I don't even want to think about, but we have to face that possibility."

Obadiah nodded but remained silent.

That's a fucking understatement.

"Obi," Eva asked gently. "Please talk to me."

"You want to talk?" He asked quietly without facing her. "Okay, we'll talk. Did I ever tell you that when I was young, I was always bored? Nothing really held any interest for me; girls, skipping school, smoking, none of it. The only thing I found that could control my boredom were the holidays we used to take. We used to camp in the Black Valley near Lough Leane. I would spend a lot of my time climbing along the Hag's Glen and then up Devil's Ladder to the col between Carrauntoohil and Cnoc na Péiste. The lake there was home to hundreds of bullfrogs. I used to spend hours stabbing them with a pair of scissors or catching them in nets and laying them on their backs, piercing their little bulging stomachs and turning them over to see their jelly eyes mist over as they died. Then I used to see how far I could throw them into the lake."

"What? Obi, you're not making any sense." Her voice trembling slightly, Eva briefly glanced back at Ellie as though seeing her would make her feel secure and safe.

"Just listen," Obadiah said, turning to face her. "Later on, I learnt that fireworks strapped to their backs made the most amazing sight, blood and lights all combined, flowerlike shapes in the sky. And do you know how that made me feel?"

Eva had pulled over onto the hard shoulder, her face one of incredulous shock at what she was hearing.

"Nothing," Obadiah continued flatly. "I felt nothing. I realised I couldn't feel anything, from that day onwards. And I never thought anything of it. Everything I ever did, I did without any consideration of the consequences, because, as far as I was concerned, there were none. But I was paying a concealed price for my actions. That was the tradeoff. I see that now. Everything I did required me to be emotionally bankrupt. I could never have achieved the things I have otherwise. But now, I wonder was the price too high? Was it a price I didn't even know I was paying?"

Eva had shrunk as far towards her door as she could go, trying to place as much distance between her and her husband without leaving the car. She glanced furtively at Ellie, playing on her tiny laptop, the little girl unaware of what was being in front of before her.

"Oh my God, Obi." Glistening tracks snaked down Eva's face, her tears coming in slow intervals. "I'm trying to understand, but you're scaring me. These things you're saying... they're terrible. I mean, you're talking like you're a monster."

Obadiah dropped his head as he spoke. "I am."

Eva reached out and touched his face gently. "No, you're not. You're sick, but we can get through this. You just need to let me in. Please, Obi, let me in."

Reaching up, Obadiah placed his hand over hers and held it on his cheek for a moment before gliding it back towards her lap.

"You got in. You make me feel stronger than I've ever felt before and yet I'm weak around you. And I should hate you for it, but I don't." Obadiah shifted uncomfortably in his seat. "You want to know the closest I've ever come to being afraid? Being here, with you and Ellie. And you know why... because you don't see me. Everyone I've ever met, they all gave me a look, like they could see the real Me, the Me waiting to come out. The bad Me. The one not here with you."

Tears in her eyes, Eva looked at Ellie, as though trying to get some comfort from seeing her daughter. "Obi, this is insane."

"Just listen. Feeling that fear makes me relieved, relieved that someone can see something else in me besides evil. It makes me believe it could be real. It makes me believe that even someone like me can feel things. A little bit… a tiny piece of empathy. I always believed empathy was the greatest weakness mankind could possess, a vestigial limb, making people vulnerable. But I see now it isn't a weakness, it's your greatest strength. Where it makes you strong, my lack of it left a hole in my psyche that I know now I can't fill. Where I should have had the most evolved of all human functions, I ended up with emptiness."

Eva looked as though her world were collapsing around her, but Obadiah held his gaze, as though trying to burn Eva's face into his memory before turning to look at Ellie. He saw she had fallen asleep, her head resting against the side of the window. He wanted to remember this moment and their faces, feeling sudden apprehension for reasons he couldn't explain. He realised that right here was his opportunity to experience something that he'd never thought possible, a chance to exist outside the dark life he'd fashioned so carefully for himself over so many years.

But he knew it would be something he could never accept as anything other than a distraction. Obadiah had made his peace with who he was a long time ago. How could he ever expect anyone else to do the same?

"Compassion, Eva," he said softly, as he looked at Ellie before turning back. "That's what I should have had. Instead, there was… is… nothing."

Smiling softly at her, he opened the car door and stepped

out. The evening air was bracing, a cold breeze washing over him like a sign of approval at what he was doing.

"Obi, where are you going?" she gasped, scurrying into the passenger seat.

"I have to leave," he replied. "I know you don't understand, despite what I've just told you, but I do. It's for your own safety, yours and Ellie's. You need to leave me."

"Why?"

"Because, if I stay… I'll hurt you."

She clasped her hand to her mouth, tears flowing down her face. "Obi, you're breaking my heart. What can I do? Tell me. I'll do anything."

He surprised himself with his genuine attempt at a smile. "There's nothing you can do. Just know you've already done so much. I'll be back… I just need time."

"Where will you go?"

Obadiah looked around himself thoughtfully. "Oh, don't worry. I grew up around here, remember? I'll just walk and see where I end up. I'll be fine."

He glanced one final time at Ellie asleep in the back of the car and gently closed the door. Eva leaned over and placed her hand on the glass, her face sad but full of compassion for the man she loved. He nodded acknowledgement of her gesture and walked around the rear of the car, not looking back until the car had made its U-turn and disappeared into the distance.

Turning up the collar of his jacket, he shoved his hands in his pockets and headed towards the lights of Caragh, the distant sound of the Liffey enticing him to approach.

———

THE SUN HAD ALL BUT SET WHEN OBADIAH WALKED INTO Cooke's Pub.

The place reminded him of Coffey's Bar. While in care as a

teenager, he had belligerently walked out of the home on a few occasions to go and watch the Raheens when they played at Tom Lawlor Park. After the match, he would go to Coffey's and blag himself a few drinks with his false ID before returning back to the home to face the wrath of whoever was on duty that particular night. He'd ensured he would always drink enough to numb the discomfort of the beatings he knew he would receive.

Standing at the bar, he ordered a Jack Daniels and perused the pub while waiting. The Smiths played quietly from the jukebox, intermingled with the low, background chatter of the pub's few patrons, whispering while they finished their food. The gentle atmosphere of the pub calmed Obadiah, allowing him to slow his mind for the first time since he'd awoken this morning.

Being around Eva and Ellie was distracting. Not because he felt a desire to harm them, but because they made him feel. Yet somehow, he felt that having walked away from them felt like a failure, something he'd never accepted; a conceit he would never submit to.

In his former life, he had strived to make himself the most proficient and successful serial killer, honing his art until it became muscle memory. Even when facing execution, he had refused to succumb to the societally dictated pressure that you must be contrite when confronted with death. And he had died knowing he'd devoted himself to the idea of becoming a unique agent of death.

But could he so readily accept the idea of being 'normal'?

A sudden air of disquiet seemed to descend, causing him to shiver. It was as though the temperature had dropped momentarily.

He hadn't noticed the man take up the position next to him at the bar. Slight, with broad shoulders, wearing a black suit and shirt. He was staring at Obadiah, methodically running his finger around the top of his shot glass.

"Problem, mate?" he asked, his tone laced with menace.

The man smiled, his cheeks wrinkling with the movement. "Not at all."

Obadiah took a long mouthful of his drink. The stranger was still staring at him when he put down his glass.

"Listen, do yourself a favour and fuck off!"

Unfazed, the man continued looking at him intently.

Obadiah turned round full in his seat. He went to speak but found himself lost for words, staring back at the man.

Unable to process what he was seeing, he tried to make sense of how the person before him could look exactly the same as he had the last time he'd seen him. His mind told him it was impossible, that it apparently had a memory of standing at the back of the cemetery as they'd lowered his body into the ground.

Obadiah could also distinctly remember the time he'd spent with the man who had killed him. He considered his time with Richard Bullen, four nights later after the funeral, as one of the defining moments of his career. He'd thought it impossible that someone could suffer so perfectly until that night. But Bullen had exceeded his expectations. Screaming and begging almost right on cue. Even when Obadiah had stuck the screwdriver slowly into his spine, he hadn't disappointed, squirming and gasping in an almost staccato pattern.

It had been beautiful.

And yet now, the reason for his revenge all those years ago was seated beside him, as though they were just out for a beer.

"Tommy?"

"Hey Obi, how you doing?"

Obadiah ran his hands over his shaven head, rubbing it vigorously before returning to stare at Thomas Jacques.

"What the fuck's going on? You're dead!"

"If that's true, then what does that make you?"

"Riddles? From a dead man? What the fuck, Tommy?"

Obadiah glanced around the pub, expecting to see a sign that something was amiss; some indication that this wasn't supposed to be. But all he saw were the pub's few remaining customers, finishing their meals and talking quietly, oblivious to the impossibility that was sat before him.

"This is insane."

"This is insane? Let's face it, you were one of the world's most infamous serial killers, you have more Google hits than Paris Hilton's sex tape and were probably the most celebrated guest ever to grace Absolom and kindly take his place at the executioner's table. Seems to me, this is probably the most normal thing ever to happen to you."

"Normal? Nothing that's happened to me from the moment I was executed has been normal, so my dead friend visiting me is par for the course. You here to tell me I'll change at the next full moon, Jack Goodman?" Obadiah said with a chuckle.

"I'm not here to tell you you're going to become a monster, Obi."

Obadiah smiled a dark smile. "You don't have to. I'm one already."

"I know," Tommy replied quietly.

"Okay then, why are you here?"

Tommy moved his chair closer. "Well, I don't mean to sound arrogant, but trying to explain to you my being here would be like trying to explain quantum mechanics to a slug. For the sake of simplicity, let's pretend that you're down the rabbit hole, Alice and that this weirdness is just the norm around here."

Obadiah looked around the pub, as though trying to ascertain if what he was seeing was real. No one was paying any attention to them, which either meant he was hallucinating or that Tommy was here and the two of them, sitting at the bar, was perfectly reasonable. He turned back to his friend.

"Okay, assume for a moment that I can believe that I'm sitting in a pub in Ireland with the only person in my life I could have called a friend... who happens to be dead... what purpose could you have here?"

"I'm here to help you."

"Help me with what?" Obadiah studied his dead friend with unblinking eyes, looking for any hint of a clue as to whether or not this was all a trick.

He'd always prided himself on being able to read body language, knowing it would always say more than what was actually coming out of a person's mouth. But he had nothing.

"With your suffering to come."

He took in Tommy's emotionless expression. "My suffering?" he snorted. "What do you even know about the word?"

"I know you've always believed that your way of existing in the world was superior to everyone else," Tommy replied with a sneer. "I remember you used to speak of other people's ridiculous morals and their pathetic unwillingness to manipulate others, even to service themselves. You twisted it to mean that perhaps everyone was like you and that they were simply pretending to have this mythical concept of conscience. By believing that, you could, therefore, claim to be the only straightforward and honest person in the world... the reality in a society of fantasy."

"You never really knew me, Tommy," he noted in a flat tone. "You only like to think you did."

"You're wrong, Obi. I know that somewhere, buried so deep inside you it's probably never even been aware of the existence of light, there's the faintest murmuring that something is missing. You even said in your interview with Franklin that you felt 'hollow'. Everything you ever did, from the moment you took a life, was simply because you envied what others had that you believed you didn't. You sought to destroy that which you lacked, always choosing those people whose characters were defined by conscience; mothers, fathers, nurses, doctors. You wanted to play with the people around you, but what you were doing was illustrating that there's an intrinsic link between you and the rest of humanity. As one-dimensional and inborn as it is, you desperately wanted to be a part of the world, even as you fought against it."

Obadiah grinned and clapped slowly. "Bravo, young Jacques. You were never this insightful when you were alive. That's the afterlife for you. Offering you gifts you would have wanted when you were alive, only to give you them when you're dead and no opportunity to ever use them. Until now, that is."

Tommy took a deep breath and looked at Obadiah with an air of resignation. "Well, that's not my real reason for being here."

Obadiah looked suspiciously at his friend. "Why are you trying to help me, Tommy? We weren't that close."

"You're right, we weren't. And honestly, you're the most despicable man in this or any other plane of existence. The things you did Obi, you should never be allowed to forget or even approach any sort of closure. You're an evil man. But even the evilest of men should be allowed the chance to atone for their sins."

"Is that why I'm here? To atone?"

"No, Obi," Tommy said. "You're here to suffer, plain and simple."

"Don't sugarcoat it, Tommy, just tell me straight," he replied glibly.

"I'm telling you everything you need to know, my old friend. You need to look with better eyes to see what's right in front of you. You'll suffer here, that much is already prologue."

"And when will this alleged suffering begin?" Obadiah asked, his tone slightly less arrogant.

"It already has," his friend replied assuredly.

Obadiah looked around him again, noting the normality of the pub's patrons and then back at the surreal presence of Tommy.

"Fuck off!"

An almost cruel smile spread across Tommy's face. "You're afraid, afraid of what is beyond and immediately ahead of you. You were an unstoppable force, and the world was the unmovable object, giving you stability, both equal and opposite. But here, you are at the mercy of a higher power, one that has plans for you. And Obi, it's so close now, so terrifyingly close you can almost taste it. It's going to get worse for you my old friend. I just wanted to warn you. Not that you can stop it, but just so you're prepared for what is to come."

"And what's that exactly?" Obadiah demanded, letting out some of his anger as he leaned towards his friend, his eyes narrow slits.

Tommy's expression became forlorn as he rose from his seat. "It was good to see you, Obi."

"Tommy, wait!" he called as his friend left his seat and headed for the door, the cold draught blasting into the pub as it was opened. His friend paused for a moment, looking back with a dead expression before stepping outside.

Obadiah slowly sat back down and continued to stare at the door long after it had quietly closed.

Dr. John Franklin, BS.c. (HONS), PH.D. M.A., M.CLIN, PSYCH. A.F.Ps.S.I.

Subject: Stark, Obadiah James (a.k.a. The Tally Man) cont.

Victim history continued: Between January 1991 and March 1993, the subject murdered a further seven women; Amanda Eagles, Lynda Portman, Rachel Wheet, Joanne Armstrong, Ann-Marie Sutcliffe, Sharon Bantame and Lynette Bouza.

The locations of the victims' bodies varied by as much as 200 miles; Amanda Eagles' body was found in Spanish Town in Baton Rouge, not far from the location where Meredith Clements' body had been discovered, whereas Lynette Bouza's body was found in Pensacola, Florida.

Such distances made it difficult for law enforcement agencies to focus their investigation and served to illustrate Stark's insight that he needed to keep the murders separated by, not only time, but also geography.

During this twenty-seven month period, Obadiah moved between jobs, always staying long enough to avoid unwanted attention, but not long enough for his inept social skills to become apparent. Indeed, the subject had by now become a consummate actor, making complete use of the social roles he understood could make excellent masks for him to wear on a daily basis. For short periods of time in his variety of outwardly professional careers, Obadiah distracted people from his true nature by presenting himself in a creative and *faux*-thoughtful way, using his insight to understand what people really desire from others in order to be accepted. This ability to abuse people's aptitude of conscience provided him with the power to render those around him blind to his actual personality.

This is perfectly illustrated in an excerpt from a police statement provided by one of Obadiah's former colleagues at an Outreach Association he'd worked at in New Orleans.

Excerpt taken from interview with Angela Boyes (dated March 18th 2004):

"I worked quite closely with Obi during the winter of '91. We would always get busy around Christmas, with folks being ill with the flu and the like, all wanting to know how to get hold of the best healthcare, being poor and all. Obi was always kind and courteous, taking his time to advise those that would call in when they were real sick. He had a kind tone to his voice, really gentle. He could always put people right at ease, with his talk on how they would be okay and which was the best hospital to go to with the best doctors. He was real smart too, always telling us on our breaks about different cultures and the things they did for fun.

"… I couldn't believe it when I saw it on the news all those years later… that Obi was that man they'd been looking for all that time… who'd murdered all those poor women. And I got scared. I mean, I used to sit next to him and let him drive me home. He was always kind to me, never tried anything on. But seeing him on TV, that look in his eyes… empty. It was as though he were someone else… and his voice. He didn't sound kind anymore when he spoke… he sounded lifeless, as though he was talking in his sleep."

During this time, the media were now comparing Obadiah's crimes to those perpetrated by Theodore 'Ted' Bundy and Richard Ramirez, whose crimes consisted of thirty homicides that were known of and thirteen counts of murder respectively.

Though his identify was still unknown, the subject remained on FBI and law enforcement watch lists. Indeed, Obadiah was once again interviewed at his home following the discovery of Ann-Marie Sutcliffe's body, but no arrest was made due to lack of evidence.

In was apparent during our conversations that the subject held an extensive knowledge of law enforcement methodologies, subsequently utilising many simple techniques to avoid detection such as ensuring he'd never leave fingerprints at the scene or DNA evidence on any of his victim's bodies.

Though it's widely considered virtually impossible to leave no physical evidence, one can compare, once again, the subject to Ted Bundy, who used the fact that his fingerprints were never found at the scene of any crimes as part of his defence case and up until his execution in January 1999.

Obadiah Stark's application of the above and his use of expansive geographic locations across widely disparate jurisdictional locations for disposal of his victim's bodies, ensured that he was able to elude capture for nearly fifteen years.

A meticulous researcher, the subject can now be considered as a sufferer of low latent inhibition, a condition that would link into his power/control classification as a serial killer. Whereas, in someone of a low I.Q., such a characteristic can result in distracted behaviour, general inattentiveness and a tendency towards other absentminded habits, in someone with a high I.Q like Obadiah, such a behaviour could allow an individual to stream stimuli in a more effective manner, thereby allowing it to power their creativity and increase awareness of their surroundings. Depending on the sufferer's intelligence, it can either cause psychosis bordering on schizophrenia or, with an above average intelligence, a higher level of creative achievement. However, as this is the author's assessment and not a clinically-endorsed theory, the aforementioned may be viewed as an observed personality trait rather than a mental disorder.

Throughout this period of time, the subject was attentive to one additional thing; his tattoo. Looking at it as a record of achievement for his crimes, Obadiah Stark continued to add tally marks to the tattoo on his back.

As during the eleven-year investigation of the subject's crimes, the individual responsible for the application of the tattoo remains unknown, despite many tattoo artists being interviewed following the description given by Sara Morgan. Often, serial killers may take a souvenir which holds no value other than to them in their fantasy world. The subject, never accredited with psychotic breaks or delusions despite his obvious sociopathic nature, chose to have applied a tattoo as his symbol of achievement and constant reminder of his crimes. Conversely and completely in keeping with the subject's paradoxical nature as a serial killer, this tattoo held no significance other than to Obadiah Stark himself, in that it did not have any links to his *modus operandi* nor motive for his committing the crimes.

It was a simple yet elegant representation of a stele, adorned with a weeping angel or 'The Angel of Grief' held within its epitaphic area of two inch lines in blocks of four, with a strikethrough signifying, in the subject's case, his number of victims tallied in blocks of five.

Excerpt taken from interview with Obadiah Stark (dated 15th April 2010):

"I was never one of those narrow-minded individuals who believed he would never be caught. I knew that, one day, I would be. But unlike Bundy, Gacy and all those other wannabe pretenders to the throne, I realised that it wasn't just the act you had to be remembered for, it was the manner

in which you acknowledged it. Ramirez had a pentangle tattooed on his hand to signify he believed he had been working for Satan; Gein used the skin of his victims to fashion a flesh suit; all these things captured headlines certainly. But what if someone has something so simplistic, elegant, and yet representative of something so horrific that you cannot get past the fact that someone measures up the things he's done by simply putting a solitary line onto a design. That's something you'll always remember... that I could quantify those women by placing a mark on a tattoo and that that's what their lives amounted to as far as I was concerned.

"I knew it would never leave people... the simple, horrific nature of my record of achievement. They would always mention it whenever I was discussed. In the beginning, I was only ever going for notoriety, but I ended up with infamy. I made certain they would never forget what I achieved. The legacy of my actions forced its way into them, penetrating their minds. You could say, physiologically speaking, I raped it into them."

Three things cannot be long hidden: the sun, the moon and the truth.'
Buddha

15

OCTOBER 2ND

14:17

Northern Ireland Regional Forensic Mortuary
Belfast, Ireland

TRUTH IS ONE OF THE CENTRAL SUBJECTS IN PHILOSOPHY AND ONE of the largest.

Yet problems arise due to the fact that truth can be objective, subjective or, as Arthur C. Clark once said, far stranger than you could imagine. The nature of truth eludes us, but not because it has no nature, instead because it has more than one. And while hiding behind a myriad of disguises, the search for truth can lead to our most beautiful moments or most painful epiphanies.

Whether stumbled across or actively pursued, just like the bell which cannot be unrung, once the truth has been learnt, you cannot unlearn it. Yet the truth, whether it provides us with a bright moment or a dark hour, always has attached to it an element of discomfort and fear which propels us towards the courage we need to ultimately confront it.

LOOKING OUT ONTO THE INTENSELY LIT COLD AREA FROM THE coroner's office, Joe couldn't shake the prescient feeling that something terrible was going to happen.

Though it was only his interviews with Stamford and Sabitch which had intrigued the investigative side of him, he couldn't shake the feeling he now had that something had been amiss with Stark's execution.

Joe didn't know whether he was becoming obsessed with a conspiracy that existed only in his head, or if there was something more to it, but he'd figured that whatever it was, the best place to start corroborating Stamford's claims would be at the facility where Stark's body had been handled. With any luck, Joe was hoping that William of Occam was right and that out of the few assumptions he had, the simplest one would be the truth, though what principle William would have formulated to explain why anyone would want to cover up the execution of a serial killer, he couldn't even hazard a guess.

The mortuary, a part of the Royal Victoria Hospital that was kept out of the public eye, wasn't quite the X-Files location Joe had expected. Instead of cavernous spacing and stark, flickering lights, he'd found himself in an ineffably routine place where technicians busied themselves organising autopsy instruments awaiting Sterile Services and pathologists, dressed in their blue, reversed gowns and purple nitrile gloves, carefully examined bodies with surprising gentleness.

The building housed a four-table post-mortem examination room and refrigeration capacity for fifty-six bodies, a dedicated homicide suite, police interview rooms and a training facility for junior pathologists. A water hose was fixed to the wall with a number of drainage-type plug-holes placed beneath each of the countertops, a set of large scales accompanying them.

Joe was pulled from his observations by the coroner entering the office, medicinal-smelling air floating in behind him. The overhang of chlorine and disinfectant reminded him of the swimming baths.

"So, Mr O'Connell," Andrew Evans announced, pulling out the chair at his desk. "What can we do for you today?"

His smile was well practised, but his tone was brusque, indicating that this conversation had no intention of lasting long.

Joe extended his hand, shaking the coroner's firmly before sitting down. "Thanks for seeing me on such short notice. I know you're busy, so I won't take up too much of your time. And please, call me Joe," he said taking the notepad from his shoulder bag.

Evans smiled. "How can I help?"

"As you may know, I reported on the Stark case extensively, but I just need some contextual details to tidy things up... the process for the receipt and transportation of bodies, that kind of thing."

Evans nodded acknowledgement before speaking. "Well, on arrival at the mortuary, the deceased is labelled with their identity before being placed in the cold chamber. The Gardaí fill out a P1 form, the deceased's belongings are catalogued, and the body is undressed or left clothed depending on whether there's to be a post-mortem in the event a crime is being considered."

"And if a crime is considered?"

"The process would generally be the same, but we would have to liaise with the Senior Investigating Officer in charge of the case regarding storage and handling of the body. We usually keep the bodies in a positive temperature chamber between two and four degrees, which allows the body to be kept for several weeks but doesn't prevent decomposition. For suspected victims of a crime, we store the body in a negative temperature chamber, which ranges between minus ten and minus fifty degrees Celsius. This renders the body completely frozen and therefore good for the collection of forensic evidence."

"Do the Gardaí have influence in regards to your standard operating procedures?"

Evans thought for a moment. "Not really. They can arrange to have the body moved if necessary, but other than that…"

"And in the case of Obadiah Stark, everything was procedure? I imagine you'll be aware of the concerns raised following his execution, so I was just curious to know if you had to take extra measures regarding his transportation, security for the body, decoy transfers etc."

The coroner held a short silence before snorting. "I wasn't aware of any concerns, but to answer your question, procedure was followed, as usual, the only difference being that the PSNI contacted us ahead of his transportation to ensure a technician was going to be on hand to receive the body."

"PSNI?"

"Police Service of Northern Ireland."

"Right," Joe acknowledged with a smile. "And this was all before Stark leaving Absolom?"

"The warden informed us the execution had taken place, we were then contacted by the PSNI regarding the time of his arrival."

"Are all executed prisoners transferred from Absolom brought by boat?"

"The execution of prisoners is a rare occurrence, Mr O'Connell," Evans replied with annoyance. "Maybe one every year or so, depending on the efficacy of the prisoner's solicitor. Richard hates the perception that Absolom is there purely for the capital punishment of prisoners. He believes that it stands for more, that simply being there isn't enough for the inmates to appreciate the gravity of their actions. For that reason, he takes consultation from justice organisations as to how he can better facilitate the rehabilitation of their minds, especially those awaiting execution."

Joe considered his response. "So, he seeks advice on how he can teach them remorse before he puts them to death?"

Evans rubbed his cheek slowly. "That's a crude way of putting it, but yes. Not everyone considers the death penalty enough of a punishment, Mr O'Connell. Some people feel that they have to at least appreciate the gravity of their actions before they die. Otherwise, true justice hasn't really been achieved."

Joe met the coroner's intense gaze, uncomfortable with his rhetoric. "These organisations… how much involvement do they have?"

"It's purely on a consultative basis as far as I know."

"I can't imagine it's a service they provide out of altruism."

Evans shrugged. "You'd have to speak to Richard regarding their arrangement. Consider the other side of the coin, Mr O'Connell. Society demands these people suffer for their crimes, not live comfortably in their final days. As I said, sometimes death isn't considered enough."

"Isn't enough?" Joe said flatly. "I wasn't aware capital punishment was at the whim and demands of a capricious public."

"You obviously don't agree with the death sentence," stated Evans

"I've never agreed with an eye for an eye, though in Stark's case I can see how an exception could be made. Still, I fail to see how incarceration therapy of any kind could have made that man feel any remorse."

Evans smiled. "A debate for another time perhaps."

"Going back to transportation," Joe continued. "The boat came straight here following the execution?"

"As far as I know," Evans replied. "Not certain what time. The duty-attendant will have that information in the log at reception."

"You might be interested to know that records indicate there was a delay in the Absol's return to Dunquin that night. Any idea why?"

"I don't take note of shipping lane traffic, as a rule, Mr O'Connell," Evans said curtly.

"You mentioned before that everything was procedure... so there was no autopsy?"

"Wasn't necessary. We knew how he died and politically, no one was curious about anything else. His death was by lethal injection, and that's what's on his death certificate."

Joe took advantage of his opportunity. "Funny you should mention that. I was looking into the necessary paperwork required following an execution before a death certificate can be produced, just to make certain I had all the information before I went ahead and published it..."

"And?" Evans squinted at Joe.

"... and, I found something unusual."

The coroner furrowed his brow. "I'm sorry, I don't follow."

"Correct me if I'm wrong, but I have it on good authority that a death certificate can only be issued once the execution has been critiqued by the warden and filed in the Master Execution File."

"That's right" The coroner tensed in his seat, his eyes narrowing.

"Yet I have a source who states that Obadiah Stark's file is empty. There's nothing in it relating to his execution. If that's the case, how can he have a death certificate on file at the local registry office?"

Silence punctuated the air, allowing the low buzzing sound of the overhead light to makes its presence felt. Joe noticed that Evans' skin had begun to turn pink and blotchy. The part of his shirt visible along the top of the lab coat appeared to be clinging to him as though he were sweating.

"I wouldn't know, Mr O'Connell. Are you often compelled to indulge the whims of someone who may only be telling you this for their Warholian fifteen minutes of fame? Assuming it's true and not simply a filing error, do you have any proof to support this potentially libellous allegation?"

Joe shook his head and continued, despite knowing that the man before him would continue to be obdurate. "No. But I do have proof that the boat transferring Stark's body appeared to take four hours to make what is generally a ninety-minute journey the night of his execution. I also have a source that claims Stark's master execution file is empty, therefore citing irregularities regarding the completion of his death certificate. As a journalist, I'd like to know why. Given the high profile of the case, a simple 'procedural error' coming to light regarding the keeping of poor paperwork would be a bit embarrassing for all concerned, don't you think? His crimes, victims, not to mention the fact he evaded the authorities on both sides of the Atlantic for the best part of a decade... it would be a travesty if something as incidental as a death certificate could cast doubt on whether procedure was followed at his execution."

The coroner responded quickly. "Well, I can't help you with the boat you mentioned and access to any of the deceased's information is only for employees of this facility."

Evans was becoming jittery and fractious. He fished a packet of cigarettes from his pocket and lit one, ignoring the country's no smoking laws and exhaling the blue smoke with a sharp breath. It was evident from the body language that he wanted to be anywhere but here and was eager to get Joe out of the room as quickly as possible.

"Is Stark's body still here?" Joe pressed.

Evans turned his head to stare at the door, as though indicating Joe to leave.

"Why?"

"Just curious."

Evans refused to take the bait. "Sorry, we have rules to follow as well, you know. You can see what time his body was booked at the front desk, but other than that…"

Joe smiled dejectedly but held the coroner's stare. "Well, it was worth a try. I guess I could edit my piece to exclude the need for those details. I mean, it's not as though you've got anything to hide, is it?"

Evans raised his eyebrows, his expression one of subtle disquiet. "Is there anything else I can help you with, Mr O'Connell?"

It was more of an insistence than a question.

Joe considered his answer, refusing to let his doggedness at calling him 'Mr. O'Connell' irritate him.

"No, thank you," he replied as he slowly put his notepad back in his bag. "I think I've got everything I need."

He turned towards the door, the coroner right behind him, almost ushering him out the office. Joe turned and held Evans' stare for a moment before smiling.

"Oh, just one more thing. You didn't tell me the name of the group working with Sabitch."

"The Brethren," Evans snapped, flicking a piece of fluff from his lab coat. "Now if you don't mind, I have a lot to do."

"Right," Joe replied with a slow nod before moving down the stairs.

A petite, pretty young girl behind the desk returned Joe's smile as he approached her and placed his hands on the countertop.

"Hi. I've just been speaking to your boss, and he told me that if I needed anything, you were the girl to see…" He leaned forward to look at her name badge. "… Kelly."

He continued to flash his most charming smile as he

subtly looked her up and down. Her black hair was long and flowing, with large, brown doe eyes that seemed to take up her whole face. Joe thought there was almost something childlike and mysterious about the way she was looking at him. As though she was thinking something dirty.

"And what do you need exactly?"

Joe gave her a playful look.

"Ten minutes would probably be enough, but actually I was wondering if you could tell me what time the boat that brought in Obadiah Stark's body arrived on September 7th?"

Kelly's smile quickly disappeared. "Sure," she said, her fingers flicking across the keyboard in front of her.

"You okay?" Joe couldn't help notice that she'd gone from looking seductive to troubled in a matter of seconds.

"Yeah, it's just hearing that guy's name. It gives me the creeps."

Joe smiled softly. "I know what you mean."

"Okay, here we go… his body was booked in at 21:14."

Joe frowned. "Are you certain?"

Kelly nodded. "Uh-uh, it's right here. They were preparing for his arrival before my shift finished that night. I remember being glad I wasn't going to have to be the one who was here when he arrived."

Joe turned away from the desk as he thought. The Absol did dock here that night, pretty much on time. So why didn't it arrive back in Dunquin until after midnight?

Joe felt Kelly's large, brown eyes boring into him. "Is there anything else I can help with?"

"No," Joe said thoughtfully. "You've been very helpful, thank you."

She gave him one last beaming smile as he slowly headed for the exit.

"You're welcome."

———

EVANS WATCHED JOE APPROACH THE RECEPTION DESK BEFORE closing the door and picking up the telephone.

He paused halfway through dialling the number as though uncertain whether to proceed before completing the digits and leaning back in his chair.

Evans realised that he was holding his breath while he waited for a connection.

There was a click as the phone was picked up at the other end, but no one spoke.

"It's me. I've just had a reporter asking to see the booking log for the night of Stark's execution. I didn't give him anything, and he seemed satisfied, but I don't know. You told me that no one would ask questions. This is my career on the line here. If I'd have known people were going to start poking around, I would have…" he was about to say 'asked for more money', but caught himself.

He knew better than to bite the proverbial hand.

The line remained silent.

"What should I do?" Evans asked nervously.

"Was it O'Connell?"

"How did you know?"

There was a pause. "Do nothing,"

The line went dead.

The coroner cradled the handset against his chest before slamming it back into its receiver. Clasping his hands together to try and stop them from shaking, he took a final drag before stubbing out the cigarette so hard ash plumed into the air.

It was still gently falling as he made his way out of the office and across the mortuary floor.

————

IT WAS EIGHT O'CLOCK AND DARK BY THE TIME JOE HEADED BACK to The Daily Éire.

He had felt the need to freshen up after leaving the

mortuary, thinking that a shower and a few cups of coffee would help him put things into perspective. Instead, he'd fallen asleep on the sofa and woken up just after seven with a desire to revisit some of his interviews before trying to make some sort of sense out of the myriad of scenarios he had flying through his mind.

Parking at the top of Denny Street and stopping to have a quick chat with the Daily Éire's security guard, Paul Helm, or 'Buster' as he was better known, Joe had proceeded to walk through the lobby and straight for his office.

Choosing to leave the larger expanse of the room in darkness, he had flicked through the filing cabinet, occasionally stopping to pull out a brown folder and place it on his desk before putting them all in his shoulder bag and heading back up the street.

"Shit."

Approaching his car, he noticed that his offside front tyre was flat.

Throwing the bag onto the back seat, he bent down and saw the long slash horizontally across the front of the tire. Joe fingered it curiously, recognising that it couldn't have happened by accident and could have only occurred in the last thirty or so minutes he'd been in the office.

He stood and moved to the boot, shifting the requisite car essentials to one side before lifting up the base. As he was unscrewing the spare, Joe became aware of the black Audi pulling up, its headlights momentarily blinding him.

He shielded his eyes, hearing the engine die and a door open and shut before a figure appeared beside him.

"Need a hand, mate?" the voice asked.

On any other day, Joe wouldn't have been suspicious, but after his discussion with Evans, his growing disquiet about everything Obadiah Stark and the now obviously slashed tire, Joe found himself unusually keyed to the convenient

Samaritan's over-enthused smile, slicked back hair and black jacket.

He also couldn't help noticing the Audi's heavily tinted windows. But it wasn't the tinting that had him uncomfortable so much as the fact that they were so black it was impossible to see inside.

Joe smiled up at his would-be helper. "No, I've changed one before. Cheers though"

He glanced past the man to see Paul Helm, the security guard, in his usual spot in the booth by the door outside the office. Instead of feeling safer and less alone with him in his sights, Joe found himself in a whirlpool of anxiety and negative emotion. The man stood before him with his offer of help did little to dissuade Joe's dispirited sentiments.

"You've had a slashed tyre before?" the stranger asked, peering over Joe's shoulder. "You must be popular."

"I'll be okay, thanks."

"Go on," the stranger insisted. "It can be a pain in the arse changing these things. You get the spare, and I'll get the nuts loose and the car up. The name's Milton."

Joe shrugged and passed him the torque wrench before reaching into the boot for the jack.

"Joe," he replied, shaking the man's outstretched hand.

As Milton began working on loosening the nuts on the wheel, Joe placed the jack besides him and pulled the wheel out of the boot, bouncing it on the floor before rolling and resting it against the passenger side's door. He grabbed his cigarettes from his pocket and lit one, taking a long drag on it before exhaling slowly. He watched his convenient helper straining to turn the nut counter-clockwise before it twisted free and he began to spin it off the wheel.

"So, you from around here?" Joe asked.

Milton carried on working on the nuts as he spoke. "Not, really. Just passing through. But I saw you and figured I'd lend a hand. Wouldn't do to have one of Ireland's most famous reporters stranded at the side of the road."

Joe frowned. "Do I know you?"

Milton gave a look of mild derision and idle curiosity, his obsidian eyes twinkling playfully in the reflection of the streetlights. "Relax, everyone knows who you are, Joe. You're the man who kept the country up to date with one of the world's most famous serial killers. And given the fact you're just up the road from The Daily Éire, I didn't really need a slide ruler and a pencil to figure it out."

He nodded as he watched Milton twist off the last nut, place the wrench on the floor and begin jacking up the car. Though the exchange still had him feeling a little uneasy, he began to wonder if he was letting everything that had happened recently cloud his better judgment and make him a little paranoid.

"How's it going there," he asked, flicking his cigarette on the floor and crushing it out with his heel.

"I think…" Milton replied with a grunt. "… that we're done."

He twisted the jack twice more before standing and handing the wrench to Joe.

"Cheers," Joe replied, placing it on the roof of the car. He rolled the tyre in position and bent down to fit it into place.

"No worries, Joey," said Milton with a conceding nod before moving back towards his car.

Joe grabbed the wrench and bent to tighten the nuts. As he moved down past the window, he noticed Milton's reflection behind him, his arm rising up towards the back of Joe's head and the click of the hammer being cocked.

"What the fuck?" Joe yelled as he turned and instinctively grabbed Milton's hand.

The gun fired softly into the space his head had just been occupying, the suppressor muffling the bang to a quiet hiss.

Joe hit Milton three times in the sternum, sending him

crashing back into the wall, the gun spinning from his hand. He glanced in shock at the gun on the pavement, trying to process what was happening as Milton jumped to his feet and charged at Joe, the precise right hook connecting with the side of his head and sending him stumbling against the car.

He blinked, trying to focus on the man standing in front of him as Milton grabbed the gun from the floor and aimed it at his head. Joe managed to force his legs to work, diving out the way as a bullet whistled past his face and smashed into the passenger side rear window.

"What the fuck are you doing?" he shouted at his attacker.

Milton placed his foot on Joe's chest and checked the street around him. Usually, you body checked enough people on Denny Street to be a UFC fighter, no matter what time you were out. Tonight though, there was no one.

As Joe watched Milton tighten the suppressor and point the gun at him, his hand groped clumsily for the wrench. He felt his fingers curl around the cold handle as adrenaline brought on by the fear of death surged through him.

He swung it into Milton's kneecap, taking a small amount of satisfaction at the crunching sound he heard accompanied with Milton's loud scream.

Joe reached up and grabbed the barrel of the gun, aiming it away from his face and swung the wrench again, this time connecting with the side of Milton's head. He ignored the sickening crack it made as it struck his cheekbone, blood spraying from the now open wound as his attacker fell sideways and onto the street.

Joe glanced up the street towards the office and saw Paul staring back at him. He felt relief and irritation that he apparently hadn't moved during the attempt on his life.

Joe began to move towards him, his legs suddenly feeling like two columns of concrete.

He glanced back a few times to see Milton moaning on the

floor, holding his face as though his hands were all that was keeping it together.

Paul stepped quickly towards Joe as he reached the office and pulled him into the building. He offered himself as support but was immediately waved away.

"I'm okay," Joe insisted. "Where were you when I needed you?"

He noticed the confused look on Paul's face that told of the value he placed on his own life.

"Never mind. Have you called the police?"

"Yeah, they're on their way, though I'm not sure they believed me. Don't often get armed gunmen on Denny Street."

"No shit." Joe's legs gave way from beneath him, and he slumped down against the wall, his ears still ringing from the blow he'd received.

He found himself shaking from the sudden release of adrenaline. In between shudders, he realised that whatever he was onto had people worried. Powerful people. And that meant, whatever it was, it was real and tangible, not the fantasy he'd begun to suspect it could be.

Why else would they send someone to kill him? It was a new experience for him. He'd had death threats before, but never any that had actually followed through.

Joe listened for the sound of sirens in the distance but heard nothing.

"Jesus. Someone riots about student fees, the police are here in a flash," he said. "Someone tries to shoot you in the street, and they're nowhere to be fuckin' seen."

Paul stepped outside and looked around the corner of the building. He moved back in and touched Joe gently on the shoulder.

"I wouldn't worry about it too much, son. You're the only person they'll be talking to."

He pushed himself up and followed Paul's pointing finger back outside and up the street towards his car.

Milton had gone.

"Shit!" At that moment, he realised something else.

Wherever his investigation went from here, Joe knew it would be a place far from good.

'Man cannot remake himself without suffering, for he is both the marble and the sculptor.'

Dr. Alexis Carrel

16

22:58

"It's going to get bad for you, my old friend."

Those words had played repeatedly in Obadiah's head all the way back from Cooke's Pub. Tom Jacques, his only friend in life, had delivered those baleful words in his melodic Irish lilt – not as the shy reticent boy from Killarney, but as a poised advisor delivering a threat.

And now, standing before the front door of the house, bathed in the night that had once embraced his solitary existence, Obadiah experienced a gut-wrenching emotion long-denied to him by his cold, calculating immorality: fear.

Tommy had been right. Obadiah had always wanted to be part of the world, and Eva and Ellie had given him the chance to reclaim his place in it. He'd been allowed to imagine what life would have been like had he taken a different path.

The thought that his chance at redemption could be stolen away from him was terrifying.

You will suffer here…

Obadiah moved to the front door, noting it was slightly ajar. Giving it a gentle push, he let it swing open as he stood on the threshold, listening.

Moving through the silent hallway into the kitchen, he

sensed the ambience of death. His pace quickened with his pulse.

Moonlight bathed the downstairs rooms, illuminating recognisable objects - Ellie's toys, an empty wine glass. Ascending the stairs, his heart pounded so hard he thought it might knock him over. His legs became lead, forcing him to grip the handrail as he reached the landing.

Soft, ambient light shone softly from beneath the master bedroom door. Reaching for the door handle, his palms clammy, Obadiah entered the bedroom.

'You're here to suffer, plain and simple.'

Eva lay face-down on the bed, her legs spread apart, arms fastened to the posts. Her nightclothes had been lifted and placed around her lower back, bloodstains spreading out across the sheet beneath her neck like a Rorschach image. Ellie was lying next to her mother, curled up under the crook of her arm, the child in her pyjamas, Snoopy pulled in tightly to her chest as though it was a protective guardian.

Obadiah moved slowly towards the bed, numb with grief that impaled his heart, leaving him feeling something he'd never considered possible – powerlessness.

The butcher of dozens leaned forward to examine the remains of the one woman he could never have harmed, his hand gentle as it graced her forehead.

Eva's skin was already cold – Obadiah estimating her death had been a good four hours ago. Her blue eyes remained open, the colour now sapphire due to their lack of oxygen. All the joy and happiness they'd held was gone, vanquished by an act that had left her mouth slightly parted in its final cry for help.

The side of her face was bruised, her jaw broken. The horror of it all washed over him in waves, and he recognised the emotion as shame.

Welcome home, Tally Man, you've come full circle.

Trying to instil order to his racing thoughts, he reached

over and gently stroked Ellie's face, the extension of his hand seeming to come in aching, strobe-like moments. He was surprised to find her skin warm, her body shifting gently beneath his touch… alive!

Moving with purpose, he strode around the bed and scooped her up in his arms, pulling her close to him, her face in the crook of his neck. She was most likely in shock, either from what she'd found or what she had been made to witness.

As he turned around, he saw the note. It rested beside Eva's body, the handwriting neat and concise. The message pulled at Obadiah's memories, its words taunting and gleeful.

Nature doesn't recognise good and evil, only balance.

The words sat like a stone in his stomach. He crumpled the note, Ellie stirring in his arms.

Obadiah felt her body begin to shake from the adrenaline being released in such a small frame. She pulled Snoopy tightly to her and opened her eyes, looking at him with a vacant expression.

"Daddy?"

"I'm here," he replied - so softly it surprised him. Shifting her away from the horrific remains of her mother, his hand hovered tentatively over her head, as though he were afraid to show affection. Yet he did it anyway, without really understanding why, as though his body were guiding him to behave appropriately given the circumstances.

Obadiah remained motionless for what seemed like an eternity, his hand nestled softly on Ellie's head, her small frame shaking in his arms. He glanced once more at Eva's body, almost sad that he had to leave her behind.

Through her, his mind had irreversibly been opened up to other possibilities, possibilities that had allowed him to see what he looked like through a glass darkly – a hateful bastard allowed one last chance to see life that existed outside darkness. Eva had been one half of the light which had enabled him that chance. The child he now held in his arms was the other.

He would be damned again if something was going to happen to her.

Seeing his wife lying lifeless and barren, he felt anger that made him suck the air through gritted teeth. Concerned about his daughter, he stepped into the hallway and pulled the bedroom door closed, sealing in the horrors behind them.

Moving to the stairs, Obadiah suddenly shuddered in pain, as if his back were being stung by a thousand wasps. Dropping to one knee, he lowered Ellie gently onto the floor before he rolled over and collapsed.

"Daddy, what's happening?" Ellie cried, her hands pressed to his chest. She was almost frantic with terror as she watched him writhe in agony against unknown torture.

As had happened before, the pain slowly eased, allowing Obadiah to push himself up. Reaching around he touched the top of his shoulder blade, knowing that if he were to look in the mirror, he would see that more tally marks had reappeared on his back.

"Daddy, are you okay?" Almost hysterical, Ellie placed her hands frantically over Obadiah's face and body as though making sure he was real.

"It's okay," he assured her weakly. "I'm okay."

Ellie began to cry, the unimaginable suffering she'd experienced breaking free from her small frame, her voice spiralling up as she spoke.

"But Mummy... she's in there, and she won't wake up. I lied down next to her to try and wake her up, but she wouldn't. Someone came and was hurting her... I tried to stop him... I shouted for him to stop hurting my Mummy but he didn't, so I hid in my room with Snoopy and waited for the shouting to stop, and when I went in to see Mummy she was sleeping, but I couldn't wake her up..."

Ellie pressed herself into Obadiah's chest, now shaking

uncontrollably, her body wracked with emotions. He picked her up again and moved stiffly down the stairs, grabbing the car keys from the table and continuing to scan the darkness of the house while moving through the hallway and out the front door.

The street was deserted as they crossed the moonlit pavement, Ellie whispering quietly to her beloved stuffed toy that everything was going to be okay.

The air was silent, breathless, shadows marking their route as though illustrating the safest way to travel. He swapped Ellie's position in his arms and opened the car door, placing her gently on the back seat.

Climbing behind the wheel, Obadiah leaned back and closed his eyes. In his prior existence, his sole purpose had been the taking of human lives. Now everything had changed – he had to keep Ellie safe.

As he started the engine and pulled into the road, Obadiah found the night that had once been his friend was now a vast and lonely place.

Dr. John Franklin, BS.c. (HONS), PH.D. M.A., M.CLIN, PSYCH. A.F.Ps.S.I.

Subject: Stark, Obadiah James (a.k.a. The Tally Man) cont.

Victim history continued: The subject murdered a further two women during 1993; Rebecca Collins and Wendy Marrin.

Sara Morgan, attacked that same year but surviving her assault, has been the topic of much debate over the years, with a suggestion that the circumstances surrounding her kidnapping and subsequent ordeal were deliberately orchestrated by the subject in order to enhance the legacy he was creating for himself: however this is pure conjecture. As far as I am aware the subject didn't know she'd survived.

Twenty-four year-old Sara Jayne Morgan was living and working in Monroe, Louisiana at the time of her kidnapping. Picked up in a bar by the subject on 18th June 1993, she was subsequently discovered lying at the side of Highway 80 just outside Ruston. Unconscious and barely alive, the lower half of her face appeared to have been blown off, with little remaining of her jaw. During my interview with the subject, he acknowledged that he'd taped a firecracker inside her mouth and lit it. When asked why he had done it, he replied that whilst "she was extremely attractive and one half of me wanted to get to know her, the other half of me was curious to find out how pretty she would be if part of her face was missing."

Sara Morgan was treated at Northern Louisiana Medical Centre and to everyone's surprise, survived the ordeal, though not without having to undergo intensive facial reconstruction and skin grafts. Unable to speak at the time and to this day without using an electrolarynx, she was however, following her extubation in Intensive Care, able to provide the police with a crude drawing that would associate the subject with the name that would forever be linked with his crimes.

Sara had drawn a picture of a tattoo seen on the subject's back; a tombstone etched with the tally marks in batches of five. From that point onwards, though the police had tried to keep the information hidden from the newspapers, the subject would be known as The Tally Man.

Though her survival was seen as a small victory, it was believed in some quarters of law enforcement that she'd been allowed to escape rather than procure release herself, lending itself to the theory that the subject had let her escape in order to garner publicity. A key analyst within the FBI stated that Obadiah Stark was too meticulous and calculating an individual to let something as easy as an escape route go unnoticed and it was more than likely he was unaware of her survival.

Excerpt taken from interview with Obadiah Stark (dated 15th April 2010):

"Legacy? I don't know about that, but what I do know is that there are two types of people in the world; those who make things happen and those who wonder what happened when all is said and done. I made things happen. Those people don't know how to make things happen for themselves, so how can they hope to make things happen for others?

"As to the legacy issue, that isn't something which can be left to chance. It's something that requires determination, based upon the life you lead. I fashioned my life to ensure that I touched people, made a difference in my own way. I wasn't trying to make the world better than I found it. I was

trying to show those who try to structure the world and make it fit into a specifically shaped box, that they were wasting their time. I simply showed them how pointless their efforts at controlling everything is. Besides, a legacy is just an idea that encompasses the past, present and the future. It shows you where you've been and where you're going. My actions were a journey from success to significance. I'm not a monster; I was just ahead of my time."

It was following the murder of Wendy Marrin that Obadiah Stark appeared to pause his activities for a six-month period. The reasons for this sabbatical remain unclear.

During our interview, the subject failed to divulge exactly what he' done during the aforementioned period, but whatever his actions, December 1993 saw the discovery of Siobhán Duggan's body in an alleyway in Slane, Ireland. No link was made initially between the subject's crimes in America and a murder in a small town on the bank of the Boyne. However when Katherine Keld's body was discovered in a cave outside Ardfert near Tralee, the local Gardaí theorised a link between the murders due to similarities with the victims in the USA.

Subsequent liaisons with the FBI and Interpol identified a high probability that Obadiah Stark had proceeded to continue his work on the shores of Ireland.

The subject's links to the country were not realised at the time and therefore it was implied that his choice of location was arbitrary.

'The basic tool for the manipulation of reality is the manipulation of words. If you can control the meaning of words, you can control the people who use them.'
Phillip K. Dick

17

OCTOBER 3RD

00:26

Fenit (*An Fhianait*)
County Kerry, Ireland

THE ACT OF DECEIT IS SOMETHING THAT SOME FIND MORE comfortable to commit than others.

Some may do it to protect those they care for; others to gain a stronger position for themselves. Deceit is often seen as the raison d'être of the politician, whose very existence is seen by some to be solely for the purpose of inveigling and obfuscating the truth.

It must be used delicately for, like a snake coiled around the wrist, it can have a nasty habit of causing a severe injury if you don't handle it with care. For those who use it to serve their own ends, very few would weep when it all comes tumbling down around them. But for those who use it in the pursuit of protecting those they care for, it can become an altogether different beast.

In those circumstances, deceit can be seen by the deceiver as the right thing for the wrong reasons. It is always a matter of perspective and how the deceived will choose to view it.

Will they see it as a noble sacrifice or a selfish act?

———

JOE CLOSED THE FRONT DOOR WITH MORE RELIEF THAN HE CARED
to remember.

Moving through the living room to the kitchen, he poured himself a large JD and grabbed a packet of peas from the freezer before crashing onto the settee. Swirling the bourbon around the glass, he took a large mouthful, enjoying the warm, astringent sensation before swallowing it.

After the Gardia had finally arrived to interview him, Joe had realised that for all the use they were going to be, he might have been better merely writing off the attempt on his life as an aggravated subscriber and left it at that.

"No need for that tone, Mr O'Connell," the Officer had said. "We're simply trying to establish the facts."

"The facts? The fact is that a complete stranger tried to shoot me in the face and you're asking me stupid questions. He must have left fingerprints on the car somewhere. Go and find out who he is instead of making me wish he had shot me."

The officer had glared at Joe. "I understand your angry and upset, Mr O'Connell, but I can assure you, we will do everything we can. In the meantime, I suggest you go home, put something on your face for the swelling and get some rest. We'll contact you if we need anything further."

Following the officer's advice, Joe pressed the peas to his cheek and allowed himself a moment to consider how he'd ended up the focal point of a murder attempt.

The intricacies surrounding Stark's execution were becoming a little more sinister and suspicious with every passing day. Someone's cage had obviously been rattled, someone who perhaps stood to lose a great deal if he actually uncovered anything substantial.

Right now all he had was supposition, hearsay and chary behaviour, but based on tonight's escapade he knew he must be close to something others would rather keep hidden.

He stared at the ceiling, hoping for a revelation. Something was linking a number of people involved in and witness to Stark's execution, he just couldn't put his finger on it.

Acts committed by someone like Obadiah Stark left a resonance, lingering in silence. The family members bore him enmity: he'd seen it during his interviews. Animosity, from evil gone unpunished.

Beginning to irritate himself, Joe rose from the settee and poured himself another JD, placing the peas back in the freezer to chill again. The glass was almost to his lips when the doorbell made him start, causing him to spill the drink down his shirt.

"Shit!"

He placed the glass on the bench and grabbed a tea-towel to wipe his front as he approached the door. Joe noted the small shape through the glass before he opened it, subconsciously registering her frame.

Vicky waved a bottle of wine gently in front of his face.

"I figured we'd give Sean Og's a rest tonight…"

Joe felt slightly uncomfortable as she registered his injuries, her eyes scanning him repeatedly.

"Jesus, Joe, what happened to your face?"

"I was attacked by a Crayola. Come in."

He pushed the door open wider and ushered Vicky into the hall. She slowly traversed under his arm, staring at him as she moved into the living room.

"When did this happen?" she asked as he closed the door behind them.

"Just this evening, or should I say yesterday," he replied glancing at his watch and standing awkwardly still. "Don't worry, it's not as bad as it looks."

Vicky frowned. "Figuratively or literally, because it looks pretty bad to me. Have you been to the hospital?"

He shook his head. "No, my bag of Bird's Eye is currently recharging in the freezer... better than anything they could do. Besides, after the Gardaí were done with me, I honestly couldn't be arsed."

She moved in front of him, frowning. "Gardaí? What are you going on about?"

"I had a flat tyre at work," Joe replied while massaging his bruised jaw. "This guy offered to help me change it, I was tired, so I accepted. Then he attacked me."

"Do you know who it was?"

"Oddly, he didn't introduce himself."

"Why'd he want to hurt you?" Vicky pressed, ignoring his sarcasm as she sat down, resting the bottle of wine between her legs.

Joe looked at her with an exasperated expression. "You know, it's funny, he didn't punctuate kicking the shite out of me with exposition, so I don't really know!"

"How do you know he wanted to kill you?"

"He had a fuckin' gun, Vicky, so I figured he wasn't simply trying to get my attention."

Noticing her hesitant gaze, Joe sat down beside her. "Sorry, just been a crappy day."

She gently touched his arm while raising the wine bottle and giving it a shake. "It's okay. We now have a better excuse to open this. That's if you don't mind downgrading to something a little less inebriating?"

She nodded towards the empty glass on the bench. Joe smiled. "No, it's okay. Most of it ended up down my shirt anyway."

Following her into the kitchen, Joe leaned back against the bench and pointed towards the drawer holding the bottle opener as she glanced around.

"So, what do you think it's all about," Vicky asked as she

began removing the cork. He acknowledged her with a sigh and accompanying frown.

"Honestly? I'm not sure, but I think it all has something to do with my digging into Stark's execution."

Vicky looked puzzled as she grabbed two glasses from his cabinet and filled them, handing him the fuller of the two.

"How so?"

Joe hesitated for a moment, his expression closed. "The night Stark was executed… something's 'off' about the whole thing, and I think tonight pretty much confirms it."

Vicky gave a startled laughed. "Joe, being beaten up is hardly confirmation of a global conspiracy."

"Ordinarily, I'd be inclined to agree with you, but aside from being a shite raconteur there's nothing else I'm doing that would get under someone's skin enough for them to want me dead. When aforementioned beating involves someone actually trying to shoot you, it tends to indicate they want you dead for a reason."

Joe noted her sceptical look before taking a drink. "Yeah, I know. But it still doesn't change the fact that something's not right about it all."

Vicky studied Joe's face. "Okay, Sherlock. Let's assume for a moment that I believe you…"

"I know it sounds a little mad, but bear with me. Stark was executed last month, big event, the world's media in attendance, the victim's relatives and yours truly. The lethal injection seems to go as planned and aside from Stark having some sort of seizure and scaring the crap out of everyone, dies on schedule. Curtain down, exit stage left, case closed, right?"

"Okay," Vicky replied cautiously.

"Boat visits Absolom where Stark's body is loaded onto it, standard procedure. Boat sets sail for the mainland where the body is to be delivered to the Royal Victoria."

"They take the bodies of prisoners to a hospital mortuary?"

"Well, the site isn't directly attached to the hospital, and they have a contract with the Government regarding the storage of bodies. I imagine if you boil it down to its common denominator, it comes down to money. Anyway, there they're supposed to stay until the state decides on the funeral arrangements, that sort of thing."

"Okay," Vicky said rolling her eyes. "It's fascinating, but I'm not really feeling conspiracy here, and I already know all of this."

Joe drew in a deep breath and held it for a moment before releasing it slowly as he spoke. "The boat transporting his body took nearly four hours to make an hour and a half trip."

"And?"

"… and, his body never made it to the mortuary."

Vicky frowned. "You can prove this?"

"Well, not exactly, but I think what I have is pretty conclusive. When an hour's trip takes three times longer than it's supposed to and there's no record of problems or weather issues, it's a fair bet that something's a little funky."

He could tell she wasn't satisfied with his answer. "Okay," Vicky announced. "Let's just say for the sake of argument that you're right and that something unusual is going on, what purpose does it serve?"

"I don't know," Joe replied, his gaze falling to the floor and then back up again. "Yet."

He sighed and stood up, moving back towards the living room shaking his head. He was tired and miserable and aching from head to foot. It was all fucked up, and he knew it, but really needed someone to believe him.

He slumped onto the settee, folding his arms across his chest. "It's not just the boat, it's everything. I've interviewed every witness, relative, prison guard and criminologist this side of the Liffy because I felt like I owed a service to the relatives. To ensure that instead of reporting crap like other papers did, I could give what had happened to them some gravitas. And then, after Stark's execution, I had this idea to write a book about the man, his life and crimes. I didn't want it to be just another cash-in, I wanted it to be justified and balanced. Your offer of help came at the right time. You've given me the credible stuff that adds more than just the 'he was a killer because his parents held him too tight or not enough', shite.

"But since looking into it all further, something's wrong. I don't know what or why, but it is. Before Stark died, these people were angry, now, they're like a bunch of hugger-muggers."

"Hugger whats?"

"Hugger-mugger; cloak and dagger kind of thing."

She started to laugh, but then looked at Joe's expression and fell silent

"I'm not imagining it, Vicky. Stamford started this whole thing and had nothing to gain by lying to me. Sabitch and Evans are definitely hiding something to do with his execution file and death certificate, and…"

"And?"

"… and, Evans got all funny when I challenged him about something called The Brethren."

"The Brethren," Vicky repeated, her face twitching slightly.

"You've heard of them?" Joe challenged.

"No," she replied quickly, her face flushing as she averted her gaze. "Wow, I feel a little lightheaded all of a sudden. Must be this wine."

Joe watched her as she moved into the living room and sat down in the chair opposite. Vicky's gaze cast towards her feet before rising again.

He felt his head tilting wearily, prompting him to give an exasperated sigh.

"I don't know, maybe you're right. I'm tired, getting slowly drunk and look like I've gone four rounds with The Rock. I think I just need to go to bed. I don't blame you for thinking it's a little far-fetched. I'm not sure I believe it myself. I guess after everything today, I just needed to share it with someone. And why not a beautiful, smart criminologist…"

His voice faded as though afraid to say anything else. A moment passed between them and seemed to hang in the air.

Joe cleared his throat and rose quickly from the chair.

"Definitely time for bed I think. I'll walk you to your car."

Vicky smiled and stood up, following behind him. She placed her hand on his shoulder and spun him around to face her.

"Time for bed, you said."

She touched his face before kissing him, her body folding into his and forcing him back against the front door. Shocked by her sudden actions, he nevertheless found himself pulling her closer to him, his hand sliding beneath her blouse and pulling it loose.

Her hands moved across his chest, unbuttoning his shirt and moving down towards his trousers with an unexpected urgency. Joe pushed her back, staring directly into her eyes and seeing a stark need that forced his body to unconsciously react.

"I don't think this is a good idea," he uttered in a low voice.

Vicky gazed back at him, biting her lower lip. "Why not? You promised me a good time the other night at Sean Og's. I just want to collect."

She kissed him again, her hands exploring his body as she pulled him down towards the floor. Joe pulled his shirt over his head and lay down beside her, his hands pulling at her blouse and finding her bra strap.

"Don't lose respect for me if this doesn't happen with one hand."

"Just get it done," Vicky murmured.

Mindlessly colliding with her body, Joe found himself thinking that his evening had taken a dramatic turn for the better. And yet, the darkest corner of his mind continued to process his refusal to give up on the fact that he was close to uncovering something about Stark that was desperately trying to stay hidden.

And like any secret, he knew that the only thing you got when digging up the past was dirty.

'While every human being has a capacity for love, its realisation is one of the most difficult achievements.'
Erich Fromm

18

23:18

Obadiah turned off the engine outside the cottage and leaned back into the seat.

The silence around him seemed almost prescient, a pulsing reminder of what had just occurred and what he knew was to come.

Nature doesn't recognise good and evil...

He remembered the words; he'd said them to Franklin the day of the interview. That, someone, was trying to send him a message was apparent.

What the message was he hadn't yet figured out.

That they'd used Eva to do so, a mistake.

He breathed deeply, quelling the rage within him. He couldn't allow himself to lose focus as to why he had driven here. The compulsion he'd felt to keep her safe was powerful, driven by feelings he still didn't understand. Yet he knew whoever had come for Eva would come for Ellie.

And that he would not allow.

Obadiah climbed from the car and gently closed the door. Leaning against the roof, he gazed up at the ecliptic, noting the full moon in its eerie glow. It was a harsh reminder of his current place in the universe; cloven and powerless. He forced himself to think when all he wanted to do was close himself off from everything around him.

What had happened to Eva shouldn't matter to him, yet he couldn't shake his sense of righteous indignation. Seeing her face flash before his eyes, Obadiah realised they'd been closed. Forcing them open he shook the image away, scooped up Ellie from the back seat and placed her on his shoulder.

She stirred slightly when he knocked on the front door, the sound of footsteps approaching from the other side a few minutes later.

"Obi?" Mark Thorne's voice was laced with concern at the late hour visit.

"Can we come in?" he asked flatly.

"Of course you can," Mark replied, opening the door to allow them passage.

Obadiah moved into the living room and placed Ellie gently on the settee. He stared at her for a few moments before turning away and standing by the window.

"What's happened?" Mark asked from the living room doorway as he tightened his dressing gown belt.

Obadiah remained silent, turning to look at the picture on the mantelpiece he had seen the last time he'd here before everything had reset. Eva and him enjoying a moment frozen in time.

A moment he still had no recollection of.

He felt a weight on his chest as though underwater, the recollection of her voice and touch pressed against his memory as though trying to force their way to freedom.

Mark moved to his side, gently touching his arm. "Obi, are you okay?"

In an instant, Obadiah's hand was around his throat, slowly squeezing his windpipe. Mark grabbed at him, trying to free himself, eyes wide with fear and panic. The sensation of someone's life being gradually extinguished and their accompanying high-pitched wheeze washed over Obadiah like cleansing water, reminding him of a time when he was the apex predator, and people were merely cattle for his pleasure.

Eva's body, cold and silent on the bed, strobed through his mind, her killer's hands around her throat, her violation harsh and brutal.

As he felt Mark's energy bleeding away, he momentarily felt ashamed and relaxed his grip. Mark fell to the floor, his stridor becoming less laboured. Obadiah glanced over at Ellie, and satisfied she was undisturbed turned calmly back to the window as though nothing had happened.

"What the fuck!" Mark exclaimed, massaging his neck. "What's got into you?"

"Eva's dead," Obadiah stated coldly.

"What?"

He turned to face him, his expression causing Mark to take a few steps backwards. "She's dead… murdered sometime tonight."

Mark spluttered with laughter at the matter-of-fact delivery. "You're joking?"

"She's lying on the bed, her throat cut."

Mark stumbled and fell into the chair behind him. "What do you mean, her throat cut? You're not funny, mate. Why would someone have killed Eva?"

"To get to me," Obadiah acknowledged. "I seem to have brought something down on the people around me. Ironic really, given that once upon a time it would have been me… being played at your own game is distinctly un-amusing."

"Get to you for what?" Mark sprang up from the seat, his hands shaking as he moved for the door. "You're fuckin' delusional, mate. I'm going to the house."

Obadiah was in front of his host before he had a chance to open the door, his hand firmly grabbing the handle. "I wouldn't do that. Not unless you want to be implicated in something particularly unpleasant."

He stared at Obadiah as though trying to assess the reality of the situation before shaking his head and sitting back down.

Obadiah sat on the edge of the settee beside Ellie, his hands clasped together and resting on his knees as though about to pray.

"Someone broke into the house and murdered her to get to me. Who, I don't know, but the message was unambiguous."

"Which was?" Mark asked despondently.

"That I can't care about something without losing it. It's punishment, you see. For the things, I've done. Eva saw someone she believed me to be, maybe the man I could have been, but not the man I am."

"You're not making any sense."

Obadiah continued without elaborating. "Have you ever seen a dead body? The face swells in a matter of hours after death, the body bloating as it fills with gas. They tend to take on the appearance of over-ripe fruit, the skin taut yet at the same time withered, mottled. There's an accompanying smell, of course, but this occurs later, perhaps three or four hours later. And then, there are the eyes. Often they take on the last expression the person had, peaceful or horrific depending on the circumstances. They can be discoloured, burst blood vessels and so on, but usually take on a milky appearance, post-mortem cataracts obscuring any warmth they once held.

"Eva isn't at that stage quite yet, but she will be soon, and therefore if you wish to remember her as she was, you will stay away from the house."

Obadiah took a deep breath and moved back towards the window. He noted the look of surprise on Mark's face as the phone rang, a call at this time obviously unusual.

His surprised expression turned to unease as he answered it and then handed the phone to him.

"It's for you," he said, puzzled.

Obadiah glanced at Ellie, watching her stir slightly before putting the phone to his ear only to hear a tut of disapproval.

"You've been a naughty boy."

"Tommy," Obadiah announced. "I didn't speak to you again after I'd moved to America and since my execution, I've spoken to you twice in the space of an evening. How did you know I was here?"

Tommy chuckled under his breath. "I know, almost prescient, isn't it?"

"It is," Obadiah agreed. "which also means you know I'm going to kill you for this."

His hands were clenched so tightly he could feel his nails cutting into his palm.

"You haven't learnt anything, have you?" Tommy said with disapproval. "But you'll figure it out soon enough. I wish I could be there to see it when you do... your big brain finally slotting all the pieces into place. Your apotheosis will be something to behold. But you're obviously not quite there yet."

Obadiah ignored his monologue. "So, come on then, fill me in."

"Obadiah, I can't do that," Tommy mocked. "Besides, I don't really need to. You've always known what this is all about, your brain just hasn't quite caught up."

"I gather this is all part of the grand plan you were regaling me with to make me suffer. You need to do better."

"Of course I don't," Tommy said gleefully. "The intention behind it has already been set in motion. Did you really think that you could do all the things you've done and not be punished?"

"Isn't that what Death Row's for?"

"Theoretically, yes. But for some people, it's just not enough. There's no return to balance after your actions. This, however, may come close. You just need a little more of a push to make you start to see."

"See what?"

Tommy laughed. "You'll see."

Obadiah clenched the phone tighter in his hand. "When I find you…"

"You'll what? I'm already dead dumb arse. You're not paying attention, and it's getting a little irritating. None of this is my doing, nor anyone else's… it's yours. It's all yours."

"I didn't touch her."

Tommy tutted again. "Oh Obi, for someone with an I.Q as high as yours, you're fuckin' thick mate. But don't worry, you don't have long to wait. Once Ellie is taken care of…"

"You won't get anywhere near her," Obadiah interrupted.

"Oh, I believe you. I just want you to know it won't make any difference. There's nowhere you can go where you won't be found. You can't hide from yourself, Tally Man."

Obadiah placed the phone back in its cradle, ending the conversation without a reply.

As he moved back towards Ellie, Mark intercepted him. "What the fuck is going on?"

He knelt before Ellie, gently stroking her hair. She stirred at his touch and mumbled something incomprehensible but didn't wake. He paused for a moment, staring at her intently as though trying to memorise her face.

"I have to keep her safe," Obadiah said softly under his breath.

Sighing, Mark shook his head. "Obi, I don't understand. Who the fuck was that? You come in here in the middle of the night with your daughter, tell me Eva's dead, give me no explanation as to what's going on… Eva was right, you are getting worse. Whatever is going on in your head, it's making you ill, mate. Don't you see?"

"I see perfectly, but I have to keep her safe," he repeated, his voice still a whisper.

"Safe from what?"

"From me," Obadiah replied, his tone flat and emotionless.

He lifted Ellie gently from the settee and moved towards the stairs, stopping to look at Mark with a silent question about where to take her.

"You can put her in the spare room, top, on the left."

Obadiah nodded and climbed the stairs. He placed Ellie on the blue duvet and covered her with a blanket. She drew her knees up in a foetal position and turned over, pulling Snoopy closer to her breast.

He sat down beside her in the darkness, his stomach beginning to heave at the thought of someone hurting her.

He knew they would come - whether it be Tommy or a stranger, someone would come and try to take her. Obadiah would be ready. Whatever the reason was for his being here, it had all begun to spiral apart, something Obadiah now suspected had been the intention all along.

He'd arrived here a monster, but had discovered a man hiding in plain sight. Eva and Ellie had loved him, trusted him, cared about him. He'd been allowed to feel, for the briefest moment, something he never thought possible; hope.

But the man had gone, leaving behind only the monster.

A monster forced into being once more.

Damn them for making me care.

Obadiah stood and gently tucked the hair on Ellie's forehead behind her ear.

"Thank you," he whispered in her ear before moving out of the bedroom and down the stairs.

Mark was standing in the space Obadiah had previously occupied. He turned as Obadiah entered the room.

"So, what happens now?" he asked.

"Now, we wait."

Dr. John Franklin, BS.c. (HONS), PH.D. M.A., M.CLIN, PSYCH. A.F.Ps.S.I.

Subject: Stark, Obadiah James (a.k.a. The Tally Man) cont.

Victim history continued: The discovery of Katherine Keld's body in Ardfert caused outrage across Ireland the likes of which would not been seen until Gerald Barry murdered Manuela Riedo in Galway City in 2007.

At the behest of the Gardaí the FBI sent a liaison to assist in the search for Katherine. Alan Dark, a thirty-four year-old profiler from the Louisiana field office, had been involved in the search for the subject ever since the murder of Tammy Porto in 1989 and was believed to be the most knowledgeable agent in regards to Obadiah Stark.

Following Stark's arrest in 2003, the offender profile created by Dark was found to have been a fairly accurate description of not only his physical appearance, but also motivation and personal history. This profile however brought Dark a great deal of criticism due to the fact that, whilst precise, it had ultimately not helped in his capture.

Yet regardless of Dark and the Gardaí's best efforts, the body of thirty-two year-old Wendy Dutton was found in Waterford on the South East coast of Ireland in October 1994.

Located in one of the oldest quarters of the city known as the Viking Triangle, her body was discovered with the hands bound and throat cut: once again the wound had been so deep, it had almost severed her spinal column. Following this murder, the subject's pattern abruptly changed, with the only murder in 1995 being that of Ruth Kipling in County Clare.

Excerpt taken from interview with Obadiah Stark (dated 15th April 2010):

"I remembered County Clare from when I was a boy in Ireland, so when I picked her up, I felt slightly sentimental about being back there. Indulgent I grant you, but it seemed almost prophetic. I was initially going to just throw her off the Cliffs of Moher, but then I thought it seemed a bit of a waste. Why be back home and hide my work? I'd gone there to show my immigrant relations just how I had taken control of my own destiny and carved a little niche for myself in the world... no pun intended."

The subject did not kill again until two years later, when the body of Niamh Kelly was found in March 1997 in Kerry.

She had been stabbed in the head thirty-nine times. When questioned, Stark announced that *"... Stano stabbed Toni Van Haddocks thirty-eight times, so I figured, why not go for thirty-nine?"*

The reason for the subject's lengthy periods of time between crimes seemed to indicate that he was becoming cautious, in spite of the fact the Gardaí had very few leads at this time.

The local press were vitriolic in their anger at the apparent slow-moving nature of the case and the fact that the authorities appeared to be no closer to identifying and arresting a suspect.

Though Stark had no regular job during this time period, he was found to have moved around the country, holding positions in various establishments ranging from public houses to voluntary services. These occupations had allowed the subject to once again be in a prime position to both identify and meet young women whose deaths could satisfy his desire to kill.

Excerpt taken from interview with Obadiah Stark (dated 15th April 2010):

"I know who and what I am... what I have done defies belief for some and cannot be quantified by others. It isn't for them to understand why I did the things I did, it's only for them to accept that there was a reason behind it all. You asked me earlier if I received any sexual gratification from my crimes? Of course I did. Until you've done the things I've done, you can only imagine the raw energy you feel from being in control of another's life. How could you not be turned on by that? But just because it aroused me, doesn't mean I wanted any reciprocity from them. I managed fine in that department, thank you very much.

"I find women attractive and have had many relationships with women, sexual and otherwise that haven't ended in their deaths. I don't need to sexually dominate and embarrass them to feel like a man, that isn't true power nor is it a display of greatness... anyone can take whatever they want from a woman. But taking their life, taking the very essence of what makes them who they are... now that's power without equal."

'Doubt, the essential preliminary of all improvement and discovery, must accompany the stages of man's onward progress. The facility of doubting and questioning, without which those of comparison and judgment would be useless, is itself a divine prerogative of the reason."

Albert Pike

19

OCTOBER 4TH

08:15

Fenit (*An Fhianait*)
County Kerry, Ireland

ALTRUISM AND COMPASSION ARE INEXPLICABLY LINKED TO ONE another in an oddly subjective way.

Viewed as part of a larger picture, compassion from someone who had never been altruistic in their life could lend itself to the question of whether the individual was genuine.

On the other hand, continued and sustained altruistic acts without any semblance of understanding as to the reasons behind them and what they mean to the recipient, could be seen as motivated by a naïve duty to the right thing.

Being altruistic is seen as the defining characteristic of many charities and organisations all over the world run by people who believe their desires and wants are secondary to others, be it animal or human.

To commit an act of kindness knowing that no one will ever know it was your actions which saved them, made them perform better or gave them something they'd always wanted, is hard.

The motivation behind the act can be contentious, even ambiguous in nature, but ultimately they'll be motivated by compassion. And it is that compassion that ends up forming the structure upon which altruistic acts are built.

This structure must be maintained and cared for as with any structure. For if left alone, it can become weathered and weakened, leading to it becoming less than it was.

If this were to occur, what began as a selfless act can soon become motivated purely by a personal motivation, hidden within an act of trying to do the right thing.

———

JOE ROLLED ONTO HIS BACK AND STARED AT THE CEILING, uncertain what had woken him. He hadn't felt Vicky get out of bed and nor heard her leave, so he put it down to his internal alarm clock.

The oppressive, musky smell of sex still hung in the air. Joe smiled, remembering how Vicky's enthusiasm had taken him by surprise. His assumption had been her well-educated, buttoned-up demeanour would have inhibited her, despite her flirting with him the other night. On the contrary, she had been extremely adventurous, making their spontaneous night together memorable.

Climbing out of bed, Joe pulled on a t-shirt and shorts and headed for the kitchen. He flicked the switch on the kettle, spotting the note which stood against the bread bin. Leaning back against the counter, he unfolded it.

JOE, SORRY I HAD TO DISAPPEAR. REALLY ENJOYED LAST NIGHT. WILL SEE YOU LATER. VICK X

The kettle clicked off. He made himself a cup of coffee and sat down on the settee, the note still in his hand. After everything that had happened yesterday, the night had undoubtedly ended better than it had begun. Joe found himself smiling as he realised he could still smell her on him, provoking his body slightly. He only hoped it wouldn't have too much of an effect on their work relationship. After all, he still had a book to finish and a few mysteries to solve, one of which included The Brethren.

His mind kept drifting back to her expression when he'd mentioned them. Her face had momentarily betrayed she'd either heard of the group or knew more than she'd been willing to share.

His gut told him The Brethren were significant.

Draining his cup, Joe placed it on the kitchen bench and headed upstairs to shower and change. He checked his bruised face in the mirror before heading back downstairs. He quickly spread some peanut butter on a slice of toast, locked the front door and made his way to the car.

Sitting there eating with the engine idling, Joe considered his options. Last night he'd wanted to start searching for anything on the man who'd attacked him. This morning he wanted to start an earnest search for information on The Brethren.

As he headed off the drive, Joe felt his skin momentarily chill at his suspicion that one investigation would lead into the other.

———

THE DRIVE TO WORK WAS REFRESHINGLY UNEVENTFUL.

Joe belligerently parked his car in the same spot where he'd been attacked and headed into the office, nodding knowingly at Paul as he passed by security. He felt a few intrusive gazes in his direction as people around the office noticed his face, their conspiratorial whispers floating through the air as they wondered who had beaten him up and why.

He imagined a few of them wished they'd been the ones to do it.

Dropping his bag on his chair, he grabbed his second cup of coffee of the morning and headed over to Alison's desk. He knew she'd know something about The Brethren, given that she had a proclivity for knowing something about everything. That was why her entertainment section of the paper was always so up to date; she seemed to always be in the loop for relevant news.

"Good morning gorgeous. How are you this morning?" he asked as he flopped into her chair.

"What do you want, Joe?" she replied with a courteous smile which rapidly disappeared when she saw his face. "Jesus, what happened to you?"

"It happened when I was changing a tyre."

"With what, your face?"

"Cute," Joe replied. "But sidestepping that for a moment, what do know about The Brethren?"

"The Brethren?" Alison repeated. "You're usually pursuing something a little more insidious than goodwill organisations."

"Is that what they are? Fighting for truth, justice... that sort of thing?"

"You could say that," she responded cheerfully. "I think the Stark case was their biggest, certainly in regards of the publicity it got them. They had an office in Kerry a few years ago," she replied, moving round to the photocopier behind him. "But now I think they work out of Dublin. They gained a lot of funding from the Government which gave them the opportunity to expand. Bigger offices and all that."

Joe frowned. "So, why had I never heard of them until a few days ago?"

"Been the victim of injustice recently?" Alison asked sarcastically.

"Aside from you turning down my offer of a date? No... fair point."

"I know a few people who've used them before," Alison continued. "Spoke really highly of them."

Joe looked troubled. "I know more about Obadiah Stark than anyone in this place, and I had no idea they existed."

"Because you know so many people whose lives have been affected by a serial killer?"

"I do at the moment," Joe said wryly.

Alison turned and smiled at him. "They deal with abuse cases, sex crimes, that sort of thing. They aren't a legal company, so much as a group of people who offer support to those who feel the legal system didn't give them what they thought they deserved."

Joe sighed. "I feel a little out of the loop. All the work I've been doing and this falls out of the blue into my investigation."

"You've actually never told me what it is you're working on?" Alison said.

"Let's just say my work on Obadiah for the book has opened up other avenues of investigation I hadn't considered, which include being beaten up," Joe acknowledged. "This 'Brethren' have only been mentioned a couple of times, but the circumstances and reactions have been... unusual. I guess I'm a little disappointed that I might have missed something important not being aware of them."

Alison turned away from the photocopier and moved to sit on the edge of her desk. "To be fair, you've only ever been looking at the case from a criminal perspective. Don't take this the wrong way Joe, but before all the work you've been doing for your book, you were never really that concerned about altruism, only the truth. You always nail the truth aspect. But sometimes a little justice feels good too. And besides, if investigating them has resulted in you looking like Rocky Balboa's punch bag, maybe you're overstepping an invisible line in the sand."

"Possibly," he conceded knowingly. "You respect them?"

"They do noble work," she replied, touching his arm protectively. "Just be certain about whatever it is you're considering..."

"I'll be tactful as always," Joe interrupted, spinning playfully in her chair before standing up.

He walked back to his desk and logged into Google's Yellow Pages for The Brethren's number, the advertisement and slogan appearing seconds later alongside a large picture of the CEO of the company identified as Gideon Archard.

When justice fails, we will succeed

Grabbing a pen from his desk and chewing on it thoughtfully, Joe gazed out at the muted office as he ruminated on the pros and cons of being so blatant in his curiosity. It was out of character for him to use such an intrusive tactic during an investigation, but part of him was becoming frustrated with the mysteries stacking up around Obadiah Stark.

Retyping the Brethren's name into Google, he clicked on the first link that took him to their official webpage, noting the grandstanding slogan emblazoned across the top of the screen. Returning to the results page, he accessed a link further down which took him to some customer reviews.

One detailed a sexual abuse case which had been thrown out of court for lack of evidence, with a girl named 'Haley', describing how they'd helped her secure a law firm whose investigation had subsequently led to the offender receiving eighteen years. Another covered a hit and run where the driver had received, what the victim's family had considered, a lenient sentence. The Brethren had apparently lobbied the Government for a review of the case, resulting in the driver being retried and prosecuted.

Further comments all detailed success stories of the company and how they were paragons of virtue when it came to justice for the underdog.

Joe flicked through the pages of hits, finding it hard to

believe that a company he'd never heard of could have so little negative press about them. There were plenty of testimonials and platitudes regarding their almost philanthropic work in regards to the justice system, but nothing at all suggesting they were anything other than perfect.

No company so big and powerful could be that clean unless they had one hell of a PR representative.

Mel Gibson could have done worse than to hire them. He got shafted every step of the way, Joe thought.

Gingerly, he flicked down the links, scanning the various headlines and statements: BRETHREN SCORE ANOTHER LEGAL WIN FOR INJUSTICE... FAMILIES OF MURDER VICTIMS PRAISE BRETHREN FOR VERDICT... ARCHARD POSSIBILITY FOR HUMANITARIAN AWARD... FAMILIES OF TALLY MAN VICTIMS SEEN OUTSIDE BRETHREN OFFICE.

Clicking on the last link, Joe read with curiosity about how some of Stark's victims' relatives had been discussing in an interview how they wished to engage The Brethren regarding some sort of recompense for their suffering. It went on to describe their feelings on the death penalty and how Stark's punishment had been quick, whereas theirs was never-ending.

He once again found himself caught off-guard by a discussion of The Brethren and their involvement in criminal justice. He had thought he knew every facet and fact surrounding Stark and his murders yet had never once caught wind of the fact that the relatives had been soliciting such attention. His arrogant assumption concerning his knowledge of Obadiah's crimes was diminishing rapidly.

Joe pinched the bridge of his nose and sighed. He was about to close down the browser when his attention was captured by a link reading 'BRETHREN EMPLOYEE CLAIMS SMEAR CAMPAIGN AGAINST HIM.'

The link took him to the front cover of a newspaper with the headline black and bold across the top. The photograph beneath showed an earnest-looking, middle-aged man who was sitting in what looked like a living room. The article beneath detailed how the man, identified as Lewis Dunwall, had been in their employ for eight years only to find himself dismissed when he'd accused them of engaging in questionable ethical practices. Though Dunwall refused to state in the interview what they'd done precisely, he alluded to their altruistic nature not being entirely genuine and that they sometimes achieved results for their clients in a manner that contradicted the very notion of what people would consider justice. The article ended with details regarding an out-of-court settlement for an undisclosed sum of money.

Joe printed off the page and scribbled Dunwall's name on a piece of paper before briskly walking over to Ciaran's office. He knocked and entered without waiting to be invited.

"Just come right in," Ciaran stated with irritation. "Shouldn't you be at home resting?"

"I haven't got time for that," Joe replied curtly. "I was wondering if you remember anything about this?"

He placed the printout on the desk. Ciaran looked down to the section Joe was pointing to and scanned it quickly. "Why? What's this about?"

"Would you just tell me if you remember anything about it?"

Ciaran raised his eyebrows in response to Joe's insolent tone.

"Okay, I'm going to assume that your attitude is down to you having the remnants of a concussion, but aside from that, yes I remember it. The guy was employed by The Brethren, was sacked for a reason known only to them and the next thing he starts spouting off to anyone who'll listen that the company occasionally gets results for its clients by less than above-board means. What more do you want to know? He was just pissed at being fired and had a vendetta against them."

Joe frowned. "Why didn't they try to sue him for libel? Further down it says they settled out of court. Isn't that a little funny for such a big company, whom I've never heard of, by the way, to do? Paying him off smacks a little of buying his silence rather than recompensing him for lost earnings don't you think?"

"I try not to overthink when it comes to you, Joe," Ciaran said exasperatedly. "What are you angling for now? What has any of this got to do with Stark or your book? I've given you a lot of latitude with this project of yours. Don't try my patience, which is already fuckin' wafer thin at this moment in time."

"I think it has everything to do with Stark, I'm just not sure how."

"And you think this because…?" he asked, trying hard to contain his temper. "If you say a hunch you're fired."

Joe paused thoughtfully. "There are discrepancies in the log regarding the transfer of Stark's body, the coroner was cagey and evasive, to say the least, Sabitch virtually threatened me when I went to see him and Stamford was the one who set me on this path in the first place with his conspiracy theory about Stark's execution being… whatever the fuck it was supposed to be. The only thing connecting any of this randomness together seems to be The Brethren. They have something in common with the victim's families, they have something in common with the prison. Jesus, Ciaran, someone tried to kill me last night virtually right outside your fuckin' office window. Why would someone bother to do that if I wasn't getting close to something connecting all this? Even you have to admit it stinks just a little."

"Dunwall lives out past Leixlip," Ciaran replied with a sigh. "At least he did after all of this." He waved the printout in the air. "Go speak to him and see what he has to say, but be careful. He said he had proof about The Brethren being into something dodgy, but no one ever saw it as far as I know. If there was anything, they probably took it in exchange for the money he received."

Ciaran moved around his desk and sat on the edge of it, his look becoming concerned. "The Brethren are powerful, Joe. How you claim to have never heard of them, I have no idea, but that aside, be damn certain wherever you go with this that it's one hundred per cent reliable. I'll be behind you every step of the way, as long as you're right."

Joe nodded gently. "I'll be careful. My face can only take so much."

As he headed out of the office and back to his desk, he suddenly felt as though he was about to open Pandora's Box.

Once opened, if he found something, would he ever be able to push everything back in again?

'The secret is not to give up hope. It's very hard not to because if you're really doing something worthwhile I think you will be pushed to the brink of hopelessness before you come through the other side.'
George Lucas

20

03:48

Obadiah sat motionless on the floor outside the room where Ellie was sleeping, pricking the knife tip methodically into the end of his fingers.

He'd spent the last few hours quietly bubbling with suppressed rage at Tommy's phone call. The threat to Ellie apparent, he wanted to understand why he cared so much about what happened to her.

Searching his heart in an attempt to locate some trace of compassion that might be lingering in a dark recess had yielded what he thought was the tiniest vestige of hope, naked and shivering somewhere in the void of his mind.

He knew it had been forced there by Eva and Ellie. Diminished with his wife's death, it existed nevertheless. But Obadiah knew compassion and hope were two separate things.

The hope he still clung onto was driven by the uncertainty which had followed him here, the uncertainty that somewhere in his soul he had always wanted to be loved. And that hope which remained, however flickering, was something he intended to hold onto with every fibre of his being.

Compassion, on the other hand, that active desire to alleviate someone else's suffering, was anathema to his soul. Maybe it had shone momentarily in the intimate moment he'd shared with Eva, but if so, her death had driven it away.

All that now remained was Obadiah Stark.

The Tally Man.

The hush engulfing the house seemed a pending epoch. It unnerved Obadiah, not in a fearful way, but like kismet, as if the reason behind all that had happened was about to be revealed.

Since waking here, he'd suspected someone was playing a game with him. Whether God or some other sentient being, he didn't know. It didn't matter.

Obadiah Stark was no one's puppet.

Mark's presence at the bottom of the stairs broke his reverie.

"Something's not right," Mark said nervously. "The lights have just gone out in the street."

Obadiah glanced back at Ellie before rising to his feet and walking down the stairs.

"Grab Ellie and take her somewhere, anywhere. If anyone tries to stop you who isn't me, kill them."

He held the knife out, handle first.

Mark looked at it, then at Obadiah, shook his head and pushed it back towards him. "What the fuck, I'm not killing anyone!"

"You will if anyone tries to take her," Obadiah replied, gently pushing the knife back. "Nothing can happen to her. I need your help, Mark. You have no idea how difficult saying that is, but I do. You have to protect her for me if I fail."

"Fail what?"

"Killing them."

"Who?"

"The people about to come for me… and for her."

Mark sunk slowly to the floor, sad bewilderment caressing

his face. "Jesus, Obi. What the fuck have you got me into? You're insane."

Obadiah stared at him, thinking that where once he would have been disgusted at such a pathetic display, he felt only pity.

"You have no idea," he snorted in reply. "Now stand up, get Ellie and go. Somewhere safe, you understand?"

Mark looked up at Obadiah, resignation replacing bewilderment.

"I understand."

The sound of glass breaking downstairs forced Obadiah to the top of the stairs.

"Go," he barked. "Out the window in her room and onto the garage. NOW!"

He waited until he heard Mark whispering to Ellie that they had to go on an adventure as he lifted her from the bed before slowly descending the stairs.

Dizziness came upon him suddenly, broadsiding him across the head. Grabbing hold of the bannister Obadiah couldn't stop himself from falling back onto the stairs. He tried desperately to pull himself up, wondering if someone would use this opportunity while he was incapacitated to kill him.

Lying back down, the pain began to arch across his back accompanied by voices all around him. The familiar tearing sensation that was his tattooed tally marks being slowly re-etched onto his skin consumed him. Multiple layers of pain in different areas of his back slithered their way across his spine while voices echoed around him. Their overlapping nature made it hard for him to focus, auditory and bodily sensations unrelenting and torturous.

The voices jabbered endlessly, anxious and intense, incomprehensible syntax yielding emotion rather than intent. He felt as though he were suddenly caught in a physical and mental web.

Helpless.

He wondered if his being here was merely a delusion trying to harbour meaning for himself, opaque as it was. Perhaps it was his mind's way of injecting a determinate meaning into perplexity.

Still, in pain, he pulled himself up using the bannister again as support. The figure before him seemed to appear from nowhere. He instinctively spun around, smashing his elbow into the stranger's temple before falling backwards, off balance. Using his momentum, he pushed both of them off the stairs, hearing a gasp of expelled air as his fall was broken by his attacker.

Obadiah rolled off to the side, his forearm connecting with the stranger's head. Satisfied the figure was incapacitated and smiling at the wet, guttural sound of someone choking on their own blood, he rose to his knees and stood slowly. The dizziness returned immediately, but the pain seemed to have receded, probably from adrenaline.

He paused to listen for the voices, but heard only the figure next to him, gurgling and gasping for air. Irritated, Obadiah knelt back down and grabbed his head, ramming it repeatedly into the floor until he felt the body go in his hands. Stimulating memories of the power he'd once held flooded his mind, making his body ache.

A shadow flashed up ahead, forcing Obadiah toward the kitchen. He grabbed another knife from the holder and held it by his leg. The arm that locked around his neck caught him momentarily off guard. Spinning around quickly, Obadiah broke the hold he was in and kicked the attacker's legs out from beneath him. Kneeling on his spine and pulling his head back violently by the jaw, Obadiah moved the knife quickly from side to side before the man realised what was happening. Arterial spray pirouetted across the walls as the man panicked, trying to buck Obadiah off.

Blood soaked into the carpet as Obadiah climbed off him and watched the body become limp.

Wiping the knife blade against his trousers, he moved to the front door and looked through the window. The street was deserted, but he knew the two men he'd just killed were only an opening salvo. Tommy was not going to stop whatever he'd started tonight. Why his former friend had taken this role, Obadiah had no idea.

But everything occurring tonight was a message, sent via Tommy, to ensure it was received loud and clear.

As he headed into the living room, shadows falling across the floor made it hard for Obadiah to initially spot the third man standing in the corner. The figure moved forward quickly, blocking Obadiah's knife slash and countering it with an elbow to his temple. Stunned by the blow, the man spun around and followed up with the back of his fist, sending Obadiah sprawling across the floor. He sprang to his feet, ready for a second assault. Yet the man just stood, bathed in the shadows.

Waiting.

"Well, come on then. Isn't this what you want, a shot at the big time?"

The man remained still, his face hidden yet his stance familiar. Obadiah moved towards him slowly before stopping as laughter began to echo around him.

"Jesus Christ, Obi. You have no idea how to protect someone, do you? 'Out the window!' What kinda silly bastard suggests that as an escape plan?" Tommy appeared as though the darkness were melting around him. "If you could protect someone as well as you can kill, they might have stood a chance, but as it is, nul point."

"Where is she?" Obadiah demanded.

"Who? Your little Eleanor? She's... somewhere. Your mate Mark, on the other hand, I wish I could tell you he was safe and in one piece."

"What have you done?" Obadiah asked softly, his eyes glowing eerily in the moonlight.

Tommy gestured behind him. Another figure entered the room holding Mark's severed head. The expression on his face one of surprise, eyes wide and staring.

"I did ask him nicely for the girl, but he was absolute in his resolve that she wasn't to come to any harm. Your influence I fear. You do have a way of scaring the shite out of people. I think he was more terrified of what you would do to him if he let anything happen to her. Guess he worried about the wrong person, eh?"

Obadiah sensed someone behind him, their presence again familiar, the face obscured. "Why, Tommy? What do you hope to accomplish with all this?"

Tommy moved to the chair in front of Obadiah and sat down. "To make manifest what we discussed earlier. When I said your suffering had already begun, it wasn't hyperbole. If you take a moment to think about it, about why you're here, it will start to become clear. If you think this is me doing all of this, it isn't. It's you. You created misery and torment in your life, committed unspeakable acts and brushed them off as though you had lint on your jacket. Nature doesn't recognise good and evil, only balance. Weren't those your very words at your trial? Your way of explaining yourself to all those family members whose loved ones you'd taken. Profound, yes. Adequate... not by a long shot, sunshine.

"But you were right... nature does require balance. And this will be yours. Think of me as your scales of justice, one hand holding your past and the other your future, both patiently waiting to see what will tip them one way or the other. Tick-tock, Tally Man."

Obadiah clenched the knife tightly in his hand, subtly registering the position of the other figures in the room. "I'm obviously a little slow here, Tommy. You think I don't know this is all a little Twilight Zone? You're not executed, awake to find yourself in your childhood town, kill a bunch of people and have everything reset itself the next day without realising something is a little 'off' about the whole thing. Add to the mix I ended up with a wife, child and an alleged brain tumour, and you see that the afterlife is one fucked up place."

Tommy threw his head back in an exaggerated fashion and laughed. "Afterlife? That's what you think this is? Ah, bless ya, Obi. That genius level I.Q of yours is obviously on vacation."

"So, tell me what this is then?"

"I don't have to, you already know. You've just been so caught up in your 'save the cheerleader, save the world' complex, you've missed the small print. By the way, hearing voices yet? Sound so clear don't they? Like they're in the next room or something."

Obadiah made his move, darting across the room. He stopped just short of Tommy's position as he saw Ellie being brought in through the kitchen door. His anger was innately replaced by joy at seeing her safe.

"Daddy," she called out, her voice trembling with fear and relief at seeing him.

The words that left his mouth seemed natural where once they would have felt alien. "It's okay, baby. Don't worry… everything will be okay."

"That's right, Obi," Tommy taunted as he rose from the chair and moved behind her, stroking her hair. "Lie to her like you lied to all those other girls. Tell her she'll be safe, that she has nothing to worry about."

Obadiah moved a step closer to them both, the man behind Tommy who had brought Ellie in taking a step back as though afraid.

"Ah, ah, Tally Man." Tommy lowered his hand to the little girl's neck, caressing it gently. "I'd snap it before you got anywhere near me. Think very carefully about your next move. Can't you sense it, Obi? The pieces falling into place, the resolution beginning to set in? Your apotheosis is almost upon you."

"You're insane."

Tommy began to laugh hysterically. "Hello, this is the pot calling the kettle... you're black!"

Ellie was crying uncontrollably, both at the situation and the raw emotion flowing from the people in the room.

Obadiah could feel it. Death was coming, the sensation as familiar to him as his own face.

The voices began again, imperceptibly at first and then slowly growing louder. Obadiah shook his head, trying to remain focused. All around him he could hear conversations, laughter, anger, mixed together in a cacophony of sound. Over the top of it was Tommy's voice, jocular, teasing.

"You look a little peaky there, mate. Can I get you anything?"

Obadiah's vision began to blur at the constant bombardment of sounds slamming through his head. He wobbled backwards but managed to steady himself, changing his position, so he was facing them all.

"Let her go,' he demanded, shaking his head to clear it. "This has nothing to do with her. Neither did Eva. You killed her just to send me a message, didn't you? Fine, I get it, I have to be punished. So punish me, but leave her out of it."

"Obi, my old friend. She is your punishment... or rather losing her is"

The tip of the knife burst through her sternum, stifling her cries for Obadiah. She was silent for a moment, her eyes fixed on her father as tears ran down her cheeks.

Obadiah's face crumpled, all the voices around him seeming to be replaced by a vacuum. At the same time, he felt the burning sensation return to his back, signifying another tally being added, almost as though it had been waiting for this very moment.

Though the pain was intense it was insignificant to the

stabbing pain he felt in his chest, as though the knife had penetrated his own soul.

All the death he'd caused, the lives he'd taken, had prepared him to face his own mortality, his own execution the antithesis of that knowledge. Being here had changed nothing, always understanding his time here would eventually come to an end. But now, he felt the ultimate deprivation he'd forced upon so many others.

Before his eyes, the loss of innocence, the death of someone most vulnerable had occurred. The darkest recess of his soul held nothing compared to the emptiness now consuming his heart. Grief so sudden and yet boundless, signifying the loss of the future, of hopes and dreams, crashed into him like a tsunami.

He watched Tommy smile as he slowly pulled the knife from Ellie and let her collapse to the floor. The whole scene was in slow motion, seconds becoming minutes around him.

He found he couldn't move, the adrenaline which had powered him leeching away as though caught in the vortex that was his daughter's life-force draining away.

The voices became more intense, as though reacting in response to what had just occurred.

Tommy stepped over Ellie's tiny body and knelt in front of Obadiah, casually wiping the blade of the knife on his jacket.

"I know you won't understand these feelings you're having, how could you? You've only ever imposed them on others… never had to face them yourself. The Tally Man, capricious, cruel and resoundingly evil… in the end, seeing the truth of everything." He tapped Obadiah gently on the forehead with the knife blade. "Those voices you can hear, the ones bouncing around your head. They're not a figment of your imagination. They're real. Real in the sense that those people are talking about you right now. It's quite a journey you've been on, Obi. But every journey, though it has a first step, also has an end. And you've almost arrived at yours."

Tommy stood and signalled for the masked men to move Ellie's body. Obadiah watched as they grabbed her by the arms and dragged her into the corridor, all the time finding himself unable to move, as though the very voices around him were paralysing him.

Tommy circled around behind Obadiah, striking him hard on the back of the neck. Falling to the floor, his vision blurred, he saw the men return and stand around him in a semi-circle.

"I think it's time you looked upon the real face of evil, Obadiah. Time you saw whose been guiding you down this path all this time."

Tommy knelt behind him and pulled his head back so he couldn't avert his gaze.

One by one, the men removed their masks, their movements familiar and yet alien. It was as though he were watching someone doing an impersonation of himself.

"Say hello to darkness, Obadiah Stark."

He looked upon the men before him, their faces an exact reflection of his.

"Meet the man responsible for all of this... you."

Obadiah's scream reverberated through the house, its echo carrying high into the night.

'Discovery consists of seeing what everybody has seen and thinking what nobody has thought.'
Albert Szent-Gyorgyi

21

OCTOBER 4TH
14:36

Leixlip (*Léim an Bhradáin*)
County Kildare, Ireland

SECRETS.

Aspects of information marked by the habit of discretion. Dangerous though they can be, secrecy is often utilised to protect others from that which may cause harm or damage. Whether unavowed or esoteric, the secret can be kept dormant for the longest of time. But like anything buried, it will eventually find its way to the surface.

This is when the secret can become a something more than initially intended. Once discovered and dependent on its nature, it can often become a weapon. Held over someone or something, the secret can take on a life of its own, bidding all of those who share it into its web of unavoidable deceit and deception.

To the keeper of the secret, it can be a source of high power.

To those who wish it kept, it can become motivation like no other.

———

JOE GAZED UP AT THE HOUSE, TAKING NOTE OF THE ACCUMULATED rubbish in the front garden.

A car in the throes of being cannibalised sat on the drive, propped up on bricks. The surrounding garden was akin to a miniature jungle, overgrown hedgerows and knee-high grass. Climbing from his car and making his way through a gate hanging on one hinge, Joe considered whether he would be attacked by some feral beast hidden in the undergrowth. Making it up the path unimpeded, he knocked on the front door before turning to look around.

Beyond the wilderness that was Dunwall's garden stood The Wonderful Barn, its external flight of ninety-four steps curling round its corkscrew shape. Built to function as a grain barn, Joe had always thought it made an interesting folly on the Leixlip horizon.

He knocked on the door again and waited a few moments before opening the letterbox. He could hear a television in the background, but peering through saw nothing.

"Mr Dunwall," he shouted through the opening. "My name is Joe O'Connell. I'm a journalist with The Daily Éire. I was wondering if I could have a few minutes of your time?"

Listening intently, he heard nothing. "It concerns The Brethren."

Joe noticed the front curtain flick aside, followed by the sound of keys being turned and latches being released moments later. An unkempt, grey-haired man stared through the opening, his eyes glazed as though intoxicated.

"Can I see some I.D, please," Lewis Dunwall asked.

Joe produced his press card from his pocket and held it up. His eyes flitted between the pass and Joe's face before he seemed satisfied he was talking to the card's owner.

"So, Mr O'Connell... what do ya want?"

"I'll get right to the point, Mr Dunwall. During my

research into Obadiah Stark, I've come across The Brethren's name. One or two things don't quite add up..."

"Isn't the Stark story old news?" the man interrupted.

"Well, some new information has recently come to light, and I think you can help me with the details."

"You're the journalist. Isn't uncovering details supposed to be yer job?"

"It is. And they produced your name."

"I can't help ya," Dunwall snapped as he began to close the door.

Joe stuck his foot in the opening. "It's important. I wouldn't be here otherwise. It'll be strictly confidential, I promise."

"For every promise, there's a price to pay, Mr O'Connell," Dunwall replied, anxiously scanning the street behind Joe. "I'll give ya ten minutes," he conceded. "Then ya leave, understand?"

Joe nodded. "I understand."

Dunwall opened the door wider to allow Joe passage, his body language failing to hide contempt for the journalist. Stepping inside, his senses were immediately assaulted by a musty smell which he could only assume was coming from the books and newspapers piled high along the passage.

Glancing into one of the boxes as he passed, Joe saw references to both The Brethren and Stark on the newspapers inside. Brittle and yellow, their advertisements showed wasp-waisted women in full-skirted, calf-length dresses with gingham prints, indicative of the 1950's. Joe frowned, confused at his thinking The Brethren were a relatively modern company. He pushed the detail to the back of his mind and continued looking around him, the peeling wallpaper and signs of damp on the ceiling indicating its inhabitant had little pride in his house or its value.

As they moved towards the kitchen, Joe scanned the living

room, seeing it was in the same state of disrepair, with more boxes stacked against the surrounding walls.

Lewis Dunwall had apparently become a hoarder during his time away from the world. Joe felt sadness at seeing how one man's life had become desolate.

Ushering his unwanted guest to a seat around the small kitchen table, Dunwall sat down opposite, his twitching hands scratching at the stubble on his chin.

Joe glanced around, noticing the pots and cups piled beside the sink and takeaway boxes scattered across the kitchen bench, more evidence of the man's pathetic existence.

"So, what do ya want to know? How much they paid me fer my silence? How they discredited me after firing me? How they ruined my life and made me so afraid I daren't even step outside anymore? Whatever I tell ya is off the record... I'm not being held to anything I say."

Joe pulled his chair in towards the table. "I appreciate this must be hard for you, Mr Dunwall. But all I really need to know is a little about the events leading up to you leaving The Brethren."

"Leaving? Fired, ya mean."

Joe shrugged in acquiescence.

Dunwall dropped his head, mumbling to himself. He began to speak without making eye contact.

"I worked in the legal team. We dealt with cases as they came in, reviewed them and decided whether they qualified as suitable."

"What were the criteria for suitability?" Joe asked.

Dunwall lifted his head to stare at Joe. "Archard's criteria," he replied flatly.

Joe nodded but remained silent. "When I first joined, we would get maybe six or seven cases a week. A year later, we were taking six or seven a day. They were mostly high profile cases, but we did receive the odd small one... traffic accidents, fraud, that kind of thing. People looking for justice where they'd felt the system had let them down.

"Anyway, I remember the day the Stark case came in… files as thick as War and Peace, all from relatives who felt that Stark's death sentence hadn't been enough. Ironic isn't it, the death sentence not being enough."

Joe smiled but remained silent.

"That's what The Brethren do. They do things fer those who don't think enough was done."

"Which is what exactly?" Joe pressed.

Dunwall stood suddenly and moved towards the back door, pacing. "I don't think yer appreciate how powerful they are. They hold a lot of sway with the government, mostly because of what they offer. Yes, a lot of it is above-board, but they have another agenda beneath the public façade."

"Such as?"

Dunwall stopped pacing and looked directly at Joe. "Providing unique solutions to the perceived inequality of justice," Dunwall replied.

Joe stroked his chin thoughtfully. "And these solutions are… illegal?"

Dunwall's answer came in a hesitant, staccato reply. "They're... less than… moral."

"I'll need a little more," Joe said gently.

Dunwall hesitated. "Mr O'Connell, the last time I tried to tell this story I ended up out of a job, my pension frozen, divorced, with my house repossessed and branded a liar in the media. I mean, look around ya. I don't live in the world anymore, I just exist in it. They took everything I had away from me. Forgive me if I'm not fallin' all over ma'self to tell ya everything."

Dunwall began pacing faster, his agitation evident. "I believe in justice. I believe in the law and that just and equal punishment should be meted out to those who deserve it. I've followed everything those bastards 'ave done since I was fired, buying every newspaper, following up on every story, wanting to see how they could continue to get away with it. The justice they offer feeds on people's basic desire for revenge when wronged, but..."

"I can assure you, I treat all my contacts with the strictest confidence," Joe reassured him. "There'd be nothing linking you to anything I used."

Dunwall sat back down, his head in his hands. "It wouldn't matter," he replied with a heavy sigh. "They'd figure out it was me who'd talked soon enough. I don't think you'd even believe me if I told you what they were capable of anyway."

"Try me." Joe challenged.

Dunwall looked around in an unquiet manner, his eyes wide and fearful.

"Stark wasn't the first. They've been doing this for years. You saw the boxes, right? They're full of articles, newspapers, going all the way to the early thirties. They're not new to this game, they've just been ahead of the curve enough so that no one ever really latches on to what they do... hiding in plain sight ya might say. Sure, most of their work is mainstream stuff and always has been, but the really dark cases, the ones where people want justice for terrible things... that's where The Brethren shine. Go back, to the West Mesa murders, Lisbon Ripper, Connecticut River Valley killer... ask ya'self why these killings stopped abruptly. Go back further... Monster of Florence, Cleveland Torso Murderer... ya know better than most, serial killers don't just stop, but these did."

"You're not seriously telling me that The Brethren were involved with any of that?" Joe responded incredulously.

"They've done all of that an' more, wielding more power than ya could possibly imagine or that anyone has the right to possess. And this power was never more evident than with Obadiah Stark. Let me ask ya a question, do you think he's dead?"

"No," Joe responded flatly. "I don't know why I think that, but my investigation seems to be alluding to the fact that his execution was more a performance."

Dunwall leaned forward, his eyes displaying an intensity Joe found unnerving. "An' you'd be right to think that."

"So, where the hell is he?"

Dunwall held Joe's gaze, as though still uncertain whether to continue. "Obadiah Stark is currently being held in a Brethren-owned facility on Tearaght Island, just west of the Dingle Peninsular and has been there since 7th September following his 'execution'."

"And he's still alive?" Joe asked with palpable excitement.

"They have him in an artificially-induced coma for want of a better word. This allows them to do what they need to and what they're expected to."

"Which is?"

"Ensure he suffers."

Joe fell against the chair's backrest, staggered at what he was hearing.

"Why?"

"Because the victim's relatives wanted something done and were willing to pay handsomely for the privilege. But money doesn't spend in Hell, Mr O'Connell. The devil deals in a different coin. I keep telling ya, sometimes justice isn't enough," Dunwall insisted. "Obadiah Stark, at this very moment, is probably experiencing more pain and anguish than he ever imagined possible. But not physically... mentally. The Brethren would never lower themselves to something as crude as physical torture. What they do is far more sophisticated. Subject evil to darkness and all you will do is harden its resolve. To get to a monster like Stark, you have to give him something to believe in, someone to care for. You have to give him a heart. Only then can you tear it out."

Joe was reminded of Evans' comments.

"Some people feel they have to at least appreciate the

gravity of their actions before they die. Otherwise, true justice hasn't been achieved."

"Can you prove any of this?"

Dunwall absently looked around him, all tenacity gone from his face as though realising the consequences of what he'd done.

"I can give ya a name... someone who was involved from the start. I saw her meet Archard on many occasions. She knows about Stark, about everything."

"Who is it?"

"Carter," he replied with a sigh. "Victoria Carter."

Dr. John Franklin, BS.c. (HONS), PH.D. M.A., M.CLIN, PSYCH. A.F.Ps.S.I.

Subject: Stark, Obadiah James (a.k.a. The Tally Man) cont.

Victim history continued: Though the subject was yet to realise, his time as a serial killer was slowly coming to an end.

From 1998 until his capture in 2003, Stark murdered four more women; Philipa Mallory, Phoebe Loughrin, Patricia Duffey and Melissa Farrell. Though all matched the same *modus operandi*, each murder appeared to increase in ferocity.

At this point, Kevin O'Hagan was brought in by the Gardaí to assist in the manhunt, now the largest in Ireland's history. A former FBI profiler, unlike Dark's months earlier, O'Hagan's profile provided not only an accurate physical description, but surmised certain behavioural characteristics Dark had missed. O'Hagan theorised that Stark deliberately increased the severity of his latter four killings in the hope of being caught. Stark seemingly confirmed as much to this author during the course of the interview.

Excerpt taken from interview with Obadiah Stark (dated 15th April 2010):

"I began having a presentiment about future events. When you've done what I have for long enough, you take note of hunches and suspicions... at the end of the day, they keep you alive. I'm not suggesting I have extrasensory perception, far from it. I simply have an unquenchable desire to survive, whatever the cost. Yes, I was caught, but not because some profiler thought he understood me. I was caught because it

was my time. People believed it was because I made a mistake or that O'Hagan was smarter than me and provided some insight that enabled them to arrest me at the airport. I was caught simply because I had nothing more to prove. Twenty-seven tallies equalled twenty seven souls... I would say my legacy had been secured, wouldn't you?"

Like David Berkowitz three decades earlier, hubris was ultimately the sole cause of Stark's capture. Whereas Berkowitz had been arrested due to a parking ticket he'd received due to parking in front of a fire hydrant, suspicion was directed towards Stark following an incident in which he was arrested for a fight in a bar.

Upon his arrest, the subject was identified as having no permanent residency in the United Kingdom, having stayed under the radar for so many years through his taking 'under the counter' employment. Released on bail, no initial concerns were raised about Stark other than his being in the country illegally, however the description and sketch provide by the FBI from Sara Jayne Morgan's interview resulted in Stark's re-arrest at Dublin airport during his attempt to return to America.

Subsequent visual confirmation of his tattoo as described by Morgan finally brought an end to The Tally Man's murderous rampage across two continents and over sixteen years.

Following his trial and sentencing and despite much legal wrangling between the American and British Government as to where he should be imprisoned, the subject was incarcerated in Ireland's maximum-security prison, Absolom.

Taking inspiration from America's supermax penitentiaries such as ADX Florence and Varner Supermax, Absolom was designed to hold prisoners awaiting the death penalty, a sentence only recently introduced in Ireland shortly before Stark's arrest.

Stark made the most of his notoriety whilst in Absolom, even going as far as to offer the Gardaí assistance during their search for the Shannon River Killer in 2007. The subject refused all requests for interviews from both the media and professional psychologists until 2010, when this author had a meeting approved.

Stark gave no reason for his acquiescence, though my impression is that he simply wished to pander to his ego and ensure there was a written account of his crimes.

The subject is due to be executed on 7th September 2011.

Excerpt taken from interview with Obadiah Stark (dated 15th April 2010):

"I have known people who simply exude vulnerability. Their faces say 'I'm afraid of you'. Such people invite abuse; by expecting to be hurt they encourage it. I mean, what is one less person on the planet? All these human cattle do is go about their daily, mundane business without a single, solitary thought about others and what the impact of their actions can be. People are solipsistic by nature; they are only interested in themselves, not the well-being of others. I simply took their selfishness and turned it on them, proving that one person can exploit the shallow nature of humanity. I had the attention of the entire world, by basically doing what they already did and not giving a crap. Ironic isn't it? That they then decided I was the enemy."

'The resolution to avoid an evil is seldom framed till the evil is so far advanced as to make avoidance impossible,'
Thomas Hardy

22

OCTOBER 4TH

19:12

Tearaght Island (*An Tiarcht*)
  County Kerry, Ireland

OBADIAH HEARD A SOFT BURST OF CHILD'S LAUGHTER ECHOING IN the distance as he came to.

He didn't know how much time had passed since his confrontation with Tommy, but the room he was in appeared, defused somewhere between darkness and light, told him he was now somewhere different.

The air felt warm and musty, the smell of his own body odour suggesting that he'd been here for a while. Trying to sit up he found he could only raise himself up a few inches, his body securely bound.

He tried to speak but found his throat sore and dry, the words coming out somewhere just above a croak.

"Where am I?"

He heard no reply.

"Where the fuck am I?" Obadiah demanded, his tone stronger.

His eyes slowly focused, revealing the vast expanse he

found himself in. High ceilings ablaze with bright strip lights, the rear of the room so distant it was enveloped in darkness.

He looked down to see he was strapped to a trolley, wearing linen trousers and a shirt similar in design to the ones he'd been wearing on the day of his execution. Equipment surrounded him, some of which he recognised as infusion devices and syringe drivers, attached to him via cannulae in his brachial arteries. Some of it was less familiar, almost futuristic in its design, sleek and chrome.

"This is Hell, Obadiah," a mechanical sounding female voice announced from behind him.

"Your Hell to be more precise."

———

Fenit (An Fhianait)
County Kerry, Ireland

Joe felt bereft during the journey home.

Dunwall's revelation regarding The Brethren and Vicky's part in it had forcibly removed something from him. The extent of their actions was more significant than he could have imagined. He was left with the confusion as to why and how she fitted into the mosaic he was piecing together.

Stepping into the house Joe dropped into the nearest chair, his legs suddenly unsteady, stomach queasy. Not only did he now have to consider Vicky involved in the conspiracy surrounding Obadiah Stark, but that everything she'd told him was a lie.

When he'd started this investigation, he'd wanted to uncover details and depths which would have set his book above all others about serial killers and their motivations. Instead, he had ended up with suspicion, murder attempts and a conspiracy involving a seemingly charitable organisation and one of the most secure prisons in the world.

He rubbed his eyes and rose from the chair to make a drink. The knock at the front door came as he popped ice-cubes into the half-full glass, swirling the Jack Daniels around as he opened it.

"Hey you," Vicky said, greeting him with a smile.

"Hey," Joe acknowledged with more surprise than he would have liked.

An uncomfortable moment passed between them.

"Can I come in?" she asked.

"Sorry, of course," he replied, opening the door wider to allow her passage.

Moving into the living room she sat down, straightening the hem of her long coat beneath her. "I haven't disturbed you, have I?"

"Not at all. Was just working myself up to a mood that involved getting drunk actually. Fancy one?"

"I like your thinking," she replied with a chuckle. "That would be great, thank you."

Joe stepped into the kitchen and held up the bottle towards her. She nodded her approval. Half filling another glass, he took a deep breath and returned to the living room, handing her the drink before sitting down opposite.

"So," Joe asked as naturally as he could. "What have you been up to?"

"Not much… thinking about you mostly."

"Oh," Joe replied.

"That's all you can manage?"

'I'm sorry,' Joe responded. 'You just caught me off-guard, that's all. To be honest, I was thinking about you too."

Not actually a lie.

"That's good because I was also thinking that you need to be careful about where you're going to take your Stark theory."

Joe gave Vicky a puzzled look. "What's brought this on?"

"I'm worried about you. Last night was wonderful, Joe. But I can't help thinking you're letting all of this get to you."

She sat forward, her coat slipping open slightly allowing Joe to see she was naked underneath. "The things you were saying last night, conspiracies and cover-ups… you sounded a little crazy. So I thought you might need something to still your mind for a while."

She finished the drink in one mouthful and moved to kneel in front of him, placing the glass on the floor. Rising up, she kissed him passionately, biting his lip as she pulled away.

Joe felt himself become quickly aroused.

"Crazy?" He asked in a low tone. "I might have been a little agitated, what with someone having tried to kill me, but I'm not crazy, Vick. I didn't just fall off a turnip truck, you know. I've been doing this journalism stuff a while and trust me when I say someone is trying to cover something up about Stark's execution."

"Such as?" Vicky asked firmly, slowly undoing the belt on his jeans.

"Does it really matter? Someone doesn't try to kill you unless you're on to something, wouldn't you say?"

"Perhaps. But maybe it was just a coincidence. Wrong time, wrong place."

She began working on his shirt buttons.

"Do I look like John McClane?" Joe asked wryly. "It wasn't random… he knew my name and happened to be there to help me change a tyre that had suspiciously gone flat? Give me a break."

Vicky slowly reached into his loosened jeans and took hold of him.

"It must have been terrible for you. And that's the other reason I came, to try and take your mind off it."

She moved his right hand and placed it beneath her coat, allowing him to feel her warm body beneath.

"Please, Joe. Let it go."

"Why?"

Vicky gripped him harder, causing him to moan softly. "Because I care about you."

"No, why did you come here, Vicky?"

"To get naked with you."

"I mean here, to Ireland?"

Vicky leaned into his ear, breathing heavily as he moved his hand down between her legs. "Because you asked me for help. Why else would I have come?"

Joe moved his hand, making her moan loudly and push against him. "I think you came because you were invested in something, though why you would need The Brethren's help is beyond me."

Vicky stopped gyrating against him and dropped her head to his chest.

"Oh, Joe. Why did you have to keep digging? Let me guess, Dunwall?"

Joe pushed her back gently and cupped her face in his hands. "You know I can't tell you my source. But please try to understand it's my job. I just couldn't let it go.""

Trust me, I understand more than you know." Vicky stroked his cheek gently before reaching into her pocket. "Which is why I need to do this."

He saw the taser in her hand moments before it touched his neck, his body tensing up as he experienced one colossal cramp.

Joe rose onto his tiptoes, his arms being pulled into his body as though suddenly magnetised.

As he collapsed to the floor, Vicky knelt beside him and stroked his head, tears in her eyes.

"I'm so sorry, Joe. But it's for your own good."

She pulled the phone from her pocket and dialled a number.

"It's me. You were right, he knows... no, I've taken care of it. I'm at his house... just hurry."

She hung up and sat down beside him, placing his head gently in her lap. Tears began to well in her eyes as she stroked his hair again.

"Damn you, Joe O'Connell. Damn you."

———

TEARAGHT ISLAND (AN TIARCHT)
County Kerry, Ireland

"HOW MUCH LONGER ARE YOU GOING TO KEEP ME WAITING before someone tells me what the fuck is going on?" Obadiah insisted.

"You'll find out soon enough," the woman replied, still behind him and out of sight. Her voice sounded metallic, almost comical.

Obadiah looked around the empty, sterile expanse once again. "I assume we're waiting for something or someone?"

"In the assumption, we're waiting for someone, you are correct. Then we'll be ready to begin."

"Begin what?"

"What has been in preparation for so long, Obadiah."

He pushed against his restraints again but found there was no give. "I want to know what this is all about."

"You are in a position to demand nothing," the woman replied in a robotic tone. "I, on the other hand, am in a position to grant nothing. Therefore I suggest you calm down and wait."

He heard a phone ring behind him, followed by the woman's footsteps as she approached it. There was a slight pause before she spoke.

"Excellent." He heard the phone placed back in its cradle.

"You're in luck, Obadiah," the voice stated. "Your wait is over."

He heard a door open to his left and footsteps before two men moved into his periphery. They stood on either side of his trolley and spun it around before wheeling it back in the direction they'd just come. Obadiah closed his eyes and tried to make sense of his sudden change of circumstances.

Was this another part of his death cycle, which had started with him returning home? He needed to know what had happened to Ellie's body after Tommy had stabbed her. He needed to know what had happened to Tommy.

Maybe this was more of his games to torture him.

Moving through a large double doorway, they entered a smaller room that again held numerous pieces of equipment along either side of the walls. He was placed directly in front of a sizeable opaque window, the men who'd brought in him securing the trolley in place before moving away. Moments later he sensed someone behind him again.

"At some point are you planning to introduce yourself? You seem to have gone to a lot of effort to get me here."

Getting no reply, Obadiah heard the doors open again and was able to turn his head enough to see that the man being wheeled in next to him was still unconscious, strapped to a trolley similar to his.

The window before him slowly lost its dark tint revealing people on the other side. He saw at least three rows with a dozen chairs in each, occupied with a mixture of men, women and children.

"And this is?" Obadiah asked sternly.

"Your execution," the woman announced still out of sight. "Your actual execution, not the showcase you went through in Absolom. Tonight, Obadiah Stark is the night you die."

He pushed hard against his restraints. "Who are you?"

He realised the person who moved to stand in front of him was a woman only from the curvature of her figure accentuated by the tight white shirt and knee-length skirt she was wearing. Her face had very little in the way of feminine features, with the lower half of it below the jaw appearing to have been reconstructed. The procedure had worked in the sense that rather than an actual jaw, there was a veil of skin starting from just below her nose that rolled around to the top of her neck.

It gave her an appearance akin to a Cabbage Patch doll whose face had been melted.

In the middle of her neck was a circular, metal disc to which she placed an electrolarynx.

"You don't recognise me, do you?" The reverberation of her voice was jarring.

"Miss World?"

"A sense of humour... brave considering your circumstances. I'd forgotten how arrogant you could be. I wouldn't expect you to remember me, of course. I looked a lot prettier in 1993. Well, before you left me in a ditch on Highway 80 that is. Ringing any bells now, Tally Man?"

Obadiah stared at her, eyes unblinking. "You're the charming individual who provided the world with my travelling name. Quite inventive I have to say. Though I never expected to see you again."

"That makes two of us."

"What was the name of the firecracker again?" he continued. "Thunderking, if I'm not mistaken."

"You're not," she replied. "And for the sake of completion, my name is Sara Jayne Morgan."

Obadiah remained outwardly impassive, trying desperately to hide the feelings of confusion and loss he felt at his new circumstances.

The man who'd tried to take her life was not the man before her now. But he knew it was something he could never expect her to understand.

He wasn't sure he understood himself.

Sara had moved beside the other trolley. She opened some smelling salts and waved them under the unconscious man's nose, before standing back. His face wrinkled briefly before he came to, his expression immediately one of anxiety at his situation.

"Where am I?" he demanded loudly. "What the fuck is this?"

Sara moved in front of him. "Please try to remain calm, Joe. We have no intention of hurting you. That's not your purpose here."

"Here?" Joe asked, wrestling against his restraints. "Where is here exactly?"

"Somewhere we can proceed uninterrupted. It's for everyone's safety, I'm sure you can understand."

"No, I don't fucking understand. I was just tasered by someone who I thought I knew and now I wake up to find myself being confronted by someone who sounds like a Dalek. I want to know what's fucking going on. Where's Vicky?"

"Be patient, you will see her soon enough. But in the meantime, Joe O'Connell," Sara announced. "Meet Obadiah Stark aka The Tally Man. One of the world's most prolific serial killers and sentenced to death at Absolom Maximum Security prison. Tonight, you will perform an interview before he dies. His last interview and the one you have wanted for a long time."

Joe, still feeling stung by Vicky's betrayal, looked to his left at Obadiah. "I'll be damned. You are alive."

Sara made a coughing sound that Joe guessed would have been a laugh if she'd had a mouth. "You don't seem surprised."

"I suspected something was going on... hadn't quite got to this scenario, though thinking back about the taser, I guess I was on the right track. So, his execution at Absolom?"

"What we intended you and the world to see."

"And 'we' is…?"

"I'm sorry, how rude of me to not have introduced ourselves. We are The Brethren that you've been so diligently honing in on. The company is more than what you see here of course, but we represent its core values."

"And you've brought me here to what, chat to him? Are you fuckin' insane?"

"Don't you want the chance to speak to the man you've researched and studied for so long in person? This is that chance, Joe. The chance to ask the questions you've always wanted to before he dies."

Joe gave an exasperated sigh. "And what are you going to do with me after I'm done? Kill me?"

"Don't be so melodramatic. We simply brought you here to show you the extent of our power, given that you have such an intrinsic involvement in Obadiah Stark's story. Nothing you learn tonight will ever leave this room. It will be for your benefit alone. Take it as the acknowledgement of our respect for you. You got so close, Joe, you have no idea. Closer than anyone has ever got before. You should be proud of yourself. Giving you this opportunity of a lifetime is our way of saying thanks. And I know you'll be thinking you will go and tell everyone about us, but think about it for a moment. Do you really think anyone will believe you? Look what happened to your friend, Dunwall. His is an important lesson to remember when considering challenging us."

"A threat?"

"An observation," Sara alluded. "One reiterated to you earlier this evening if I'm not mistaken by my sister."

He felt his mouth go dry. "Who?"

"Come on, don't play coy about it. I know how fond you've become of her, as she has of you. Trust me, it made convincing her to do the right thing that much harder."

Joe felt suddenly dizzy. His mind fought with everything it could against what he knew was coming. He heard a door open behind him followed by footsteps. And then there she was, standing in front of him.

"I'm so sorry about this, Joe," Vicky said.

"You've lost the trench coat… shame," Joe said sarcastically. "So, you're part of all this?"

Vicky nodded sadly. "My sister was one of Stark's last victims before he left the USA. And 'victim' is probably right, despite the fact she survived. I mean, look at what he did to her. The Brethren approached her after she'd left the hospital and asked her to help the families set all of this up."

"And you're involved in this because…?" Obadiah interjected.

Vicky turned sharply to face him, her tone venomous. "Because I wanted to be there for her. What we've achieved with you, it's never been done before. Frankly, it's less than you deserve. If I had my way, you'd repeatedly die until the end of time."

"You sad, pathetic little insect. In your little dominion of superiority and you think you have all the answers. None of you understands true power. If you did, you would have let me die at Absolom. All you've done is prove to me that what I did will never diminish with time. Otherwise, we wouldn't be here, would we?"

"Shut up," Vicky snapped, as she turned back to face Joe. "Please tell me you understand what we're trying to do."

"I understand you used me."

"No," she denied. "I never used you. I am a profiler and my offer to help you was genuine. By working with you, I thought I could make you see a different perspective on things and show you how justice isn't straightforward. You were never supposed to be involved. Stamford contacting you was something we hadn't foreseen, but once he did, I realised you wouldn't let it go until you discovered what actually happened. I tried to distract you, but underestimated your tenacity."

"So the man who tried to kill me, you arranged that?"

"No," Vicky insisted. "That was The Brethren's idea. They didn't trust I could divert you from the truth, so they decided on more... drastic measures. I had no part in that, I give you my word."

"Well, forgive me sweetheart, but at the minute your word doesn't mean shit."

"I hate to break up the reunion," Obadiah interrupted. "But at what point is anyone going to tell me what you intend to do with me."

"It's simple, Obadiah. After Joe's interview, we intend to execute you in front of the audience beyond this window."

Sara pulled a black curtain aside, revealing neat rows of people staring intently at what was now visible.

"Of course, you've been through this before, but on this occasion, you will die knowing what it truly means to be bereft."

Obadiah looked at the people through the window, recognising many of the faces from his execution. He could see Sabitch standing at the back, a smug expression on his face. The remainder of the people appeared to be exhausted, as though having to see the whole process of his being put to death again was too much for them.

"Right then," Obadiah said, nodding towards Joe. "Let's get on with it."

Joe looked himself up and down. "It would go a lot smoother if someone would consider not leaving me tied to this fuckin' trolley!"

Sara nodded to Vicky who moved towards him and began loosening the straps. She avoided eye contact with Joe as she worked, instead quickly moving back beside her sister when she was done.

Joe rose and straightened out his clothes. "Can I begin by saying this is Vanilla Sky insane. You want me to simply sit and interview a man who is supposed to have died already, never mind the fact I was tasered and brought here by force?"

Sara's reply was simple. "Yes."

"I imagine you're recording this."

"Of course."

"And if I refuse? Try to escape?"

"Your body will never be found."

"Glad we got that all cleared up then," Joe replied wryly. "Can I get a pen?"

Sara shook her head. "Of course not."

"A chair then?"

Vicky who left the room and returned with a chair, placing it in front of Obadiah. Joe sat down without acknowledging her and gazed at the prisoner.

She was right, this moment had him buzzing with excitement. Coupled with the fear he felt, Joe was completely wired as though he'd drunk ten cans of Red Bull.

"Well, I have to say this is probably the most surreal experience of my life. You don't mind if I call you Obadiah, do you?"

"Given the circumstances, it would be slightly pedantic to complain," Obadiah replied.

"Fair point," Joe agreed. "Okay then, I guess my first question should be why do you think they've gone to all this effort, faking your death, doing whatever the hell they've been doing with you?"

Obadiah laughed. "Ironically, your first question is one I cannot answer. You'll need to ask Cindy Crawford behind you."

Joe sighed with exasperation and turned to face Sara. "Go on then. Why?"

Her response was bland and unemotive through the electrolarynx.

"From his arrest and incarceration up to the execution, all of it was leading to this moment for right and just punishment - meticulously planned for and implemented as intended. Death was never going to be enough for Obadiah Stark. He had to be made to suffer, as the people before him had. As I did. But for him to suffer, his Hell had to be very special. It had to be unique. A Hell to experience the pain, anguish, hurt and anger that he caused others or who suffered as a result of his actions. A Hell he created for himself within his own soul by turning his back on unconditional love, compassion and peace. Exposing Stark to evil would only have hardened him and tempered his resolve. At the end of the day, how do you torture someone who has nothing to lose? We were tasked to make him care, to make him feel, to make him love and then tear it away from him violently, as a reflection of his actions onto others. And it wasn't easy. Creating subliminal conditioning for someone requires technology far more advanced than the world is used to. Fortunately, The Brethren have unlimited resources, so money wasn't an issue."

Joe looked confused. "So that night at Absolom?"

Sara made a gurgle he presumed was a laugh. "The world had to believe he'd died, otherwise we couldn't do what we needed to. He was given a chemical variant of benzodiazepine, a dash of a psychotropic drug to cause his mind to see and feel what they'd been programmed to and an element of psycho-stimulant to ensure he reacted violently to any stimulus contradicting his fabricated reality. A little tetrodotoxin was added to complete the compound, and the rest was done by technology you saw around you in the other room, feeding him suggestions, concepts, ideas, all into his subconscious mind."

"Tetrodotoxin... the zombie drug derived from puffer fish," Joe confirmed.

"That's correct," Sara acknowledged coldly. "Freud, Napoleon Hill worked on similar projects, so we can't really take the credit for any it. We just made it... more effective."

"So basically it was just a fancy form of hypnosis?" Joe asked.

"Implantation," Sara corrected. "Imagine the mind is split into two halves, the conscious and subconscious. Separating them is what you could call a line of belief which acts as a filter. The trick is to bypass this line to gain access to the subconscious mind. According to dear old Freud, when we are sleeping, we enter what's called the Theta phase where our subconscious mind can be accessed much more easily. Now you can implant suggestions in the subconscious mind that you couldn't have before because the conscious mind was alert and would have rejected anything it thought was ridiculous. From that point, it is simply a matter of audio messages directed towards the subject and a few drugs to ensure the mind remains in a relaxed state. What I'm telling you isn't anything ground-breaking, hypnotists use it to make someone fall asleep on stage and act like a chicken."

"I wouldn't really equate what you've done here to making someone cluck," Joe retorted.

"You're right. Once Stark had emptied out his mind we just provided him with the Lego to build his own Hell in it. If the afterlife is the realm of the mind and spirit, these hellish conditions exist merely by creating them in your own psyche. You have to be careful what you put in your mind and what you build there."

He turned back to face Obadiah. "What did you see when you were under? What was it like?"

Obadiah felt tears well in his eyes, quickly blinking them away. "I had a wife," he said after a long pause. "And a child. They loved me. I was someone else to them... something else. I was sick, dying of a brain tumour. And they weren't afraid of me. If what they're saying is true, I made them up because that's what I'm supposed to believe my heart wanted the most, in spite of everything I've done. But it was real... it felt real."

Sara made a noise similar to a snort. "So, your soul simplified the evil in your subconscious to having a brain tumour? How pathetic. If only those whose lives you took had been so lucky. At least they would have had a chance to say goodbye."

Joe ignored her comment and leaned back in the chair, folding his arms. "You know, no one feels sorry for you. How could they after what you've done? I think this whole situation is fucked up and can't help wondering how they could have got away with it for so long, but I can't say that whatever they've put you through really counts as suffering. What do you think?"

"I think they expect me to be afraid. They're mistaken. I'm no more afraid than I was the first time around." Obadiah paused before continuing. "The first time around... it sounds odd saying it, as though people experience dying twice. The difference this time is that whereas in Absolom I lay on the table full of venom and nonchalance, this time I feel grateful. They think they punished me by keeping me here and making me dream an imaginary life. At first, it was punishment - feelings so abhorrent to me, I couldn't even process them. But then I found something through a little girl and a woman that I thought I'd sold so very long ago."

"Which was?" Joe asked.

"My soul," Obadiah replied.

Joe scoffed "Someone like you doesn't have a soul. You're evil, plain and simple."

"You're so certain of that, aren't you? And in the most basic respect, you are correct. I would kill everyone in this room and think nothing of it. My heart remains dark. But my soul, that's something I had no concept of before. And I understand it now. I was empty. And out of that emptiness, I found a little girl called Ellie and a woman called Eva who loved me and cared about me. None of this will change how you all feel about me, nor should it. But they shouldn't be afraid of what they're about to do."

"We're not afraid," Sara interrupted.

"Really?" Obadiah challenged. "Because you look it to me."

"And Sabitch, Evans," Joe asked, turning towards Sara. "The people on the other side of that window, they were all in on this, right?"

"Of course," Sara confirmed. "The Brethren are powerful, but not arrogant enough to concede that we can't do everything by ourselves. To achieve something the likes of which we have with Obadiah takes a great deal of planning and organisation. Sort of a multi-agency approach you might say."

"So, these people Stark spoke of. They were just figments of his subconscious?"

"They were," Sara confirmed. "The subconscious mind doesn't comprehend or discern between good or bad, right or wrong. It's created to store exactly what you give to it, and that is what it then does, always saying yes and accepting what it's provided."

"Stark's body?"

"It will be taken somewhere where no one will ever find it."

"And me?" Joe asked cautiously.

Sara moved in front of her sister and held a syringe up in front of Joe's face. "You are going to be given this and will wake up in your own home, safe and sound."

"Sounds like you've covered all the bases," Joe acknowledged flatly before facing Obadiah once more. "And how do you feel about all of this? Was it better to have loved and lost than never to have loved at all?"

Stark smiled at Sara. "It was. . . exquisite."

Sara moved and stood at the side of the window, allowing the observers to maintain a clear view. "Obadiah Stark, in front of these people you have been deemed guilty of murder and are therefore sentenced to death. Do you have anything to say?"

Obadiah smiled. "You want me to apologise?"

"No Tally Man. We just want you to die."

"Straight to the point, I respect that. In that case, get on with it. Dying twice is so boring."

He looked defiantly at the myriad of faces before turning his head to look at Sara, feeling more alive than he'd ever felt before. He was conscious of every muscle as he strained against his restraints, his senses amplified.

He knew this moment was the most important of his life. For the first time since being a child, Obadiah felt calm, his mind purged of all the hatred he had kept trapped there for more than three decades.

He closed his eyes and saw Eva and Ellie.

His family.

They had been part of a manipulation that would have made Machiavelli proud, yet his feelings for them were not false. It felt like a gift to him, one he had finally earned.

Sara nodded to the men at the back of the room who quickly moved and flanked Joe, securing his arms behind his back and dragging him back towards the empty trolley.

"Get the fuck off me," he shouted as tried to fight them.

Sara handed the electrolarynx to her sister and moved beside Joe once he had been strapped back down, placing the syringe in his arm and quickly administering its contents. He glanced over at Vicky, feeling his body begin to tingle and go numb.

"I trusted you. How could you do this?"

"I wish I could make you understand."

"You never could. It's not the way it should be, Vicky. You now that."

Joe felt his eyes grow heavy as his head slowly lowered self to his chest. He turned his head towards Obadiah, feeling the energy and power emanating from him, despite his silence as he slipped into unconsciousness.

Vicky moved forward and gently stroked his cheek. "I'm so sorry, Joe. I really am."

Sara signalled the man Obadiah assumed by now was a doctor, forward again. He held another syringe that he gently attached to the end of the cannula. He looked at Obadiah briefly, his eyes sad as though bearing a heavy burden before slowly depressing the plunger.

Obadiah's eyes grew heavy as his vision blurred. He felt no sadness at what was about to happen. It was as it was meant to be.

A monster like him only ever wanted to live long enough to make a mark on the world. And make a mark he had done. His legacy would never be forgotten. But in return, it had given him something. Something a man like him should never be allowed to have. He felt grateful that he'd had the chance to discover it for himself.

Life through death. Maybe even salvation for his black soul.

Drifting away, he felt a burning sensation on his back. Though too tired to react, it felt similar to an incision, working its way down his shoulder blade as though someone was carving a line into his skin.

A line that would sit alongside the previous twenty-seven tally marks. A line that now represented the loss of twenty-eight souls.

A final tally signifying the death of Obadiah Stark.

The Tally Man.

'Man is not what he thinks he is, he is what he hides.'
Andre Malraux

EPILOGUE
OCTOBER 9TH

09:16

Denny Street, Tralee (*Trá Lí*)
  County Kerry, Ireland

Joe spun idly in his chair, glancing at the clock with every rotation and desperate for a cigarette.

His conversation with the Gardaí about the events a week ago had proven fruitless. Not being able to provide them with the location of where he'd been held nor willing to explain how a previously dead serial killer had been re-executed, had left them with little to act on. Instead, he had decided to try and locate Vicky, though that had proven just as useless. Her mobile phone number had been disconnected, and the hotel where she'd been staying had her as checked out on the 5th of October, the day after everything had taken place.

A few phone calls had uncovered that Evans had taken

362

extended leave and Stamford had suddenly resigned his position at Absolom. Sabitch had not yet returned Joe's requests for an interview, with his secretary claiming he was 'swamped and would be for the foreseeable future.'

A visit to Dunwall's house had been equally unsuccessful, with him finding it forebodingly deserted. Door unlocked, Joe had let himself in to see even the materials from his hoarding habit gone, with only outlines in the dust on the floor to indicate that anyone had ever been there.

As the office thrummed with life behind him, Joe found himself feeling completely isolated, with a profound uneasiness in his heart and a crawling feeling on the nape of his neck.

Everything he'd discovered about The Brethren, about Obadiah Stark, about Vicky, was being systematically erased or covered up.

Ciaran had been unimpressed with the fact that Joe had decided to put his book on hold, especially given all the latitude he'd been given. He hadn't wanted to shelve it, but with Sara's not-so-veiled threat still fresh in his mind, he didn't dare pursue his findings regarding The Brethren for fear of the repercussions.

For the first time in his professional life, he felt he had no options.

"Penny for them?" Alison said, sitting on the edge of his desk.

"You wouldn't have enough money, trust me," Joe replied wearily.

"You look like shit if you don't mind me saying."

"I feel like it. What can I say, rough week."

"Haven't seen your little blonde criminologist around recently. Repelled her with your overt sexuality?"

"Let's just say that I learnt more than I intended to when I procured her services."

"Ah, the old 'woman with skeletons' scenario."

"More like fossilised dinosaurs," Joe said with a sigh.

"Seriously, Joe. Are you okay?"

"I'm wondering if this is for me," he replied following a long pause. "A few things I've learned have made me wonder if there's any point. I mean, how can you report what's happening in the world, about all the horrible shit that goes down, if your hands are being tied?"

"Some people like that kind of thing," Alison flirted.

"I'm serious," Joe fired back. "What if you discovered something that would send everything into a tailspin? That would make people question their trust in the powers that be? I took this job to report the truth so that I could make a difference in some way. I wanted to let people know that they could trust the media, or some of us anyway. That we're not all interested in sensationalism. Only recently, the closer I got to something, the more questionable the truth actually became. Some people deserve what happens to them, no doubt about it. But the methods… that's the thing I'm struggling to understand."

"You're not making any sense," Alison said in a worried tone.

"I know" Joe replied. "I might never make sense again. At the end of the day, all my sources for the Stark story have dried up in the most extreme way possible, and I'm facing repercussions from a huge corporation if I share what I discovered, which makes all my work a waste of time really. Basically, the whole things a fuckin' mess. And yet…"

"And yet, what?"

"Yet some things are just niggling away at me."

Alison placed her hand on his shoulder. "Well, in that case, don't give up. You're one of the best reporters in this place and a decent guy. Whatever you've gone through, don't let it jade you. You seek out the truth, that's what you do, and you do it well. If you can't do it by conventional means, go unconventional. You'll figure something out."

Joe smiled as Alison moved back to her desk. She was right, it wasn't like him to just give up. He felt completely drained by the whole experience and was seriously wondering if he should take a break from journalism, but wasn't able to shake Dunwall's suggestion that Obadiah Stark hadn't been the first person The Brethren had carried out their little experiment on.

He'd mentioned the Monster of Florence and the West Mesa murders amongst others. The Florence murders had taken place between 1968 and 1985, the West Mesa murders in 2009. Both cases remained unsolved, despite the Florence crimes leading to the conviction of men whose guilt has always been contentious. Sara told him they'd been doing it for a long time. But for how long and why?

Joe needed to know before he could let it go, however dangerous it would be for him. And if he was going to pursue it, he needed to be careful. No more book pursuits or publicity. If he was going to try and uncover the extent of The Brethren's reach, he needed to change his methods and style.

Swinging his chair back round to face the desk, he grabbed his phone book and flicked to the back. He made a quick look around the office, at Alison, at his colleagues going about their oblivious, daily business. If he followed this path, he would potentially have to give all this up.

Well, I'll know one way or the other after this phone call.

He dialled the number, twirling a pen between his fingers as it rang. A man answered with a firm hello.

"Kev O'Hagan?" Joe asked.

"Who wants to know?"

"Joe O'Connell. I need your help."

———

THE ROOM WAS VAST, BATHED IN SHADOW THAT BLENDED INTO the darkness towards the back. Sconces set along the wall gave off the only illumination.

The chambers were equally spaced, each containing the body of either a male or female. Two men were busy securing a man's body into one of them with straps across his forehead, torso and legs. One of them adjusted a display at the side of the chamber before pulling the door down from above, which closed with a soft hiss of air. A mist began to coalesce, crystallising on its occupant's face and exposed skin. The second man fixed a metal plate to the side, designating the occupant with a name, number and year.

"Have you finished?" the woman asked as she approached.

"Yes, Miss Morgan," one of the men replied. "Subject 28 is secured. Cryogenesis has begun and should be completed in thirty minutes."

"Excellent. That will be all."

"Of course," the man replied, indicating to his colleague that they were to leave.

Sara moved closer and touched the glass. "Finally, you're here. Granted, not our most famous occupant - that privilege belongs to Subject One. But I think you might be my favourite. After all, we have such a history together don't we, Obadiah?"

She kissed the glass and stared at The Tally Man's slowly freezing body before turning and making her way towards the exit.

She stopped at the chamber for Subject One, gazing through the frosted window at its occupant.

"And to think it all started with you, my dark soldier. Our gain became Whitechapel's history."

Sara caressed the glass and ran her fingers over the designation plate, the curves of its inscription so familiar to her now.

SUBJECT ONE. JACK. 1888.

She turned and made her way up the stairs and through the metal door which slammed shut, the echo reverberating through the room and down into the darkness.

AFTERWORD

THE TALLY MAN is a work of fiction, but many of the elements that helped define it are real.

The Blasket Islands exist; ADX Absolom does not. I merely chose somewhere in the world that was both beautiful and remote to place an imaginary supermax prison.

The drugs and toxins used to induce Obadiah's dream-like state are real; the processes used to create elements of his torture are not.

Many of the roads and locations described in Ireland are real, but I have taken some artistic licence with others to mould them into something suiting my literary requirements. I hope I can be forgiven. Obadiah's profile is fictional (or is it?), but for a professional insight into the world of psychological profiling and criminology, I would highly recommend you read anything by Paul Ekman, the BRACE® organisation, Robert Ressler, Tom Schachtman, Akira Lippit, R.T Kraus, A. Hoffer, R. M. Holmes, S. T. Holmes, Robert Hare and, for a deeper understanding of how evil, love and redemption exist in our world, seek out anything written by M. Scott Peck.

Any mistakes are my own.

Thank you for spending time in my world. It means more than you could know.

ABOUT THE AUTHOR

David is the one on the left; the attractive one on the right thinks he's someone else.

David McCaffrey was born in Middlesbrough, raised in West Sussex and now lives in Redcar. He worked in the NHS for many years, his last position being Lead Nurse in Infection Prevention and Control at James Cook University Hospital.

He started writing following the birth of his first son and in 2010 was accepted onto the writing coach programme run by Steve Alten, international bestselling author of *Meg* and *The Mayan Prophecy*. *The Tally Man* was the result and the rest, as they say, is history (cliche, cliche).

Though psychological thrillers are his *raison d'etre*, David is also an activist for bullying and harassment in the NHS. His book, 'Do No Harm: Bullying and Harassment in the NHS' went to Number One in the Nursing and White Collar Crime categories of Amazon Kindle charts in November 2018 and was the Number One bestselling book in the U.S Amazon Kindle charts for more than three weeks in the Issues, Trends and Roles category.

David is a proud supporter and donator to the Ben Cohen StandUp Foundation which tackles bullying across the board, from schools to the workplace. He had the honour of being invited to speak at the Standup Foundation's Inaugural Conference in November 2018.

Half of all profits from 'Do No Harm' go to the Ben Cohen Foundation.

David lives with his wife Kelly, has a Jakey, a Liam (a.k.a Gruffy) and a Cole (a.k.a Baby Moo Man) They also have an Obi… who's the dog.

facebook.com/www.davidmccaffrey.net
twitter.com/daveymac1975
instagram.com/mccaffreydavid

ALSO BY DAVID MCCAFFREY

In Extremis: A Hellbound Novella (Book Two in the Hellbound Anthology)

Nameless (Book Three in the Hellbound Anthology)

The Warmest Place to Hide

Do No Harm: Bullying and Harassment in the NHS

By Any Means Necessary (ghost writer) by Stephen Sayers

Printed in Great Britain
by Amazon